Steiner _____ _____ at the supports under the shelves that lined the rear wall. The structure collapsed, raining bottles down on the two figures that bolted upward. The assassins covered their heads, trying to protect themselves from the descending wave of glass and liquors. A wooden piece from the shelves sparked from Steiner's blasts. Flames burst out around the two men, exploding upward, consuming the falling liquids in flight.

The heat from the sudden eruption forced Steiner to shield his face. He stumbled back in surprise. Never had he expected such a reaction from low-alcoholic substances, unless—

One of the burning assassins aimed a gun. A bolt from Steiner's AT-7 ripped through the man's chest before he could open fire. The lifeless body sank into a flaming grave.

Before Steiner had a chance to seek out the other assassin, he saw something being swung at him from a corner of his vision. He ducked, but not in time to avoid being clipped in the shoulder by a chair. The force of the blow threw him to the floor. When he collided with the cold unyielding surface, he lost hold of his weapon . . .

PRISON SHIP

MICHAEL BOWERS

ACE BOOKS, NEW YORK

THE BERKLEY PUBLISHING GROUP
Published by the Penguin Group
Penguin Group (USA) Inc.
375 Hudson Street, New York, New York 10014, USA
Penguin Group (Canada), 90 Eglinton Avenue East, Suite 700, Toronto, Ontario M4P 2Y3, Canada
(a division of Pearson Penguin Canada Inc.)
Penguin Books Ltd., 80 Strand, London WC2R 0RL, England
Penguin Group Ireland, 25 St. Stephen's Green, Dublin 2, Ireland (a division of Penguin Books Ltd.)
Penguin Group (Australia), 250 Camberwell Road, Camberwell, Victoria 3124, Australia
(a division of Pearson Australia Group Pty. Ltd.)
Penguin Books India Pvt. Ltd., 11 Community Centre, Panchsheel Park, New Delhi—110 017, India
Penguin Group (NZ), 67 Apollo Drive, Rosedale, North Shore 0632, New Zealand
(a division of Pearson New Zealand Ltd.)
Penguin Books (South Africa) (Pty.) Ltd., 24 Sturdee Avenue, Rosebank, Johannesburg 2196,
South Africa

Penguin Books Ltd., Registered Offices: 80 Strand, London WC2R 0RL, England

This is a work of fiction. Names, characters, places, and incidents either are the product of the author's imagination or are used fictitiously, and any resemblance to actual persons, living or dead, business establishments, events, or locales is entirely coincidental. The publisher does not have any control over and does not assume any responsibility for author or third-party websites or their content.

PRISON SHIP

An Ace Book / published by arrangement with the author

PRINTING HISTORY
Ace mass-market edition / January 2010

Copyright © 2010 by Michael Bowers.
Cover art by Scott Grimando.
Cover design by Judith Lagerman.
Interior text design by Kristin del Rosario.

ISBN: 978-0-441-01815-4

ACE
Ace Books are published by The Berkley Publishing Group,
a division of Penguin Group (USA) Inc.,
375 Hudson Street, New York, New York 10014.
ACE and the "A" design are trademarks of Penguin Group (USA) Inc.

PRINTED IN THE UNITED STATES OF AMERICA

10 9 8 7 6 5 4 3 2 1

Thanks, Bonnie, for the encouragement
and for introducing me to Jack

CHAPTER

1

2435: Six years after the start of the Galactic Civil War

"BATTLE stations," McKillip barked as he stepped into the command center.

Commander Jacob Steiner activated the alarm and watched from his console as each deck of their vessel, the U.S.S. *Valiant*, acknowledged the alert. He glanced up at McKillip, who strolled through the command staff, monitoring them as they prepared the ship for combat. At six feet two, the fifty-nine-year-old captain stood three inches taller than Steiner and possessed the strength of a man twenty years younger. Around his waist, he wore a sash in his family pattern, with an embroidered crest as a tribute to his storied ancestry. His dark, silver-streaked beard dominated his wrinkled face, creating an aura of fatherly wisdom that Steiner found most appealing about the man. Steiner had grown his own sandy-colored beard in the hope that it looked half as dignified.

"Lieutenant Riggs, plot a course into Sector 489, deep into enemy space," McKillip finally announced.

Suzanne Riggs shot Steiner a fiery glance. She had never liked surprises. She prided herself on staying in the loop, but Steiner was in the dark as much as she was. A slight shrug of his shoulders confirmed that when she looked his way inquiringly. Pursing her lips together, she spun back to her console and worked furiously at her assigned task.

McKillip stepped up to Steiner. "Activate the ship's intercom."

Steiner opened a channel to the hundred other crew members on board.

The captain took a deep breath. "We have been ordered into Sector 489 of enemy space to assist the *Excalibur* and the *Cheyenne*, both returning from a reconnaissance mission. It will be dangerous because of all the enemy activity in the area." McKillip's gaze froze on Steiner as he closed the intercom. "These orders came from *him*," McKillip whispered.

Steiner knew instantly whom he was referring to, Admiral Ralph Jamison on the War Council. Their history with the admiral had begun six years ago, right before the Galactic Civil War broke out. Back then, when loyalties were divided among the officers of the United Star Systems, it looked more and more likely that the democratic planetary union would fall to the Separatists' New Order Empire without a fight. Captain McKillip had begun forming a close-knit team of officers he knew would not be tempted by Separatist bribes. A student of history, he'd called this newly formed covert team the Cyrian Defense, after Cyrus the Great's unchallenged, overnight conquest of Babylonia—the exact fate he worried awaited the U.S.S. McKillip had asked Steiner to join his undercover team, and they had succeeded in exposing a massive conspiracy and preventing an assassination attempt on the President of the United Star Systems. By chance, Admiral Jamison had had a peripheral involvement in the operation, and he had exaggerated his role and assumed all the credit, making himself a national hero. Happy to keep the profile of the members of the Cyrian Defense low, McKillip had remained silent as Congress and the president promoted Admiral Jamison to Chief Military Officer of the U.S.S. Fleet.

But then the New Order Empire had attacked. In the aftermath of the Day of Betrayal, as the attack became known, Jamison showed his true colors. He did little to stop the rampant piracy plaguing a hobbled fleet, and when a cruise ship of civilians was taken hostage, McKillip sent a team, which infiltrated the vessel, freed the captives, and captured the leader of the pirates. But after being convicted in U.S.S. courts, the man received a pardon from President Lindsey at the behest of Admiral Jamison without any explanation. Since then, McKillip had made it his personal mission to use all his remaining contacts to collect any evidence connecting Jamison to the pirating ring. He blamed himself for enabling Jamison to become a leech on the United Star Systems.

And now Jamison was giving them orders.

"Do you think he knows you've been investigating him?" Steiner whispered.

McKillip stood confidently in the middle of the command center, meeting each uncertain glance by the crew members around him as they prepared for battle. He replied softly, his eyes averted, "Well, if the *Excalibur* and the *Cheyenne* are not there, we'll know for certain."

"Have you notified Judith?" Steiner asked, referring to McKillip's wife.

"She'll deliver my files to the rest of the War Council if anything happens to us."

"Course plotted, sir," Suzanne called out.

"Thank you, Lieutenant. Commander, inform the crew."

"All stations, prepare for a starspeed jump," Steiner announced over the ship's intercom. His stomach tightened in expectation of the dimensional shift about to occur. He had never quite become accustomed to it. His hands tightened on the console, yet he willed his facial muscles to show none of his inner anxiety. Barely audible whines could be heard around the command center as the crew activated the energy-stasis fields securing them to their seats. McKillip strolled to his command chair and activated his.

"Phase to starspeed," McKillip said.

Steiner clenched his console tightly. The stars in the viewports disappeared as his insides lurched. His vision blurred. He swallowed hard to keep the bile from coming up his throat. Slowly, his stomach began to relax, and his vision cleared.

"Phase successful," Riggs announced.

The star field flashed briefly every few seconds as Suzanne phased the ship back and forth in a rapid succession of short hops, directing their path toward enemy space.

As Steiner stared at the hypnotic flickers on the viewscreen, his thoughts drifted to how tragic it would be if this mission was to be their last. All the efforts they had made to preserve the Union might be rewarded with death by the hand of a criminal they had unknowingly helped into power. Steiner glanced down at the white-gold ring on his finger. If death did await him, at least Mary would be there waiting for him. On February 18, 2429, six months before the Day of Betrayal, a tragic accident had stolen his wife away from him, forever. The white-gold ring on Steiner's finger began to feel heavier and heavier. Steiner closed his eyes, remembering the scent of her perfume. Her emerald eyes glistened at him as she pulled back her dark hair to reveal the star-shaped earrings that he had given her to celebrate his promotion to Executive Officer. Her musical voice penetrated his being, melting all his defenses. "If you miss your own child's birth, Commander, I'll make sure you're court-martialed." She lifted his hand and kissed his wedding band. "I love you." She headed toward the shuttle on the launching pad, touching his hand with hers until their fingertips lost contact.

"Commander," McKillip said sternly, snapping Steiner back to reality. The captain's gaze scolded him. "Any sign of the *Excalibur* or the *Cheyenne* on your sensors?"

"No, sir," Steiner replied.

McKillip gave a short nod.

Steiner cursed himself under his breath. McKillip needed him now more than ever. He had to remain alert. A light appeared on his console, followed by a warning tone. His heart sank as he interpreted the readout.

"How many?" McKillip asked.

"Three enemy battlecruisers are on an intercept course. No sign of the *Excalibur* or the *Cheyenne*."

"Abort the mission. Lieutenant Riggs, take us back."

Suzanne dephased the ship, reversed course, and phased again.

Steiner didn't even feel it this time. His insides were already burning with fury. Another vessel suddenly appeared directly in their path, blocking the way, but it was no ordinary battlecruiser. "Dreadnaught directly ahead," he said.

McKillip locked gazes with him, his expression hardening.

"Enemy ships are thirty seconds from jamming range," Riggs announced.

"What's the nearest U.S.S. outpost on the border?" McKillip asked.

"Falcon two-six is within range," Riggs replied, her short-cropped red hair spinning with the movement of her head.

"Adjust course to get us as close as possible. Lieutenant Majors, contact the commanding officer and tell him that we will require assistance."

Steiner fought back the anger, focusing on the multicolored displays before him. "They have already sensed us and have deployed armed drones to help protect us once we are in United Star Systems territory."

"Good. Put me through to the entire ship." McKillip paused as Steiner opened the intercom. "We are nearing the border and help is awaiting us on the other side. Four enemy vessels are closing on us. We cannot fight them all single-handedly. Our only chance is to run blind until we reach the border."

Riggs's hazel eyes met Steiner's, reflecting something he'd never expected to see in them. Terror. She knew, as well as he, that ships rarely survived a blinded flight at starspeed without colliding with an asteroid or other stellar debris. Without precise navigation, the interdimensional jumps could not be controlled. They would have no idea even of the direction they were traveling in.

"God will protect the just and upright this day," McKillip continued. "We shall survive."

Steiner resented any deity that would deny him a future with Mary. God had nothing to do with their current situation—Jamison did. On the tactical display, the gap between the *Valiant* and the intercepting vessels narrowed. His fingers rubbed his wedding ring.

The helm console's readouts went dark. Riggs pivoted around. "We're being jammed, sir."

"Maintain course the best you can."

Beads of perspiration dotted Riggs's brow as she continued her succession of jumps blindly.

McKillip's left hand gripped his patterned sash. His wrinkled cheek twitched.

Steiner kissed his ring.

"We should have crossed into U.S.S. space by now," Riggs shouted.

Steiner's breath caught in his chest.

"Dephase," McKillip ordered.

When the light of the stars reappeared, a collective sigh of relief rose from the back of the command center.

A warning indicator lit up on Steiner's console. Something was headed straight at them.

"Plasma missile closing in from directly astern," Steiner said, as the blinking object penetrated their defensive grid.

"Evasive man—" McKillip began, just as the *Valiant* shuddered violently.

Primary powered lights blinked as distant eruptions were heard. Damage reports from all over the ship clogged the communication channels.

Steiner focused on his display. His heart sank when he noticed the unusual pattern of lights on the interior sensor grid. The engine chamber had been decompressed. Franco, Ching, Mac, the shipmates he had grown to know for the last ten years, were gone in a millisecond. Even as he stared, the landing bay went dark. Doc and Miles were probably in there. He fought to keep from thinking about it as his world unraveled around him.

"How bad did they hit us?" McKillip demanded.

"Engine chamber and landing bays have been compromised. Engines inoperative. Primary generators fluctuating."

"Position report," McKillip barked.

"We missed our mark, sir." Riggs triangulated their course on the holographic viewer as she continued. "We are in United Star Systems space, but we are too far from Falcon two-six to get immediate cover from them."

"The enemy vessels must have projected our exit point for the jump and fired a missile early," McKillip said, moving to the tactical display.

A new alarm sounded as a red object appeared in the display, next to the dreadnaught.

McKillip frowned. "They must be determined to destroy us."

Steiner glanced at the readout. "Countermeasures are barely operative."

"Signal all hands to abandon ship," McKillip said.

Steiner activated the alarm on his console. The tones echoed throughout the ship.

"Lieutenant Riggs," McKillip said, "oversee the evacuation."

"Yes, sir." She bolted up from her chair and helped the rest of the command crew to file down the outside corridor.

Before the second missile reached midpoint, a third was launched.

"Go, sir," Steiner said. "I'll stay to the last moment."

"Not yet." McKillip went to the communication console and unlocked the panel's hood. He lifted the instrument panel, exposing the brightly lit interior.

"What are you doing, sir?"

"We need the communication logs. It's the only evidence that we were ordered on that suicide mission."

The readout on the tactical display flickered a few times. Steiner had resigned himself to joining Mary, but now he wanted only to give McKillip enough time to obtain the evidence against the admiral. When the missile closed within forty thousand meters, Steiner fired the countermeasures. The missile evaporated harmlessly into a flash in the darkness outside the viewports. Within the flash, he saw Mary. He blinked back the tears starting to form. On his readout he saw twelve lifepods departing the ship just like Mary's shuttle had departed the depot that fateful day.

Mary waved to him as she embarked on the shuttle. He watched himself press his hands against the transparency in the guest lounge in reply. The craft lifted into the air, trailing liquid across the launching pad. When he realized it was fuel leaking out, he beat against the window, shouting in vain for the craft to return.

Sparks erupted from the open communication console.

McKillip jumped back, then immediately put his hands back in.

Two more warning tones sounded, indicating two more objects had been launched from the dreadnaught. "Hurry if you can, sir. We now have three incoming missiles."

"I have it." McKillip said, lifting a small object from the inside of the console. "Our insurance policy."

Steiner readied his hand to activate countermeasures for the first missile.

The tactical display went dark. All the lighting in the room dimmed to emergency levels. McKillip met Steiner's gaze for an instant. A bright flash erupted from the exterior viewports, a wave of disorientation, then blackness. The sound of groaning metal made Steiner open his eyes. Smoke hovered in the room. He lay sprawled on the floor. When he tried to climb to his feet, a sharp pain ran through his right leg. Then he remembered the two missiles en route. They had about thirty seconds before impact. He forced himself to his feet, searching the haze for the captain. His body lay across the tactical console, facedown. Blood dripped from the console. Steiner raised McKillip's head; his face looked peaceful. When Steiner felt for a pulse, McKillip's eyes opened, and he coughed. Steiner tried to lift him and found a piece of communication equipment embedded in his abdomen. McKillip's dark eyes flickered, then met Steiner's. "Get out while there's still time."

"I was supposed to die, not you."

McKillip shook his bloodstained beard. "One of us must survive," he barely managed.

Steiner felt frozen. Within his mind, Steiner saw Mary's shuttle hover above the depot just outside the window of the lounge where he stood. Fire ignited from the rear of the craft, spreading to engulf the entire vessel. The flaming wreckage crashed against the pad, bursting into a blossom of fiery debris that pelted the transparency of the lounge.

Then he remembered the incoming missiles.

Eyes tearing, he threw himself away from the captain and stumbled to the door of the command center. He looked back at the man, who stared blankly into nothingness.

He limped into the smoke ahead of him, trying to keep his bearings. His fingers found a control panel for a lifepod. A shining red light indicated it had already been launched. The next one was still green. He stumbled inside, pulled down the emergency release lever, and fell into the first seat. The automatic harness closed about his body. He felt the thrust of the lifepod as it propelled itself from the *Valiant*. Then he closed his eyes.

CHAPTER

2

MARY'S hair flowed like a silk sheet in the breeze. Eyes glistening, she smiled, then turned and ran playfully down the street, beckoning him to follow.

"No," Steiner pleaded. "Stay for a while."

She threw him a kiss as she danced into the chapel at the end of the block.

"Don't go in there," he yelled, running to catch her.

The chapel shimmered in the light. The steeple sank into the distorting mass as it morphed into a shuttle sitting on a landing pad.

Steiner forced himself awake before the dream could steal her from him again. In the darkness of the early morning, he sobbed silently. Someday to hold her again so that she would never leave.

A cough sounded from behind the wall next to his cot, reminding him of where he was. In the faint light, he could make out the toilet in the corner and his prison-issued orange jumpsuit hanging over the back of his chair. He climbed out of bed, picked up the green marker next to his cot, and checked off another day from hand-drawn calendar on the metallic white wall. It had been six months since the destruction of the *Valiant* and the series of events that occurred afterward. As he took a shower in the corner of his cell, he reminded himself of why he needed to keep living. He recalled going to McKillip's home the day after the tragedy and finding that Judith had been murdered the previous night by a prowler, who had conveniently stolen all the computer records within the house. His pulse began to race. Dressing in his prison jumpsuit, he remembered the news services blaming the destruction of the *Valiant* and the loss of half its crew on the captain's dismissal of counterorders that Jamison had sent, but Steiner knew they had never received any counterorders. Someone had falsified the computer records. His breathing became rapid. His hands trembled from rage as he shaved. He thought of the face of Admiral Jamison, expressing fake pity for the great loss Steiner had suffered. Steiner threw the disposable razor on the floor. He closed his eyes, imagining Jamison smugly sitting behind his desk, just as he had when Steiner confronted him that fateful day. When Jamison had the gall to blame McKillip for the incident, Steiner had decided if the Cyrian Defense had installed the admiral in power, then it seemed right that one of the last surviving members should take him out. That was when Steiner had jumped over the man's desk and punched him with all his might. His fist hit the concrete wall of his cell, and pain shot up his arm.

Footsteps sounded outside his cell. Steiner licked the blood from his knuckles, relishing the sting of his wound. The door slid aside. Two guards stepped through, both armed with stun guns.

"You have a visitor," one of them announced.

Steiner laughed to himself, enjoying the irony. It had been two MPs who had kept him from killing Jamison that day in the admiral's office. He had subsequently been court-martialed for attempted murder and incarcerated.

After the guards frisked him, Steiner exited the cell, with both guards trailing behind him half a step. He marched with pride, as if he were on his way to meet an admiral. The only visits he had were when his lawyer needed to update him on the military tribunal he had called regarding Jamison's connections to the pirating ring within

U.S.S. space. The judge had agreed to the investigation on behalf of McKillip and his wife. The coincidental timing of both of their deaths had raised suspicions among the other admirals, but they were hesitant to believe any accusations of treason against the Chief Military Officer of the U.S.S. Fleet. Steiner wanted to live to try to change their minds, or at least cast enough doubt to put a stop to Jamison's illegal activities.

Steiner entered the vacant visitation chamber, where the guards proceeded to shackle his legs to the single chair on his side of the table. The cool air chilled his body and his rage. Freshly used cleanser burned his nostrils. He caught a glimpse of his own reflection in the laminated surface of the table in front of him. Within the glint of his determined gaze, he could still see the shadow of the officer he once was. With his fingers, he combed out the tangles of sandy hair. His bare face looked pale and weak without a beard covering it. The warden expected all his inmates to be clean-shaven, or he would have the barbers do it for them, painfully.

A knock stole his attention away. When the door opened, a businesslike woman clad in a power suit entered, her flame red hair tied up in a bun.

Steiner could not believe his eyes. "Suzanne?"

"It's a long story, Jake—one best told in private."

As both guards exited, Steiner stared at his old shipmate in utter disbelief. He hadn't seen Riggs since their rescue from the *Valiant*. Even though he felt a small measure of joy at seeing her again, it was overwhelmed by shame because of his appearance.

She guided her slender figure into the chair sitting on the opposite side of the table, her perfume competing with the acidic odor surrounding them. She eyed him as if pitying an injured pet. "You don't look so good, Ja—"

"How did you find me?" he cut her off. "No one but my lawyer knows I'm here. Did he tell you?"

"No, I accidentally discovered you on my own. From all the reports, I knew you had been incarcerated for—" She swallowed. "Why did you attempt to murder Admiral Ralph Jamison?"

Steiner sighed. All the news services had labeled him an insane officer, driven over the edge by the destruction of his ship. If only they knew the whole truth.

"Jamison slaughtered half our shipmates," Steiner shouted. "Close friends of both yours and mine."

"I've been told Captain McKillip ignored the counterorder."

"That's a lie. There was no counterorder."

"What if he made a mistake?" Suzanne asked.

"No. I spoke to him right before the mission began. He didn't make a mistake."

"All right," she said. "Tell me what he told you."

"For the past year, McKillip had been collecting evidence linking Admiral Jamison to the pirates plaguing the border systems. Before we went into Sector 489, he warned me that Jamison had signed the orders, and there was a possibility it was a trap—in fact, he died trying to remove the communication array to preserve the logs."

"Did he save the logs?"

"No, it was too late."

"So, you have no proof?"

Steiner's anger grew at her skepticism. "He told his wife to take his computer records to the War Council if he was killed."

"Did she?"

"She was murdered by a burglar on the same day. The computer files were stolen."

"So you think her murder was orchestrated by Jamison." She gasped. "I can't imagine how you must be feeling right now. You and McKillip had a very special relationship. You were like the son that he and Judith never had. But why would you waste your career in order to murder Admiral Jamison?"

"I just wanted a confession, but—"

"That temper of yours got the better of you," she interrupted. "I told you it would land you in trouble eventually."

Steiner hated it whenever she lectured him, especially since he no longer possessed the rank to stop her. "Why are you here anyway? How did you find me? My lawyer moves me around regularly and keeps my identity a secret."

Her mouth compacted into a fine line. "I work for Ralph Jamison now."

Steiner came to his feet, the shackles restraining the movement. "You what?"

"He's my boss," Suzanne replied, standing up as well.

"I knew you were ambitious, but to sell out for a promotion . . ."

"Just hold on there. You have no proof of your accusations."

Steiner slammed his fist on the laminated surface. "He's a murderer."

The door slid open. One of the guards peered through. Suzanne glared at Steiner for a long heartbeat as if to remind him she controlled the proceedings. After he resettled himself in his chair, she motioned to the guard to close the door again.

Blood began to leak from the reopened scab on Steiner's knuckles. "Does your master also know I'm here?" he managed in a civil tone.

"A memo on his desk said you were located here. After a glance through the list of convicts, I found a Jake Smith. I took a chance that Jake Smith was Jake Steiner."

Steiner's fury dissolved into fear. If Jamison knew he was there, his life was in great danger. "I've got to get out of here."

"Why?"

"I called for a formal tribunal into your boss's activities," he said. "If he gets the chance, I'm sure he'll try to silence me, too."

"When is the trial?"

"Six months from now, unless he twists more arms and postpones it again. Do you have something to write on?"

After Suzanne produced a pad and pen from a pocket, Steiner recited his lawyer's name and number.

"Tell him that I require an immediate transfer," he said.

"You really think Ralph will try to kill you?" she asked.

"Assassinations are quite easy in here, that's why I'm hiding under an alias. I want to live to testify."

A gleam danced in her eyes. "Transfers take time, more time than you may have. I can get you out quicker."

She was up to something. Steiner could feel it coming. "What are you talking about?"

"I'm the director of the P.A.V. Program—Penitentiary Assault Vessel. Convicts man a spacecraft to raid enemy installations in return for points toward their freedom. The ship is still docked in orbit. I can get you on board today."

Steiner sighed. "So that's why you came to see me. You're not interested in my well-being. You just want to recruit me for your personal gain."

"That's not true. I care about what happens to you. You're my former commander, my shipmate, my friend."

Steiner shook his head. "Jamison could find me there just as easy."

"But on the P.A.V., you'd be armed," she replied.

"What? The convicts have weapons?"

"No. Just the captain."

Steiner chuckled at the absurdity of her proposition. "You want me to command a prison ship?"

"Penitentiary Assault Vessel," she corrected with an edge of irritation. "Besides, I can't think of anyone more qualified. You served as McKillip's executive officer for seven years. You were born to be a leader."

"Not of a prison ship," he shot back. "What's to keep the convicts from taking off with it?"

"Security passwords control all the major functions of the vessel. If anyone mutinies, they couldn't go anywhere. All you have to worry about is training them to fight."

"Impossible," Steiner said. "A bunch of inmates could never function as an assault force."

"I handpicked all of them. They have both the military experience and the desire to make this work. Most of them are like you. They made a mistake and want to start over."

Steiner rubbed his chin, scraping slight stubble. "If you have already chosen a crew, then you must have had a captain already singled out. Why isn't he doing it?"

Suzanne hesitated and lowered her gaze. "He's dead," she admitted. "He was found murdered before the ship launched."

The answer didn't surprise Steiner. "One of your hand-picked men, of course?" he said sarcastically.

Her gaze narrowed. "We don't know who did it. Ralph

Jamison almost shelved the whole program. I asked him if I could take it over."

"How do I know you're telling me the truth? Perhaps you're helping him to get to me that much easier?"

"How dare you suggest such a thing after all we've been through in the last ten years," Suzanne said. "I'm offering you a second chance."

"You're not doing this for me. You're interested in whatever can get you to the top the fastest. Go find yourself another pawn." Steiner turned toward the door, and called out, "Guards, we're done in here."

When the guards stepped into the room, Suzanne signaled them to hold back for a moment. She leaned forward. "Jake, you're only thirty-four. By the time you're released, you'll be in your fifties. The United Star Systems needs good captains now. At least think about my offer." She held out the pen. "Write my number down somewhere. If you change your mind in the next two days, call me. After that, the P.A.V. program will be dead."

To appease her, Steiner curled a corner of his shirtsleeve and let her write it on the inside fabric.

Suzanne stood up from the table. "Good luck, Jake."

"Thanks. If Jamison knows I'm here, I'll probably need some."

When she turned to leave, there were tears in her eyes.

CHAPTER

3

STEINER stood in a line of convicts waiting to be served meals. The digital clock on the wall read "12:36," the time when the west-wing cellblock assembled for lunch. The cavernous dining hall resonated with the roar of conversing voices, riotous laughter, and the continuous scraping of trays. The rice dish being served possessed the same lack of smell that every other meal seemed to have.

Steiner searched through the room's occupants for potential assassins. Thankfully, no one showed any interest in him.

Maybe he was overreacting. He might be transferred out before Jamison could try anything.

His mind replayed the encounter with Suzanne. Her offer enticed him the more he thought of it. He missed command, but when he looked at the convicts eating in the dining hall, he couldn't imagine them manning a warship.

Steiner smiled when he saw Sam Perez threading a path toward him. When he had first learned that the "Teenage Wrath of God," as the news links had labeled the seventeen-year-old youth, was being held at Atwood Penitentiary, he made an effort to befriend him because he sympathized with his plight. Both of them were being punished for seeking justice for crimes against people they loved.

Born the son of a famous crime lord, Sam was given up by his mother when he was five years old. She left him with Father Jose Perez at a local parish, begging him to hide the boy until she could return for him. Sam served as the grounds-keeper for the parish, waiting every day to see his mother return for him, but she never did. After the New Order was formed, its supreme leader, Christophe Staece, made the Catholic Church the official religion of his new empire, which immediately brought suspicion against the Catholic parishes throughout the United Star Systems. During the following five years of growing unrest between the two superpowers, Jose Perez spoke out for a peaceful resolution. After August 15, 2429, the Day of Betrayal, the mistrust of the Catholic Church within the U.S.S. territories ignited into rage and resentment. During a candlelight vigil for peace, a mob from the neighboring township rose up and burned Father Perez's parish to the ground. The candle-holding parishioners scattered in fright as the priest attempted to plea for the mob to stop. They trampled him to death in front of Sam, who had watched from under his overturned wheelbarrow. Forced to live on his own, ten-year-old Sam started stealing food from the same townspeople who had mobbed his parish. Enacting what he thought to be divine justice, he set fire to the houses and businesses of those he remembered seeing during the attack. After he had terrorized the township for seven years, Planetary Police managed to catch him. At age seventeen, he was prosecuted in Pennsylvania as an adult, for postwar rioting, and received a ten-year sentence at a maximum-security prison, as an example to the populace.

"*Buenas dias*, buddy," Steiner said, welcoming Sam into the lunch line.

The teenager twisted about suddenly, attempting to punch Steiner in the gut, but it was blocked easily.

"Not bad," Steiner commented. "You're getting there."

Afraid for the boy's safety among the hardened prisoners, he had volunteered to train him in some defensive skills. But the skills he had been able to teach him were no match against "Big Al," the leader of the underworld within the prison itself. Steiner suspected the warden was in for a take of the money

Big Al was bringing in selling contraband, like drugs, ciga-
rettes, and sometimes alcohol, to the other prisoners. This way,
the warden kept his hands clean while Big Al muscled the
other convicts. When Big Al had tried to bully Sam to run
drugs for him, Steiner had jumped to his defense.

Moving forward in line, Sam said in a hushed tone, "Big
Al has been telling everyone that he's going to break my
legs."

"He's just trying to save his image after what I did to him.
Just stay close to me during the recreational breaks. He won't
try anything, not after what happened last time." Just then
Steiner remembered that he wouldn't be there much longer
once his lawyer transferred him to another prison. What would
happen to Sam then? The boy possessed no combat skills, except what few defensive moves Steiner had been able to teach
him so far. Who would protect him once Steiner was gone?

"You call those vegetables?" a familiar voice broke
through the surrounding noise. At the end of the food counter,
Rick Mason stuck his tongue out at a server and gagged.
Snickers spread down through the line. In retaliation, the cook
heaped a mound of the greenish brown substance on Mason's
tray, then indicated the sign posted behind him. It read, ALL
INMATES REQUIRED TO FINISH EVERYTHING ON THEIR TRAYS
BEFORE LEAVING.

Pushing his midnight black hair out of his face, Mason
sneered at the server, then walked into the dining area. A group
of men followed, slapping his back and congratulating him.

Maybe Mason was the answer to Sam's dilemma.

Even though the man was small in stature—only five feet
tall—his entertaining personality attracted others to him.
With so many friends, he never had to worry about protection. At twenty-seven, Mason was old enough to be Sam's
guardian yet young enough to still relate to him.

After proceeding through the gauntlet of cooks, Steiner
led Sam down the center aisle, which separated two rows of
ten long, rectangular tables with attached benches. As they
walked through the front of the hall, Steiner saw Big Al,
surrounded by muscular bodyguards and criminal cohorts.
The tattooed-covered kingpin glared back at him. Steiner
continued on to the rear table against the wall and set his tray

down near the group huddled around Mason, listening to another one of his smuggling adventures.

"When I heard the sensor alarm blaring, I knew it was going to be a bad day," Mason said, rolling his eyes for added drama. "I activated my rear monitor. There was the most monstrous U.S.S. destroyer I've ever seen." He extended his arms, sizing up his imaginary craft. "Some weak-looking captain with a woman's eyebrows demanded my surrender. I laughed at him."

Chuckles rose from his audience.

Steiner smiled at the comical description of Captain David Cole, a former friend of McKillip's.

Mason continued with his story, describing the three hours he had outmaneuvered Cole's destroyer before being captured. When he finished the tale, a clatter of applause rewarded him.

Steiner admired the smuggler's ability to hold his fans under his spell.

"Hey, Ironhand," Mason shouted at Steiner, using his newly coined nickname. "You're becoming quite famous around here. I heard you sacked 'Two Ton'—I mean, Big Al."

The smuggler's friends shared quiet snickers along with cautious glances toward the front of the room.

Steiner refused to reply. He didn't want anyone to know of his military training—especially now.

Mason turned his attention toward Sam. "I heard he was defending you, '*El Niño*.'"

Sam leaned across the table. "I'm not your '*Niño*.'"

"No offense intended, little brother." Mason backed away. "I'm quite impressed that you stood up to the 'Beast.' It took guts. I admire that. But I wouldn't make any vacation plans without your guardian angel."

"I've been taking care of myself since I was five. I don't need any help."

"Everybody needs friends—except maybe 'Ironhand.' He doesn't need anyone." Mason smiled at Steiner, leaning forward. "I heard you nailed Big Al with one punch. Where did you learn to fight like that? Military?"

"Eat your vegetables, Rick," Steiner said. "You earned them."

Mason broke out in a knowing grin. "Anything for a war hero." In mock compliance, the smuggler dug his spoon into the grotesque substance, raised a dripping heap to his mouth, then flicked it against the rear wall. Laughter erupted from the others as it oozed down the surface.

When Steiner turned away to escape the antics, he noticed a guard exiting an outer door. Another one slipped out the front entrance. His nerves jolted. They never left during mealtimes. A sickening sensation built in his gut as the last three guards disappeared through the kitchen door.

He realized that Jamison must have some influence over the warden here. With no supervision, one convict could murder another without compunction.

Steiner expected one of Big Al's minions to come after him, but they appeared to be immersed in their meals. If one of them were going to try something, the others would be watching expectantly.

It had to be an outsider masquerading as an inmate.

A brief scan of the serving line hit the jackpot. A braided ponytail—something the prison barbers would never have allowed—hung down the back of one of the men's necks. His shirt concealed a bulge near the waist. A short, squat man, nicknamed the Squealer, whispered into Ponytail's ear and pointed at Steiner.

When the assassin's heartless stare found its target, the corners of his mouth rose.

Steiner fought to keep himself from panicking.

He glanced around at Mason and his friends. Should he ask for help? He doubted any of them would risk their life for someone else.

Ponytail and Squealer passed by the first of the cooks.

Steiner inspected his dull-edged utensils for potential weapons. He wished he had a gun or knife. The vegetable mush running down the wall inspired an idea.

"Rick, if you're having problems finishing that, would you like to trade with me?" he said.

Mason appeared startled at first. Then a cunning grin creased his features. "Believe me, this stuff tastes great. I'm just not hungry."

"Save your cons for a fool," Steiner snapped. "Give me your tray."

Without hesitation, the smuggler passed it down the table.

Steiner added his own portion of vegetable substitute to the pile on the platter.

"I had no idea you were so fond of that stuff," Mason said with a smirk.

"It might keep me alive a little longer."

All indications of silliness vanished from the smuggler's face. He scanned the room until he locked onto the man lacking the standard haircut.

When Steiner stood, Sam jumped up as well.

"Sit down, little brother," Mason snapped. "If he wanted your help, he would have asked for it."

Steiner nodded his agreement, then waited until the boy returned to his seat.

Steiner headed toward the front of the dining area at the same time Ponytail and Squealer left the serving line. He tilted his platter up against his chest to keep its contents hidden from view. Warm liquid from the vegetable substitute seeped through the fabric of his tunic and trickled down both sides of his abdomen.

Steiner closed distance with his adversaries, eyes fixed on theirs. His anxiety mounted with each step.

Ponytail unveiled an AT-7 military-issue pistol from under his shirt.

Steiner catapulted his ammunition. It scored a direct hit in his target's face. He ducked to the right as two fiery blasts discharged in random directions from Ponytail's pistol.

Mayhem burst out as convicts dove for cover.

A couple of more stray bolts from the blinded assassin's AT-7 ripped into a nearby table.

Steiner tumbled into a roll, coming up near his opponent. A well-placed kick sent the weapon flying from Ponytail's grasp.

Two of Big Al's muscular bodyguards, hit by vegetable projectiles, rose from their benches. While Ponytail wiped his eyes, Steiner shoved him into the two men's dinners. One of the angry inmates grabbed Ponytail's hair and dragged him across the tabletop, while the other beat him.

Squealer charged forward with a knife. Steiner blocked the thrust of the blade and used the informant's own momentum to send him sailing across a nearby table.

"You're mine this time!" a familiar voice shouted.

Steiner spun around and gazed up at the tattooed kingpin towering over him.

Big Al.

The monstrous figure reached for him. Steiner dodged the attack, then focused all his remaining energy into one strike at the man's nose. Cartilage cracked. Blood sprayed. Steiner backed off in anticipation of a response.

Big Al's eyes rolled up into his head as he toppled backward to the floor.

Gun blasts sounded from the front of the hall. Steiner ducked, wheeling about to hunt down the source. Convicts scattered from the tables to the walls. An intensified beam sliced into the digital clock above the serving line, igniting it into a shower of sparks. The burning fragments outlined a lone figure next to the food counter with a pistol raised in the air.

Ponytail.

Bruises disfigured the assassin's face. A trail of blood seeped from his mouth. His gaze burned more intensely than before. Two of Al's bodyguards lay at his feet, their blood spreading out over the floor.

Steiner upturned the nearest table. Abandoned trays of food crashed to the ground.

A bolt of energy tore through the barrier as if punching through paper. Steiner jumped back as another one penetrated directly in front of him, digging into the bench of a neighboring table. His eyes watered from the stench of smoldering metal and plastic.

He thought he heard Sam cry his name through all the shouts from the onlookers. He couldn't worry about the boy—Mason would take care of him.

A careful peek through one of the smoking holes saw Ponytail advancing on the shelter, grinning confidently. Keeping low, Steiner crept toward the table edge his attacker approached. His foot scraped against a fallen platter. He dove to the ground just before an eruption of fire ripped through the tabletop where he had just been. Burning debris rained down on him as he scrambled under the fresh puncture.

He was still more than four feet away when he heard footsteps coming from the corner of his barrier. Ponytail stepped around the upturned shelter and took aim. Steiner's muscles tightened in anticipation of death.

Ponytail's head jerked backward. The AT-7 discharged into the ceiling. When the assassin thrashed about, Steiner saw Sam tugging on his braided hair.

Steiner launched himself from all fours, sprinting through the spilled food, determined to save his friend.

Ponytail twisted about, bringing the gun to bear on the boy.

"No," Steiner screamed as he charged the assassin.

Sam thrust the gun muzzle away from him, sending a bolt high into a wall. Before Ponytail could fire again, Steiner pounced on him, slamming him against the ground. His fists pounded into the assassin's face until the man lost consciousness. The temptation to kill the man almost overwhelmed Steiner, yet he held himself back. He couldn't give the warden another reason to keep him there.

Holding his opponent's head up by the ponytail, Steiner stood to his feet. Sam's hands trembled as he handed over the fallen AT-7. Steiner smiled a thank-you to his young friend.

Taking the gun, Steiner hauled the assassin across the floor like a sack of grain toward the serving line. The frightened stares of the cooks cowering in a corner followed him all the way. He dropped the AT-7 into a pot of soup, then dumped the bowl of vegetable substitute over Ponytail's head.

Cheers rose from Mason and his friends at the back of the room.

Guards stormed in from the side doors, forcing a path through the crowd. Steiner knew they would carry him off to solitary confinement, where who-knows-what-else might happen to him. He ripped the end of his sleeve off, sprinted over to Sam, and thrust it into his hand.

"Call this woman immediately. Tell her Jacob Steiner is in trouble, and he'll accept her proposition."

A question began to form on Sam's lips.

"I don't have time to explain. Please call her."

Still looking confused, the boy nodded.

The sting of a stun gun sent Steiner spinning into a world of darkness.

CHAPTER
4

STEINER gazed out the window at the Earth far below, a giant orb radiating colors throughout the spectrum. Streaks of lightning danced at the eastern edge. To the south, a deep blue ocean showed through the brushstrokes of pure-white clouds.

It had been six months since Steiner had been in space, and he had forgotten how much he had missed it.

After being rescued from Atwood, he had been brought to Earthstation's medical center. Once he had bathed, shaved, and combed his hair, an elderly male doctor treated his facial bruises, covering them with a flesh-colored camouflage salve.

The door to the examination room opened. Suzanne Riggs stepped inside with a satchel.

"Well, Jake, you look much better today."

"I feel bett—" Something stung the back of his neck. He twisted around to see the doctor putting an implanter back into his bag. "What was that for?"

"I injected your tracer, of course," the elderly man answered.

Steiner glanced at Suzanne. "Tracer? For what?"

"All convicts in the P.A.V. program have them implanted

in their necks, so that we can keep track of them," she explained.

"Even the captain?"

"You're not a free man yet. The military just wants to protect its investment."

After the doctor picked up his bag and left the room, Steiner grimaced at Suzanne. "I bet you're enjoying this situation. Me, a prisoner, and you, a military director."

She glared at him for a second before opening her satchel. "Atwood finally released your personal possessions." She produced a container from inside the bag and handed it to him.

When he opened the lid to the box, he saw Mary's holodisk sitting on top of a pile of other items. The smooth wafer that held his wife's image felt cool against his palm. She had given it to him as a present on their only anniversary, five months before she died. He slipped it into one of his pockets, then dug around in the bottom until he found his wedding band. The white gold glistened as he slipped it back on his ring finger.

"Wearing that won't bring your wife back," Suzanne said.

"Psychoanalyze someone else, please."

She said nothing for a moment. "I've arranged for you to go aboard the P.A.V. secretly, as you requested." She reached into the mouth of the satchel a second time. "But I question the necessity of it."

"I need to see how the other 'investments' act when they're not trying to impress anyone."

A frown creased her lips as she pulled out two P.A.V. uniforms. "I still think it's dangerous."

"What's the extra uniform for?" he asked.

"Me. I'm going on board with you."

Steiner nearly fell as he jumped off the table. "Forget it."

"I can take care of myself," she replied. "I'm not as helpless as you think."

"A woman on an all-male ship would be asking for trouble."

"Who said anything about my going on board as a woman?" She put a cap over her head, tucking her hair up into it.

"It's too risky. I'm going alone."

"No more arguing, Jake. My decision is final. The convicts are more likely to ignore you if they see you're with someone else."

She was right about that, but he wasn't about to admit it. Biting his lip, he grabbed one of the uniforms.

After getting into the blue-trimmed gray outfits, they made their way through the traffic of engineers, technicians, and security people in the midst of their daily routines.

They stopped at one of the long windows, overlooking the ships in the dock. Suzanne pointed to a smaller vessel than the rest, which resembled an octagonal cylinder with rows of half-spherical gunnery ports bulging from all eight sides. From the front of the ship protruded a cone-shaped energy collector, which channeled stellar gases to the cubical thruster assembly at its rear. From that angle, Steiner could see its port-side, rectangular nacelle, held out by an extension arm to keep its older-styled dimensional shifters safely away from the central hull.

How much worse can this get? Steiner thought to himself. The Stellar-Four Class, or "Peacemakers" as they were commonly called, had served as the watchdogs of the galaxy for over thirty years before the Galactic Civil War began. He thought they had all been destroyed. The last time he had seen one was six years ago on the Day of Betrayal, when the United Star Systems had used every vessel it had to repel the initial surprise attack by the Separatist fleet.

"What do you think?" Suzanne asked.

"You don't want to know," he replied.

With a groan of irritation, she proceeded to the security checkpoint for the docking tube. After she showed the guard her identification card, the young man opened the gateway.

Steiner followed her through it, onto a metallic walkway encased within a transparent cylinder. As they walked the length of it, Steiner surveyed the outside of the vessel. Pulse-cannon damage from ancient battles scarred its rough hull. One section appeared to have been recently repaired where, he imagined, the hull had been breached. Brand-new shield generators dotted the exterior, every five meters, connected by wires, which looked a bit sloppy but were a welcome addition. The eight rows of gunnery ports gave the vessel the advantage of firing at any angle, but each port had to be manually operated by an individual gunner, a severe disadvantage when facing ships with computer-synchronized weaponry.

After following Suzanne through the open outer hatch into the extended gangway of the P.A.V.'s air lock, Steiner watched as she paused before unveiling the interior of the ship. "Welcome aboard, Captain." She pressed a keypad, and the door slid open, giving Steiner his first view inside.

A dimly lit landing area stood before him, with corridors running forward, to the right, and to the left, each leading to its own ramp, which elevated the walkways to meet darkened hallways five feet above the landing. Steiner peeked inside to see if anyone was hiding at the sides of the hatch. With a frustrated huff, Suzanne confidently stepped through the opening. Following her, he thought back to the last time he had been on one of these ships, almost ten years ago. He vaguely remembered its having three main decks and a command center sitting atop the outer hull. The air-lock landing area seemed to be situated between decks.

"Why is it so dark in here?" Steiner asked.

"The head engineer wanted to conserve as much power as he could until the launch."

The silence felt deafening. The metal walls and floors amplified his footsteps. The air tasted musty, probably because of the outdated ventilation system, but at least it contained the correct oxygen mixture.

"Is anyone on board?" he asked.

"All forty-eight men," Suzanne answered.

"Where are they?"

"Does it matter? This will make your tour much easier."

As they walked, Steiner touched the deep scars in the metallic walls from handheld weapons, as if someone had done it for fun.

Suzanne stopped at an adjoining passageway, which stretched the length of the ship in both directions. Loud voices came from the aft section.

"What's going on down there?" Steiner asked.

"It's the ship's bar."

"A bar?" he repeated, unable to believe it. "Aboard a prison ship?"

"It's an incentive for convicts to join the program. I refitted the recreation hall."

"Wouldn't it be wiser to keep them sober for battles?"

"The beer has extremely low alcohol content. It would be next to impossible to become intoxicated."

Loud cheers erupted, followed by thunderous laughter.

"Tell them that," he said.

Suzanne sighed. "Ignore them for now. Let's get on with the tour."

She climbed a stairwell to their immediate right, which led to the upper-deck level. For the next fifteen minutes, she guided him through the vacant crew quarters, explaining how each door to all fifty cabins had been refitted so that the doors could be locked individually or locked in groups from the command center in case he wanted to secure the convicts during their off-hours to encourage them to sleep. Finally, she brought him to massive closed doors at the far end of a wide hallway. Accessing a computer panel embedded in the side of the frame, she entered a series of digits, then stood back as the entry split apart. On the opposite side, a stairway rose into a brightly lit chamber.

"This is the command center," Suzanne said. "Like most of the vital areas of the ship, it can only be opened with a password."

Together, they ascended the dozen steps to the main deck. Viewports surrounded the rectangular room, giving a 360-degree view of the space dock in which the ship sat. The floor sloped down to the helm console at the very front. At the heart of the center stood the captain's seat. It differed from any Steiner had ever seen. A flat, semicircular control board with a domed cover over it was molded to the left armrest.

"I had this specially designed," Suzanne pointed out. "The shielded section is where you can enter passwords without any of the crew seeing you."

"Just how many different codes are there?"

"Ninety-seven." She produced a computer pad from inside her uniform jacket. "I suggest you try to memorize them, so you won't have to carry this around with you."

Listed on the tiny screen on the pad were passwords for the command center, the armory, the landing bay, the two main air locks, and every single pressure door on board. The top code was highlighted. It read PAV:73993.

"What's this one used for?" he asked, pointing to it.

"It's the most important. That prevents other U.S.S. vessels from firing on you."

Steiner's stomach tightened. "Run that by me again."

"Anytime another U.S.S. spacecraft passes near the P.A.V., it will request this password to be transmitted. If it isn't, the ship will automatically assume that your crew has mutinied and open fire."

"What if I'm occupied when that happens?"

"They'll give you ample time to respond before they attack."

"With my luck, I'll meet up with an impatient, trigger-happy captain who will blow me away before I can."

"You've got to think more optimistically. No one in the fleet would do such a thing."

She guided him down a narrow stairwell on the right side of the center and introduced him to his personal conference chamber. The nameplate on the door read: CAPTAIN JOSEPH BARKER.

"This must be the man who was killed," he said.

"Sorry, I'll have it changed tomorrow," Suzanne replied.

"No, leave it up."

"Why?"

Steiner traced the carved letters with his finger. "It will serve as a constant reminder to me never to let my guard down."

The stairwell on the opposite side of the command center led to where the star charts were kept. Suzanne guided him to the rear of the circular control console, which was elevated a foot above the main deck. The weapons console faced the front viewer. Six darkened monitors lined the rear wall. When Suzanne pressed a keypad on the console, the screens flashed to life, depicting vacant corridors.

"Surveillance cameras have been positioned throughout the ship," she explained as she demonstrated by changing the images.

Steiner watched the quick succession of deserted areas on the screens. "Wait, what was that? Back them up just a little."

Suzanne reversed the order, stopping on an overhead view of the massive engine chamber. Three small figures worked near the end of one of the long, cylindrical reactors.

"Who are they?" Steiner asked.

Suzanne zoomed the image in on one of the convicts, an ebony man with thinning gray hair. "That's Phillip Daniels, the head engineer. He helped restore the P.A.V."

Daniels guided a young-looking black man and a lanky white man in reattaching a piece of coolant tubing.

"What's Daniels in prison for?"

"Does it matter?"

"I want to know each of my men's crimes. Now, tell me."

"A few years ago, he worked as a hit man for Mikey Calandra."

"Oh really. Our old friend Mikey, the most sadistic crime boss in the galaxy."

"Jake, nobody is in prison for picking flowers in someone else's yard. Many of these men have brutal pasts. Remember—you were arrested for attempted murder."

"I sought justice."

"A judge didn't think so."

Steiner held his tongue.

After Suzanne locked the command center, she returned to the stairway they had come up and proceeded down to the central hallway, where they could still hear the loud voices coming from the aft area. She headed toward the bow of the ship, showing him the training firing range that she had had converted from a cargo hold, with a row of training assault rifles aimed at light-sensitive targets on the far wall. Finally, trying to avoid the central junction where convicts might be, she directed him to a ladder well that descended into the lower decks. She opened the large landing bay, which held a shuttle and an Armored Transport Carrier to transport assault teams to planets or provide air support. Lining the back walls were four TRAC vehicles with pulse cannons for ground attacks. She ended the tour with the armory. The assortment of assault rifles, AT-7 pistols, handheld missile launchers, and portable laser cannons pleased Steiner. He had expected the ordnance to be as outdated as the ship, but they were top-of-the-line models. Before leaving, he packed two AT-7 pistols and a dozen grenades into Suzanne's satchel and grabbed a hand-held blast shield. He then asked her if she could take them to his assigned cabin, where he could set up his own personal emergency arsenal. She insisted he was being a pessimist but gave in. After they had deposited the armament, he tucked one of the AT-7s under his belt and pulled his jacket over it.

"You'll have to give that back to me when we disembark," Suzanne said.

"I won't need it then," he replied. "I assume our next stop is the bar. I want to be prepared to meet my crew."

She rolled her eyes. "You won't need to be armed for that."

"I'm not as optimistic as you are."

Suzanne shook her head, muttering to herself.

As Steiner exited the cabin, a flicker of light from down the corridor caught his attention. When he turned to look, it was gone. He walked to the end of the passageway and stared up at a lifeless camera embedded in the ceiling.

"Where are you going?" Suzanne asked, following after him.

"Someone just used this camera."

"That's not possible. They can only be operated from the command center. You saw me lock it after we left."

"The indictor light was on."

"It must have been a malfunction. The restoration team probably missed something."

Steiner continued to stare up at the camera, hoping it would relight to confirm what he had said.

"Are you going to watch it all night or finish the tour?" she asked.

Steiner sighed and walked away from the camera. This was an old ship. He couldn't afford to be paranoid over every malfunction. He followed her to their next destination to meet the rest of his crew.

CHAPTER
5

SONGS and laughter mingled with the voices flowing from the bar as Steiner and Suzanne stood at the entrance. A sign labeled the place HELL.

"Part of your crew seems to be religious," Steiner whispered, taking a cautious look through the open doorway. Cigar smoke screened out all but vague images. The odors of liquor and sweat permeated the air, testifying to the number of low-alcohol drinks being served and the patrons' lack of cleanliness.

Steiner walked through the curtain of haze into the establishment. Hell it was, a place of cutthroats, thieves, liars, and murderers. No decent person would want to be there, yet it was filled.

Circular, varnished tables dotted the room, all occupied by groups of convicts. An antique, wooden bar counter, complete with stools, stretched the length of the rear wall. A burly man served drinks from behind it.

Steiner led Suzanne between the tables near a large poker game. Distrustful eyes stared, and cards were concealed as they passed by. A gathering to the left burst out in laughter as someone finished the punch line of a comical story. Vulgar limericks set to song rose from the far right. A couple of convicts huddled in a corner, engaged in an arm-wrestling match.

The bartender, a fat, balding man with a scraggly beard, wiped the wooden counter, oblivious to the proceedings. A smoldering cigar stuck out from his mouth. When he moved, he used a cane to support his left leg. His upper body was well muscled, making his movements quick, despite his disability. The shape of a knife scar on his right cheek matched the scowl on his face. He might have been mistaken for just another brawny thug if not for the glint of intelligence in his eyes.

"Two mugs, please," Steiner said, trying to ignore the nauseous fumes of the cigar.

Without a word of acknowledgment, the bartender poured the drinks. Steiner took the opportunity to admire the assortment of various multicolored bottles shelved behind the counter. The man must collect them. The countertop vibrated when the bartender slammed two full mugs down. Just when Steiner expected him to demand payment, he returned to his cleaning.

Mystified, Steiner picked up the beers, then trailed behind Suzanne to a darkened corner of the crowded room. They found one empty table cluttered with abandoned mugs. She pushed them to one side, providing enough space for both of them to set down their own.

"That bartender," he said, just loud enough for her to hear him over the noise. "What's his story?"

"His name is Bryan Sicket," she replied. "He uses the nickname Bricket." She pressed a few keys on her computer pad, and a personnel file appeared on-screen. "He was a corporate embezzler."

Steiner glanced through the information, noting that Bricket was an expert hacker. That would explain the hint of intelligence but not the rest of his appearance. "Has he always looked that rugged?"

"Eleven years in prison takes its toll." With another touch of her finger, the screen changed to a picture of a gullible-looking, chubby man barely resembling the bartender. "He was disabled during an escape attempt seven years ago.

Since then, he has been highly involved in reform programs like the P.A.V."

Steiner peered over at the bartender, who grudgingly refilled a mug for another customer. "He doesn't seem too excited about his current job."

"On the contrary, he's part owner of the bar. He splits the profits with the prison system. While the ship is docked, the drinks are free in order to keep the crew happy until the launch."

Steiner took a sip of his weak beer, swished it around his mouth, then swallowed the bitter-tasting liquid. He watched as Bricket shoved back a drunken convict who had fallen asleep at the counter. *How could anyone drink enough of this swill to get intoxicated?* Steiner wondered.

For the next half hour, Suzanne went over the records of each member of the crew while Steiner observed their behavior in the bar. Most of their pasts sounded the same— murders, thefts, armed robberies, rapes, and assaults. Steiner found that small doses of his beer temporarily distracted him, making the time pass quicker.

"You have one more officer—the best one out of the lot," Suzanne said. "He's got a previous service record with the United Star Systems. In fact, you've worked with him before."

"Really?" Steiner asked. "What's his name?"

"Maxwell Tramer."

Steiner had taken another sip from his drink when he heard the name. He coughed, liquid spraying out of his nostrils.

"Before you go crazy, hear me out," she said.

Steiner was so furious, he almost forgot where he was. "You have the 'Killer Cyborg' on this ship?"

"Before the accident, he was one of the best weaponry specialists in the fleet," she replied.

"It murdered two innocent men."

"He was forced back into duty before he had time to adjust to his new form. The transition was too much for him. He's had eight years to assimilate. He's ready to serve again."

Steiner fought to keep his temper under control. "I refuse to work with that thing."

"Stop referring to him as an inanimate object. He is alive. I've spoken with him. His warden described him as a quiet, solitary individual who never harmed, or attempted to harm, any other inmate."

Steiner huffed. "If it murdered once, it will again. Maybe that's who killed Barker."

"That's not fair. Give him a chance. When you reach your first port, if you still feel you cannot trust him, you can have him transferred off."

"I don't want Tramer here at all—not after what it did."

Suzanne rolled her eyes. "Many other members of your crew have murdered people."

"But not crumpled their victims."

"Listen to me, Jake. I've interviewed him in depth several times. He's the same man who helped us upgrade the *Valiant* eight years ago."

"No," Steiner shouted, pounding his fist on the table.

The noise startled several of the convicts close to them. They turned to stare. Steiner ignored them and sipped at his drink as if nothing had happened. The men lost interest.

"Maxwell is dead," Steiner said much softer. "Some cyberneticists created their version of life using what was left of his body. Don't ask me to treat it like anything except what it is: a killing machine."

"I would transfer him off if I could, but no facility in the area is equipped with the security needed to house him."

"What about its previous prison?"

"It's located in the Southern Territory of the galaxy. No vessel is available to transport him there before the P.A.V. launches. I'm sorry, but you'll have to take him as far as the Tycus base. That's where you'll get an encrypted Orders disk."

"That's two weeks away. I don't want that thing on board for a day. Use your prestigious rank to influence someone to take it."

Her countenance darkened. "There's nothing I can do. You're stuck with him for a while."

Steiner wanted to hit the table again but couldn't afford any more attention. "I can't understand why you ever enlisted Tramer to begin with," he said.

"I gave him a second chance, just like I gave you," Suzanne replied.

Loud cheers rose from the counter, where a group of prisoners had rallied together. Bricket grumbled as he backed away from the assembly. A man climbed up on the bar and danced around, shouting for everyone's attention.

When the room quieted, the man stood erect. "Do you know who I am?"

The crowd responded in an unintelligible chatter of individual voices. Steiner recognized him as one of the maintenance personnel but couldn't remember his name.

"I'm Captain Barker, raised from the dead," the man shouted. Boos and hisses rose up in reply. "I'm here to make soldiers out of you all. We'll start with our daily exercises." He did jumping jacks while being assaulted by wadded-up napkins.

"I'm sure they're just venting their frustrations," Suzanne whispered.

Steiner imagined the real Joseph Barker acting like this caricature. Maybe that was why he was killed. Maybe he tried to make this ragged bunch into a model crew.

"If anyone does anything wrong," the phony captain threatened, "I'll punish all of you."

"Kill him," several people chanted.

Reaching under his tunic, Steiner's fingers tightened around the handle of his AT-7.

"Don't do anything yet, Jake," Suzanne pleaded. "They're just fooling around."

Louis Rathen, one of the pilots she had briefed him about, jumped onto the counter. The audience went wild as he bowed. "Time to die," he bellowed at the other actor. He reached into his shirt and pulled out a pistol.

Steiner sprang to his feet and stormed through the crowd, shoving convicts out of his path. Somewhere behind him, he heard Suzanne shouting for him to stop.

Louis Rathen pretended to shoot his gun. The "captain" grabbed his chest and fell into the raised arms of nearby patrons. When the mob lowered the actor to the ground, Steiner greeted the man with an uppercut to the jaw. Rage constricted the faces of all the spectators. When Steiner whipped out his AT-7, they backed away.

Louis Rathen stood motionless on the counter, staring down in apparent bewilderment.

With a powerful swipe of his free hand, Steiner knocked the pilot's feet out from under him, sending him crashing down against the hard surface. While Rathen was still dazed, Steiner whisked the pistol from his grasp.

"Jake," Suzanne screamed.

Steiner spun around in time to see a convict grab her by the wrist and rip her hat off.

"It's a woman," the man exclaimed.

Steiner aimed both gun muzzles, causing everyone in their sights to drop to the ground. "Let her go," he ordered, then squeezed the triggers. Energy bolts dug into the table right next to the man holding Suzanne, shattering all the glass mugs on it.

The convict released her and threw up his hands.

Silence engulfed the room as all eyes fixed on Steiner. "I'm your new captain," he shouted. "I won't be as easy to kill as Barker."

Suzanne stepped through the gathering, giving him an irritated glare.

"I expect all of you to be cleaned up for the launch tomorrow," he bellowed at the men.

After handing the confiscated pistol to Suzanne, he yanked Rathen off the counter and dragged him toward the exit. A path split apart for them as they passed through the crowd. Before leaving the establishment, he took a last look at his future crew, making sure they didn't make any sudden moves. They appeared too surprised to do anything but gape. Behind the counter, Bricket's bearded face grinned with pleasure.

Steiner led his prisoner some distance from the bar, then shoved him up against the bulkhead. "Where did you get a pistol?"

"I can't remember."

Steiner pressed the barrel of his AT-7 into Rathen's nostrils. "Since I'm a convict, too, it wouldn't make much difference if I burned your head off right now."

"One of the visiting technicians sold it to me," the pilot blurted out.

"How many more weapons are on board?"

"I don't know—maybe a dozen."

Steiner leered at Suzanne. "So much for your tight security."

She ignored the remark. "What are you going to do to him?"

"Throw him off this ship as an example to the others."

"You need three pilots. How am I going to find a replacement by tomorrow?"

"Can you enlist anyone?"

"Just about. Why?"

"I know a pilot."

CHAPTER

6

"I can't believe I agreed to do this," Mason said as he looked out a window at the docked P.A.V. "A Peacemaker. They haven't made one of these in about thirty years. We'll be outmatched by every vessel we encounter."

As Steiner expected, Suzanne responded immediately with her defense. "As I pointed out to you earlier, Mr. Mason, you won't be required to engage any enemy craft. Your missions will only be of an information-gathering nature."

"Oh, I forgot. We're pirates, working *for* the U.S.S."

Suzanne rolled her eyes, muttering something under her breath.

Steiner hadn't been surprised that Mason had joined the program. The man probably would have done anything to escape his mundane prison life.

Sam pressed his face against the transparent glass. "What's it like traveling through phased space?"

"You've never experienced the fifth dimension?" Mason asked.

The teenager's eyes widened as the pilot exaggerated about interphasing in order to traverse the galaxy at greater speeds than physically possible. Mason emphasized the need for highly skilled hoppers, like himself, to make sure that they didn't collide with anything along the way.

Steiner smiled, amused by Sam's innocent excitement. When he had visited Atwood to enlist Mason, he had never intended to bring Sam along. But the boy had begged to come, and suddenly it had seemed like a sort of solution since the alternative was leaving him behind at Big Al's mercy. Besides, Jake needed a friend he could trust.

Suzanne drew Steiner back from his fellow shipmates. "How do you know Rick Mason is any good at space piloting? When I did a background check on him, I came up empty."

"The stories he told in prison were too technical to have been made up," Steiner replied. "He even described some of the captains perfectly."

"Can you trust him?"

"More than Tramer."

The retort earned a glare from Suzanne. "Let's go. Your meeting with your crew is in fifteen minutes." She started down the corridor.

Steiner called Mason and Sam from the window, then led them after her.

Three station personnel passed by in the opposite direction, eyeing Steiner and his convict friends with looks of disgust. Steiner ignored them. He expected this kind of behavior from other military personnel.

Mason scratched his neck. "Regardless of what that old medicine man told us, I can still feel that piece of circuitry he shot into me."

"It's your imagination," Suzanne said from the front. "The tracers are painless."

"That's what you think, Legs," Mason replied.

"Get used to it, Shorty," she shot back.

Mason grinned. "A beauty with a mouth."

Suzanne stopped at the security checkpoint for the docking tube.

A young male guard saluted.

"Has the vessel remained secure during the night?" she asked.

"Yes, ma'am. All the prisoners are accounted for."

The way the guard answered her aroused Steiner's suspicions. He stepped forward. "Has anyone gone on board?"

The guard didn't even acknowledge him but kept his attention focused on Suzanne.

"Did you let someone pass?" Suzanne repeated his question.

The guard hesitated. "A technician went through earlier this morning to retrieve a tool. He only took a minute."

Suzanne flushed. "I explicitly told you no one goes on or off without my permission."

The young man stiffened. "I'm sorry, ma'am."

"Did the technician have anything on him?" Steiner asked.

The guard ignored him again.

Steiner reached over, grabbed him by the collar, and dragged him half over the desk. "Answer me, now."

"The security sensors didn't detect anything," the man stammered.

When Steiner released his hold, the guard drew his sidearm. Steiner slapped the weapon from the young man's hand. It clattered across the floor.

"At ease, Private," Suzanne shouted. "I'll handle it from here."

The guard scowled at her as he picked up his pistol and departed.

"With security like that, no wonder half the convicts are already armed," Steiner grumbled.

"Why did you do that, Jake?" Suzanne shouted. "Nothing gives you the right—"

"While we were at Atwood, I got the impression the warden was stalling us," he cut her off. "I think this technician might be the reason."

"You think Ralph sent him?"

"Of course—who else? I want my gun back."

"Not until we get on board."

"I don't want you coming with us."

Her countenance darkened. "If you're worried about my safety, don't bother."

"That wasn't my concern. If I'm going to succeed, I need to portray myself as a strong leader. Having my superior with me might tarnish that image."

She glanced over at Mason and Sam, watching a few feet away, then nodded. "You win." She extracted a holster with an AT-7 from her handbag. "Just don't kill anyone yet." As she handed the belt to him, she kissed his cheek. "Keep in touch."

Steiner strapped on the pistol. "If you don't hear from me, it means I'm dead."

Suzanne frowned. "Your crew is better than you think."

Steiner beckoned Mason and Sam to follow him into the docking tube. When they were all inside, Suzanne wished them well, then closed the entrance.

Steiner walked in silence through the transparent tunnel, gazing out at the old ship he was about to board. During last night's visit, his disguise had offered some protection. Today, the gold-and-silver rank emblems on his black jacket made him a target. When he focused on his reflection in the heavy glass, he was reminded of the way corpses were dressed up before being laid in their coffins.

"Did I understand you and Legs correctly?" Mason asked. "Is someone still gunning for you?"

"That's why I got this," Steiner said, as his hand slapped the holstered AT-7.

"Just make sure I don't get caught in the middle."

As he stepped into the P.A.V.'s air lock, Steiner pulled out Suzanne's computer pad and searched for the password to open the interior hatch. "Don't worry. I can handle myself." He punched the designated code into a keypad. A gush of air blew into his face, forcing him to blink, as the door slid aside.

The bright interior lighting blazed into the darkened air lock, stinging Steiner's eyes. Despite the luminance, the ship's walls appeared bleak and colorless. Steiner stepped on board hesitantly and looked around. The three branching passageways were empty, but voices and noises echoed from deep within them.

After sealing both hatches to the air lock, Steiner led Mason and Sam toward the heart of the vessel. Steiner's throat felt as dry as the air flowing out of the ventilation ducts. He caressed the inviting handgrip of his AT-7.

He tensed when he saw two crew members turn the corner toward them. They talked casually, then froze upon seeing Steiner. They stood at attention and saluted. When Steiner returned the gesture, the men continued walking by, casting a couple of curious glances behind until they disappeared down the junction by the air lock.

Steiner exhaled with relief. Maybe this wouldn't be as bad as he expected. The scorched walls reminded him otherwise.

When Steiner rounded a junction leading toward the cafeteria, he stopped just short of running into a seven-foot-tall metallic mass. The hairs on the back of his neck stood on end as he looked into the two eyes staring down at him. One, a human ocular cavity, gray and lifeless, the other, a glowing blue sensor orb. They were centered on a grotesquely deformed head, half-covered with apparatuses. The facial tissue was deathly pale and scarred, overlapping in areas where it had been sewn together. The arms and legs were entirely mechanical, fashioned to resemble oversized human appendages. A polished breastplate hid the body's torso from view. Small see-through gaps protruded through the servos and gyrating components around the metallic pelvis frame. The scent of something like embalming fluid and rot hung in the air.

Mason spat a curse under his breath.

Steiner had seen pictures of this "thing," but they couldn't prepare him for the utter terror he experienced standing next to it.

"Captain Steiner?" The blackish lips moved, but the synthesized voice emanated from a device embedded in the neck.

Steiner fought to keep his voice from betraying any fear. "Yes. Are you Tramer?"

The hideous face remained an expressionless mask. "I am he."

He? Steiner repeated to himself. How could it possibly think it was a man or even close to one? This monstrosity was an "it," never a "he."

"Hi. I'm Sam." The boy stepped forward, extending a hand.

Tiny motors whined as Tramer's head tilted down to look at the boy. Mason pulled Sam back. The blue sensor orb rose to shine at Steiner once again. "Captain," the disembodied voice said. "Your officers have assembled in the cafeteria."

"Inform them that I will be there shortly," Steiner replied.

Mechanisms inside the cyborg's body danced to life, turning it around in preparation to depart.

Steiner clenched his fists. How could Suzanne have possibly thought that this was the person that had once worked with them on the *Valiant*? It looked and acted nothing like the man he once knew. Despite its previous murders, Steiner refused to be afraid of it. If it killed him, too, he would be with Mary again.

"Tramer," Steiner shouted, before the cyborg got far.

A hum emanated from a joint in the mechanical man's hips as its entire torso pivoted around to face him. The unnatural stance further testified that it was only a machine.

"You forgot to salute," Steiner said.

Mason cringed like a trapped animal ready to flee.

One of Tramer's metallic arms rose, its spiny, clawlike fingers lining together before reaching the top of the disfigured head. The legs began moving, drawing the backward-facing body away. The torso spun to its forward position as it continued down the corridor. In a few seconds, the thuds of its heavy footsteps faded into the distance.

"Please don't tell me Gruesome is part of the crew," Mason growled.

"Our weapons officer," Steiner answered.

Mason's gaze burned. "Why didn't you mention that earlier before I agreed to come on board?"

"I don't want Tramer here any more than you do, but I didn't have a choice. It was Suzanne's idea."

"Of course it was, since she won't be cruising the galaxy with it."

"Don't worry," Steiner said, motioning them forward again. "I've already made plans to get rid of it."

Steiner followed the path that the cyborg had taken, each step bringing him closer to that monstrosity. A cold, forbidding feeling began to invade his soul. Death awaited him just ahead.

When they arrived at the doorway to the cafeteria, Sam started off by himself. "Since I'm not an officer, I'm going to do some exploring."

"Why don't you wait until one of us can join you?" Steiner asked.

"I can take care of myself." With that, Sam tramped away.

Steiner was tempted to chase after him but held back.

"He's tough," Mason said. "He'll be fine."

I hope so, Steiner thought, entering the cafeteria. He winced as he passed Tramer, who stood along the inside wall. He doubted he would ever become accustomed to its hideous appearance.

The dining area was similar to the one at Atwood, about a hundred feet long and sixty wide. An adjoining kitchen lay on the opposite side, oversized pots and pans hanging from ceiling hooks.

Seven other officers sat alone, scattered about long, rectangular tables with attached benches. Their sitting positions confirmed how much work it would take for Steiner to teach them to think as a unified group. He called them all forward to a single table at the head of the room. When the men had moved to the selected seats, Steiner glanced over at Tramer, who hadn't budged from its position by the door. He wasn't about to invite it closer. He wanted to stay as far away from it as possible.

"I'm Captain Jacob Steiner," he said to the convicts gathered around the table. "Please introduce yourselves and tell what position you hold."

The gray-haired hit man rose first. "I'm Phillip Daniels, the head engineer."

"How many are in your staff?" Steiner asked, trying to keep his gaze from drifting to the cyborg's glaring sensor orb.

"Seven, including myself."

"How long would it take to complete a visual survey of all the vital systems?"

"Half an hour. Is there a problem?"

"An intruder came aboard this morning. I want to make sure nothing has been tampered with."

"I'll make sure everything is checked before we depart." Daniels sounded too eager to please. Steiner wondered what the head engineer might be secretly planning.

The bartender tapped his cane against the floor and grinned. "Bricket's my name. I'm the senior computer specialist, and I also moonlight as the keeper of the well."

Steiner nodded.

A lean, muscular man with a mustache that bulged out over his upper lip came to his feet. "Benjamin Richards, chief of security." Steiner remembered how proud Suzanne had been when she had told him about her choice of Richards. The man was a former police officer, convicted for beating information out of his prisoners. He held belts in three different forms of martial arts.

"These are my assistants in charge of keeping the peace," Richards said, signaling for two men to rise. "Larry Hulsey and Eddie the Giant."

An average man of five and a half feet, Hulsey was small-boned, built for quick mobility. At first glance, he looked like a college student on the honor roll, but this seemingly harmless man had teeth. He had gunned down three drug dealers because they had overdosed his girlfriend. Steiner recalled his amazement when Suzanne had told him it had taken a SWAT team to capture Hulsey.

Towering over his colleagues at nearly seven feet, Eddie was a former professional wrestler, in prison for raping a senator's daughter. His dark-skinned arms rippled with muscles twice the size of Steiner's. The mountainous swells of his chest stretched his uniform to the limits, but farther down, his contour narrowed into an overhanging stomach. Even out of shape, he looked like he could easily fight three people at a time.

"Weapons have been smuggled aboard, gentlemen," Steiner told them. "Your job will be to search out and confiscate any weapons on the ship."

"May we be armed with anything more than stun guns?" Richards asked.

"Not at this time."

The security chief frowned as he and his assistants returned to their seats.

The two remaining men at the table showed no enthusiasm as they announced themselves.

"Julio Sanchez, pilot."

"Mack Palmer, pilot."

"Rick Mason, the best pilot," came a shout from the opposite end of the table.

The two stared at Mason, who smiled triumphantly.

Since all the men at the table had introduced themselves, Steiner turned toward Tramer. It remained silent.

"Tramer is our temporary weapons officer," Steiner said. "It will be leaving us at Tycus."

The cyborg didn't react in the slightest.

"I understand my predecessor had many rules," Steiner said, casually walking around the table to escape the blue glare from the cyborg. "I have only one—stay alive. To do that, we must function as a team. Anyone not willing to do so will end up in the ship's brig." He purposely glanced over at Tramer. It was a meaningless threat. A detention cell probably couldn't hold it.

While he outlined their upcoming raids, he found himself constantly reminded of Tramer's presence. The sensor orb glistened in the pots hanging above the adjoining kitchen. When he looked at the floor, he saw a pale blue glow bordering his shadow on the floor.

He passed out lists, which divided the forty-eight-member crew into three groups of sixteen and designated them by a color code, RED, BLUE, and GREEN. According to his schedule, each crewman would spend eight hours a day in ship operations, followed by another eight of weapons training.

The stench of the cyborg grew more prominent in the room as each moment passed. Steiner began to taste it in his mouth.

"From now on, the bar will be restricted," Steiner said. Bricket's mouth dropped open. "For each successfully completed work shift, everyone will be awarded time to use it. This will give the crew an extra incentive to perform."

"You'll put me out of business with rules like that," Bricket said.

"Your money would be worthless if we don't survive the first mission. Any other questions?"

No one spoke.

"All stations, report ready at 0930. RED shift leads out. You're dismissed."

Steiner watched the men leave. Tramer stared at him for a long, uneasy moment, then marched out through the door.

"Ironhand—I mean, Captain," Mason said. "If I were you, I would try to make friends with Gruesome, not anger the thing."

The mutilated bodies of the cyborg's two former victims flashed into Steiner's mind, but he quickly discarded them. "There's a half hour left before the launch," Steiner said, changing the subject. "Would you check on Sam before you head to the command center?"

"Sure," Mason replied, heading toward the door.

Steiner sat alone in the spacious sanctum, enjoying a moment of silence. He reached into his jacket and pulled out Mary's holocard. When he activated it, her face flickered to life before him. Green eyes sparkled under waves of dark hair.

"I may be joining you soon," he whispered to her.

STEINER waited in his custom-made chair as each of the RED shift reported to the command center for duty. While he watched them prepare their posts, he wondered which of them might be planning his demise. Heavy footsteps warned him of Tramer's entering and moving to the weapons console. Steiner didn't look back at it. The sight of it disgusted him.

"Captain, all stations have reported in, except for the engine room," Tramer announced.

The mechanical hardness of the voice grated on Steiner's nerves. He refused to acknowledge the cyborg's report.

Down at the helm, Simmons, the navigator, was showing Mason what course had been plotted. Ever since Mason had entered the center, he had been so busy that he hadn't found time to talk. Steiner wanted to ask where Sam was but refrained.

To get his mind off the boy, Steiner stepped up onto the raised platform behind him. He passed by Tramer at the weapons console and stopped at the security station against the back wall. The monitors displayed several scenes of the crew hurrying with last-minute preparations. One view depicted three engineers searching along the cylindrical reactors that stretched the length of a massive chamber.

"Daniels hasn't finished with his inspection," Tramer said.

The deck vibrated several times. Miniature motors

whined closer. Steiner looked up at the lifeless face looming over him. He fought back the urge to shrink away.

"He estimates a fifteen-minute delay," Tramer added.

"Thank you," Steiner replied with a forced smile. "I'll wait in my conference room."

When he retreated down the stairwell into his private sanctuary, the nameplate on the door reminded him of his predecessor's fate and perhaps his own. Footsteps followed behind him. He whirled about, half-expecting to see Tramer. Instead, it was Mason.

"Have you seen the instruments I have to work with? I've had better on most of the freighters I used to operate. Isn't this supposed to be a warship? A senior citizen's mobility unit is better equipped."

Steiner smiled. Mason's colorful exaggerations always cheered him up, even when they weren't intended to. "This, coming from the man who bragged he could master anything that flew."

"I can fly it," Mason replied. "But it's going to be a real long trip. Most ships are equipped with third-generation phase drives. This bucket has the original model. It'll take weeks to get to the border."

"Two weeks," Steiner corrected.

"Whatever." Mason glanced up the stairwell, then pressed the keypad to close the door. "I don't like being up there that long with Gruesome. He makes me nervous—like he's always watching me. And, his body smells like it's decomposing."

"We've got to work with it for now. Did you find Sam?"

"He's in the bar, chatting with some of the off-duty men. He's a smart kid. He'll be fine."

Steiner had already suspected that, but it set his mind at ease to hear confirmation.

The ship shuddered, then mellowed into a slight drone.

"The engines are active," Mason said.

"Captain," Tramer's voice erupted from the intercom, "Daniels reports that all the vital systems are clear of tampering."

Steiner touched a keypad on the desk. "I'm on my way." After closing the channel, he found Mason grinning at him.

"I see I'm not the only one that shakes whenever that thing speaks," the pilot said. "It's almost like death calling your name, isn't it?"

Without a reply, Steiner made his way to the door. After climbing up to the center, he slid into his command chair, while Mason took his place at the helm.

"Earthstation, this is Captain Steiner, requesting departure instructions."

"P.A.V.," the controller responded, "you are cleared for launch on path seven.

"Take us out, Mr. Mason," Steiner said.

"My pleasure," Mason replied as he manipulated their vessel forward.

The low grinding of metal vibrated from the hull. An alarm rang out.

"Collision alert," the controller shouted. "P.A.V., adjust your course immediately."

Mason flushed as he worked frantically to correct his error. After the ship backed away from the side of the dock, one of the mooring clamps could be seen bent up against the superstructure.

Steiner's faith in the smuggler's skill wavered for a moment, then strengthened when the P.A.V. glided gracefully away from the station. Their ship never deviated from its flight path again—not even by a meter.

Sunlight pierced through one of the side viewports, maneuvering the shadows around the room as the P.A.V. banked on its course. Other vessels passed by, arriving on neighboring paths. A few minutes later, they had cleared all other traffic. The starry expanse stretched out forever, waiting to accept them.

"Increasing to top velocity," Mason said.

The Earth shrank away in the rear viewport until it was a speck lost in the vast field of space.

"Phase," Steiner commanded.

His stomach sank as the universe around them faded into the darkness of interdimensional travel.

CHAPTER

7

WITH his AT-7 holstered at his side, ready to be drawn at the slightest provocation, Steiner walked through the P.A.V., inspecting the performance of his crew. His muscles ached from the constant tension he exerted on them to keep himself ready to defend against an attack. At any moment, someone might jump out at him from one of the open doorways or shadowy corners.

During the six hours since the launch, he'd noticed that the other convicts were always silent in his presence; some even stared until he left. He sensed they were afraid of him. He liked that. It might keep him alive longer.

He fastened another button on his jacket. Why was he so cold all the time? An hour earlier, he had checked the environmental controls just to make sure the temperature gauge was set for the mid seventies. Perhaps it was malfunctioning, too. He shivered. The lifeless gray surroundings strengthened the chill that gripped him. Even as he passed by workmen repairing the seared walls, it couldn't melt his utter despair. He knew he was probably only there to die.

When he ascended a stairway to the second level of the crew quarters, he caught a glimpse of someone following far behind him. Impulsively, his hand went to the handle of his pistol.

No, he scolded himself, easing his fingers off the weapon. Paranoia might be stealing his judgment away. He would first test his suspicion.

He entered one of the ladder wells and climbed down to the lower decks, where the landing bay and armory were located. Rarely did anyone go down there.

After walking a short distance through a vacant passageway, he pretended to stop in order to use Suzanne's computer pad. While he faked pressing its keypads, he ventured a quick glance behind him. The straggler wasn't there. Just as relief began to flood through him, his peripheral vision caught a face peeking around a corner in the direction from which he had just come.

There was no mistake about it this time.

He continued on as if he hadn't noticed the man, picking up his pace just enough to get out of visual range. When the corridor curved slightly, he slipped into a niche in the bulkhead. He pressed himself into it, feeling the icy touch of metal against the back of his head. His breathing quickened.

Less than a minute passed before he heard the scuffle of footsteps. He lifted his AT-7 from its holster and sprang from his hiding place. His pistol muzzle was pointed at—

Sam?

Steiner lowered his gun, paralyzed by the fear that he might have shot the boy. Sam must have been the one trailing him all along. Steiner checked to make sure no one else was in sight, then thrust Sam into the concealment of the niche.

"What do you think you're doing by following me?" He whispered what he wanted to scream. "I could have killed you."

"I'm watching your back," Sam answered.

"I don't need your protection." Steiner realized his voice had risen too loud. A deep breath calmed him enough to continue. "I don't care what happens to me, but I want to make sure you're safe. If you're seen with me, it could put you in jeopardy."

"You saved me from Al," Sam replied. "I owe you."

"I didn't bring you along so that you can repay me."

"That's the only reason I came."

Steiner sighed. From past experience, he knew it was useless to try to change the boy's convictions about anything. If Sam was determined to protect him, then nothing would keep him from doing so. However, there was a chance that his mission could be modified.

"Sam, if you truly want to help me, then you must pretend you don't know me." When the boy tried to speak, Steiner covered his mouth. "Hear me out first." He waited for a nod before he removed his hand.

Sam's eyes sparkled with the fire of determination, yet he remained still.

"Blend in with the other convicts," Steiner told him. "Act like them. Get them to trust you. Then, you can function as my eyes and ears for any approaching danger."

The boy's gaze softened. "I'll agree if you watch your back better."

"I spotted you, didn't I?"

"After being followed halfway across the ship. If I had a weapon, I could have—"

Sam deflected Steiner's hand as it came up to silence him again. The memories of their defense-training matches at Atwood came back to Steiner. He twisted the boy's arms together. Sam fought vainly to release himself, but he had never been a match for Steiner physically. A grin cracked the boy's strained face as his strength gave out.

"I'll beat you someday," he said between gasps for breath.

Steiner couldn't prevent himself from chuckling softly. "But not today, amigo. Are we clear on your role?"

"How can I warn you if I can't be seen with you?"

"Use Mason as a messenger."

When Sam nodded, Steiner freed his arms.

"Be sure to keep one eye behind you," the boy said.

"I will. Now, get out of here."

Sam punched him in the arm lightly, smiled, then slipped out of the niche.

Steiner hated to think how much he would miss the teenager's company.

* * *

THE next two days passed as the first, long and filled with anxiety. Steiner didn't allow himself to sleep even for a few hours. Above all else, he had to maintain an unpredictable schedule, which would make it difficult for anyone trying to kill him.

Nobody had tried yet.

The effects from lack of sleep finally caught up with him as he patrolled through the firing range. Inside the darkened arena, his vision blurred worse than it had all day. When he closed his eyes to allow them to adjust, the haze building in his head seemed to ease. After a few seconds, he opened them, determined not to be tempted to sleep again.

He toured behind the BLUE team as they stood in a line, armed with fake assault rifles, shooting light rays at targets on a far wall. The camera in the back corner of the room panned along with Steiner. He could feel Tramer's stare boring into him. Since the beginning of the voyage, the cyborg had never left the command center. It kept watch over the entire ship through the security monitors.

Steiner stopped behind one of the gunners, James Grant, impressed by the accuracy of his shots. The man might be the best marksman they had. As Steiner watched, the flashes on the target began to blur together into a fuzzy, twinkling star. All the surrounding sights and noises faded out. The sparkling orb grew in radiance until it was all he could see. His mind floated into its grasp.

Mary looked up into his eyes, sharing a secret smile with him before placing the wedding band on his finger. Her eyes watered as the minister pronounced them husband and wife. They kissed.

A shout pierced his ears.

Steiner cried out as his attention snapped back to the range. James Grant froze in the midst of what seemed to be a celebration dance. His target blinked with the symbol for a perfect score.

Grant and the men around him stared at Steiner, startled by his sudden outburst. An uneasy moment passed as Steiner tried to think of a way to rationalize his odd behavior. His mind was too clouded by weariness to be creative.

"Continue with the next set." Tramer's voice echoed throughout the arena.

At the command of their leader, Grant and the rest of the BLUE shift began firing at the targets once again.

When Steiner looked up into the rear corner, he found the camera still aimed at him. He tried to swallow the shame welling up in his throat.

Faint snickers sounded from the trainees as he left the range. Steiner was disappointed with himself. The incident would be all over the ship within a few hours. It might cause the crew to lose their fear of him.

As he continued with his rounds, he found that his mind strayed more often. It became a struggle to focus his attention. Shadows played at the corners of his vision, causing him to flinch for no reason. Maybe he needed some food? He stopped by the cafeteria, got a meal, and took it to his cabin. He refused to eat in view of the convicts since it would be a sign of his own mortality. They needed to believe him to be an indestructible man, requiring no nourishment or rest. His mistake earlier might have tarnished that image. He couldn't afford any more displays of weakness. Not ever.

The synthesized entrées tasted bland, but at least they were nourishing. He closed his eyes momentarily and found it difficult to open them again. His muscles ached with fatigue. He had to have rest, even if it was just a brief nap. He couldn't risk being asleep for long, since he still had to maintain his hourly rounds. He stretched out on the cot, his body welcoming the softness of the mattress.

For reassurance, he dragged out the weapons that he had put under the cot during his tour with Suzanne. He positioned the satchel of grenades next to him on the mattress, then propped the blast shield up against the bed frame, directly in front of his body.

Satisfied, he surrendered himself into the tender grasp of his pillow and let his thoughts go.

It wasn't long before sleep embraced him, a dreamy haze of images and colors, swirling around in giant whirlpools. Peace replaced all worries. He wanted to stay there forever.

An irritating sound echoed throughout the rainbowlike landscapes. He recognized it as the call of pain and suffering.

When he tried to flee from it, his legs wouldn't move. The noise grew in intensity until he couldn't bear it any longer.

When he awoke, he found his portable comlink flashing, its message alarm beeping. He brought the device up to his face. "Steiner here," he said.

"Captain," the synthesized voice of Tramer replied, "we have a U.S.S. ship requesting transmission of your password."

"How long have they been waiting?"

"Nearly five minutes. They have forced us to dephase into normal space and armed their weapons."

Steiner bolted from his cot, almost falling down from a head rush. "Why didn't you call me sooner?" he bellowed as he strapped on his gun belt.

"I have been signaling you since the ship first appeared. Only now have you answered."

The mysterious noises in Steiner's dream must have been the message alarm. It was his own fault for not responding to it earlier. "I'm on my way," he said, softening his tone.

He splashed water on his face, jarring his senses back to life, and sprinted from his cabin. As he ran down the corridors, dodging crew members, he scolded himself for dropping his guard again. Twice now, his mistakes had weakened his image.

When he bounded up the steps to the command center, his heart stopped at the sight of the cyborg standing at the top. His hatred of it paled in comparison to the threat of attack. He raced past it without a second thought.

A small gunship closed distance in the front viewport, all weapons trained on them.

The navigator, Simmons, sat at the communication console, begging the other vessel's commander to wait. He backed away from the mouthpiece to allow Steiner to speak into it.

"This is Captain Jacob Steiner. Hold your fire."

"Transmit the appropriate password," came the response.

"I was asleep. Stand down."

"You have twenty seconds left to comply." The channel went dead.

Idiots, Steiner shouted silently. Even though he and his crew were prisoners, they deserved to be treated with the same respect due other U.S.S. personnel.

He slid into his command chair to access the shielded keyboard. His fingers hesitated above the pads. A wave of panic swept through him when he realized that he had forgotten to bring Suzanne's computer pad. In his hurry, he had left it next to his bed.

He searched frantically though his memory. What was the password? It started with "PAV." What were the numbers that followed? It had been a simple series with several repeating digits. If there weren't any urgency, he would probably be able to remember.

"Captain," Tramer said emotionlessly. "They have been waiting too long already."

Steiner glanced up at the cyborg. Its words hinted urgency, but its face showed none. Even in a crisis, this thing still didn't show a trace of emotion. No fear. Nothing.

The gunship made a wide loop as if it were about to make an attack run. Would it actually fire on one of their own?

"Captain, transmit the password," Simmons cried out. "They're going to destroy us."

The password. Didn't it start with a seven? Two nines were in it too. What was the last pair of repeating numbers? One, two, three—three. That was it. He typed into the keyboard, "PAV:73993."

The gunship broke off from its charge at the last second and sailed over them. It sped off into the distance.

Simmons gave a heavy sigh of relief.

Julio Sanchez glared back at Steiner from the helm. "Any orders, sir?" he asked in a low tone that seemed to hint at contempt.

"Continue on previous heading," Steiner replied firmly.

After a brief hesitation, Sanchez phased the ship into starspeed.

Steiner's insides felt like they were dropping into his knees as the star field faded away. He stayed in the command center for a moment to allow the sensation to pass. Shame burned within. Whatever fear the convicts had of him had probably been destroyed.

Steiner stood up as proudly as he could and departed. Tramer's sensor orb followed him out.

CHAPTER

8

"THE odds are favoring me today," Mason said as he laid his cards on the table. He had a full house.

With a growl, Bricket threw his cards down, revealing only a pair of sevens. "Not again. You must be the luckiest pirate around."

Standing inside the entrance of the bar, Steiner watched them from a distance, rubbing his chin, letting his new beard growth prickle against his palm.

Eddie leaned against the doorframe, keeping out any passing crew member who didn't qualify to enter the establishment.

Steiner smiled at him, but the man just ignored him. He returned his attention to the poker players across the room.

Nearly a week had passed since the launch, and no one had attempted to harm him yet. Since Joseph Barker never made it out of the space dock before being killed, Steiner had expected someone to have come at him already. What were they waiting for? The impending danger had begun to sprout up like weeds of paranoia within the gardens of his mind, beginning to undermine his rationality. He couldn't fight the feeling that something was building on the horizon, preparing to explode soon.

The air in the bar was clear of smoke and only slightly stank of stale liquor. Quiet rumbles of voices flowed from three small groups of convicts, sitting in the far corners. While Bricket gambled with Mason, the bartender's assistant stood behind the counter, polishing the collection of stylish bottles lining the shelves against the rear wall.

Steiner took a couple steps closer to the poker players, then hesitated, unsure whether he should bother them.

Loneliness had driven him here to find Mason. He knew the pilot played poker with the bartender daily during his off-duty hours. Besides Sam, Mason was the only person on this ship he could trust.

Mason brushed his slick black hair out of his face and looked up at Steiner. A devious grin curled his lips. "Hey, Ironhand, would you care to play with us? I could use the extra money."

Steiner was thankful to hear someone address him. "Chess is the only game I'm interested in."

Mason grimaced. "Too much thinking for my taste." His feet shoved out a chair across from him. "At least join us for a moment."

It was the invitation Steiner had been waiting for. He threaded his way through the vacant tables dotted with abandoned beer mugs. The sticky floor sucked at his boots as if screeching out to all the listening ears that he was lowering his defenses for a moment. Nevertheless, he continued forward.

He sat on the edge of the offered seat and tried to open the conversation casually. "It's become much more civilized in here than before."

"That policy of yours cleaned it up, along with half my profits," Bricket grumbled.

Not a good start, Steiner scolded himself.

Mason relieved the tension with a snicker. "Earlier today, a couple of guys tried to sneak past that mountain guarding the entrance." He pointed at Eddie, posted inside the doorway. "I doubt they'll ever try again." He broke into laughter. "They got tossed out like rag dolls."

A shout tore through the subdued noises in the bar, jarring Steiner's defenses to life. His fingers instantly found the grip of his AT-7 and he wheeled around in his chair. On the far side of the room, a convict shoved Simmons away from his table, cursed at him, and told him he'd kill him if he ever bothered him again. Simmons left the room while a couple of other men barked insults at him.

"Calm down, Ironhand," Mason said reassuringly. "It's just the navigator getting what he deserves."

"What do you mean by that?"

"The backstabber gossips about everyone."

The man at the other table started quieting down. Steiner's hand eased away from his weapon.

"I'm betting you'll survive longer than he will," Mason said. He cast a sideways glance at Bricket.

The bartender shifted uncomfortably, lit up a cigar, and eyed Steiner. "Rick told me how you evaded death in prison. Takes audacity to stand up against those kinds of odds and win. I admire that."

"Rick could always spin a good yarn." Steiner held his breath against the pungent fumes the bartender puffed out.

Mason picked up his perspiring glass of orange liquid, took a sip, and hummed pleasantly. "Bricket, why don't you make one of these for the captain?"

A drink? The mere thought of the bitter-tasting liquor repulsed Steiner. "No, thank you."

"Believe me, Ironhand, you'll love this drink," Mason said. "It's better than the one that guy with the braided pony-tail served up."

"Ponytail," Steiner breathed the word before he realized it. Mason must be trying to get rid of the bartender for some important reason. "Maybe a cool drink would be soothing."

"Com'on, Bricket," Mason coaxed. "Make him one."

The scarred face tightened. "My assistant can make it."

"He can't make it like you. Believe me, I've tasted them."

Bricket shot a hard glare at the pilot and mouthed a few silent words.

Mason smiled, lifting his glass. "Give the captain what he wants, a nice cool drink just like this."

The bartender pursed his lips.

Mason gathered a handful of poker chips from his winnings. "I'll give you some of your losses."

With a groan, Bricket grabbed his cane. He jabbed it into

the floor, lifted his body from his chair, and limped toward the counter, a trail of smoke following in his wake.

Cards sputtered as Mason shuffled the deck until the bartender was out of earshot.

"Sam dug around and found out the reason the mysterious technician came on board the morning of the launch," Mason whispered. His mouth spread into a toothy grin. "He came to tell everyone that a price has been put on your head—a *high* one."

Steiner groaned. The news didn't surprise him. Since no bomb had been discovered on the ship, the only other reason Jamison would send a man on board was to offer a reward for his assassination. What really grated on him was how much Mason was enjoying telling him such disturbing news.

"Wait, you haven't heard the best part yet," Mason said, barely suppressing another snicker. "Nobody's cashed in because they're afraid of you. He told them you were a coward—an easy kill. But no one believed it because you proved him wrong by the way you threw Rathen off the ship the night before the launch."

Steiner let the information soak in for a few seconds.

"Don't you get it?" Mason seemed to be irritated that he didn't find it as funny. "You saved your own life."

"Only temporarily. They still might try to cash in on Jamison's offer later."

Mason shuffled the cards again. "Well . . . maybe. Just keep that gun of yours handy at all times."

I always do, Steiner thought, as his hand instinctively went down to handle of the weapon.

His thoughts turned to Sam. Five days ago, when he sent the boy out on his mission, he never expected any results. "How is my amigo doing?" he asked.

"Fine," Mason replied. "He's been bugging me to teach him how to fly, so I've been training him on the flight simulators. He's probably in there now. When he learns to fly this old Peacemaker, you can get rid of one of those two other hoppers. I don't trust either of them."

Steiner didn't like Sanchez and Palmer either. They knew their skills were needed, so they didn't bother to conceal their resentment toward him for throwing their friend Rathen off the ship.

He changed the subject by pointing to the pile of chips in front of the pilot. "You seem to be lucky today."

"Bricket is loaded with money," Mason said as he whisked five cards to Steiner. "I can't believe someone can be so rich and still be stuck in prison." He indicated that Steiner should look at the hand he had been dealt.

"Rick, I don't have the time or energy to play this game with you."

"Go ahead. Take a look."

Steiner curled the glossy cards back with his fingers and found a royal flush staring up at him.

Mason's grin broadened. "Sweet, isn't it?"

Bricket hobbled toward the table with a second glass of orange liquid.

Disapproving of the pilot's greed, Steiner slid the cards, facedown, back to him. He hated it that Mason was cheating but wasn't about to give him away. He couldn't afford to lose his support.

A foaming mug thudded down onto the table. "I hope you like it," Bricket said as he dropped his body back into his seat.

Steiner smiled, sipping the drink in gratitude. It was the best one he had tasted so far, but the bitter taste still dominated it.

"How about those chips you promised," Bricket demanded of his opponent.

Mason passed over a generous pile. "I'll win them back with no trouble."

"We'll see about that. Deal."

"My pleasure." The pilot smirked as he dealt the cards.

Steiner finished the drink while watching Bricket lose another hand. Just before taking his last swallow, Steiner noticed a slight variation in color between his drink and Mason's. A terrifying realization swept through him. What if it had been poisoned? Fighting back the desire to panic, he swished the remainder of the liquid around in the bottom of the mug, searching for an oily film. It looked clean. He breathed deeply with relief.

The drink must have been mixed a little differently. How could he have been so careless—especially after learning of a bounty on his life? He promised himself never to accept another drink from anyone. It had been harmless this time, but maybe not the next.

Later, as he continued with his inspection of the ship, the bounty shadowed his thoughts. He wondered why Jamison would even bother offering one since the previous captain had been killed before leaving space dock. If the convicts had taken out one leader already, surely they wouldn't need an added incentive to remove another.

When Steiner entered the engine room's control cubicle, he found only one attendant standing watch at the consoles. Everyone else was missing. That was strange, considering he had always seen the engine room staff servicing at least one of the components at any time during the day.

Suspicion kicked in.

After the attendant greeted him, Steiner pretended to depart, then hid in the shadows.

Daniels and his staff were very close. Individual men might have been dissuaded by what Steiner did to the technician, but maybe not a combined group. Perhaps, together they were planning something against him. After all, that was how mafia families operated.

Adrenaline pumped madly through his body as he waited.

When the attendant used the washroom, Steiner sneaked into the reactor chamber. Four giant cylindrical devices stretched a hundred meters to the far end. He started down one of the aisles between two of the powerful machines, creeping low as if behind enemy lines. The steady drone of the engines masked his footsteps.

Somewhere in that massive room, the engineers were plotting something, but where?

The air temperature increased the farther Steiner moved into the interior. Under his jacket, a droplet of sweat traced the contour of his spine all way to his waist.

About halfway to the other side, voices from somewhere ahead froze him. He flattened himself against the side of one of the reactors as two men casually walked across a gap, deeper in the interior.

If he followed them, they might lead him to where the

other engineers were holed up. He ran lightly to the end of the aisle.

The voices argued about the right way to clean out waste materials from storage units.

When Steiner peeked around the corner, he found no sign of the two men even though he could still hear them, echoing from deep inside something.

Then he saw it. A ladder disappeared into a tunnel in the bulkhead above.

Inching up to the base of the ladder, he risked a look up into the shaft. A distant light shone from a hatch opening on the far side. The voices of many people conversing floated down from it. All of Daniels's staff must be up there. The two men climbed up into the room and closed the hatch, immersing the tube in total darkness.

The new silence amplified the gentle roar of the engines until the noise seemed almost deafening.

Steiner considered his options. He could call Richards, the head of security, and his men down here to break up the gathering. No, that would only weaken his tarnished image even further—especially if his suspicions were proven to be wrong. His only choice was to raid the assembly himself.

He took off his jacket, inviting the air to cool his damp skin and shirt. He tucked the leather garment between two nearby components, out of view of any engineers who might pass by while he was up there.

He climbed up the ladder, rung by rung. To the left, the massive chamber swelled as he rose above the apex of the four cylindrical reactors that stretched all the way to the opposite side. Steam rose in spurts from the coolant vents, the vapors diffusing the lights in eerie glows. Far in the distance, he could see the attendant at the control cubicle.

The vastness of the scene made Steiner feel small and ineffective for the task ahead. He would have to face down all the engineers at once, including their leader, an accomplished assassin. Then it occurred to him. What if they had planted some hidden defense by which to alert them of an intruder's presence? What if they already knew he was coming? What if they were luring him into a trap?

Steiner stopped his ascent a few feet under the maw of the black tunnel into which the ladder led. *Maybe I should go back now.*

Just as he was about to lower himself, he realized that he couldn't retreat either. It would be a sign of his weakness, an act of cowardice, which would eventually lead to his death anyway. He had to go on.

He closed his eyes, focused his thoughts on Mary, imagining her beckoning him to join her in eternal bliss. If this was his time to die, he would embrace it.

He continued climbing the ladder, the darkness of the tunnel swallowing him up. He slowed, occasionally reaching blindly for the hatch. His labored breathing resounded off the narrow walls of the passageway, accented by his boots making contact with each rung. The darkness pressed in about him, crushing his resolve. His knees quivered. The formless demons in his mind played in the blackness surrounding him.

After a few minutes, he felt a handle above him. He leaned back against the sides of the tube, resting himself, gathering his nerves. His hand unsheathed his AT-7 from its holster. The utmost speed would be required. He had to open the hatch and have his gun trained on them before they could react.

He strained his ears for any noise from the other side, but it was useless. The seal was airtight. The room above must be an air lock. Since a decompression indicator wasn't lit up, it must be safe to open.

When he tugged on the handle, it squeaked in protest, echoing down the blackened hole beneath him. Steiner froze for an instant, then without a second thought about it, he jerked the metal arm into the release position. An explosive, high-pitched hiss of air escaped from the cracked seal. He flung the hatch aside and propelled himself up through the entry with his gun held out.

The sight shocked him. Five of the seven engineers were seated in a circle, singing. Their voices trailed off as each of them turned to stare at Steiner.

Daniels stood up, running a hand through his thinning gray hair. "Captain? Is everything all right?"

Steiner couldn't answer. He was still trying to comprehend what he was seeing.

"Would you care to join us for our worship service?" Daniels asked.

Steiner held the older man's gaze for a few heartbeats. He couldn't detect any visible signs of deceit. Could this actually be what he claimed it was—a worship service?

He surveyed the surroundings just to see if there was anything out of the ordinary. Just as he suspected, it was an air lock, probably used for making repairs to the outside hull. A storage cabinet of space suits occupied the side wall, near the exterior hatch. No weapons were in view.

An old, frayed book lay at Daniels's feet. It looked like a Bible. Mary had owned one once.

"Captain?" Daniels asked.

Steiner lowered his AT-7 slowly. "Why didn't you ask me before you had this gathering?"

Daniels shrugged. "I didn't think it would matter."

"It does."

"I'm sorry, sir. I'll accept full responsibility for my error. Do you wish us to stop?"

Steiner's suspicions continued to eat away at him. What if this was all an elaborate front to trick him? He looked at the book at Daniels's feet.

"Is that a Bible?"

Daniels retrieved the old volume from the ground and showed him the front cover. It was.

A tall, lanky, white man climbed to his feet. "Would you care to sing some hymns with us?"

"Who are you?"

"Everyone calls me 'Spider,' because of my long arms and legs."

"He and J.R. are my chief assistants," Daniels added, then indicated a young black man seated on the other side of the circle.

J.R. nodded in greeting.

"Thank you for the invitation, but I must decline," Steiner replied. "Carry on without me."

The group resumed singing as Steiner lowered himself down the ladder and closed the hatch behind him. He knew he probably had nothing to fear from the engineers and was thankful for it.

* * *

AT the first beep of his portable comlink, Steiner awoke from his nap. Before it could repeat, he jolted upright in his bed, raising the device to his mouth. "Steiner here."

"This is Security Chief Richards. We have a disturbance in the bar that requires your immediate presence."

Steiner stood up, stretching his muscles back to life. What could have happened that his fully capable security team wasn't able to handle? A cascade of chills ran through his body as he considered the possibilities.

"I'm on my way," he said into the mouthpiece of the comlink, switched it off, and reattached it to his belt.

When he arrived at the bar, he found Richards and both of his colleagues, Hulsey and Eddie, holding back a crowd of convicts from the entrance.

"What's the situation?" Steiner asked the chief.

"Four men forced their way inside and refuse to leave."

"Have you tried to remove them yet?"

"We couldn't," Richards answered, holding up his stun gun. "We're outmatched."

A lump built in Steiner's throat. The men inside must be armed with real weapons.

"We evacuated all the bystanders," Richards added. "We weren't able to get Bricket out, though. They wanted him to serve more drinks until you showed up."

The last words echoed in Steiner's mind. He had known all along that sooner or later someone would get up enough courage to try to cash in on Jamison's bounty.

"What are you planning on doing?" Richards asked.

That seemed to be the question on everyone's mind, judging from the stares of the crowd. Perhaps this was the test they had all been waiting for? Could Steiner defend his command?

He inched up to the doorway to survey the interior of the establishment. Someone had reduced the lighting so that shadows draped everything below the tabletops. Two of the ship's gunners stood at the counter, drinking and laughing. The taller one was a hot-tempered fuse nicknamed Torch. Steiner couldn't remember the name of chubby, bald man next to him. An angry scowl bent Bricket's scarred face, probably because he had lost his paying crowd. The other two men must be hiding somewhere inside.

With a deep breath, Steiner unsheathed the AT-7 from its holster. During his academy days, he had earned an award for marksmanship with this kind of weapon. Those skills would be put to the test.

He stepped inside, scanning the inside walls near the entry with his pistol muzzle. Nothing. Cautiously, he threaded a path through the tables, searching for the faintest of movements in the pits of darkness beneath them.

His gaze locked onto the counter. Since it stretched across the entire back length of the establishment, it offered the best mobility. He guessed that was where the other two assassins were lying in wait.

His focus shifted to the decorative bottles arranged on the shelves lining the rear wall. An idea flashed into his mind.

"So," Torch shouted, "the mighty captain himself has come to force us to leave." He turned to his companion. "Will he succeed, I wonder?"

A sinister grin split the bald man's face as he shook his head back and forth.

Torch lifted his half-filled mug. "A toast to his death."

The chubby hands of the other brought a glass up also. Both men drank, then belched in unison.

Steiner wanted to shoot the two of them down just to get it over with, but a display of cowardice like that might cause the rest of the crew's respect to decline further. If that happened, he might lose his command—along with his life.

"You have violated the bar-usage policy," he shouted, halting five meters from the gunners. "You will both report to the brig immediately."

They roared in laughter.

"And if we don't, Captain?" Torch demanded. "What are you going to do about it?"

Steiner met Bricket's gaze for a split second. The bartender's eyes shifted to the left in an unnatural fashion.

It was a hint. The two assassins must be hiding exactly where Steiner had expected, behind the counter to the left.

"You'd better leave now, Bricket," he said, motioning toward the storeroom.

"We haven't finished our party yet," Torch cut in. "He stays."

Steiner's muscles tightened in anticipation. "You're finished now."

Torch's hand slapped the counter.

That had to be a signal to the other two.

Steiner drew his AT-7 and fired at the supports under the shelves that lined the rear wall. The structure collapsed, raining bottles down on the two figures that bolted upward. The assassins covered their heads, trying to protect themselves from the descending wave of glass and liquors. A wooden piece from the shelves sparked from Steiner's blasts. Flames burst out around the two men, exploding upward, consuming the falling liquids in flight.

"No," Bricket cried as he dropped to the floor.

The heat from the sudden eruption forced Steiner to shield his face. He stumbled back in surprise. Never had he expected such a reaction from low-alcoholic substances, unless—

One of the burning assassins aimed a gun. A bolt from Steiner's AT-7 ripped through the man's chest before he could open fire. The lifeless body sank into a flaming grave.

Before Steiner had a chance to seek out the other assassin, he saw something being swung at him from a corner of his vision. He ducked, but not in time to avoid being clipped in the shoulder by a chair. The force of the blow threw him to the floor. When he collided with the cold unyielding surface, he lost hold of his weapon.

He rolled back to his feet in time to see Torch reaching for the fallen pistol. With a sweep of Steiner's leg, the weapon skidded away under the tables.

Muttering a curse, Torch picked up another chair. This time, Steiner grabbed one of his own and deflected a second swing. With a cry of rage, Steiner charged at his opponent, using the legs of his chair to pin the man against the edge of the counter.

Bright beams tore through the air inches from Steiner's face. He instinctively flung himself backward to the ground. Torch dropped a few feet away, with smoking puncture wounds through his head and upper shoulders.

Steiner dove under the protective darkness of the tables, scrambling deeper into their midst, listening as the bald man scolded the second gunman for killing Torch.

A glance over at one of the tables helped him recognize the other man as James Grant, the best marksman on the firing range. Burns had blistered his face and arms, and dark singes ran up his clothes. His body shook with apparent rage, which might explain why he hadn't hit Steiner on the first try. With a maddened cry, Grant initiated another assault, randomly cutting through the tables in search of his prey.

Steiner couldn't possibly stand against him without his pistol. He strained his eyes for any sign of the AT-7 in his blackened world below. A glint of metal caught his attention a meter from the counter's midsection. Now to get it—

One of his overhead shelters shook violently. Steiner rolled to the side as the shattered table collapsed to the floor. The smoldering wood sizzled from the intense heat of the energy-bolt strikes. He flattened himself as another table crumbled several meters to his left.

"Show yourself, Captain," Grant screamed, his voice cracking with strain.

As quietly as he could, Steiner crawled toward his weapon. Just a few more seconds—

"He's over there." The shout came from the far right. Steiner glanced over to see the bald man pointing directly at him.

Steiner lunged forward with all his strength just as the table above him was slashed apart. Brilliant streaks lanced over him as he scrambled forward, crouched low. He dove under the overhang of the wooden counter. On the other side of the structure, he could hear Grant cursing at his defensive tactic.

Steiner maneuvered to the left, picking his way between the barstools until he was close enough to reach his weapon. His fingers closed around its handle, giving him renewed hope.

A loud eruption brought him about. Two meters away, a large hole had been blasted out of the lower part of the counter. Wooden splinters exploded out as another energy bolt burst through the structure, shattering the legs of a barstool in its path.

Steiner dashed along the overhang, the destructive path following on his heels.

When he reached the wall at the far end of the room, he spun around and watched the oncoming bolts spraying through the wood, heading toward him.

He closed his eyes and listened to Grant's approach, the scuffle of his boots. He rose from his hiding place, already aiming at his target.

Grant's eyes widened as he adjusted the angle of his gun muzzle. Two of Steiner's bolts tore through the man's torso before he could fire. Grant sprawled back against the floor, where he lay motionless, blood oozing from his body.

All of Steiner's strength fled at once, replaced by a weakened state of relief. Only one of the four assassins remained.

The bald man stood alone in the center of the room, panting in apparent terror.

His knees aching, Steiner walked along the smoldering ruins that used to be the counter. The fire continued to burn behind it, lighting the surroundings in flashes of red and orange. The stench of death hung in the air. Smoke trailed from the jumbled ruins of seared furniture, filling the ceiling with a ghostly haze. The crowd outside the entrance froze to complete stillness.

When Steiner neared the unarmed gunner, he holstered his AT-7. If his prisoner went to the brig peacefully, there would be no more need of further violence.

The bald man's eyes darted wildly from his dead comrades to Steiner. He dashed his glass mug against a tabletop, leaving sharp jagged edges on its rim. With a loud scream, he burst forward.

With a reflexive draw of his pistol, Steiner severed the gunner's arm from his torso with a single blast. The man cried out, stumbled to the right, and fell headlong into a smoldering pile of furniture.

When Steiner got closer, he saw a charred piece of wood protruding from the gunner's back.

The test had ended. Steiner had survived without losing any respect. He closed his eyes, listening to the whispers of astonishment from the spectators, intermingled with the quiet crackling of the fire.

A shudder ran through the floor, followed by another, then a mechanical hum. Steiner spun around in place, aiming his AT-7 at Tramer, who had stepped through the people gathered at the entrance. The cyborg halted a few feet away. Steiner's finger tensed on the trigger.

The mechanical man remained motionless.

A long heartbeat passed.

The cyborg's black lips parted. From out of the mechanical device on its neck came what sounded like, "Behind you."

Steiner hesitated, wondering if he had heard correctly. Was it trying to trick him?

Within the reflection of the fire dancing on its breastplate, a dark shape moved.

Steiner ducked, barely missing two energy blasts rending the air where he had been standing. He twisted his body about, his pistol muzzle searching for the source.

Grant had pulled himself onto the bar counter. One bloodied arm held a smoking gun. Before the man could ignite another bolt, Steiner shot him. The headless corpse slid off the structure, leaving a red smear across the polished wooden surface.

Steiner looked back at the cyborg, which hadn't moved from its original position. Two black, charred marks discolored its shiny breastplate where Grant's energy bolts had struck it. Servos whined as the cyborg's right arm rose slowly to its head to give a salute.

Steiner blinked. He couldn't believe what he was seeing.

With a whirl of mechanical components, Tramer turned around and marched out of the room. The crowd at the door parted instantly to allow it through.

For a few seconds, Steiner remained still, trying to recover from his utter shock.

Bricket rose from his shelter behind the undamaged section of the counter. He hobbled toward the blaze a few meters away, whimpering something about how much it would cost to replace his collection of bottles.

Sheathing his AT-7, Steiner slid over the counter. He took one of the remaining bottles from what was left of the shelves.

"I had always wondered how people could get drunk from low-alcoholic drinks," he said, removing its cap.

He took a deep drink. It was the real thing—strong liquor.

Bricket choked up a sob. "What do I do about my bar?"

"Rebuild," Steiner replied, handing the bottle to the bartender. "I'm sure you have plenty of that low-alcohol stuff to sell."

The bartender frowned.

Swimming in a newfound feeling of pride from his success, Steiner hopped back across the structure and headed toward the exit. He planned on finishing his nap once he reached his cabin. As he walked through the crowd at the entrance, they stared at him in awe—even Eddie the Giant. Steiner had proved himself master of the ship. For the moment, at least.

As long as Jamison's bounty existed, he knew it wouldn't be long before someone tried to kill him again.

CHAPTER

9

WHISTLES and hurrahs erupted from the spectators, standing against the walls.

Steiner stroked his two-week-old beard, gratified by how well the crew seemed to be responding to his new game, bruiseball.

A new round began as one team gave the opening toss to the other. Snatching the yellow-painted helmet from the air, Eddie the Giant charged down the center of the cleared-out cafeteria. Since none of his opponents could slow him down, one of them jumped under his feet, causing him to topple down on everyone around him. Body armor protected all the players from injuries.

Steiner had created the game to give the convicts combat training for the raids ahead. They loved it, not just playing but watching, too, as evidenced by the cheering of the spectators.

A week ago, he had never expected to stand among a group of convicts like this, without fearing for his life. Much had changed since the pivotal battle he had fought against the four assassins in the bar. Mason, who was in the command center at the time of the attack, had watched the entire ordeal through the security monitors and had told the tale countless times to anyone who would listen. Whispers of the legendary "Ironhand" had circulated throughout the ship. Crewmen had begun acting respectfully to Steiner and strove to please him. Potential had begun surfacing among the crew. The missions ahead didn't seem so impossible anymore.

A howl broke out as another bruiseball player, nicknamed Rex, dove on top of Eddie, ripped the game prop away, and raced in the opposite direction. He tossed it back and forth with one of his teammates, Bo, then faked out the goal's protector and slammed it through the posts.

Teamwork like that had made them the best bruiseball players on board. They would be valued raiders in the missions to come.

Rex and Bo did a victory dance.

Cheers rose from the crowd, along with a couple of catcalls. Richards stood ready with his stun gun just in case a disturbance broke out.

Steiner caught a glimpse of the overhead camera panning across the room, reminding him of Tramer's unseen presence. The cyborg hadn't said a word to him since the battle in the bar. He still didn't know why it had saved his life. Its breastplate bore no trace of the energy-bolt scorch marks it had received, but had been cleaned and buffed back to its previous shine, which indicated the metallic body was impervious to small-arms fire. That was cause for worry. How could he stand against it if it opposed him?

When Steiner shifted his gaze, he saw Bricket maneuvering his bulky form through the spectators, heading straight for him.

Not again, Steiner thought.

"We arrive at the Tycus base tomorrow," the bartender said, setting up his next question. "Have you reconsidered my proposition?"

"I've told you before that I'm not interested in any percentage of your profits. I'll let you repair the bar—but that's as far as I'm willing to go."

"Okay, I'll accept your decision." Bricket's tongue ran along his lips. "I'm impressed with how much you've accomplished with the crew since you came on board. When we left

Earth, I never expected you to last the first week, but you did. I never expected all these convicts to act like soldiers, yet they are. However, they are becoming more unhappy."

"Are they now?" Steiner asked, realizing where this was leading.

"They don't want the fake liquor. Fights are breaking out more and more each day as everyone gets drier and drier."

Steiner had noticed increasing mood swings in some of the men but couldn't relent. "I need them sober for the raids," he said.

"Consider this. How much better would they perform for the chance to have a drink once in a while?"

Steiner tugged at his beard as he considered the argument. Their addiction might be an irresistible incentive, and the bartender's lust for money might make him right for policing the distribution. "All right—under one condition," he answered, noticing Bricket's face lighting up. "We store it next to the main port-side air lock, where I can jettison it if I see one drunken man."

The bartender's smile faded. After a hard swallow, he stared at the floor for a moment. "Deal," he spat, then hobbled away. Steiner knew the man's profits wouldn't be as high as before, but at least it would be better than what he was currently making.

After the bruiseball game had concluded, and the spectators had left, Steiner, Richards, and Eddie took the suits back to the armory. When Steiner started to enter the code to open the storage chamber, he noticed Tramer standing at the far end of the corridor. Steiner covered the keypads as he finished the sequence. When the barrier slid aside, the two security men dumped the suits into the interior. Once Steiner had resealed the door, he looked back down the passageway. Tramer was gone.

What was it up to?

An electronic beep stole his thoughts away. He unhitched the comlink from his belt and depressed the speaking pad. "Steiner here."

"A message for you is coming in from Earth," Simmons's voice announced.

"Who's the sender?"

"Director Riggs."

Steiner's heart skipped. "I'm on my way," he replied, sprinting toward the command center. Excitement swelled within him. He hadn't spoken to Suzanne since the launch two weeks ago, and there was so much to tell her.

When he arrived, he found Tramer once again watching the ship's monitors. The cyborg didn't even bother acknowledging his presence.

Steiner descended the stairwell into his conference room and locked the door behind him. After he sat behind the desk, he activated his wall monitor. The screen depicted the logo of the United Star Systems. Beneath that, it read: SECURED MESSAGE FROM DIRECTOR RIGGS.

After he entered a code into the keyboard, Suzanne appeared in front of him, looking the same as he remembered her. He expected her to be joyous about his success so far, but she seemed disturbed about something.

"Hello, Jake," she said. "How do you like being captain of the P.A.V.?"

"I've named my ship the *Marauder*. The title P.A.V. only reminds the men that they are prisoners. I need them to think like warriors."

"You sound much more optimistic than the last time we spoke. How's the crew?"

"If Jamison doesn't try anything else, I might be able to mold them into a fighting force."

Suzanne flinched at the mention of the admiral's name. "What has he done?"

"The technician that he sent came to inform the convicts that there was a price on my head."

"Has any of the crew tried to hurt you?"

"Four of them, armed with guns."

She frowned. "I'm sorry. I wish the security had been tighter. Where are the men who attacked you now?"

"Dead. I probably would be, too, if it hadn't been for Tramer."

Her face brightened. "He helped you?"

"Yes, but I don't understand why."

"Do you still want him transferred off?"

"No, even though I am uncomfortable around whatever he

is, or whatever he has become, I don't think I can do this without Tramer. With this bounty on my life, I won't be able to train the crew on real weapons. Tramer is the only other one who can do that."

"Believe me, Jake. You've made the right decision."

"Was that the only reason you called?"

"Not exactly." She sighed, her previous sullen mood returning. "I have some good news and bad news. The bad news is that the admiral that you were supposed to report to on Tycus has taken ill. You are to report to his replacement for your Orders disk."

Steiner didn't think that was bad, one admiral was no different from another—except . . .

"It's Ralph Jamison," she said.

The name bored into Steiner like a thorn. "I can't trust any orders coming from him, not after what he did to McKillip," he shouted. "I refuse to report to him."

"Calm down. Jamison only has the task of giving it to you—nothing else. The disk was imprinted months ago, before you were assigned to the P.A.V." Suzanne paused. "Just watch yourself when you're in his office. Don't give him another reason to throw you in prison. I won't be able to get you out next time."

Steiner opened his clenched fists and found them drenched with sweat. "What's to keep him from killing me himself when I go into his office?"

"He's an admiral. His office is in a public place. If you were killed there, it would put a lot of suspicion on him. I'm sure he'd rather have you millions of light-years away when someone tries to assassinate you."

Steiner considered her reasoning logical. Jamison wouldn't want to draw suspicion. After all, the admiral wanted Steiner dead to stop the threat of the tribunal.

"It will be difficult facing him again after what happened," he said.

"Just behave yourself, get the disk, then get out. It's that simple."

Steiner doubted it would be that easy.

"Now for the good news," Suzanne said with a little smile. "As you leave the building, check in with the guards at the front desk. I left you a surprise you're going to love. Trust me on this."

Steiner sighed. He was a little tired of her surprises.

After wishing him luck, Suzanne ended the transmission.

With the conversation still heavy on his mind, Steiner retired to his quarters, lay back on his cot, and took Mary's holocard from the table. When he activated it, her face materialized above the flat side of the wafer. Her flowing dark hair, her emerald eyes, her private smile—everything about her was frozen for all time within the tiny mechanism. Whenever he felt discouraged, just seeing her again lifted his spirits. His wedding band felt cold against his fingers, so he cupped his other hand over it to warm it.

He closed his eyes, imagining Mary with him, touching him, holding him, kissing him. Soon his conscious thoughts slipped away, giving life to his dreams. He found himself standing in Jamison's office, living out his assault on the admiral again. His murderous fury returned in full force. His fingers tightened around Jamison's throat as the rush of footsteps from the MPs grew louder behind him. He needed just a few more seconds to finish off his enemy. When strong grips began to pry him away, the vision changed abruptly.

Steiner found himself in the shuttle depot once again, facing Mary before she boarded the shuttle. Her hand trailed away until their fingertips lost contact. Desperately, he reached out and grabbed her wrist. She struggled against his hold.

Please, don't go, he cried out.

She ripped her arm free from his grasp and fled toward the shuttle.

No, he screamed. *I need you.*

Steiner jerked upright on his cot, gasping hard. Sweat covered him. He tried to calm himself but couldn't seem to catch his breath. A horrifying realization came to him. Something was wrong with the air in the room.

He moved from the bed to the oxygen indicator on the wall. It read dangerously low. An alarm should have gone off when it sank below tolerable levels. Why hadn't it?

He punched the keypad to open the cabin door. Nothing happened. He hit the mechanism again to no avail. His hand pried out the emergency hand crank. It wasn't operational either.

He searched wildly for some idea that might save him.

His head began to spin. His muscles grew weary. He had to get air soon.

In desperation, he tore the grating off of the air vent and peered inside the dark tunnel. Ten feet into it, an emergency seal closed off the shaft from the air generators.

Someone was trying to suffocate him.

Then he remembered the satchel of explosives under the cot. He dragged it out, dumping the contents onto the floor. Twelve grenades. How could he use them to escape? They could puncture either the cabin door or the seal in the air duct; however, he would surely be killed by the blast.

Just as despair started to creep in, a solution occurred to him. The blast shield. He wrenched it out from under his cot. Its construction appeared tough enough to withstand intense heat.

He put his plan into operation. After piling the grenades at the base of the cabin's door, he picked up the blast shield, then searched around for some insulation. The sheet from the cot. He ripped it from the mattress and tied it to the handle of the shield.

When he armed one of the grenades, a ten-second countdown was initiated.

He scrambled into the air duct with the sheet in tow. He pulled the excess bedding into the narrow shaft until the shield covered the vent opening. Darkness shrouded him. He braced himself against the sides, keeping tension on the sheet.

Then it happened.

It was as if his head exploded. Brilliant light, deafening noise, smoke, pain, then blackness.

He found himself riding a river of colors, trying to keep his face above the waves. Branches hung overhead just out of reach, as if they were taunting him. Something rubbed against his arm. He twisted around to see McKillip's body floating next to him.

No, Steiner screamed, almost going under. His legs fought desperately to keep him up.

Then he saw a dark mound ahead, protruding out of the surface. A blanket of black material spread out from it. When he got closer, he recognized it as hair. His blood froze as the head turned to reveal—

Mary.

With a cry of terror, Steiner released himself to the powerful undercurrent. He was drawn deeper under the swirling tide. Pressure squeezed his lungs. The colors surrounding him began to fade into total darkness.

Rest.

Something like metallic claws clenched his arms. Abruptly, he was drawn upward.

Distorted voices sounded from all around. Light filtered through his eyelids. Blurred images of people surrounded him. Something was placed over his nose. His lungs breathed in pure oxygen. His head throbbed with intense pain. When he tried to move his arm, he found it had no strength. It didn't even feel as if it belonged to him.

"Breathe deeply for a few moments," a voice said. "Don't try to move."

He turned toward the source of the sound. The hazy form of J.R., the assistant engineer, huddled over him.

"I used to be a medic," the man reassured him calmly. "You'll be fine in a while."

Steiner's senses began to sharpen. Distant voices become clearer. People were gathered all around him. His memory reemerged from the haze that had engulfed it. Someone had tried to trap him.

He bolted upright, fighting the nausea the movement created. J.R. and Daniels stood next to him, extinguishers strapped to their backs. Tramer towered over him to the right. Steiner's hand dropped to his holster to see if he still had his weapon. To his surprise, he found it there.

"What happened?" he asked.

"We all heard an explosion," Daniels said. "Tramer arrived on the scene first. He dragged you out of the burning cabin."

Steiner met the cyborg's lifeless gaze for just a split second before the machine wheeled about and thumped away.

Why had it saved his life?

The engineers helped Steiner to his feet. Smoke fogged the corridor, hiding his cabin from view. He stumbled closer, curious about the amount of destruction. The spectators, congregated around the site, backed away, giving him clear passage.

The door that he had placed the grenades by lay in a twisted heap at the base of the entry, the corners broken off in the track. Steiner was amazed that he had survived a blast of that magnitude.

All that was left of the room's furnishings was ashes and ruins. The cot had been permanently embedded in the bulkhead. Its metal posts stuck out, jagged and bent into wicked shapes. The blackened blast shield lay atop a pile of rubble, its surface showing signs of melting in several spots. Somehow, he must have kept his grip on it after losing consciousness.

Then his heart sank.

When he rummaged through the warm ashes by his cot, he discovered Mary's holocard. Cracks split its scarred surface. He tried activating it.

Nothing happened.

With a small cry of rage, he threw the worthless piece of metal against the charred bulkhead.

In his mind, he could hear the sinister cadence of Jamison's laughter.

CHAPTER

10

TYCUS, Steiner thought with apprehension as he led Mason toward the landing bay. He had asked the pilot to shuttle him down to the ground installation, where he was to have his meeting with Jamison. If Mary's holocard hadn't been destroyed, he could have used it for encouragement. He needed it badly.

Steiner still didn't know who had tried to suffocate him the previous night, but he had discovered how they had managed the attempt. The assassin had broken into the life-support control station through one of the ventilation shafts and sealed off the flow of air to his cabin. Steiner had Richards install a proximity alarm near the oxygen generator to prevent anyone from doing the same thing again.

It was frightening to consider that the assassin was still at large on the ship. It began to erode Steiner's optimism about his crew. He was determined not to let anyone get an advantage over him again, so he would plan his moves carefully, as if he were playing a chess game for his life.

"Do you really think it's wise to leave Sam here all alone?" Mason asked, breaking the silence as they walked. "What if the crew riots or something like that?"

"When we first launched, weren't you telling me he could take care of himself?" Steiner replied.

"That was before the two attempts on your life. If he were coming with us, I'd feel more at ease."

"Trust me. He's safer here on the *Marauder*."

Steiner understood why Mason worried about the teenager. Over the past two weeks, a kinship had grown between the two of them; it was as if they had become brothers.

Daniels, J.R., and Spider waited by the sealed entry to the landing bay.

"What are they doing here?" Mason whispered.

"They'll be manning the landing bay while I'm gone," Steiner answered.

"What makes you think they won't try to kill you, too?"

"If they were going to, they probably would have already succeeded by now."

After an exchange of greetings with the engineers, Steiner started to enter the password into the computer panel beside the door.

"Ironhand," Mason said, pointing down the corridor.

A blue sensor orb shone from a darkened silhouette at the far end.

Steiner expected Tramer to come forward, but it remained perfectly still.

"There's nothing to worry about," Daniels said. "Tramer won't harm us."

"You sound like you trust it," Steiner replied.

"More than most."

The reassurance didn't comfort Steiner. Keeping one eye on the cyborg, Steiner returned to the task of opening the door. The thick barrier slid aside. Darkness veiled the interior. The musty odor of stagnant air crinkled Steiner's nose. It was quite apparent that this was the first time the bay had ever been used.

Daniels vanished into the blackness. Several seconds later, the overhead lights sprang to life, illuminating a vast chamber, which housed a small personnel shuttle and a giant armored transport carrier, a spacecraft capable of ferrying troops and making aerial attacks on ground installations. An assortment of wheeled vehicles called TRACs lined the right wall, armed with massive guns powerful enough to punch a hole through the outer hull.

Daniels signaled his aides to begin their work. Spider ascended a ladder into a control booth while J.R. ran to the back of the line of vehicles. A moment later, the shuttle moved forward, suspended from a claw that moved along a track in the ceiling.

A groan rose from Mason. "A scuttle bucket? I should have expected as much. After all, why would the military give us anything that was up-to-date?"

"Hello." Bricket's voice sounded from the entry. "We're here."

The bartender stood in the doorway with another man.

"Bricket, I only planned for you to join us," Steiner said.

"My apologies, Captain," the crippled man said, hobbling into the bay. "I thought I might need a sturdy back to help transport the shipment."

Steiner should have realized the bartender wouldn't be able to do all the physical labor by himself. He eyed the assistant with suspicion. He couldn't remember anything about the man except that he was one of the maintenance personnel. It was doubtful Bricket would have chosen an assassin to come. As long as Steiner was in command, the bar stayed open.

"I can go alone if you wish," Bricket said.

"No. Just inform me next time."

At a signal from the bartender, the other man carried two gravity trucks into the room.

"What's your name, crewman?" Steiner asked.

"Frank Pearce, sir."

A loud clang echoed as the shuttle halted directly above the massive sealed doors of the air lock under the floor. A fuel vehicle, driven by J.R., backed up to the rear of the craft.

"A scuttle bucket," Mason grumbled as he made his way over to it.

Because everyone had arrived, Steiner turned toward the control panel to close up the bay. He twitched involuntarily when he saw Tramer directly outside the doorway, its sensor orb glaring at him.

"Can I help you with anything?" Steiner asked, a little angry at being startled.

"Am I to be transferred off here?" Its icy words echoed through the empty corridor.

"I've decided to keep you on board for a while."

Motors whined as it saluted.

Steiner punched the landing bay's password into the control panel. The thick pressure door closed, cutting off the resounding thuds of the cyborg's feet as it marched away.

Steiner wished he knew what Tramer's programmed motives were. Why did it always shadow him? Why did it protect him when it had brutally murdered before?

Casting the thoughts from his mind, Steiner moved toward the shuttle's hatch. The vessel's external lighting flared to life, casting colorful glows into the shadows.

When he stepped inside the passenger compartment, he heard Daniels and Mason arguing in the cockpit.

"It doesn't matter how many improvements you made, this is still a piece of junk," Mason said.

"We did the best we could with what we had," Daniels replied. "Did you expect all the components to be brand-new?"

"No, but I thought they'd at least be in operating condition." The pilot pointed to the rear of the craft. "That energy coil back there belongs in a museum."

"All of the ships in the bay, including this one, were tested three months ago when we were refitting this Peacemaker for use. They all worked fine then."

"Three months ago," Mason exclaimed. "A lot of good that will do us now."

Daniels shrugged at Steiner as he exited the cockpit. The head engineer couldn't be blamed for what the military provided him.

Steiner strapped himself into the copilot's seat.

"Ironhand, if that coil sends an intermittent flow to the engines, it'll be our death sentence," Mason said.

"Just do the best you can," Steiner replied.

A low-pressure hiss announced that Daniels had sealed the hatch to the shuttle. Steiner glanced back to make sure Bricket and Pearce were fastened into their chairs.

Mason huffed. "The prison system gave us faulty equipment just so it would kill us. Fewer convicts to worry about."

The floor parted, exposing a chasm beneath the suspended

spacecraft. With a jarring motion, they descended into the pit below. The enormous air lock, which was capable of releasing the armored transport carrier, dwarfed their tiny shuttle. The doors above joined back together, immersing them in pitch blackness.

"We're depressurizing now." Daniels's voice sounded from the communication panel.

"Oh, joy," Mason muttered. "Now we get to test our hull's integrity. What's that?" Mockingly, he put his hand to his ear. "Is that air I hear escaping?"

"Don't joke about things like that," Bricket shouted from the back. "These miniature buckets give me the creeps."

It took nearly ten minutes for depressurization. The length of time irritated Steiner. The *Valiant* used to process its shuttles within a minute and a half.

When the hatch below finally opened, the glow of the planet shone up into the chamber. The shuttle crawled downward again through the *Marauder*'s bulkhead, stopping at the bottom of the docking assembly.

"You're cleared to start the engines," Daniels's voice announced.

"If they still work," Mason muttered. The hull shuddered from ignition, then mellowed into a massaging vibration. "Well, what do you know. Release the claw."

Metal ground together overhead. Steiner's stomach lurched as the craft tumbled away from the *Marauder*. He had forgotten that these old ships lacked automatic stabilization. His discomfort didn't last long. The shuttle shot forward, pressing his body into the cushioning of his seat. The belly of the *Marauder*, dotted with its wartlike gunnery ports, raced away, replaced by a vast field of stars. The planet rose into view through the transparent dome that curved around the cockpit, its reflected glow brightening the small cabin. Mason guided them into the upper atmosphere with barely any jolts or jars. He whistled a tune while a fiery glow enveloped the shuttle.

When they reached the calm of the stratosphere, the drone of the engines cut out. Steiner's stomach heaved as the ship plummeted toward the planet.

"That coil did exactly as I said it would," Mason shouted, working furiously with his controls. The engines sputtered a few times in response but refused to ignite. He slammed his fists against the console. "Restart, you junk heap."

The shuttle began to roll. Steiner wondered if Mary had experienced this kind of terror during the last few seconds of her life. Maybe the wait to be reunited with her was over.

Cursing to himself, Mason pointed the nose of the falling craft toward the planet. When they punctured the clouds that patched the noonday sky, the distant ground became visible, rushing up at them.

"Ironhand, flood the engine chamber with fuel," Mason demanded.

Steiner looked sharply at him. "Why—?"

"Just do it!"

Steiner opened the intake valve to the chamber. Since the engines weren't active, the ship would be leaving behind a trail of fuel. If it ignited, the resulting explosion would surely destroy the shuttle.

Mason waited a couple seconds, watching the spill in a rear monitor. "When I tell you to, shut the valve."

Steiner had no idea what the pilot was up to, but anything was worth a try at that moment. He placed a finger above the keypad.

Mason tried restarting the engines once more. The trail of fuel exploded in a brilliant flash of light. "Now," he screamed as he accelerated the ship to full speed. Steiner sealed the valve. The shuttle barreled downward, away from the long dark cloud in their wake.

Steiner realized that the explosion had ignited the engines while the extra speed had kept the trailing inferno from engulfing them.

Mason struggled to regain control over the shuttle as it dashed toward the planet.

Steiner gripped the armrests of his seat, unable to breathe. A forest raced toward them. The trees became more detailed by the second. Just then, the nose of the craft began to rise.

"Com'on, baby," Mason shouted.

Steiner could make out individual leaves on the approaching oaks. *Clear them,* he screamed inside his mind.

The craft leveled out, digging into the top of the foliage.

Branches scraped wildly against the hull. A second later, they broke free, skimming across the roof of the forest.

Mason let out a triumphant cry.

Steiner leaned back and closed his eyes. He had never seen a maneuver of that type. It was innovative, even ingenious. He found he had a new sense of respect for the pilot. This would definitely be another adventure Mason could brag about.

They arrived at the U.S.S. military installation with no further trouble. Mason set the shuttle down in a grassy field designated for visiting ships.

After a moment to catch their breath, Bricket and Pearce departed to get the liquor shipment. Mason, whose ego was still soaring, agreed to watch the shuttle. Still feeling a bit light-headed, Steiner started toward the headquarters located at the center of the base.

His upcoming meeting with Jamison haunted his thoughts. In a few minutes, he would be face-to-face with the man he hated with a passion. A soft breeze cooled the sweat on his forehead. He tried to think about something else—anything that would get his mind off Jamison.

The military headquarters loomed ahead of him, nearly thirty stories high. He entered one of the four short wings extending from each side, passing through a security checkpoint, where his AT-7 had to be turned in. As he maneuvered through the shuffling personnel toward the center of the building, his hand toyed with the empty holster. He felt vulnerable without his pistol. It had become a part of him during the last two weeks.

The corridor widened into a mammoth lobby that he remembered well from his years aboard the *Valiant*. The tiled floor depicted a giant emblem of the United Star Systems. Portraits of all the famous admirals lined the walls—including one of Ralph Jamison.

As Steiner approached the elevators, he got a good look at the painted face of his nemesis, the long, narrow cheekbones, the balding head, the beady eyes. It repulsed him to see it hanging up with all the other admirals—leaders who were honest and true.

After he stepped into an open lift, he jabbed the keypad

that would send him to the top floor. During the ascent, the soft instrumental music playing inside the car raked his already tensed nerves. It was as if it were mocking his struggle to remain calm.

When the elevator opened, he found himself in a luxurious waiting room, distinguished by plush, elegant furniture. A holographic flower garden covered one of the walls.

It wasn't fair. McKillip had spent his whole career on a cold metallic ship in space. He died following the orders of a murderer who lived like royalty.

Steiner rubbed his clammy palms on his pants. His throat constricted into a tight knot. He wasn't sure if he could go through with this. The memories of his last visit flashed through his mind. He wished he had killed Jamison back then. Justice would have been served.

Straightening himself into a dignified posture, he started down the hallway leading to his enemy's lair. The hair on the back of his neck prickled as he stopped in front of the secretary's desk at the doorway to Jamison's office. The woman seated there was the same lady who had been there six months ago. Her hands trembled. Obviously, she remembered his last visit.

"Please tell Jamison that Captain Steiner is here to receive his Orders disk," Steiner managed to say calmly, but wasn't sure how.

"He's been expecting you. Go right in." The secretary pressed a keypad that opened the office door.

Steiner hesitated, feeling apprehension about entering the room. What if Jamison tried to murder him? He was unarmed. Within his mind, he reran Suzanne's reasoning. This was a public place. Surely, Jamison would wait until he was millions of light-years away before the fatal blow came. Somehow, Steiner wasn't convinced. His feet refused to move.

"He's waiting for you," the woman repeated.

I'll bet, Steiner thought.

Ralph Jamison strode through the doorway, a devilish grin imprinted on his face. "Captain Steiner, welcome to Tycus. Did you have a safe voyage?"

Steiner's pulse quickened until he could hear the blood

coursing through his head. His lungs ached with the memory of near suffocation. He wanted so much to end the admiral's existence that his hands began to rise involuntarily. He looked into his enemy's grinning face. Steiner froze suddenly.

Grinning? Why would Jamison be grinning? Surely, he remembered what had happened during Steiner's last visit. Wouldn't he be the slightest bit fearful of being assaulted again or killed? Unless he wanted to be attacked.

Steiner returned his hands to his sides.

Jamison held out a palm-sized silver disk. "These are the P.A.V.'s orders for the next six months. Many of the missions are very dangerous. I hope you have the full support of your crew."

Jamison is trying to provoke me, Steiner thought. *Why?*

What if someone was hiding nearby to shoot him down if he did assault the man? Then Jamison could claim his murder was in self-defense. It was the perfect assassination plot.

Steiner reached out cautiously and accepted the disk.

"Good health to you, Captain," Jamison hissed softly.

Another try at initiating a response.

Steiner refused to give one. He spun around, hastened back to the lobby, and escaped into the elevator. Once it had begun its descent, he leaned back against the side of the lift, emotionally exhausted, his body drenched in sweat. If he had assaulted Jamison, he was sure he would be dead.

RALPH Jamison paced about his office, disappointed that Jacob Steiner hadn't fallen for his ruse. He had hoped it would all end right then. Each day Steiner lived brought Jamison closer to losing his dream of bringing freedom to the galaxy. Had Steiner died, there would have been less for Jamison to have to worry about.

"Considering his apparent power over his crew, perhaps I should have gunned him down anyway, and be done with the matter," Travis Quinn said from the shadows.

"It would have created suspicion about me. We must have patience. Captain Steiner won't survive the next six months. I've seen what has been assigned to him. If his crew doesn't kill him, the missions will."

Quinn stepped out of the corner, his icy gaze riveted to Jamison. "The thousand credits that you offered must have produced unworthy applicants."

"It'll continue to persuade others." Jamison stepped over to the window, overlooking the eastern section of the base.

"What if he's stronger than you think?" Quinn asked. "What if he survives the missions ahead?"

"All the better for us."

AT the security checkpoint on the way out, the guards handed back his gun. Steiner caressed the handle of his AT-7. The feeling of vulnerability had faded with the return of the weapon. Before he left the building, he asked if anything had been left for him from Director Suzanne Riggs. The guard checked his records and nodded. "There is a person, who will be transferring aboard your ship."

Steiner rolled his eyes. That was the surprise Suzanne was excited about. Another convict to worry about. "Where is he?"

"Please follow me, sir." The guard led him back to a security cell.

Inside sat a familiar man, one he couldn't believe he was actually seeing.

"Pattie?" he barely managed the name.

"It's about time, 'Slugger.' Get me outta this hole. I'm ready to do some fightin'."

Steiner couldn't help but smile. It was the blessed Saint, himself. Patrick Braun.

Ten years ago, Pattie had been the sergeant in charge of the U.S.S. Ground Forces stationed aboard the *Valiant*. The short, heavyset man inside the cell had to be over fifty years of age. His once-bulging, muscular arms had softened a bit into flab, causing the Celtic cross tattoos etched on each arm to sag. His hair's buzz cut gave no indication of graying, but his eyebrows betrayed him slightly as white hairs accented the red. His gaze still looked as fierce as Steiner remembered it. The "Saint," as his men had called him, had once challenged Steiner to a boxing match aboard the *Valiant*, which the whole crew turned out for. Steiner won by a knockout. It had been his first date with Mary. Since that day, Pattie had always called him "Slugger."

"How did Suzanne find you?" Steiner asked, still not able to believe his eyes. "I haven't heard anything about you since your discharge. I even thought you might be dead."

"Dead? That'll be the day. I've been holed up here. Suzie-Q found me about a month ago, wanted me to join her little crew of convicts—I nearly laughed myself silly. 'The ship'll never make it outta the space docks,' I told her. But she didn't tell me that you were the captain."

"I wasn't. The first captain didn't make it out of the space docks."

"See, I knew it would fail. But, 'Suzie-Q' found you— a natural-born fighter—and that changed everything. Now, git me the hell outta here. I wanna bash some Separatist heads!"

As soon as Steiner signed the required line of the transfer orders on the computer pad, the guards lowered the energy field in front of the cell, and the Saint shouted gleefully, causing them to draw their weapons. He burst forward and gave Steiner a bear hug. Steiner laughed for the first time since becoming captain of the P.A.V. Suzanne was right. He loved this surprise. Maybe the prison ship could work after all.

When the guards returned the possessions he'd had on him at the time of his arrest, Pattie took only the rosary and tossed everything else in a trash can. "My good-luck charm. I'd never go to war without it." He draped the beaded necklace over his head.

"How else could we call you the 'Saint' if you didn't have it?"

"Well, now, I'm not sure I want to be called that anymore."

"Why not?"

"You see, there's too many bloody heathens in prison. I'll drink with 'em, I'll fight with 'em, but I don't want to start hearing their bloody confessions." He burst into boisterous laughter as if it was the funniest joke he had ever heard.

Steiner smiled politely.

The guards required Pattie's hands to be shackled until he

got aboard the prison ship, but Steiner unlocked them right after they left the building. As they walked through the streets of Tycus, Pattie told Steiner how he came to be in prison.

"You see, right after they drummed me out of the military 'cause I wouldn't kiss the butt of my new scumbag colonel, I went to relax with a drink in the Lion's Den, a pub right down the street a few blocks, just mindin' my own business. Some prissy boy, fresh from college, comes up to the bar and starts getting smart with me, talking trash about servicemen, so I tell him to shut his mouth. He shoves me. I shove him, harder. He pulls a knife—and *no one* pulls a knife on a Stripes, so I knocked it out of his hand and belted him like he deserved. Two of his thugs came at me, so I gave them all a beatin'. Then they pin the whole thing on me. I was just mindin' my own business."

Steiner listened to his story for the sake of his friend, but he vaguely remembered McKillip telling him about the incident a year ago. Pattie had been drinking heavily after his discharge from the U.S.S. Ground Forces. The prissy boy happened to be the son of the governor of Tycus, and the two "thugs" were his bodyguards. All three were hospitalized for weeks after the incident.

"Since that day, I've been wastin' away here," Pattie said. "It's like I always used to say, 'I ain't got the luck of the Irish, but I do have the temper.'" The burly man's mood seemed to soften. "Uh, Suzie-Q told me about Captain McKillip. I'll really miss old Pa. He brought us all together and saved the Union. How did Ma take the news?"

Steiner took a deep breath, then explained all of the events that had transpired following the destruction of the *Valiant*, including how Judith McKillip had been killed by a burglar on the same day and how he had attempted to murder Admiral Jamison for the sake of justice. Pattie turned bright red. He muttered some curses under his breath.

"I wish you had killed that moneygrubbing, two-timing backstabber. And to think, we might have helped that crook get into power. It's damned ironic, after everything we did to save everyone's butts, we get thrown into prison." His arm came up to Steiner's shoulder. "You and I are all that's left of the Cyrian Defense."

"Maybe. It's possible Isaac Steele may still be teaching at the academy."

Pattie laughed. "Good old smarty-pants. Even as irritatin' as he was, part of me misses him, too—only a tiny part. And, don't you ever tell him I said that."

Steiner smiled.

Ten minutes later, when they reached the grassy field, where the visiting ships were lined up in rows, Steiner caught sight of a hunched-over person appearing from behind a row of sleek, elegant yachts, probably belonging to some of the admirals. The man wore a gray-and-blue outfit.

A P.A.V. uniform.

The man walked hunched over, carrying a large bulk wrapped in a blanket.

It must be Pearce trying to smuggle something onto the shuttle.

"Watch my back, Pattie." Steiner drew his weapon and sprinted over to the man carrying the concealed package, while staying out of his field of vision. When he was close enough, he grabbed the man's shoulders and spun him around. The bundle crashed to the ground. Steiner found himself staring at Rick Mason. One of the blanket's corners flipped off the fallen load, revealing an energy coil hidden underneath.

Pattie ran up, winded. Obviously, he wasn't in the shape he once was. "One of your convicts, I suppose?"

Mason glanced at Pattie with uncertainty, then promptly recovered the device from the ground. "Ironhand, you almost ruined everything."

Steiner holstered his weapon. "What are you doing, Rick?"

"What's it look like? I'm requisitioning a replacement. Let's get out of here before its owner finds it missing." After picking the bundle up, Mason continued his rapid pace forward.

"This is illegal," Steiner said, jogging to keep up with him, leaving Pattie behind again.

"What are they gonna to do to me? Put me in prison? I'd

be safer there. I wouldn't have to risk my life flying the faulty machines provided for us. Besides, admirals can get new parts. We can't."

Mason had a point, but that still didn't excuse him from leaving his post. "You were supposed to guard the shuttle."

"I got that covered."

They continued until they were in sight of their craft. Bricket and Pearce were already loading the shipment of liquors on board.

Steiner drew Mason back. "I thought you had it covered. The two of them have been here for who-knows-how-long without supervision."

"Trust me. My spy approaches."

A small boy crawled out from under a neighboring ship.

Mason set down the concealed coil and handed the youngster several coins. "What have you got for me?"

The child smiled. "The men with the bottles brought guns, a whole box of them."

"Guns?" Steiner breathed the word in disbelief.

"Uh-huh." The boy pointed at Mason. "I think they were going to shoot you."

"Me?" the pilot gasped.

The boy bobbed his head with excitement. "Uh-huh. The skinny one walked all around the ship with a gun, calling for you. He saw me, but I ran away."

Steiner stepped back, a sinking sensation building in his stomach. If Mason had remained at his post, he would already be dead. Steiner gave the boy all the money in his pockets. "You were very brave. Thank you."

The youngster beamed as he accepted the gift. "Are you going to shoot them now? Can I watch?"

Steiner paused, unsure whether to laugh or be horrified. "No, you'd better go home now."

With a frown, the boy ran off as Pattie walked up, breathing heavily. "Was that one of your crew, too?"

"No, that was our intel. A couple of my men over in that scuttle bucket are planning a welcoming party for us. They brought their own guns."

"I can't believe they were going to cancel me out, too," Mason muttered.

"You wouldn't have any more pistols stashed anywhere, would ya?" Pattie asked.

Steiner drew his AT-7. "No, but I'll have one for you in a moment. Both of you stay here out of sight until I get the situation under control." With that, he darted to the shadow of the next vessel in the row of ships, crawling under its hull between the landing-gear pods dug into the grass. He paused until both Bricket and Pearce had hauled crates into the shuttle, then sprinted from his hiding place, gun in hand, making a dash for the side of the small craft. Reaching his destination without being seen, he flattened himself along the side of the vessel near the open hatch.

Bricket came out first. When he spotted Steiner, his bearded mouth dropped open. Pearce exited next, caught sight of the bartender's gaze, and followed it to the muzzle of Steiner's pistol. His hand flinched toward his belt.

"Do it," Steiner bellowed. "I'll get a lot of pleasure out of burning you through."

Pearce grinned innocently, raising his hands in the air. "Is something wrong, Captain?"

"Let me see your gun."

"What gun?"

"I'd just as soon pick it off your dead body."

The smile disappeared from Pearce's face. He slowly lifted his uniform's jacket to reveal a pistol tucked under his belt.

"Drop it."

The man did as he was told.

"Both of you, on the ground, facedown," Steiner ordered.

Bricket complied immediately, practically falling into the grass. Pearce glared as he slowly lowered himself also.

Steiner retrieved the discarded weapon.

Mason stumbled out of hiding and hurried into the shuttle, carrying the energy coil with him. Pattie walked calmly, grinning at having enjoyed the show. "If you need anyone to beat their heads into the ground, let me know."

Kneeling beside the bartender, Steiner felt for any concealed weapons. "Bricket, I can't understand why you became involved in this," he said, after his search came up empty.

"Frank was going to kill me if I didn't help him. I had no choice."

"There's always a choice. You made the wrong one."

Pattie set his weight down on Pearce's upper body, digging the man's face into the ground. "You must be 'Frank,'" Pattie said, letting out a loud fart. "Nice to meet ya." The Saint laughed, slapping his knee. "This little trip promises to be more fun than I thought."

Steiner handed him Pearce's weapon. "Welcome aboard, Saint Pattie."

"Now ya done it," the burly man bellowed with a grin. "I'll have to build that confessional for sure."

After Steiner found some cord, he gave it to Pattie, who tied up both of the prisoners. As Steiner went back to help Mason with the energy coil, he caught sight of the small boy watching from underneath a neighboring vessel. He exchanged smiles with the youngster to show his gratitude.

Ten minutes later, they lifted off. Steiner sat in the copilot's chair while Pattie, armed with a pistol, sat in the back with the prisoners, glaring at them menacingly. At one point, he snarled sharply at Bricket, causing the bartender to flinch in fear, then Pattie burst into boisterous laughter. When they reached orbit twenty minutes later, they began their approach to the P.A.V.

"Suzie-Q dug up a Peacemaker for you to use?" Pattie asked. "Brings back the good old days."

Steiner smiled. "I think sentimentality had a little to do with her choice."

"You both served on one these old wrecks before?" Mason asked.

Steiner shook his head. "Absolutely not, but we did borrow one for a joyride."

Pattie bellowed a laugh in response. "Right under the enemy's nose, we did."

"Captain," Pearce suddenly spoke out, "none of you are going to make it back on board alive."

Pattie's mood instantly soured, and he thrust the muzzle of his gun into Pearce's gut.

Steiner swiveled the copilot's seat around. "What do you mean by that?"

Pearce grinned, which caused Pattie's muzzle to dig deeper. "I wasn't working alone," the man replied, gritting his teeth from the apparent pain.

Steiner pointed to Bricket. "You had him."

"The idiot was only an excuse to get to the planet surface. I have an associate on the P.A.V. expecting these weapons. He is watching us right now. If I don't give him a predetermined signal, he will open fire on us."

Mason paled.

"I can still signal him before he does," Pearce added. "Untie me."

"No deal," Steiner replied.

"Ironhand," Mason cut in. "We can't outmaneuver the *Marauder*'s guns."

"We won't have to. I planned for something like this."

"That's what I love about you, Slugger," Pattie said. "You always got a backup plan."

Mason eyed Steiner curiously. "Is that why you wouldn't let Sam come with us?"

"Uh-huh." Steiner imitated the youngster who had aided them. He checked the timepiece on his wrist. "Sam should have disconnected the power supply to all the pulse cannons a half hour ago."

SAM picked his way through the electrical generators located above the engine room, searching for the relays. Steiner had instructed him to cut the power to all the gunnery ports an hour after they had left so that no one would accidentally discover it was off. It had taken him longer than he expected to sneak up the maintenance stairway without being seen. When he arrived, he found the massive upper level to be filled with all kinds of crackling electrical equipment.

Lightning flashed from a nearby conductor post, startling him. He moved on, determined to fulfill his promise, even if he was a little late.

Finally, he found the row of relay levels. One of them read PULSE CANNONS. Taking a firm grip on it, he pulled down.

* * *

AN energy bolt shot across the shuttle's bow. Steiner gasped. The blast originated from one of the *Marauder*'s gunnery ports. How could that be? Sam should have already cut the power—unless someone had stopped him.

"That was intended as a warning, Captain," Pearce said. "There's still time to reconsider."

Pattie glanced at Steiner as if looking for what to do next.

Steiner swiveled his chair to the front. "Rick, try some kind of evasive maneuver."

"Evasive maneuver?" the pilot exclaimed. "In a scuttle bucket?"

Another bolt flashed by on the port side of the tiny craft.

"That was closer than the first," Mason said. "Where is that kid?"

Steiner wondered the same thing.

DESPITE Sam's efforts, the lever refused to budge. He kicked at it desperately in hopes of loosening it.

An alarm sounded. Static discharges erupted from a giant assembly ten meters away. Someone must be firing at the shuttle.

Panic swept through him. His friends might already be dead. It was all his fault for not coming here sooner.

Viciously, he pried at the jammed lever. With a loud wail, he threw all his weight against it.

WHEN Mason shoved the control stick forward, the shuttle dove toward the planet, evading two more shots from the *Marauder*.

"Pearce, your life is in danger too," Steiner shouted. "What's the signal?"

Pattie removed the muzzle from his prisoner's gut and pressed it into the man's temple.

Pearce closed his eyes and gritted his teeth but didn't answer.

Steiner glared at his accomplice. "Bricket?"

"I don't know anything," the bartender whimpered.

The hull jolted as an energy bolt grazed it. The power systems started fluctuating.

"No, not now," Mason cried out.

The interior blacked out. The engines died.

Steiner's stomach tightened as the shuttle tumbled out of control. He dug his fingers into the armrest, trying to keep his eyes off the spinning panorama through the front window.

Bricket screamed from the darkened passenger compartment.

Mason cursed as he turned on the emergency lighting. He opened a maintenance panel under the main controls. "I should have stolen a whole shuttle instead of just an energy coil."

The *Marauder* spun into view of the cockpit window. The gunnery port was silent.

Steiner looked back at Pearce, who appeared equally mystified.

"Why haven't they dusted us yet?" Mason asked as he worked under the console. "Nobody can be that bad a shot."

"Sam must have cut the power," Steiner replied.

"If that's the case, I owe that kid some real flying lessons."

The electrical systems sprang to life. With a sigh of relief, Mason propelled the shuttle forward, wheeled it about, raced to the exterior docking assembly under the belly of the *Marauder*. From that angle, the active gun couldn't hit them. Once he had the craft positioned inside the claw, the engineers, inside the landing bay, started the retrieval process.

Fifteen minutes later, Steiner exited the shuttle into the bay. The engineers were waiting, full of questions but no answers. After shoving his prisoners out of the hatch of the tiny vessel, Pattie introduced himself to the engineers as an old friend of their captain and began to explain what had happened on the planet surface. More concerned about what had happened to Sam, Steiner went and opened the door of the landing bay. Sam stood on the opposite side, tears running down his face.

"You're alive?" the boy exclaimed.

"Didn't you cut the power?" Steiner asked.

Sam shook his head. "I couldn't move the lever."

Steiner stared at him, dumbfounded. If Sam hadn't saved them, who had?

His comlink beeped.

"Steiner here."

"Captain," Security Chief Richards said, "we have a murdered crewman in one of the gunnery ports, the same one that fired on your shuttle."

"How was he killed?"

"You should see this for yourself, sir."

"Send Eddie or Hulsey down here to escort two prisoners to the brig. I'll meet you at your location as soon as I can."

After Bricket and Pearce were taken away, Steiner secured the bay, then left with Pattie to see the murder victim. He smelled burnt flesh as he neared the designated gunnery port. When he arrived, he found a virtual bloodbath. The targeting chair had a body in it that couldn't be recognized because it had been shredded by energy bolts.

"Holy Mother of God," Pattie muttered under his breath, crossing himself.

Wounds like that couldn't have been caused by conventional pistols. Only high-powered assault rifles were capable of that kind of damage—the kind of weapons that were only found in the armory. No one could have smuggled one on board. Even Suzanne's weak security measures would have detected it.

Why had it been used to save Steiner rather than kill him? Who would want to protect him?

Steiner stared up into the camera in the upper corner of the corridor. It was fixed directly on him.

CHAPTER

11

STEINER stood alone inside the brig, staring through the glass portal of the detention cell, which held Bricket. The bartender lay stretched across the cot, with his back against the wall, staring into nothingness. When Steiner had first met him, he had thought him to be a hard, unshakable person, but now he saw quite the contrary, a man who had lost his most-treasured possession, terrified of what fate awaited him.

Pattie burst around the corner, causing Steiner's hand to reach for his holster. The big man had changed into a gray-and-blue P.A.V. uniform, with the sleeves rolled up, proudly displaying the Celtic crosses on each biceps. "I just saw Archimedes, and by the Blessed Virgin, I can't believe my eyes."

"You mean Maxwell Tramer?"

"Yes, of course, Maxie. We used to call him Archimedes, way back before he became that godforsaken creature."

"When did you have a chance to talk to him on the *Valiant*? You weren't even in the same department."

"Everyone has to eat, and I made it my point to meet everyone when they did. Maxie got into making weapons because he admired this Greek fellow named Archimedes.

Apparently this fellow could walk around in front of a large group of soldiers, and they would be terrified of him because he created inventions that could defeat entire armies."

Their discussion must have been heard by Bricket in the cell because he was sitting up now on the cot, staring at the glass portal in the door.

Pattie glanced inside. "What are ya goin' to do about the pansy?"

"I don't know yet."

"Remember how many pansies got killed on Day of Betrayal for followin' the leader, and how many good *men* they took with 'em? Space him, and be done with it."

A beep from the comlink on his belt sounded before Pattie finished.

"I can't do that," Steiner replied before reaching for the device.

Pattie frowned. "It's your funeral."

"Steiner here."

"Captain," Richards said. "We've completed a search of the crew quarters but couldn't find any trace of an assault rifle."

"What about Tramer's cabin?"

"Totally empty. I don't think it has ever been used."

Steiner was tempted to demand another search, but it would probably turn out to be useless as well. "Keep an eye out for it," he told the chief, then signed off.

Somehow, Steiner knew Tramer was responsible. Because the cyborg monitored the security cameras constantly, if it hadn't fired the weapon, it was sure to know who had. Steiner rubbed his eyes, wearily. All he had to do was remain patient until the next day, when they reached Baiten II, a remote planet used by the U.S.S. to train troops. Once there, Tramer would leave for three weeks of battle exercises with the crew on the surface. He couldn't wait to be rid of it.

Pattie's stomach grumbled. "Archimedes already assigned me a cabin and a shift, so I'm gonna see what the grub is like—maybe it's as old as the ship." Pattie laughed again, slapping the side of the wall. "Maybe I'll rub shoulders with some of the other grunts." He placed his pistol in Steiner's hand. "Thanks for lettin' me borrow it, but I'll be fine without it. I've been dyin' for a good fight."

Turning on his heels, Pattie whistled "When the Saint Goes Marching In," his own version of the old hymn, as he marched around the corner.

Steiner again met Bricket's gaze though the glass portal. Steiner wished he could keep the bartender inside the cell until the man could be transferred off, but some of the ship's computers were already beginning to malfunction. No one else knew how to fix them. When the raids began, they would need all their systems fully operational if they hoped to succeed. The chances of Suzanne's finding another computer genius before then were slim, perhaps even nonexistent.

Could he trust Bricket after what had happened?

Steiner opened the door to the cell. The bartender raised his gaze, then lowered it, with apparent shame.

"I gave your assistant control over Hell," Steiner began, stepping inside. "I made the same deal with him that I made with you. He can keep the shipment of liquor as long as I don't see any drunken crewmen."

Bricket's expression turned blank. Steiner realized that had been the wrong way to open the discussion. Before he could think of a better way to continue, the bartender surprised him with a question.

"Do you play poker, Captain?"

"Not much. I don't like the chance factor. Chess is based more on skill."

"Success in poker requires skill, too," Bricket replied, his disposition brightening slightly. "You have to be able to sense if someone is lying by their facial expressions. Some men twitch nervously. Others blink too many times. It's a skill to interpret signs like that."

Steiner smiled to himself, remembering how Mason had cheated the man.

Bricket toyed with his cane, his glum deepening. "Another important factor is knowing the odds." He hesitated for a moment, then met Steiner's gaze. "Frank would have cut my throat if I hadn't brought him with me. I didn't want to help him. It's just that the odds were in his favor."

Steiner huffed, revolted by the bartender's attempt to rationalize his cowardice. "I've seen you play poker. You're not as skilled as you think."

Bricket frowned. "Are you referring to Rick cheating me?"

Steiner swallowed hard.

"Did you also notice that he only won enough to cover his bar tab?" Bricket asked.

Steiner blinked. He had underestimated the bartender completely. "Why did you let him get away with it?"

"I needed the companionship. Most of the crew, including Rick, envy me because I am wealthier than they are. They merely tolerate me because they want my liquor."

Steiner thought back to the night that he and Suzanne had secretly entered the bar. He remembered how all the patrons had acted disrespectfully toward Bricket. A small part of him sympathized with the man. Bricket was as much an outsider among the crew as he was.

"What do you think I ought to do with you now?" Steiner asked.

"Lock me up like you have, if you can afford to." Bricket poked his cane against the floor. "I assume the computers are already beginning to malfunction—not that I sabotaged them or anything devious like that. Those machines are ancient. Some of the components are not even compatible with each other. I have to fiddle with them daily just to keep them functioning."

"Can I trust you not to betray me again?" Steiner asked.

Bricket sighed heavily, his body sinking into the cot's mattress. After a moment of silence, he spoke. "Someone betrayed me once, and it cost me the use of my left leg." He looked up at Steiner. "I vowed to myself never to have faith in anything but the odds. Until now, they've never failed me. If I were in your place, I'd say the odds were against trusting me."

Steiner stood up and held out his hand. "I'll give you another chance."

Bricket's eyes fixed on the offered hand, then shifted to Steiner. "Why?"

"Call it a judgment based on your facial expressions."

Bricket opened his mouth, but he seemed so stunned that

he couldn't speak. After a moment, he grasped the offered hand and lifted himself to his feet. "You won't regret this."

"I hope you're right." Steiner led Bricket out while Pearce glared at them from the window on the neighboring door.

"What about my bar?"

"Consider this a probationary period. If you do well, I'll let you have your bar back, too."

Bricket bit his lip. "Anything to be free of that cell."

As they made their way from the brig, Steiner wondered if Bricket might be acting. Bricket might be leading him along until another opportunity to betray him arose.

Steiner took the bartender to the command center first. When they arrived, Steiner found it odd that Tramer wasn't anywhere around. The cyborg rarely left the security monitors unattended.

"Rick's been complaining that the left screen on the helm is emitting ghost images," Steiner told Bricket. "Make that your first priority."

At the mention of his name, Mason, who sat at the opposite side of the defective console, glared over at his old poker partner. It was a look of contempt, perhaps even hatred.

While Bricket detached the maintenance panel, he glanced over at Mason, who was doing his best to ignore the bartender.

"I'm sorry, Rick," Bricket whispered.

Mason instantly tensed, growling something in response. Steiner couldn't tell what he had said, but the threatening tone was unmistakable.

"Bricket," Steiner scolded, then shook his head.

The bartender's gaze fell to the floor. He gave a weak nod.

After waiting for a few minutes to make sure the bartender completed his work quietly, Steiner descended into his conference room to review the orders given to him by Jamison. Extracting the disk from his pocket, he accessed it using his personal computer. As he glanced through a listing of current events that preceded their orders, he noticed that Captain Cole had been promoted to the position of commodore for the northern border region. Since Cole had been sympathetic toward McKillip, Steiner might be able to convince him to help get Jamison's tribunal bumped up.

After reading the war statistics of the past year, Steiner discovered that the United Star Systems hadn't won a major victory in ten months. A couple of admirals boasted of new offensives being worked out, but he knew it was just a smoke screen to keep the captains thinking optimistically. The underlying fact was hard and undeniable. The U.S.S. was losing the war against the Separatists.

When he looked over the *Marauder*'s assigned missions, he found they wouldn't do any good whatsoever to the overall picture. The five enemy outposts that they were scheduled to raid were so close to the border that they probably expected to be attacked. He couldn't remember all the times that the *Valiant* had been given crucial missions that determined the direction of the war. Back then, he had made a difference. It was so frustrating for him to be trapped aboard a prison ship while the future of the galaxy was decided without him.

Someone began pounding frantically on the door to the conference room.

With his hand on his pistol, Steiner stepped to the side of the entry, then opened it.

Bricket scrambled inside, his face ashen. All he said was, "Tramer," and pointed up the stairwell.

When Steiner looked up at the cyborg at the top of the steps, his body went rigid. Before, the mechanical man had always been cold and emotionless, yet now its face glowed with rage.

"Mr. Tram—?"

"Captain," it interrupted. "May I speak to you in private?"

Steiner couldn't believe what he'd just heard. The cyborg had barely spoken to him since the outset of the voyage. What had caused it to do so now? Even though he was apprehensive about speaking to it alone, he was also anxious to discover the reason for its unusual behavior. "Please come down," he said, almost immediately regretting his invitation.

The cyborg's joints hummed as it descended the stairwell. Bricket backed away from it, waited until it entered the room, then fled up the stairs.

When Steiner sealed the door, a feeling of vulnerability

swept through him. His AT-7 was useless against Tramer's armor. Its powerful mechanical limbs could easily rip him apart before he could escape. With all his willpower, he concentrated on maintaining a firm posture.

"What seems to be bothering you?" he asked.

"Why is a mutineer allowed to return to his duties?" Its synthesized voice echoed within the small room.

"I believe he made a mistake and is remorseful. He may still be an asset to the—"

"Execute him," it cut him off abruptly.

The statement shocked Steiner so much that he was speechless for a few seconds. "Execute him?" he asked. "For what reason?"

"If you don't, the convicts will no longer fear you or the consequences of defying you."

Steiner was surprised that the cyborg was concerned about his image as captain. "I need to gain their trust, not their fear."

"You will create unrest among the crew. *Death* is the only deterrent for mutiny." It spoke with an iciness that sent chills through Steiner's bones. Ending a man's life meant nothing to it.

"I will not kill him."

The cyborg stared at him as if it was challenging his stance.

Steiner's comlink sounded.

"Steiner here."

"Captain." Benjamin Richards's voice came from the device. "We just found Frank Pearce dead."

"What?" Steiner exclaimed. "How could he die if he's locked inside the brig?"

"Someone cut off the air supply to all three detention cells. Pearce suffocated."

"That's impossible. You and I set a proximity alarm inside the life-support station. Isn't it still operating?"

"My console indicates it is. No one could have broken in through the ventilation shafts without setting it off."

Steiner swallowed hard. If he hadn't freed Bricket when he had, the bartender would be dead, too. His breath caught in his lungs. That was exactly what Tramer had wanted.

"Captain?" Richards asked.

"I'll call you back in a minute," Steiner said. "I think I may know who did it." He closed the channel and looked up into the deathly pale face above him. "Did you execute Frank Pearce?"

Tramer remained silent.

"Answer my question."

"Frank Pearce trapped you in your cabin without air," Tramer replied.

"How do you know that? Did you see him?"

"People do not hide their words from what they *think* is just a machine."

Steiner gasped. Could the cyborg be programmed to respond as if it thought it were still a man? That might explain the rage he saw within its human eye.

"Did you break into life support and kill Pearce?" Steiner asked again.

"His death was necessary."

"Were you responsible for it?"

Tramer didn't reply.

Steiner fought to keep himself from shaking. He was angry at the cyborg's failure to give him a direct answer and a little frightened of what it might do if provoked. He stepped back from Tramer and took a deep breath to calm himself.

"Who is in command?" he asked.

"You are."

"Bricket lives."

The mechanical man saluted, then marched from the room.

Steiner stared dumbfounded after it, recalling its nickname, "Killer Cyborg." It could murder without hesitation. Because it thought it was still human, it was more dangerous than before. It might be insane.

CHAPTER

12

"AMAZING Grace" echoed throughout the small service air lock, which served as a chapel. The engineers worked together harmoniously to give the hymn a beauty Steiner had never known. Some waved their hands in the air as if having a religious experience. Steiner didn't share in their worship, nor did he understand it. It hadn't helped Mary. He was here for only one reason—to seek counsel from someone who knew Tramer.

When the hymn ended, Daniels led the congregation in a final prayer. After the men began dispersing, Steiner approached the head engineer, who was gathering his notes into his frayed Bible.

"May I speak to you for a moment?"

"Sure," Daniels answered. "Is this of a professional nature or a personal one?"

"Both."

Daniels indicated for him to sit on the floor beside him. "Please, go on."

"On the professional side, I need your assistance again in operating the landing bay during the transporting of the trainees to and from the planet."

The ebony man smiled. "No problem."

"But there could be problems," Steiner replied. "If there are any attempts to overtake the bay, I'll be forced to blow its emergency hatch."

As Steiner had expected, the head engineer gave no facial response—not even one of concern.

"I'll provide a space suit for you in case that does happen, but it won't protect you against the suction," Steiner added.

Daniels chuckled. "I don't care for one. Thank you for offering. What's the personal question?"

Steiner stared at him blankly for a second, then remembered what he had wanted to ask him. "I need some advice about Maxwell Tramer. You've known it longer than I. It seems unstable, perhaps dangerous. Do you have any insight to offer?"

Daniels sighed. "The best suggestion I have is to try looking at life from *his* point of view."

Steiner stopped him there. "You think that Tramer is a man?"

"He's not a normal person like you and me. He's a living soul trapped inside a mechanical shell."

"Then you believe its humanity is intact?" Steiner asked, genuinely curious.

"Yes."

"How can you tell?"

"I've seen flashes of it occasionally. He likes me."

"Why you?"

"Because I treat him as a real person."

"I've never seen you and Tramer together. If it—or rather, he—likes you, why doesn't he spend time with you?"

Daniels smiled. "Maxwell isn't comfortable being around other people. He secludes himself."

"Any ideas as to his reasons?"

"Maybe it's too painful to be reminded he was once a man. It might be easier to live as a machine." Daniels paused. "Have you ever seen how everyone treats him?"

"Most keep their distance."

"Exactly. They fear him. A few others act impersonally to him like they would toward an appliance."

Steiner swallowed against the bile climbing up his throat.

Hearing Tramer being referred to as Maxwell was growing too uncomfortable.

"What do you think that does to him emotionally?" Daniels asked.

Steiner shrugged, unwilling to make that stretch.

"But it's so easy, Jacob. Maxwell acts like a machine to protect himself from his own emotions."

A sliver of doubt cracked through Steiner's stone-hard convictions. Could Maxwell be alive? No, he refused to accept that. Maxwell was dead—that was the only way it could ever be.

"He likes you, too, you know," Daniels said.

Steiner looked sharply at the head engineer.

"More importantly, he respects your authority," Daniels said. "I saw how he acted toward Captain Barker. That man behaved like a fool. Maxwell resisted him. However, he deals with you respectfully. He wouldn't do that if he didn't like you."

That was as much as Steiner could bear. "How can you say that? That monstrosity has no regard for human life. I believe it's been involved in the recent murders. It might even be insane."

The head engineer shook his head. "If Maxwell had lost his mind, everyone on this ship would have been his victim by now. He is completely rational."

Steiner jumped to his feet. "Seven years ago, it mutilated two defenseless people. Does that sound rational?"

Still seated peacefully on the floor, Daniels picked up his frayed Bible and held it close to him. "I've assassinated many people throughout my lifetime. If anyone is more worthy of being condemned as a murderer, it's me."

Shame flooded through Steiner. He shouldn't have lost his temper with a man who had done nothing but help him since the beginning of the voyage. "I can't compare you to Tramer. You've changed, found God, or something like that."

"Maybe he has changed as well."

"I doubt it. All I see is the infamous 'Killer Cyborg.'"

"Behind the hardware, under the deformities, a tortured soul cries out in agony—in some ways, just like me."

"I don't see that."

"Look into Maxwell's human eye. The pain is evident."

BEFORE retiring for a nap, Steiner decided to go to the command center and verify Daniels's theory. One by one, the ship's cameras followed him. In his mind's eye, he could see the cyborg's frozen stare boring into him.

He likes you, too, he could almost hear Daniels say.

With forced steps, Steiner ascended the stairway to the main deck of the command center. Tramer stood in front of the security monitors. It didn't turn around to acknowledge his presence but continued flipping through the images on the screens.

"Mr. Tramer," Steiner finally managed. The cyborg turned to face him. "I am putting you in charge of training the combat teams on the planet surface."

"An intelligent choice," the synthesized voice said.

"I'm wary of sending you alone. I would like you to include Patrick Braun as your second. He used to be a U.S. Ground Forces sergeant."

"He is undisciplined."

"He is out of practice. Once you get down there, I think he may prove to be an asset to your team."

"I will comply and notify him of the change in his schedule. However, if you wish to oversee the training for yourself, a transmitter can be connected to my sensors. The signal can be received on the security monitors. You would then be able to modify my training procedures as you see fit."

The suggestion took Steiner by surprise. "Is that hard to set up?"

"The bartender is capable of the procedure," Tramer replied. "I can guide him through the process before I leave."

Steiner wondered why the cyborg was being so helpful. It didn't have to volunteer for the transmitter. It could have kept silent. Then he realized it might be looking for an opportunity to execute Bricket.

"If you try to harm him—"

"I have and will continue to respect your orders. So far,

his pardon has not caused the rest of the crew to lose their fear of you."

Steiner hesitated, wondering how to respond. "Thank you," he finally said.

"Is there anything else, Captain?" it asked.

"Yes," he forced himself to say. Every instinct in his being told him to leave, but he stood firm. It was time to test Daniels's theory. He would apologize to Tramer for treating it like a mechanical device. If it was just an inanimate object, it wouldn't respond. If it was Maxwell—no that wouldn't happen.

He looked past the glare of the blue sensor orb, into the gray, seemingly lifeless, human eye on the left side of the deformed face. He realized he had never seen it blink before. Could it? *Look deeper,* he told himself. The pupil shifted slightly back and forth, as did many people's when they were looking at another person.

Are you Maxwell Tramer? he asked silently. *Are you hiding your emotions for your own protection?* Steiner didn't want to believe it. It was more comforting to accept it as a machine. The possibilities were too horrifying. But he had to know.

"Mr. Tramer, I wanted to say . . ." He trailed off, not knowing if he could finish. His stomach tightened into knots. He forced himself to continue. "I want to apologize for the way I've behaved toward you during the past few weeks. I've acted as if you were only a machine. You were my friend once, and I hope you can be again."

The eye blinked.

Immediately, Tramer turned away. When Steiner inched closer, he saw the cyborg's reflection in one of the darkened monitors. A single trail of wetness ran down the ghostly countenance.

Feeling sick, Steiner steadied himself against the wall. Daniels had been right all along. Steiner stumbled back down the stairs out of the center, his discovery too mortifying to imagine. Maxwell had survived the explosion over seven years earlier.

When Steiner returned to his cabin, sleep didn't come well. He lay on his cot, thinking of his first meeting with

Maxwell. It was about a year before the Day of Betrayal, when there was still hope for a peaceful resolution to the unrest between United Star Systems and the newly formed New Order Empire. Steiner had joined Captain McKillip's Cyrian Defense and gone with them on a covert mission to uncover evidence that the New Order was building new warships, called battlecruisers, which outgunned the typical U.S.S. Destroyer-class vessel. After McKillip had secretly released the evidence to the interstellar media sources, the U.S.S. Congress reluctantly approved a weapons upgrade for all their U.S.S. warships, enlisting Maxwell and Candice Tramer, a renowned team in the field of particle physics, to upgrade the particle cannons. Candice oversaw the production while Maxwell oversaw the installations, visiting the *Valiant* first because it was already in the space docks at the time. Steiner had been assigned to assist him personally, following him around the ship and making sure he got everything he needed. Maxwell had a quiet demeanor, and his voice had lacked inflection, making him sound machinelike even then. But he had possessed a sharp wit, which he interjected randomly throughout his monochromatic drone just to see the unexpected reactions from his intended audience. When he was inside the *Valiant*'s cafeteria, Maxwell had witnessed a fight between Mary and Steiner and quietly observed that she might be pregnant because he had gone through a similar struggle with his wife before the birth of their daughter. He had been right.

Steiner wondered what had happened to his wife, Candice, and his daughter. She had visited the *Valiant* only once, to discuss a production problem with her husband, and Steiner got only a brief introduction to her. Where was she now? Steiner suspected she and her daughter were no longer a part of Maxwell's life. He couldn't blame them. Wiping a tear from his face, Steiner rolled over and thought about how Mary might have reacted if something like that had happened to him. He wanted to think that she would never leave him, no matter what. It wasn't long before he fell into a deep sleep.

Steiner and his newly pregnant wife, Mary, were walking behind Maxwell past a row of pulse cannons as he droned on about how he had enhanced their output. A pulse cannon exploded, blinding Steiner. When he looked up, there was Mary with a sad look on her face. Steiner raised his hand to her, but realized it was a metallic arm—Maxwell Tramer's arm. He was in the cyborg's body. Mary turned, blowing him a small regretful kiss, and ran out onto the launchpad for her shuttle. He couldn't move his mechanical legs to stop her. The shuttle erupted into flames.

Abruptly, the dream changed.

Steiner, back in his normal body, stood in the command center of the *Marauder*, face-to-face with Maxwell Tramer, the cyborg he had been forced to work with, trying to determine what its most horrifying trait was. Its smell? Its appearance? Its lifeless stare? No. It was the possibility that this grotesque creation of human hands could be his former friend. He found himself turning in utter disgust and walking away.

Steiner awoke at the sound of his comlink. "Steiner here." His own voice sounded ragged to him.

"We have achieved orbit around Baiten II."

"Thank you, Mr. Tramer. Have your first team assembled within two hours."

As Steiner washed himself and put on a fresh uniform, he thought about how he had treated Maxwell over the last few weeks. He had abandoned Maxwell in his waking life as surely as he had in the dream.

As he made his way toward the lower levels, he passed by the bar and noticed someone had painted a letter "S" in front of the sign "HELL" and a "Y" on the end of it. Immediately, he suspected Pattie had something to do with that. Upon reaching the engine room, he evacuated the crewmen out of the area except for Daniels, J.R., and Spider and sealed the lower-level pressure door. He led the engineers into the landing bay and opened the pressure door for them to begin their preparations. All three men sang hymns as they prepped the armored transport carrier, which they had nicknamed the *Stormquest*. J.R., a bass, and Spider, a tenor, blended their voices together to form such majestic tapestries of music that Steiner thought they might try to start a singing career together once their sentences had expired. Steiner helped J.R. drive six of the armored TRAC vehicles into the cargo hold of the *Stormquest*. Then he aided them in making a trek to the armory and bringing back carts filled with assault rifles, missile launchers, grenades, suits of body armor, and six portable laser cannons.

At just before 1200 hours, Steiner's comlink beeped. "Steiner here."

"Captain," Tramer's synthesized voice answered. "The RED team has been assembled at Pressure Door C-3, awaiting your orders."

"We're almost done, Mr. Tramer. I'll open the door in five minutes," Steiner said into his comlink.

J.R. and Spider hugged Daniels as if saying good-bye to their own father. Daniels climbed into the control booth for the crane and waved to his assistants as Steiner escorted them out of the landing bay.

Steiner went to Pressure Door C-3, which sealed off the lower levels from the rest of the ship, and entered the code to open it. Under the watchful eye of the weapons officer, fifteen men, including Mason, Sam, and Pattie, filed through the doorway and headed for the landing bay. Tramer acted as emotionless as ever. Steiner saluted him but got no response.

Why is he acting so distant? he wondered as he watched his old friend march after the trainees. Anxious to view what the weapons officer's sensors were recording, Steiner sealed the lower level, then hurried toward the command center.

After Steiner had Julio Sanchez set the *Marauder* on autopilot around the planet, he dismissed everyone but Bricket from the command center. Steiner sat down next to the bartender in front of the security monitors. Instead of interior views of the ship, several of the screens depicted various images coming from Tramer's sensor implants. One held a normal camera panorama, another, an infrared readout, and a third, a scanner that detected everything within a fifty-foot radius. The weapons officer could tell if a person was approaching even without seeing him directly. It seemed very beneficial, but at the same time, it must also be a curse, robbing Tramer of his normalcy.

"You don't trust Tramer going down there unsupervised, do you?" Bricket asked. "That's the reason you had me attach the transmitter to his sensors, isn't it?"

"Tramer volunteered for the procedure."

The bartender's brow furrowed. "He did?"

The top left screen showed the *Stormquest* descending into the massive air lock in the floor of the landing bay. The center monitor displayed Tramer's perspective of the interior of the troop compartment. He faced two rows of convicts strapped into seats along the side of the hull. Steiner could barely make out Mason and Sam through the open hatch to the cockpit on the far wall.

"When I attached the transmitter to Tramer's visual sensors, I took the liberty of tapping into the audio as well," Bricket said. "Would you like to hear what everyone is saying?"

This was more than Steiner had hoped for. "Yes," he answered.

When the bartender pressed a keypad, the speakers emitted distorted sounds. After several adjustments, he was able to clean it up to where individual voices could be heard. The convicts spoke softly among themselves, repeating obscene jokes and teasing each other. Steiner heard the bounty on his life mentioned twice. Both times, it had been referred to in a jesting manner, not worthy of reacting to. Tramer had been accurate when he had said that the men didn't hide their words from him. They probably didn't know the weapons officer's hearing was so acute.

"Why did you change the name of the bar to SHELLY?" one of the armored men shouted at Pattie.

"'Cause I'd rather spend me free time inside a woman, wouldn't ya all agree, lads?"

The other convicts cheered their response.

Bricket groaned. "My assistant says profits have increased since he did that."

The picture shook as the *Stormquest* dropped away from the bottom of the *Marauder*'s docking assembly. The horizon of the planet rose in the portholes along the hull. The sounds distorted briefly into a high-pitched whine, causing Steiner to wince.

"Sorry about that. It's amazing how powerful this audio feed is," Bricket said, working the controls on the console. "I'll bet I can isolate a single voice from a hundred feet away."

He experimented with his theory by zooming in on Mason and Sam in the cockpit. Their voices became distinct amidst all the other convicts' chatter. Steiner listened as Mason instructed Sam how to keep the ship's descent smooth when entering a planet's atmosphere. Mason let the boy try it by himself, but his flying was so rocky that Mason had to take over again.

Steiner smiled.

A fiery glow grew in all the windows. A couple of the convicts gave exuberant cries of excitement.

The images disappeared from the screens as the *Stormquest* descended into the blackout zone of the upper atmosphere.

"Tramer wants to kill me for aiding Pearce, doesn't he?" Bricket asked in the new silence.

Steiner knew better than to lie. "Yes."

The bartender groaned. "I could sense it when I attached the visual transmitter to him."

"Tramer thinks that executing you will provide discipline for the rest of the crew. I don't agree."

"What's to stop him from murdering me?"

"My order not to."

"Do you really believe you can control his actions with an order?"

Steiner didn't reply. In all honesty, he couldn't restrain Tramer from executing anyone. He could only hope the weapons officer obeyed him.

"That's what I expected," Bricket said. "I might be able to help you with that dilemma."

Steiner eyed the bartender curiously.

The images sprang back to life upon the darkened screens. Cheers from the convicts in the troop compartment blared over the speakers.

Bricket decreased the volume, then turned to Steiner. "When I attached the transmitter, I saw the CPU that interfaces with Tramer's brain. I could've easily sliced through its power cord with a laser cutter. Without the CPU, his human body can't sustain itself."

"You want to murder him?" Steiner asked.

"Yes, if it's the only way to keep him from killing anyone else."

"There's no proof that he murdered anyone on this ship."

"He did. Everyone on board knows it—even you."

"We never found the weapon that killed the man in the gunnery port. As for Pearce's death, Tramer couldn't possibly have squeezed through a ventilation shaft to get into the life-support control room."

"That's not the only way to get into life support," Bricket replied.

"Other than using the password for the main entry, it is."

"That's exactly what he did."

Steiner shook his head. "Director Riggs assured me that only she and I know the ship's passwords."

"I don't doubt that at all. But consider what we are viewing on these monitors. Tramer's capabilities are far more than either of us expected. How do we know what his limitations are?"

A sickening sensation swept over Steiner when he remembered the times Tramer had watched him from a distance entering passwords. He found himself doubting Maxwell again, abandoning him just as in the dream.

"He could have gotten an assault rifle right out of the armory," Bricket said.

Steiner rubbed his face with his hands. "If I allowed you to execute him, I'd be guilty of the exact same crime you are accusing him of."

"Can you risk not to? Considering his physical strength, I doubt any of the cells in the brig could hold him."

Steiner knew that the bartender was leading him along to the only logical conclusion, one he didn't wish to consider.

Bricket probably sensed his discomfort because he stopped his argument and watched the monitors for a while.

Almost completely barren, Baiten II had been one of the first failed attempts at terraforming a world for colonization. The air was breathable, but the sandstorms made growing things there impossible, so the United Star Systems used it for troop training, instead.

The *Stormquest* landed in the middle of a desert plain. Tramer immediately put on a metallic face shield, locking it into place. One of the monitors went dark from its camera being blocked by the helmet. The infrared image and the proximity sensor display remained active. When Tramer opened the hatch, a dust cloud poured through the opening. He began instructing the convicts on how he wanted the equipment unloaded. Steiner realized Tramer's helmet shield must be protecting the only exposed flesh on his body, his face, from the biting sand. On the screens, the convicts began to set up a large tent as a barrack.

"When Tramer returns to exchange the RED and GREEN teams," Bricket said, "tell him I have to adjust his transmitter for clearer reception. I'll do the rest."

"I'll consider your proposition and give you my decision at the end of the week," Steiner said sternly.

Bricket nodded and said nothing more about it.

Steiner tried to imagine whether Captain McKillip would have condoned murder to protect himself and his ship. Probably not. He had never compromised his beliefs. Could Steiner afford to follow the same policy?

As the week progressed, Steiner learned how to control the different feeds transmitted from Tramer's sensors by himself. Between patrols of the ship, he spent hours in the command center alone, watching everything that transpired on the planet below. The serious nature of his decision demanded that he do so.

Pattie had proven to be the valuable asset Steiner had hoped he would be. For the first day, the former sergeant teased and joked with the convicts like they were his buddies, secretly assessing their abilities. Then, on the second day, his mood toughened, and he began barking orders, pushing each and every convict to the limits of his physical endurance. At first, some complained, but Pattie explained to them all, "The Separatists are gonna want to *kill* you. If you survive me, then you'll survive them; otherwise, there's a dark cell somewhere awaitin' any prissy boy who wants to quit."

Within the tent barracks, Tramer would start each training session with a lecture, walking confidently among the armor-suited convicts, instructing them how best to use the assault rifles and missile launchers in concert with each other for maximum effectiveness. He would then give the team over to Pattie, to have him run them through battle exercises outside in the harsh wind. Tramer monitored from the tent as the convicts marched through the churning sands under the twin suns. Pattie taught the men his personal battle hymn. "Oh, when the Saint, goes marchin' in. Oh, when the Saint goes marchin' in. He'll stomp on his enemies' skulls. When the Saint goes marchin' in."

Mason had trouble keeping up with the others on some of the strenuous drills, but Sam didn't seem to have any difficulty. It had been the teenager's decision to go on the training week. He wanted whatever defense skills he could learn. Sam was far tougher than Steiner had expected, probably driven by the same survival skills that had kept him alive on the run. Together, Mason and Sam participated in a competition Tramer held with the TRACs. Mason drove the vehicle across the sandy terrain, bouncing over small dunes, while Sam fired its mounted gun at targets Tramer had set up in the distance. They achieved the second-highest score out of five competing teams. The other convicts warmed up to Sam quickly, respecting his determination. One evening, Sam told them his story, about being left as a child at a parish, being raised by Father Perez, who had been murdered by a mob, and his years on the run from the law. After the whole story was done, Mason seemed affected by it, because afterward, when he called Sam "Little Brother," it sounded like he actually meant it.

During the planet's dark cycles, when only one sun skimmed the horizon, the convicts slept soundly inside the tent barracks, exhausted from the intense workout, while Tramer positioned himself silently in a corner. Steiner learned that Tramer did, in fact, sleep. When the weapons officer stood motionless for several hours, his pulse slowed and his breathing deepened. His sensors continued to operate, awakening him whenever someone moved or shifted inside the tent. That explained why he never used his cabin. He could have been napping in front of his security station at any time while his components monitored the screens.

During the last night on the planet, Steiner sat at the screens, drinking a cup of coffee, watching Tramer use a small blower to discharge the sand from his servos and gears. In the back of the tent, Pattie got up from his sleeping roll and picked his way through the slumbering convicts until he got near Tramer. The Saint struggled for a moment, then whispered, "Something's botherin' me that I have to know before we do this all over again for the next two weeks. It doesn't matter how ya answer. I'll do my job as I've done. I wanna know for myself." Pattie looked away, gritting his teeth. "Okay, here goes. No hard feelings, right?" Pattie inched closer, staring directly into the monitors. "Seein' you marchin' around in front of the men, makin' them cower in fear, reminded me of Archimedes, don't ya think?" Pattie grinned nervously, searching for a response that Steiner couldn't see. Finally, the Saint's face broke into a wide grin, and he chuckled softly. "It is you, Maxie. Saints be praised! That's what I thought. Just had to be sure." Pattie backed away, the pleasant grin fading. "Bad luck, I guess." His gaze dropped to the floor, ashamed to look up. "You're a fine leader. Good to serve under ya." He gave another pained grin, shrugged his shoulders, and started picking his way back to his sleeping roll. His head bobbed up and down as he repeated something. Steiner pumped up the gain to hear what it was. "Mary full of grace, the Lord is with thee. Blessed art thou among women . . ." The words were rapid and breathless as he repeated them over and over. As the Saint got back into his bedroll, Steiner saw that the man's expression was pale, and his hands shook as he counted the rosary beads from his necklace.

Steiner sat back in his chair and held his head in his hands. He could now imagine a fate worse than death. Maybe it truly was easier for his old friend to relate to people as a machine because then he didn't have to be constantly reminded by the people around him of the utter tragedy of his own situation. Steiner laid his head down on the console and fell asleep.

The glaring sunlight pouring through the security screens woke him up. He yawned, stretching his arms to their full length. On the screens, Tramer had assembled the men for one last training session, using the portable laser cannons. Steiner found his unfinished cup of coffee sitting nearby and sipped the unappealingly cold liquid, hoping the caffeine might wake him up. Then he noticed Tramer calling to a trainee two hundred feet away. He told the man he had typed the wrong figures into the access panel of his portable laser cannon.

Tramer couldn't possibly have seen what sequence the man had entered from that distance unless his sensors had somehow detected it. Perhaps they had picked up the electronic pulses the keys generated? Or, maybe they deciphered the movements of the trainee's fingers?

Considering what Steiner had just seen, he realized Tramer must know the passwords to everything on the ship.

When he had learned that his old friend was still alive, Steiner had hoped to rebuild his relationship with Maxwell, but too much evidence indicated that his former colleague had turned into a heartless murderer.

Even so, he couldn't bring himself to execute Tramer. He was too much of an asset to the missions ahead. Maybe Tramer did like him, as Daniels had said. Maybe he could use that a little while longer.

When he informed Bricket of his decision, Bricket shook his head.

"The odds are against you," he said.

"They always have been," Steiner replied.

CHAPTER

13

DAWN found the New Order Empire's Commander George Williams standing out on the balcony of the lookout tower, surveying with disgust the area around his planetary outpost. The deep scarlet orb of the system's sun rose over the plains to the south. It was diffused by the carbon-dioxide dust storms rippling across the flat terrain.

A fierce gust buffeted Williams, forcing him back against the rear wall.

He hated this planet. Its atmosphere required that they all wear pressurized suits and helmets. The mountains to the north shielded the installation from the gale-force winds, strong enough to topple buildings.

Williams raised his binoculars to his facial mask and searched the storming plains for any signs of an invasion force. A half hour ago, their automated satellite had warned them of an approaching ship. Since then, they had lost all contact with it.

Williams knew that the enemy attack he had been expecting for the past week had finally come. He had few armaments with which to defend his outpost. His superiors had already decided far in advance that he would lose this battle.

Williams and his men were only to pretend to put up a fight. There wasn't much else they could do besides that.

It isn't fair, Williams thought to himself. He had originally been promised a posting at Hurot IV, the most heavily armed outpost near the border. Hurot IV was the most elite of all their outposts, having been constructed on a planet that once possessed multitudes of luxury resorts. High-ranking officials went through there all the time, increasing the possibilities of being noticed and promoted.

Admiral Richina must have given him this assignment in revenge for what Williams had done at that dinner party last month. Williams winced at the memory. His mouth had gotten him into so much trouble. In front of several other guests, he had attributed Admiral Richina's callous disposition to the fact that his wife had been executed for being openly sympathetic to the United Star Systems. When Williams had finished the account, he looked up and saw Richina glaring at him from the next room. Right then, he knew his career would take a tumble, and it had.

"Here they come." Lieutenant Ortiz's voice sounded within Williams's helmet. "They're approaching from sixty degrees to the south." Williams looked over to the suited man next to him who stared at a mobile readout. All the staff of the planetary outpost was already suited up and ready to retreat.

Williams found the exact spot with his binoculars. A large swirling cloud moved among the normal dust storms. *Three, maybe four, vehicles.*

In a few minutes, it would finally be all over.

His gloved fingers found the universal channel under his face shield. "Pulse cannons, open fire on the approaching targets." His voice echoed within the confining space.

The two gunports shot bolts of destructive energy across the barren surface at the invaders. Williams stepped back into the doorway, thoroughly disgusted by the sight of their pitiful arsenal.

"Sir," Ortiz called out through his helmet's comlink as he pointed to the east. "Enemy ship closing."

Williams looked up in time to see a dark shape materialize from behind a cloud of nearby swirling dust. The vessel passed directly over the installation, dropping small bombs over the pulse cannons. In a flash of light, his base's armament was gone.

"Damn you, Richina," he shouted without activating his comlink, hurting his own ears.

His men began fleeing from their posts up into the mountainside.

"Sir?" Ortiz asked. The atmospheric mask failed to hide the pleading expression on Ortiz's face.

Why not? Williams asked himself. He had put up a fight as he had been ordered to do. He had no idea what the convict invaders had planned for their prisoners, but he didn't want to find out.

"Sound the retreat alarm," he announced over the universal channel. He hated losing a battle, but a planned defeat felt even worse.

While the sirens blared, he and Ortiz climbed down from the tower and got into an all-terrain vehicle. By that time, no one was left inside the compound. Williams drove up the mountainside, fighting against the gusts of wind threatening to overturn them. When they reached the heights of the ridge, he looked back at the invaders, who were breaking through the front gate of the base. In seconds, they had infiltrated the massive doors and were branching out into different buildings.

They can have the entire base, Williams thought, gritting his teeth.

Something gleamed in the sunlight from inside the base.

"Why have we stopped, sir? Let's keep going." The lieutenant sounded nervous, on the verge of hysterics.

Williams ignored the man and lifted his binoculars to take a closer look at the glistening object. Some kind of robot was with the attackers. He had never seen anything like it.

"Let's go, sir, before they come after us," Ortiz cried out.

Williams glared at him, then accelerated the vehicle forward again. The raiders wouldn't come after them. They wanted the information stored within the outpost's computers. Little did they know, it was all fake.

* * *

STEINER couldn't understand it. The New Order Empire's plans made no sense. He sat behind his desk within his conference chamber on the *Marauder*. A table-sized holographic map of the known galaxy lay in front of him, with the galactic core acting as "north." Earth lay in the center of the United Star Systems, scattered within the habitable regions of the Orion and Perseus spiral arms. The Outer Colonies populated the area east of the United Star Systems, mixed within the Orion and the rich Sagittarius arms. According to the enemy-ship deployment, the New Order Empire must be planning another invasion, of the southern regions of the United Star Systems, on the same scale as their initial invasion on the Day of Betrayal. Strategically, an attack in the northern sectors seemed more advantageous to Steiner. Why would they bother with the south? He picked up a computer pad lying next to the holographic map, a pad that held all the requisitions, troop transfers, and a personal letter. He navigated to the personal letter, written by the enemy commander to his wife, which described the part that their installation would play in the planned invasion. Could the man have been so careless not to have even encoded it?

Steiner looked up at Tramer, who stood on the other side of his desk inside the conference room. "Is this all there was in their computer mainframe?"

"Yes," the weapons officer's voice rumbled.

"We tore that place apart," Pattie said, standing by the door. "We didn't miss a trick."

"I don't believe this," Steiner muttered to himself in utter bewilderment.

"Neither do I," Tramer replied with certainty.

Steiner blinked. "You think we were *supposed* to obtain them?"

"There is no other explanation. The occupants of the base made no attempt to destroy their computer banks before retreating into the hills."

Steiner tugged at his beard. What if Tramer was right? What if the Separatists had foreseen their raid and planted the misinformation? It seemed plausible. Steiner looked over to Pattie, seeking his opinion.

The Saint shrugged. "They did leave before we could even fire a shot at them."

"I have reviewed all the outposts we are scheduled to raid," the weapons officer said. "They are likely to produce the same results as this one. If we are to acquire any real strategic material, we must deviate from our orders."

"Where are you suggesting we attack?"

Tramer pointed to a planet on the holographic display, farther into the interior of enemy space. "We raid this installation."

With the press of a couple of keypads, Steiner enlarged the area where the spiny finger pointed. "Hurot IV? That's insane—it's too far in. There would be five battlecruisers on us in an instant."

"There are no battlecruisers in that area."

"What makes you so sure?"

"Because these plans say there are."

Tramer's theory seemed feasible, but Steiner still had doubts about such a bold move.

"The installation on Hurot IV will have ten times the armaments as the one both of you just raided," Steiner said. "The people there will fight to the death to protect their government's secrets. Do either of you believe our crew of convicts has any chance of defeating them?"

"Hell, yes!" Pattie bellowed, raising his fist in the air. "Bring 'em on."

Tramer stood motionless. "We must try," his synthesized voice replied.

Steiner thought back to the statistics he had seen on the Orders disk. The United Star Systems needed a victory right now. This might be his only opportunity to make a difference in the outcome of the war. "Okay, we'll raid it."

The announcement caused Pattie to dance a little jig. "I'll tell the men. We're gonna get some action this time." Whistling his theme song, he turned on his heels, opened the door, and climbed the steps toward the command center.

Tramer waited until the door slid closed. "Captain, I

must—" The blackish lips seemed to stumble on what they were about to say. The weapons officer's posture shrank slightly, then became rigid again. "In order to achieve success, we will need Bricket's help."

In that instant, Steiner clearly saw the man inside the machine, struggling to admit he had been wrong. "Thank you, Mr. Tramer. I will speak to him."

Tramer saluted and marched out the door.

Steiner marveled at how human Tramer had become to him. The three weeks he had spent watching life from the perspective of his weapons officer had changed his view of the man completely. He still didn't understand all of Tramer's motives, but he felt confident that they shared the same goals.

Upon entering the computer room, Steiner found the bartender working on the main terminal, a smoldering cigar drooping from his bearded mouth. Even though the ventilation system constantly worked to circulate fresh air, the pungent odor of burnt tobacco stung Steiner's eyes. He sat next to Bricket and waved the smoke away from his face.

"Is this a business call?" the man asked gruffly.

"I'm offering you the chance to win back your bar."

The sullen eyes sparkled to live. "I'll play any game with stakes like that."

"Can you devise a better method of jamming a satellite's transmissions? The last one picked us up for a second before we successfully disabled it."

The bartender tapped the ashes off the end of his cigar. "I could try boosting the power or widening the range of frequencies dampened. I might have to write some new software code. Maybe some adaptive algorithms."

"How soon can it be done?"

"Maybe in a couple of hours. Is there a hurry?"

Steiner hesitated, realizing everyone else might not be so determined to raid Hurot IV as he or Pattie or Tramer. "It appears we're going to raid an outpost in the interior. It's heavily fortified. Surprise might be our only weapon. If their satellite picks us up at all, we might become trapped behind enemy lines."

"Is this outpost next on our schedule?" Bricket asked.

"Yes, it is," Steiner lied.

Bricket stared at him intently for a few long seconds. Then Steiner remembered what the bartender had told him earlier in the detention cell. Poker players could determine falsehoods based on facial expressions. Was he reacting in a way that Bricket could interpret? His pulse quickened. He forced himself to maintain a calm demeanor. His neck started to burn. He felt on the verge of flushing, when Mason walked through the door.

"Nice flying down there, Rick," Steiner said, casually breaking away from the bartender's gaze.

Mason grinned. "Always." The pilot didn't even look at Bricket as he moved past both of them and headed toward the flight simulator in the corner of the room.

"He hasn't forgiven you yet, has he?" Steiner asked the bartender, thankful for the opportunity to change the subject.

Bricket removed the smoldering cigar from his mouth and blew a stream of smoke at the ceiling. "I have a feeling that may change in just a few minutes."

"How is that?"

"I know how to win people like Rick over." Bricket pointed at the simulator as Mason started it up. A holographic image appeared instead of the *Marauder*'s flight program.

"Through their vices," the bartender whispered.

A scantily dressed, voluptuous woman with purple hair danced across the simulator's screen. Steiner moved closer to get a better look, while Bricket hobbled behind him.

Mason glanced over at them. "I haven't seen a woman like that since my capture."

Exotic music played over the simulator's speakers. The pilot chuckled and leaned back to watch the show.

"I call her 'Princess,'" Bricket said.

"That she is," Mason replied.

Steiner watched as the bartender instructed the pilot how to control her actions by using the simulator's controls. The program included different kinds of dances, but Mason went wild for the striptease. The pilot acted so much like an excited schoolboy that he seemed to have completely forgotten about the bartender's betrayal.

"What about that base, Captain?" Bricket asked. "Where is it?"

"Hurot IV," Steiner answered.

"Hurot IV," Mason cried out, jumping out of the simulator.

"You've been there since the New Order Empire captured it on the Day of Betrayal?"

"I used to smuggle in that area. That place is a fortress. They even have a squadron of fighter ships there that can be scrambled out at a moment's notice. They would obliterate this vessel—I should know, they almost did it to one of my ships once."

"According to the captain," Bricket said, giving Steiner a sidelong glance, "we've been assigned to raid it."

Steiner flushed. The bartender knew he had lied.

"That's a suicide mission, Ironhand," Mason shouted. "They'd tear us to shreds."

Steiner hesitated. How could he convince Mason of the necessity of the raid? If he lied again, the bartender might expose him. Just then it came to him: use Mason's vices to persuade him, just as Bricket had done.

"It would be the ultimate high, Rick. To conquer the Separatist outpost that almost destroyed you years ago. Every fortress has its flaw. With your knowledge of the area, we would have the advantage."

The pilot shook his head. "No, it can't be done. The manned space station orbiting the planet would detect us long before we got there and send up the fighters to greet us."

"The orbiter won't be able to call anyone for help," Bricket cut in, then flashed a smile at Steiner. "I'll see to that."

Mason shrugged. "It would be exhilarating to bring them to their knees, but—"

"Consider it the story of a lifetime," Steiner interrupted, "the ultimate revenge."

At the mention of vengeance, Mason's eyes lit up. "Revenge." He breathed the word, then smiled to himself. "It would be a good tale, wouldn't it? I guess there are a couple of tricks I can use against them if we get into serious trouble."

Bricket winked at Steiner as if complimenting him for his

quick thinking. Steiner remained mystified. The bartender had seen right through his lie earlier and had still supported his venture. Perhaps he would do anything to regain possession of his bar.

When Steiner met Tramer to work out an attack strategy, he told the weapons officer all that he had learned from Mason and told him Bricket would work on a way to jam the orbiting station's communications with the ground installation. Tramer displayed survey maps of the planet and images of the orbiting station that had been taken by telescopes and automated spy drones several years ago. The small satellite station functioned as a long-range surveillance post, making their approach difficult. If they were detected, forces could respond within the hour, cutting off their retreat. Much of their success would depend on how well Mason could evade detection. Tramer pointed to the single air lock at the side of the station, explaining that the raiding party would have to enter at that point, which required that Steiner be secured inside the command center for his own protection during the operation. Steiner hated being excluded from the process. He wanted to be a part of this important mission, not stand by and watch it happen.

"If I'm to be locked up here, you'll have to open the armory yourself," Steiner said. "After all, you should already know the password."

Tramer didn't respond. Why would he feign ignorance? Perhaps he didn't understand.

"I want you to open it without me," Steiner repeated.

Tramer remained frozen, as if he had shut himself off to Steiner completely. All the progress they had made together working to save the United Star Systems from destruction seemed lost.

"Maxwell, if we are ever to be effective as a team, we have to trust one another."

The single human eye stared out into nothingness, as if deadened. Finally, the black lips opened. "I will do as you wish, Captain."

Steiner smiled. Perhaps Tramer's admission was a beginning toward building a successful partnership. After notifying Pattie to assemble a team of seven convicts at the entrance to the armory, the weapons officer left to meet them while Steiner remained locked in the command center.

Mason reported to the helm and started jumping the *Marauder* into Separatist space, skillfully skirting suns and retreating behind planetoids to avoid contact with enemy patrols. During the entire trip, they encountered no battlecruisers, just as Tramer had surmised.

When they neared Hurot IV's solar system, the helm console went dead. Steiner's first thought was that an enemy vessel had spotted them and was attempting to engage.

Mason rapped his fist against the darkened instruments. "I should have expected as much. There are automated jamming buoys throughout the system. We'll have to dephase."

Stars pricked the darkness on the forward viewer, growing in intensity until natural space appeared before them. The effects of the deceleration weighted down Steiner's body. He strained to lift himself from the command chair and walk to the helm. "We'll be spotted if we have to go in at standard speed. The fighters will be waiting for us by the time we hit the station."

"Maybe not," Mason said, punching a sequence of numbers into the helm's keyboard. "I always keep an extra ace handy for tight situations like this."

"What are you doing? Changing our identification code?"

"Yep." Mason grinned. "I'm configuring it to an older code the Separatists used to use."

"How did—?"

"It's a smuggling trophy. I escaped capture several times using this little baby."

"Why didn't you tell me earlier that you had this?"

"I never reveal my cards until I'm called."

Steiner recalled Mason saying he knew some tricks to get them in, but he never expected any Separatist codes. He wondered what other little bits of knowledge Mason was holding back.

"What if they no longer recognize that identification code?" Mack Palmer said from the standby chair at the helm.

Mason shrugged, as if the consequences meant nothing to him. "We flee for our lives."

Hurot IV grew in size on the forward viewer. White spirals shrouded almost all of the blue of its oceans. Somewhere beneath those gauzelike puffs, on one of the many islands, the fighters were hiding in wait for prey.

"Have there been any transmissions from the space station?" Steiner asked.

"No, all channels are quiet," Simmons answered from the communication station.

"Do they know we're here?" Palmer asked.

"Absolutely," Mason replied. "They're trying to determine why."

Steiner pressed his intercom button. "Bricket, begin impeding their transmissions."

"I've got them locked down tight." The bartender's voice sounded over the speakers.

"The space station's pulse cannons can still tear us apart before we get close enough to attack," Palmer said.

"Not if we skim the atmosphere," Mason replied.

"What?" Palmer shouted. "The ship could never stand the stress."

"The trick is to focus all the defensive energy screens to the bottom hull, then angle the trajectory so that the ship slides right across." Mason whistled as he swooped his hand out in front of him.

Palmer shook his head. "We wouldn't have enough shield energy to ward off the station's pulse cannons."

"If we catch them without warning, we won't need any more protection."

"Have you ever tried this maneuver before?" Steiner asked Mason.

"In a smaller ship, but the same principle should apply to any size craft."

"Why risk all our lives on one man's fantasies?" Palmer said. "I say we attack them straight on and take our chances."

"Why play fair when we can cheat?" Mason asked Steiner.

Steiner looked back at Tramer, who stood silently at the weapons console. "What's your opinion, Mr. Tramer?"

"Tactically, the more chance of surprise we have, the better," his synthesized voice replied.

Steiner pulled his harness around him. "Sound battle stations. Inform the crew to strap themselves in." He turned back to Mason. "Show them our hand."

The pilot smiled as he worked the controls at the helm. The planet engulfed the front viewport and crept up the side windows.

Buckles clicked around the command center as each member belted his body to his chair.

"Channeling all defensive power to lower screens," Tramer announced.

It was then that Steiner realized Tramer hadn't bothered securing himself in a chair or harness.

"Here we go," Mason said, leveling out the ship.

The hull rattled and heaved as they struck the atmosphere. Flashes of orange and red licked at the viewports.

The ship convulsed violently. The harness straps dug into Steiner, holding him against the sheer force jerking his body around. A burning glow wrapped around the ship, blotting out all traces of the planet below.

Despite the bouncing and shaking of the ship, Tramer stood perfectly erect behind the weapons console.

Perhaps he can magnetize the bottom of his feet, Steiner thought.

"The lower defensive screen is weakening," Tramer said. "Hull temperature is rising to five hundred degrees."

The ship's outer shell groaned with fatigue.

"How much time to target?" Steiner asked.

"Three minutes," Mason called back, keeping his gaze on the helm controls. His voice betrayed doubt.

Even under his safety harness, Steiner's body ached from being jolted about within the confines of his seat. As he watched the fiery glow ripple across the viewports, he wondered if he would feel any pain if the hull failed.

The nose rose. The burning lessened. Flickers of darkness broke through the streams of heat. Colored lights blinked from an object hanging in the space above. Steiner's excitement grew when he didn't see any warning lights flashing from the space station's windows.

"All gunners, open fire on my established targets," Tramer commanded into the intercom.

Steiner watched Tramer's hands move with inhuman

speed, pinpointing each potential threat and transmitting the information to the convicts manning the gunnery ports.

Lances of sizzling energy streaked out from the *Marauder*. As each of the space station's hidden weapon turrets rose into view, it vanished into brilliant explosions. Glowing debris tumbled out into the eternal blackness or flared into the planet's gravitational pull.

The battle ended in less than minute, with only one shot fired in defense.

Blackened scars pitted the surface of the space station. People stared out the windows, probably terrified as to what would happen next.

"The station's defenses are down," Tramer said. "I'm leaving to take command of the raiding party."

"Take prisoners, Mr. Tramer," Steiner shouted. "I don't want anyone to be killed without cause."

Tramer's frozen stare met Steiner's for a moment, then the disfigured head nodded once. He put on his facial shield, which masked the white glare of his skin. Servos groaned as the weapons officer descended the back stairway. On his way out, he used the password to seal the massive twin doors at the entrance.

"He knows how to do that?" Simmons asked.

Steiner didn't answer the navigator but watched as Mason lined up the *Marauder*'s port-side air lock with the one on the orbiter. A single jolt signified connection.

"Touchdown," Mason said.

"Mr. Simmons," Steiner asked, "are you picking up any transmissions coming from the ground base?"

"No, it's clear."

Steiner's heart raced. Could they have actually pulled it off?

"Mr. Mason, keep your eyes out for those fighters."

The pilot gave a nervous laugh. "I've been watching for them ever since we entered this sector."

Steiner moved to the security monitors and activated Tramer's transmitter. On the screen, Tramer opened the locked firing range and led seven armed raiders through the empty corridors toward the main air lock. The metallic walls amplified the clamor of the lightweight armor plates covering the suits.

When they reached the air lock, the raiders gathered in a circle around Tramer. Steiner could just barely make out each man's identity through the face shield of his helmet.

When Tramer reached the air lock, he opened the first hatch, then turned to face the group of raiders. "If anyone injures an unarmed person, I will do the same to him."

Steiner didn't doubt it, and from the looks of the raiders, they didn't either.

When Tramer opened the lock on the enemy hatch, Rex charged through with a howl as if this were another bruise-ball game. His companion, Bo, followed right on his heels. The two raiders dodged energy bolts from a sole defender and answered fire, killing the man instantly. Shouting wildly, they raced deeper into the orbiter. Tramer stayed close behind them to ensure that they obeyed his orders.

On the proximity sensor display, the procession of eight warriors followed the main corridor toward the center of the station. Tramer stayed right behind the leaders, Rex and Bo, while the five others brought up the rear.

Hot breath prickled the hairs on the back of Steiner's head. He glanced over his shoulder and found Simmons staring at the displays. The navigator smiled innocently and backed away while Steiner glared at him.

Returning his attention to the monitors, Steiner saw the scenes jerk and twist as Tramer searched for hidden traps and surveillance devices.

A rifle blast blazed to the right. Shouts rang out, distorted by the monitor's speakers.

Steiner drummed his fingers, wanting to be in the action— to be in control. He remembered the old days aboard the *Valiant*, leading missions like this. Would McKillip have hidden himself in the command center while his men risked themselves in a dangerous mission? What would he have thought of the captain then?

Two more bolts fired, followed by a scream. The image panned toward three people, holding their hands up, white with fear. A howl echoed from an adjoining passageway.

Tramer signaled Pattie to round up the prisoners and lock them together in a single room. The view bounced as Tramer raced after the rest of the raiders down a side corridor.

Steiner examined his pistol. It would be completely useless against the raiders' heavy body armor.

There was too much at stake on this battle. Surely, the convicts would understand that. Their lives were at risk, too.

He stood up and descended the stairway toward the exit.

"What are you doing?" Mason shouted.

"I'm going aboard the space station."

"Don't get killed. It took a lot of effort to get this far."

As Steiner pressed the correct series of keypads, the twin doors slid open. He knew that this might be a foolish move on his part. The first rule of chess was to protect your king, but he had seen some players use it very effectively in checkmating their opponents.

Steiner jogged the rest of the way to the air lock, slowed his pace, and entered the space station. The bloody remains of the die-hard defender lay slumped against the wall, the burnt flesh still smoking. Steiner's stomach tightened against the stench. He forced himself to look away as he passed the body.

Shouts echoed through the deserted station.

Steiner's heartbeat pounded in his head. Mason's warning returned to haunt his thoughts. Was he doing this only for his pride?

He took careful steps forward, his hand brushing a still-warm blast hole in the bulkhead. The stutter of an assault rifle came from ahead. A howl pierced his ears.

Steiner flattened himself against the wall as two raiders clambered through a junction twenty feet away.

"Cease firing." Tramer's voice echoed from somewhere ahead.

Steiner inched up to the junction, his ears straining for any approaching raiders. His fear made him feel almost desperate to leave, but he forced himself to stand firm.

"Captain?"

Steiner twisted about.

Pattie stepped out from the shadows near the room where the captives were being held. "What in the name of the Blessed Virgin are you doin' here?"

"This is my mission. I want to be here."

"What? Are you planning on using that hard head of

yours to beat down a door or something? Get outta here before one of my men gets any ideas."

"I thought you trusted these guys."

"Oh, I do. I trust them to stomp on any Separatist's head, but they're just convicts. Even I've heard about the bounty on you. There is talk that freedom might be attached to it—which is a phony, I'm sure—but when you got nothin' to lose, it starts to look temptin'."

"I can't win their respect, hiding in the command center. It only encourages more rumors—rumors of cowardice. Those are most dangerous of all."

Pattie growled in frustration. "Well . . . yes, I have heard them say—okay, fine. Stay near me. I'll keep 'em off your back while you strut around lookin' tough."

Tramer approached from behind Pattie, holding his face shield in one hand. "Captain," he said with a scolding tone.

"Was the planetary base alerted to our presence?" Steiner asked.

"Bricket succeeded in jamming the satellite's transmissions," Tramer answered.

"Have you discovered any information about the ground base, like where it's located?"

"Yes. I'll brief you later on the ship."

"My place is here, Mr. Tramer," Steiner replied. "Let's take a look at that information now."

The weapons officer remained motionless.

"I don't like it either, Maxie," Pattie said. "But some of the lads have begun to think of him as cowardly. I can watch his back."

Tramer's sensor orb shifted to the Saint for a moment, then returned to Steiner. "The command deck is in this direction." Motors hummed as the weapons officer turned and led the way down a passageway. Calling Midas over to watch the prisoners, Pattie followed behind Steiner.

Upon reaching the command deck, the weapons officer showed Steiner a layout of the surface installation on a computer screen. On the largest island, the base was built in a deep canyon, with fortifications on all the surrounding ridges. A mined jungle hemmed it in on all sides, making a ground attack impossible. If the *Stormquest* tried any bombing runs, the heavy artillery on the encompassing bluffs would shoot it down before it succeeded in hitting anything.

Mason had been right. The place was a fortress. Maybe it didn't have a flaw.

"Skyport, this is Landbase, requesting a routine check," a voice said. "Please respond."

Steiner's heart stopped. Had they come so far only to be stopped? His eyes locked with Tramer's. What were they going to do? Someone had to respond.

"Stans, where the heck are you?" the voice repeated. "If you left your post again, the commander will put you on report."

Tramer moved to the communication console and opened the channel to the base. Instead of speaking, he scraped his metallic fingers against the microphone.

Steiner froze, uncertain of what the weapons officer was doing.

Faint voices and laughter echoed down the corridor from some approaching raiders. If they were heard—

Steiner rushed to the entrance of the passageway. Rex and Bo, rifles slung over their shoulders, stopped cold at the sight of their captain.

Pattie shushed them, pointing toward Tramer. The weapons officer continued to scrape at the microphone a few seconds more, then stopped and closed the channel.

"What's going on?" Rex asked.

Tramer's torso spun around on the pivot at his hips. "We were almost discovered because of your foolishness."

Rex stiffened. "We just came to inform you that the station has been secured."

"Both of you boys, stand guard at the air lock," Pattie bellowed. "Make certain we aren't disturbed by anyone else. Off with you now."

Both raiders nodded and left.

Steiner looked at the weapons officer, trying to ignore his unnatural positioning. "What did you do with your fingers that caused them to stop their transmissions?"

Tramer's torso pivoted back to normal. "I simulated the sound of a damaged communication array. They may have been temporarily deceived by it. We should find the man they requested."

Pattie hummed. "'Stans,' they said, didn't they? I think I know which of the prisoners that might be. Short, little guy, a bit hardheaded. He tried to reach for the controls . . ."

"You killed him?" Steiner gasped.

"Nay, I didn't have to. I kicked the puny runt halfway across the room."

"He's okay, then."

"Yah, banged up a bit, but he's fine." Pattie frowned. "He's a determined little guy. I just don't think he'll help us."

Steiner thought about it, then noticed the face shield in the weapons officer's hand. "Stans hasn't seen Tramer's face yet, has he? I've got an idea how we might enlist his help." He smiled up at Tramer. "Have you ever played poker?"

Tramer looked bewildered. "No."

"Want give it a try right now?"

Both Tramer and Pattie listened as Steiner explained his plan.

Pattie broke into a laughing fit, slapping his knee in delight. "I wouldn't miss this for the world."

Accessing the station's personnel files and finding a picture of Second Lieutenant Stans Holtzman, Steiner confirmed that the man was the same one Pattie suspected. They proceeded to the room where the prisoners were being held. Whenever another raider appeared, Pattie would banter with him about their successful mission, while positioning himself as a shield between him and Steiner. When they reached the room, the weapons officer entered alone and dragged out a screaming man. Pattie snickered as he watched Tramer lock the struggling man in an empty storage chamber.

"Very good choice, Maxie. I couldn't have done better."

"Was Mr. Holtzman in the room with the other prisoners?" Steiner asked.

"Against the far wall," Tramer replied.

Steiner smiled. "Good. Give me five minutes with Holtzman, then make your entrance."

The weapons officer nodded once.

Steiner composed himself as he headed back to the room. His performance had to be convincing if their charade had a chance of working.

"This will be beautiful." Pattie's smile disappeared into a phony angry expression. "Go get 'em."

Steiner burst into the room, finding Holtzman where Tramer said he would be. "You in the corner," he said, motioning at his quarry. "Step outside."

Stans Holtzman stood up hesitantly, a bruise on his swelling forehead, and followed him out of the room. Upon seeing Pattie, the man's countenance tightened.

"Sorry about that lad," the Saint said. "It could have been far worse—if the Killer Cyborg had gotten ahold of you."

"Is that what it was?" Holtzman asked.

"Don't worry—he's a little busy at the moment," Steiner said. "I need you to call the ground base for me."

Holtzman looked away defiantly.

Steiner rubbed his forehead. "I don't want to see the orgy of slaying that occurred at the previous outpost we raided."

Pattie crossed himself with his left hand. "God have mercy on their souls."

"If you don't help me, that *thing* will butcher everyone here, including you," Steiner said. "That last man refused to cooperate." He shook his head sadly. "I wish he had."

"That robot thing killed Marco?" Holtzman asked, his voice trembling.

Steiner almost pitied the poor man. "It seems to love murdering," he said. "You should have seen the massacred bodies it left behind at the last place we raided. None of them would help us. Please, I'm begging you. For your sake, help me."

Precisely on cue, Tramer appeared in the doorway, blood smeared all over his breastplate and arms from the dead man at the entrance to the station. He gave a cold, heartless stare at Holtzman. Steiner remembered his own terror at seeing the weapons officer for the first time, but that sight paled in comparison.

"I'll help you ... help ..." Holtzman choked on the words in his hurry to get them out.

It worked, Steiner thought, trying to contain his excitement. Pattie led the way toward the command deck. Steiner escorted the shivering lieutenant to the communication console.

Holtzman looked back at the cyborg.

"It's all right," Steiner assured him. "He won't hurt you as long as you obey me." He placed his hand on the controls for the communication device. "I want you to tell Landbase that a meteor damaged your communication array. Apologize for the delay in transmitting a response to their voice check."

Their prisoner nodded. Steiner opened the channel.

"Landbase," Holtzman said with a slight hesitation. "This is Skyport, acknowledging your voice check."

"Stans, what happened up there?"

Holtzman glanced back at the cyborg, his hands trembling. "Sorry about the delay." His voice cracked. "A meteor damaged our communication array."

"If you require any additional parts, just send Marco down here in a shuttle."

Steiner exchanged glances with Tramer. This might be the flaw they sought. He closed the channel briefly and turned to their captive. "Tell them Marco will be right down."

Holtzman did as he was instructed, forcing the words out quickly, then signed off.

"Thank you, lad," Pattie said, taking Stans by the shoulder. "You've been a big help." He led the captive back toward the holding room, leaving Steiner and Tramer alone.

"Do you think our deception worked?" Steiner asked.

"Possibly," the weapons officer said, blood still oozing from his breastplate. "I did not detect any hidden messages, but that doesn't mean anything. Stans Holtzman spoke with very little inflection. The people on the other end might suspect he had been coerced."

"Are you suggesting we shouldn't go through with this?"

"If the base has been alerted to our presence, it's already too late to run. We have no other choice but to attack."

Tramer was right once again. If the fighters didn't get them, the outpost could contact Separatist battlecruisers to intercept them before they could get out of enemy space.

"I want to go down with the attack force," Steiner said.

"That would not be wise."

"I'll take the risk. Besides, if this mission fails, we'll probably all die anyway. I want to be there in the middle of it."

"What if one of the convicts tries to assassinate you?"

"I doubt anyone will risk anything behind enemy lines. They need me to get them back alive."

The weapons officer paused for a heartbeat. "Very well. Stay behind the attack team."

Steiner nodded wordlessly. He thought that was a reasonable request. Why risk himself by being out in front? At least he would be there when the computers were accessed.

Moving closer to one of the viewports, which overlooked the planet below, Steiner considered what they were about to do. It seemed too incredible. A bunch of convicts were about to attempt the impossible, to raid Hurot IV.

CHAPTER

14

ALONE inside the control booth of the Skyport's shuttle bay, Steiner put on his body armor. Tramer had insisted that he be separated from the rest of the raiders until the launch. Through a giant window, Steiner half watched Rex, Bo, and Midas strip the furnishings from the tiny craft they would soon use as a Trojan horse. He wondered if the sixteen raiders Tramer wanted to take would fit inside the barren shell.

Steiner stood up and tested his mobility within the suit. It had been such a long time since he had worn combat gear. His arms and legs moved too loosely within the padding. The sides of the plates scraped against each other as he reseated himself and began tightening the straps of his suit.

A series of tremors rumbled through the deck. The door to the booth slid open to reveal Tramer's pale countenance and piercing orb. "It might not be wise to let Rick Mason fly the shuttle down."

"Why? He's the best pilot we have."

"I agree," Tramer said, with a certainty that startled Steiner. "His skills are too refined to have been self-taught."

"What are you implying?"

"I believe he has served in the military."

"No. He has no previous service record with the United Star Systems."

"I didn't say which military."

Steiner stopped working with his suit. "Are you suggesting he might have been a Separatist?"

"That would explain the code he used and his extensive knowledge of this region of space."

"Don't jump to conclusions. If he did steal the code like he said, he could've gone anywhere he wanted within the Separatist empire without detection."

"Perhaps, but that wouldn't account for his ability to skim the atmosphere. By his own words, he claimed to have used other spacecraft to accomplish the same maneuver. No cargo vessel would have survived. Only military fighters with defensive screens equal to ours could have attempted the maneuver."

Steiner's body began to feel sticky within the armor. "Even if your assumption is correct, he has proven his loyalty to us repeatedly."

"Has he? He has done whatever was necessary to keep himself alive."

"Why would he give us information about how to defeat the space station?"

Tramer didn't answer. Steiner suspected he wouldn't.

"He'll pilot the shuttle down."

"I'm bringing Julio Sanchez as a reserve pilot in case I am forced to eliminate him."

Steiner jumped to his feet. "Mason will not die at your hands. For the mission, he will stay with me in the flank position. Is that understood?"

"Be wary of him." Tramer turned, opened the door, and thumped away.

The entryway closed up, sealing Steiner in with his thoughts. His mind spun with the possibilities of Tramer hurting Mason, or Mason betraying them all. While at Atwood Penitentiary, Steiner had never heard Mason tell any stories about his life before becoming a smuggler. He had always thought it was because Mason's earlier years were too dull to entertain a crowd, but what if the real reason was that he wanted to keep his past secret? What if he did have Separatist ties? No, there must be another explanation.

When the raiders finished removing all the unnecessary instrumentation, Tramer surveyed the barren shell of the shuttle, then ordered the rest of the assembled raiders to file in. Each man brought one assault rifle since there wasn't enough room for any larger weapons.

Picking up his assault rifle, Steiner opened the door to the control room and stepped out. Pattie, standing behind the line of raiders, nodded an acknowledgment. Steiner smiled in response. When he noticed a medical kit slung around one of the armored warriors, he moved closer to that warrior and tapped him on his shoulder pads. The helmeted head twisted about, revealing J.R.'s face.

"Captain?" the assistant engineer said.

At the sound of the title, three raiders directly in front of them peeked behind them. Steiner recognized the startled faces of Henry Stiles, Digger, and Glenn Edwards.

"Is there a problem, boys?" Pattie shouted from the rear of the line.

They all shook their heads and faced back toward the open hatch of the shuttle, exchanging whispers with those in the front of them.

Attempting to project confidence, Steiner met each of the curious glances as word of his presence spread up the line. "I'm glad you're coming even though you don't have much combat experience."

Being so vital to the ship's operations, Steiner had never risked any of the engineers on a previous raid. Since Hurot IV would be their toughest challenge yet, he thought bringing J.R. for his medical training would be wise in case of injuries to the raiders.

J.R. produced an uncertain grin. "Hopefully, nobody will need my services."

"Be sure to stay to the rear of your assigned team."

"Yes, sir."

Tramer beckoned Steiner with his spiny fingers, having prepared room for him right behind the cockpit. Steiner squeezed into the space.

Mason and Sanchez sat inside the cockpit, prepping the shuttle for launch.

Pattie helped the last few men inside the rear hatch of the

shuttle. The cramped passengers groaned and cursed as they crammed themselves in to make space for the Saint. The butt of a rifle dug into Steiner's right side while Tramer's cold metal breastplate pressed on his left. Finally, the rear hatch latched in place.

"Mr. Mason, take us down," Steiner said, trying not to betray how uncomfortable he was.

As Mason pressed a series of keypads on the instrument panels in front of him, Skyport's landing bay lit up with red lights as the decompression cycle began, lasting only a few seconds. The outside doors split apart, allowing the glow of the planet to shine into the cockpit. When the shuttle accelerated out of the bay, the momentary inertia caused everyone in the back of the tiny ship to groan in response to the added pressure.

Sweat permeated the air, mixed with Tramer's formaldehyde scent. The once-loud, boisterous group of raiders became quiet. Steiner could feel their tension mount in anticipation of the battle ahead. His head was so close to Tramer's breastplate, he could hear the mechanical heart inside pumping fluids through the oversized body.

Hurot IV's sun blazed through the front window for a few blinding seconds as Mason adjusted his trajectory to the one highlighted on the instrument panel in front of him. "We're in the preprogrammed flight path. Twenty-five minutes until we land."

Looking at the blue-and-white swirls on the globe below, Steiner thought back to the last time he had visited Hurot IV. Once included within the United Star Systems, Hurot IV had been captured by the New Order Empire on the Day of Betrayal. The water, which covered 95 percent of the surface and left only a scattering of islands available for human habitation, coupled with the weather, which created seasonal superstorms capable of engulfing the smaller landmasses, prevented any serious colonization of the world. Multitudes of automated water-collection platforms floated on the open seas, conveying the vital resource to one of two export stations, where cargo ships could transport the life-giving fluid to planets that lacked it. Back when the United Star Systems controlled Hurot IV, extravagant pleasure resorts had been built on all of the islands, welcoming guests during the calmer weather seasons, making it a once-sought-after vacation hideaway. Steiner had honeymooned there with Mary, two years before the war had broken out. She would have been heartbroken that the Separatists had installed a planetary base on one of the islands, making it a military target.

"How are you enjoying the ride, Captain?" Rex whispered in mocking fashion from somewhere behind him. Almost immediately after he had spoken, he yelped in pain.

"Show some respect, or I'll put you over my knee and whup your behind," Pattie admonished.

Rex remained silent, though stifled giggles sounded from around him.

"You heard what I said. *Show* some respect, or I'll *teach* you some."

"Uh . . . sorry, Captain, sir."

"That's better, laddie. You'll get your fill of Separatist skulls to—"

"Quiet, please." Tramer's synthesized voice filled the interior. "Listen."

From the cockpit, Steiner heard a strange voice. Mason looked back, his face pale. Leaning forward, Steiner listened intently as the message repeated.

"Marco, this is Devin, please respond."

Someone from Landbase was calling the shuttle.

No, not now, Steiner thought. If Mason responded to the signal, his voice would give away the fact that he was not Marco.

"Marco, you stubborn fool," Devin said again. "The commander wants me to remind you that the colonel is still down here on his inspection tour, so be on your best behavior."

Mason's gaze implored Steiner for help.

Steiner shook his head wordlessly. He had no ideas.

"Marco, respond now," Devin said, making it sound like a direct order.

Mason opened the channel. Everyone held his breath in expectation of what the pilot would say.

Mason hesitated for several heartbeats, then let out a loud belch into the microphone.

Steiner gasped.

"I'll give him that exact message," Devin finally responded. "You'll be baskin' in hot water tonight, ol' buddy. Landbase out."

The entire team seemed to let out its collective breath at the same time. Rex howled, followed by several cheers by his friends. Raiders within reach of Mason rewarded him with slaps on his shoulder.

"Prepare for the raid," Tramer shouted to the raiders. "We must all have our minds completely focused on that one goal."

The shuttle waded into the cloud bank, which blocked their view as they continued their descent. Droplets of condensation fanned out toward the outer edges of the glass in anticipation. Without warning, the concealed landmass sprang into view. It was one of Hurot's larger islands. Webs of mist draped the tangled tropical jungle below, masking most of its surface features. If Mason hadn't had the exact coordinates, he probably would never have found it—even if he'd known on which island to look.

Sunlight bathed the lattice of mists in a reddish glow as it hovered below the cloud bank on the horizon. If darkness fell, the station's personnel would have the advantage because the raiders weren't experienced in night combat.

A landing beacon flashed from within a canyon that split the jagged sea of green plants at the northeast end of the island. Undergrowth hid all but faint traces of the buildings and structures of the base concealed within the chasm. Overhanging trees and vines camouflaged the defensive towers set upon all the surrounded ridges.

Before the shuttle sank beneath the ridgeline, Mason extinguished all the interior lighting. Julio Sanchez ducked in his chair. From the sentries' point of view, it would appear as if only one person manned the ship. Only the sound of the raiders' breathing disturbed the stillness within the passenger compartment.

"Marco, you are cleared to set down in the center of the field," a woman announced over the speakers in the cockpit.

"Ironhand," Mason said, "if we set down on that landing pad, not one of us will make it to cover before being plowed down by those guns on the ridges."

Looking over Mason's shoulders at the center monitor in

the cockpit, Steiner saw a flat concrete slab in the middle of the valley with blinking lights on each corner. About a hundred yards in all directions, the installation's buildings protruded out of the steep slopes.

"I give you permission to crash," Steiner said.

The pilot grinned. "Any preference as to where?"

"The bunkhouse to the east," Tramer cut in. "Its walls are weak."

Steiner nodded his approval. The weapons officer's sensors were more trustworthy than the human eye.

"We're going to ram a building," Tramer told his team.

About a dozen meters above the pad, the pilot veered the shuttle toward the bunker.

"Marco, correct your cours—"

Mason silenced the woman's plea with a jab of a keypad. "Brace for impact," he shouted into the passenger compartment.

The nose of the craft dug into the wall of the bunker. The material gave way easily, just as Tramer had said it would. Steiner banged his head against the weapons officer's breastplate as the shuttle jolted and shook to a complete stop. Rubbing the knot forming on his brow, he surveyed the rest of the passengers. Everyone else appeared to be fine.

When Tramer opened the shuttle's forward hatch, the raiding party burst into the interior of the bunker. Most of the roof remained intact, concealing them from the sentries on the ridges. Two men cowered under their bunks at the sight of enemy invaders. Two of the raiders rushed over, knocked them unconscious, and shackled their hands.

An alarm sounded—not a fast-paced siren that might signify an attack but the slow wail that usually accompanied accidents.

Tramer called out instructions to each of the raiders. Rex, Bo, and Midas were in charge of disabling the guns on the ridges. The other ten men divided into two groups, one under Tramer's command, the other, under Julio Sanchez's. They raced down separate passageways, leaving Steiner and Mason alone to bring up their flank. Weapons fire exploded from both directions.

Mason slipped his helmet over his head. "I wonder why

Tramer didn't give me an assignment."

Steiner squirmed slightly under his protective suit. "You're with me."

When Mason picked up an assault rifle, Steiner's blood ran cold. What if Tramer was right? He thought he knew Mason well enough, but did he really?

"Which way?" Mason asked.

Steiner guided him in the direction Tramer's team had taken. He knew the weapons officer was heading for the main control complex. He wanted to be there when the computer terminals were accessed.

As they made their way through the corridors, they passed several dead enemy personnel. Steiner watched Mason for any reaction of anger or remorse for the deaths. The pilot showed little interest.

Some of the bodies were outfitted in full-dress uniform. That was odd. Then Steiner remembered what Devin had said when he contacted the shuttle, that the base had been in the middle of an inspection tour. The base's personnel had been so concerned with impressing the visiting dignitary that they had probably been caught completely off guard by the raid.

A massive amount of weapons fire erupted from outside the building. Steiner carefully peeked out of a nearby doorway that opened up into a corner of the grassy field. Pattie and two other raiders ran along the base of the cliffs toward a weapons stockpile, covered by camouflaged netting.

New alarms sounded, fast-paced and shrill. The base was alerted to their presence.

Guns from the ridges rained down powerful energy blasts on the convicts in the field, cutting down one of them instantly. The second raider ducked inside a neighboring building before the bolts hit him. Pattie raced ahead and jumped through a hole in the netting that covered the stockpile of armaments. The sentries on the ridges stopped firing for fear of igniting the depot. Several seconds later, Pattie reemerged from the weapons stockpile, cradling a portable laser cannon in his arms, and discharged a sustained searing beam of intensified light back at the ridge. The foliage growing around the defense tower caught fire as the shaft of particle energy sliced through it and cut a path through a section of the metallic walls of the guard post. Dark smoke from the shrubbery fire billowed, blocking any view the sentries had. The laser ceased as Pattie repositioned the cannon in his arms, obviously struggling against the heat the device's casing generated while discharging.

Steiner couldn't believe the risk Pattie was taking by holding a laser cannon like that.

A scrape of stone somewhere behind him tore his attention away from what was happening outside. He looked up and down the corridor. No one was in sight, yet the grinding continued to emanate from close by.

"Oh hell," Mason muttered, then shoved Steiner into the opposite wall. Frozen by shock, Steiner could only watch as the pilot raised his rifle muzzle toward him.

Be wary of him, Tramer's voice repeated within his head. He had failed to heed the warning and would pay the price.

The grating noise increased, resonating through Steiner's entire body. He realized it originated from the wall behind him.

A crack split to his left. A section of the wall swung open. *A hidden door.*

Mason dropped to his knees, firing into the opening as two soldiers burst out. Their legs disintegrated beneath them. They toppled on top of Mason, crying out in agony.

Another man jumped out of the maw of the secret passage. Before he could aim at Mason, Steiner grabbed his arm and swung him around into the wall, knocking him unconscious.

Three more soldiers charged through. Steiner watched helplessly as two gun muzzles leveled at him.

A piercing cry came from outside the building.

Pattie sprang through the sunlit doorway, brandishing the laser cannon. The high-pitched scream of the laser stung Steiner's ears as he watched the sustained particle beam burrow through all the men hidden inside the secret passage. It stopped as abruptly as it had started.

Steiner rubbed his eyes, blinded by the intensity of the light ray. When he looked up through orange-spotted vision, he saw Pattie dashing back outside.

Mason crawled to his feet. "I'm such a fool. I should have expected them to have secret doors to trap their enemies from behind."

Steiner stared at him for a moment, stunned by what had transpired, ashamed that he had thought Mason had turned against him. "You saved my life," he said.

"It was in my best interest to," Mason replied.

Steiner should have expected Mason to respond with a comment like that. How could he ever have doubted him? He peered into the darkened maw behind the door. "Where does this lead to?"

"Probably to the upper levels."

"Good. That's probably where the control complex is."

Steiner stepped over the smoking corpses littering the entryway. He counted ten dead soldiers who had planned to ambush them from behind. If they had succeeded, the raid surely would have failed.

Electrical lamps embedded in the rock illuminated the cutout passageway. Tangles of cobwebs hung from the ceiling. With Mason trailing behind him, Steiner followed the tunnel until it emptied into a cavern.

A stairway, embedded in the rock face, spiraled up to a door a hundred feet above. Steiner carefully climbed the steps, keeping his rifle aimed at the top.

He flinched at the stutter of rapid weapons fire ahead, accompanied by half a dozen short-lived screams.

"Be careful," Mason whispered harshly. "We don't want to walk into the middle of a firefight. We might get hit by our own people."

The sounds died off into a deathly silence.

Steiner continued at a steady pace until he reached the sealed entry. When he touched a glowing keypad set into the rock, the door slid down into the floor, revealing the control complex.

Tramer's sensor orb found them instantly. The weapons officer stood alone in the room, in front of a bank of computer terminals. Lifeless bodies lay scattered around him. Blood dripped from the consoles and spread out on the floor. The torsos had been hit by numerous precisely aimed energy bolts. Almost a complete hole had been blasted through each of their chests. It reminded Steiner of the gunner who had been killed on the *Marauder*.

For a brief instant, Tramer glared at Mason with the same hatred that Steiner had seen when the weapons officer had wanted to kill Bricket. Then the orb shifted back to Steiner. "Captain," the synthesized voice rumbled. "I have accessed the computer files with the help of the outpost's commanding officer."

"Where is he now?" Steiner asked, looking at the mutilated heaps of flesh.

"The other raiders have taken him to the conference hall, where all the prisoners are being held. It appears as if the station's personnel were in the middle of some kind of award ceremony when we attacked."

"What about these men?" he asked. "Did they all have to be killed?"

"When I found them, they were in the process of trying to destroy their files. They put up a strong fight."

Steiner noticed the multitude of charred markings covering the weapons officer's breastplate. He had been through a fierce battle. How had he defeated them? He had no weapon.

"There's some very important information stored here," Tramer said. "I even found a few personnel files on some of the Separatist officials."

Almost immediately, Steiner forgot everything else. He moved next to the weapons officer and looked over them for himself. A gold mine of current battle plans and strategies was listed across the screen.

Steiner started to let out a triumphant shout. It died inside his throat.

A Separatist officer stood in a nearby doorway, aiming an assault rifle at him. Before Steiner could blink, the defender was showered in energy bolts. The searing beams hit in such rapid repetition that they looked like one continuous ray and disintegrated the man's chest instantly. A smoldering heap of flesh dropped to the floor.

Mason gasped then fled back into the secret tunnel.

Tracing the direction of the beams, Steiner saw Tramer standing erect, his scarred breastplate hanging open, with two miniature assault guns attached to the interior. The plate closed up again, taking the hidden weapons with it. The weapons officer turned and stared emotionlessly.

Steiner was so stunned he couldn't speak.

A motorized whine rose from somewhere outside. Instantly, the weapons officer snatched up his face shield and ran out onto an adjoining balcony, which overlooked the installation.

The whine burst into a steady rumble.

The attack fighters. Steiner had forgotten all about them. They must be launching. He sprinted out onto the balcony just in time to see Tramer disappear down a moss-covered stairway to the side.

Steiner ran to the guardrail and looked down into the small valley. He found Tramer racing down a dirt path toward the clearing, where ten fighters were lined up next to the visiting colonel's yacht.

Weapons fire from the north ridges rained down on him. Some of the powerful bolts grazed his metallic body but failed to slow him. Abruptly, the attack ended. Rifle blasts echoed from atop the fortified bluffs, followed by a triumphant howl.

One of the fighters lifted off the ground, trailing a loose cable its crew had forgotten to unhitch. With incredible speed, Tramer grabbed the metal cord and wrapped it around the neighboring vessel's landing gear. The fighter, hovering in the air, blasted forward, pivoted against the cord, and crashed into the middle of its sister ships. A series of blinding explosions rocked the earth as all ten spacecraft disintegrated, one after the other.

The brightness of the inferno caused Steiner to lose track of Tramer. He searched around futilely. What happened to him? Suddenly, the weapons officer stepped into view. Small fires of ignited fuel danced upon his metal casing. He raised a smoking mechanical arm and saluted.

A buzz from the helm console of the *Marauder* caught Mack Palmer's attention. It came from the long-range sensors. When he looked at the readout, he gasped.

No, it couldn't be.

On the screen, a Separatist battlecruiser was heading straight for Hurot IV.

"Please—not now," he muttered.

Simmons, the only other person in the command center, looked up from his station. "What's wrong?"

"I'm picking up an enemy warship coming right for us."

The words had barely left his lips when the navigator stumbled over his own feet in his hurry to get down to the helm to look at the readings for himself.

Mack shoved the man's head away from his face. He didn't have the time to put up with the fool's prying. They were in serious danger.

Mack knew he had to hide the *Marauder* behind Hurot IV before they were discovered. At the press of a few keypads, he detached their vessel from Skyport and bolted toward the far side of the planet.

"Look, there's another warship approaching right behind the first," Simmons cried out.

Mack reexamined the screen. The idiot had jumped to the wrong conclusion as usual. He couldn't tell a freighter from a battlecruiser.

"That's just a cargo ship," he snapped. Then he noticed the speed of both vessels. They moved rather slowly. It must be some kind of a convoy heading for the outpost on Hurot IV. "Get Captain Steiner back on a communication channel right now," he ordered Simmons.

The navigator started back to his station, then stopped. "Why don't we leave without them?"

"Do you know the way back?" Mack shouted.

Simmons hung his head as he fumbled his way back to his station.

Mack knew the navigator had been denied all the charts for this area, probably just to make sure they wouldn't try running off with the ship. Besides, he wouldn't leave Julio behind.

Looking back to the screen, he found three more freighters trailing behind their monstrously armed escort. None of them had increased their speed. Maybe the convoy hadn't detected them yet.

"Steiner here." The captain's voice sounded from the speakers. "What's the problem up there?"

"I'm tracking a Separatist battlecruiser leading a convoy this way, sir," Mack said. "You had better get the assault team up here fast."

No reply.

"Captain, are you reading me?" he asked.

"Yes," Steiner answered at last. "We require transportation back to the ship."

"What happened to the shuttle you took down?"

"We crashed it into a building during the raid."

"Doesn't the outpost have any operational spacecraft you can use?"

"Tramer destroyed them all. That's why you're not currently under attack by the fighters right now."

"I can't leave the ship now," Mack shouted. "Not with a Separatist battlecruiser coming down on top of us."

Several agonizing minutes passed before Steiner replied. "Call Phillip Daniels up to the command center. I've got an idea how it can be done."

Mack glared back at Simmons, who had listened in on the entire conversation. "Get that head engineer up here fast."

STEINER walked through Landbase's ruins triumphantly, his pride in his crew's performance soaring. He had just visited the conference hall where the prisoners were being held. His small band of raiders had captured seventy-five members of the station's personnel alive, including the base commander and the visiting colonel.

He looked up at the reddening sky above. They had been successful in conquering the base before sunset, as he had hoped. The air danced with thousands of mosquito-type insects, awakened by the coming night. He waved them away from his exposed skin. They didn't bother him much. He felt too good to be annoyed by the pests. The crickets sang in celebration with him. He took a deep breath of the fragrant breeze coming from the tropical plants and flowers of the surrounding jungle. This victory felt better than anything he had experienced aboard the *Valiant*. McKillip would have been proud of him.

When Steiner had finished his walk, he entered Landbase's mess hall, which Tramer had converted into an infirmary. The odor of blood and sweat hung heavy in the air, accented by moans and cries of pain. At Steiner's request, Tramer had allowed the base's medical personnel to care for their wounded there.

Julio Sanchez sat at the entrance, nursing a scratch on his arm. His rifle was propped against the wall just within reach. "Is someone coming down to get us?" he asked.

"They're on their way right now," Steiner answered. He decided to keep the approaching Separatist convoy to himself for the time being. Why cause worry during their hour of triumph?

Scanning the interior of the mess hall, Steiner found Tramer in a far corner, standing watch over the medical personnel. Steiner threaded a path through the injured prisoners, listening to them exchange whispers about the "indestructible cyborg."

Weapon scars and the scorch marks from the explosions of the fighters covered Tramer's metallic body, adding to his already menacing appearance. His face shield lay on the floor next to him, looking much the same as the rest of him. He held the hand of a wounded raider on a gurney, a sight Steiner never expected to see. When Steiner got closer, he saw who the injured man was.

Pattie.

The Saint's eyes were closed. His armor had been removed. Ashen burns were speckled across his hairy chest in the area where he had been holding the laser cannon, and on the underside of each arm. Both of his legs had been burned off around the upper knee. The intense heat from the laser that must have severed them had probably cauterized both of the stumps. Steiner had suspected this could happen. The laser cannons were meant to be attached to tripod stands before firing to prevent the random dispersal that holding them by hand would cause.

Pattie slit his eyes. He grinned triumphantly. "The brightness made it hard to see what was in front of me. I tripped over somethin' . . . burned off my own legs before I knew it."

Steiner shook his head, fighting back his horror. "You crazy Irishman."

"Don't fret, Slugger," Pattie said. "I'm happy to report we only lost two men. Digger . . . and me."

Steiner turned to J.R. "Is he really that bad off?"

"His wounds are worse than I've ever seen. The left leg has been bleeding pretty bad."

"How can that be? They both should have been instantly cauterized."

"I'm sure they were, at first, but he kept fighting and opened the wound on the left leg."

"Had to protect my men, I did," Pattie announced to both of them. "Now I'm ready to meet Saint Peter."

"No, not until I'm done with you," Steiner replied.

"What do you want from me? My body is a wreck. Both my legs are gone."

Steiner touched the third-degree burns on Pattie's chest. "I've seen worse. Your body armor seems to have protected you from any serious damage." He began peeling back the gauze bandages on the right stump, smelling the burnt flesh from the wound. "The laser seems to have cauterized this leg," he said as optimistically as he could. Blood seeped though the bandages on the left leg. Steiner tested the tourniquet and found it loose. "Don't you have anything tighter than this? We have to get this stopped."

J.R. shrugged his shoulders. "I've been trying to make do with what I have."

"Slugger, don't ya worry about me," Pattie said, holding out his hand. Steiner took the Saint's hand. The grip still felt strong, drawing him closer to the man's soiled face. "For the last year, I've been stuck in a cell, waitin' to die of boredom. You gave me a chance to get back into the fight one more time. I *want* to die this way."

Steiner looked into his determined gaze. "Die a hero?"

"Exactly."

"You lost your legs, that's all. With a couple of prosthetics, you could fight another day."

"Who are you kiddin'?" Pattie replied, his voice becoming passionate. "I'm a lousy convict. The military won't pay a single cent to fix me up. Look at our ship, a Peacemaker, for God's sake. That's what we're worth to them."

"Nonsense. I'll get them to fix you up, just like they did Tramer."

"What? You want them to turn me into a godforsaken creature, like Maxie? You can't be serious. There's no way I'm doin' that. Maxie would've chosen death before allowin' someone to do that to him. Ask him. I'm sure he would tell you that."

Steiner regretted mentioning Tramer. He glanced up at the weapons officer, who betrayed no emotion whatsoever. "Is that why you're just giving up, like this?" he said to the Saint. "Too afraid of living?"

"I'm not afraid of anythin'. There's just no point anymore."

Steiner grabbed the beaded necklace around the Saint's neck and unsnapped its clasp. "Then you won't mind me taking this."

Both the Saint's arms came up to stop him. "How dare you, you godforsaken heathen!"

Steiner pulled the rosary away from him.

"Put that back on, you bastard!"

"We need a better tourniquet," Steiner said, moving down to the left stump.

"You're denying me my last rites!"

Steiner wrapped the beaded strand around the wound, pulling the two ends as tight as he could and twisting the beads together to hold it closed.

Pattie cried out in pain, stifling a curse.

"The *Stormquest* is on its way down here right now to carry you back to the *Marauder*," Steiner explained as he removed the gauze from the stump. He fought against his own revulsion at the sight of the blackish wound, wet with blood. Opening a fresh package of gauze, J.R. wrapped the wound and taped it up.

"Bastard!" Pattie screamed at Steiner. "I'll rip your cold heart from your chest and eat it."

Steiner laughed in a mocking style, staying out of reach of Pattie's arms. "Tough words from the same punching bag that I laid out in the ring ten years ago."

"You cheated," the Saint spat. "I should've won that match!"

"Cheated? You tried to sucker me with a quick left upper-cut, so I responded with my right to your gut."

"You denied me a rematch 'cause you know I would've buried ya!"

"I hereby accept your challenge, so I can lay you out again."

Pattie spluttered with rage. Immediately, Steiner put his ear against the Saint's chest. The breathing remained strong. Feeling for a pulse, he noticed it was a little weak. "He needs some blood. Prepare for a transfusion." He looked up and saw J.R. and the six other convicts standing behind him, staring in utter shock. Behind them, the enemy's wounded all looked on. "Would any of you volunteer to donate blood?"

All six convicts raised their hands without hesitation.

"J.R., test each of them for A-negative blood type."

"Are you sure that's Patrick's correct blood type?"

"Absolutely. It's not the first time he's been badly wounded."

The six men formed a line.

Steiner got out of way as the engineering assistant started testing. Looking down at his bloodstained hand, he found his fingers trembling. He took a deep, cleansing breath. There would be hell to pay once Pattie was back on his feet, if he ever could get on his feet again. The Saint was right. The military wouldn't pay for prosthetics for a convict, but if he could convince them the Saint was a war hero, responsible for their victory, maybe there was a chance they would change their minds. Either way, he couldn't simply let his old friend die there.

"Perhaps you should have honored his request," Tramer said.

"I don't leave anyone behind," Steiner replied. "How many others were hurt?"

"Digger is dead. Stiles has a simple flesh wound. Sanchez has a minor scratch."

Steiner knew that the death toll among the raiders would have been much greater if Pattie hadn't used the laser cannon the way he had. The Saint had sacrificed his safety to turn a probable defeat into an overwhelming victory.

"The *Stormquest* should be here within a half hour," Steiner said. "Have your men ready to go by then."

Tramer nodded once.

Steiner looked back and saw J.R. hooking up a transfusion between Pattie and Warren.

Weapons fire shot in the air in the direction of the field.

Steiner's military instincts took over. He reached for his rifle.

"It is ours." Tramer said, looking in that direction as well. "They are celebrating our victory."

Steiner relaxed. "They deserve it."

He walked over to the edge of the grassy area and found Rex, Bo, and Midas dancing around on the landing pad in the center, firing their rifles into the air in celebration. Rex howled, and the other dancers cheered.

On a small incline, near the canyon wall, he found Mason sitting alone against a palm tree, tossing pebbles into his overturned helmet, which lay in the grass several feet away.

"It's not like you to be out here alone after such a victory," Steiner said. "Is something bothering you?"

Mason tossed another small stone at the helmet's mouth. It bounced off the rim and tumbled into the grass. "I think Gruesome has it out for me. I need to stay as far as I can from him. Did you see how he looked at me when I first came into the complex?"

Steiner sighed, thinking about Tramer. "I saw."

"If I stayed there, he would have shot me next."

"I wouldn't have let him."

"How can you say that? When that thing decides to kill someone, nothing can stop it. For some reason, it has determined I'm the one to die next."

Steiner knew he had no choice left but to confront Mason with Tramer's observations about his abilities and their source. Using as much tact as he could, he explained the whole exchange between him and the weapons officer before the mission began.

Mason slammed a pebble into the overturned helmet. "Did Gruesome ever consider that the Centri System might have their own military? That's the only way we keep ourselves from being invaded by either the Separatists or the United Star Systems."

"I knew there must have been another explanation. That's

why I insisted that you join us on this mission. I think you proved your loyalty to Tramer by now."

"Just the same, I'm still going to keep my distance."

The distant drone of a spacecraft's engines echoed from above the canyon. Mason stood up. The three raiders stopped dancing. Rex pointed to the sky.

Steiner looked up, searching for any signs of the *Stormquest*. Stars showed through the gaps of the mist that draped the jungle surface. A black shape materialized from out of the clouds and descended toward the valley.

The other raiders began meandering out of the complex's buildings, cheering and waving their hands.

"Palmer finally came down for us, I see," Mason said. "Now we can get off this rock."

The *Stormquest*'s landing gear tore through some palm branches on the ridge.

Steiner tensed at the sight.

"What's the matter with that idiot?" Mason asked. "Even he can't fly that badly."

Rex, Bo, and Midas fled from the field as the vessel swayed uneasily toward the ground.

"No—it can't be," Mason muttered then ran out into the field.

The *Stormquest* touched down thirty feet from the concrete slab, its landing gear digging deep into the grassy soil. When the hatch opened, Sam staggered down the ramp.

Steiner smiled. He knew the boy could fly the vessel. That's why he had called Phillip Daniels to the command center. He had entrusted the head engineer with the password to the landing bay, so that Sam could launch the *Stormquest*. It was the only way to get back aboard the *Marauder* without Palmer's leaving the ship open and vulnerable to attack.

Mason ran up the ramp and bear-hugged Sam.

The same kinds of sentiments were expressed in the bar among the rest of the raiders after they had returned to the *Marauder*.

Steiner sat alone in the command center, watching the party on one of the security monitors. On the neighboring screen, Pattie lay on the bed in his cabin, sleeping, as J.R. watched over him. Someone shouted a toast to Tramer from another display as the weapons officer stood expressionless next to the bar counter while the raiders cheered his leadership. At first, Tramer had refused to attend, but Steiner convinced him that it would be uplifting to the men, especially since they would be losing Pattie.

Steiner felt relieved that their retreat from Separatist space went as smoothly as it had. Besides missing the convoy by forty-five minutes, they hadn't encountered any other enemy ships during their race back across the border.

Once they were safe inside U.S.S. space, Steiner transmitted the stolen computer files to the flagship, *Magellan*. Commodore Cole congratulated him on his initiative and asked him to rendezvous with the *Magellan* the next day. After explaining Pattie's great service in bringing down the base, Cole agreed to have him transferred to the *Magellan*, where the doctors could provide better care.

Steiner looked back at the monitors and saw Mason douse Sam with beer, then laugh. The boy retaliated by tossing a mugful into the pilot's face. Steiner wished he could join in the festivities, but something gnawed at him—something he had to discover the truth about.

He accessed a nearby computer outlet. After a few moments, he found a visual record of Captain Joseph Barker's body as it had been discovered on the ship before Steiner had become its captain. The picture confirmed his suspicions. The man's chest had been blown out by energy bolts, just like the defenders on Hurot IV, just like the murdered crewman in the gunnery port.

He stared back at Tramer's expressionless face on the monitor. Maybe it was only a matter of time before the cyborg turned against him, too.

CHAPTER

15

STEINER sat alone in the seat of one of the TRAC vehicles in the landing bay, gathering his resolve for what needed to be done next. The drone of the *Marauder*'s engines vibrated through the hull and the TRAC's frame like a relaxing massage. The loudest sound in the empty bay was his own heartbeat. It was ironic that this quiet arena would soon be the scene of a vicious confrontation, one that he might not survive.

He tensed when the door to the landing bay opened. Tramer stepped inside, then resealed the entrance.

Steiner climbed down from the seat and positioned himself behind one of the thick tires. No doubt, Tramer's sensors had already pinpointed his location. Looking up, he could see the blue light from the sensor orb reflecting off the top of the armored vehicle.

"You wished to see me?" The weapons officer's synthesized voice echoed within the empty landing bay.

"Come closer," Steiner shouted from his hiding place.

The hum of the mechanical body grew nearer. "We are two hours away from our rendezvous with the *Magellan*. Do you have any further orders for me before we arrive?"

Steiner recalled the many hours he had labored over the decision of confronting the weapons officer there.

"Is something wrong?" Tramer's voice sounded about thirty feet away.

Steiner closed his eyes for just a moment to calm himself. Visions of Barker being torn apart without mercy by the hidden assault guns behind Tramer's breastplate tormented him.

Steiner grabbed a handheld missile launcher that he had hidden under the seat of the TRAC. He stepped out into the open and took aim at Tramer.

"Captain?" Tramer asked, stopping fifteen feet away, close enough for Steiner to see his reflection within the shiny breastplate.

Looking into the pale face, Steiner swore he could see bewilderment and concern—not anger. That would soon change.

His finger tensed on the trigger, ready to pull it back if he detected any movement around Tramer's chest region. "Why did you kill Joseph Barker?" he asked, trying to sound calm.

Tramer's gaze shifted toward the back wall, breaking eye contact with Steiner. An emotionless mask replaced the hint of compassion in the pale face. It was as if he had reverted back to acting like a lifeless machine.

"During the celebration last night, I accessed the visual records of Barker's death," Steiner said. "He has the exact same wound as the one you inflicted on the enemy personnel of Hurot IV. It is also the same as was found on the body in the gunnery port four weeks ago."

Still, Tramer didn't respond. The silence was so deep that Steiner could hear air being sucked in by the respirator on the back of the weapons officer's neck.

Steiner swallowed hard. "I wanted to believe you were the same Maxwell Tramer I once knew, but that's impossible now. You've murdered people at your own discretion. Maxwell would have never done that."

"Barker was a spy," Tramer answered abruptly.

The sheer absurdity of the statement stunned Steiner. "That's exactly what you claimed about Mason, and you were wrong."

"No. I only suspected Mason."

"Yesterday, you were ready to eliminate Mason because of his military training. Did you ever consider he might have received his military training from the Centri System to protect against an invasion?"

"I would not have harmed him unless he tried to betray us."

"How do I know that?"

"He makes me laugh, just like Pattie made me laugh."

A lump climbed up Steiner's throat. He stared deep into the human eye and saw sincerity. "What proof did you have that Barker was a spy?"

"He was attempting to smuggle U.S.S. tactical reports to the Separatist Empire. I saw the data myself."

"Why didn't you inform Military Intelligence instead of acting as judge and executioner over the man?"

Tramer's human eye found Steiner. "Would they have listened to me?"

"You could have shown them the data."

"The military information came from one of Barker's superiors. If I'd tried to expose their operation, I would have been silenced and the data, destroyed. My only choice was to eliminate Barker and prevent his superior from making further attempts at smuggling the information."

"Further attempts?" Steiner repeated. "So you thought I was part of this operation?"

"Yes."

"Is that why you watched me all the time?"

"Yes."

"What changed your mind about me?"

"The raid of Hurot IV."

Steiner kept the launcher pointed at Tramer as he considered what he had just heard. If it was true, it explained Tramer's behavior toward him throughout the voyage. A spy ring would also account for the U.S.S. doing so poorly in the war. But it still wasn't enough to convince him.

"Do you have any evidence left?" he asked.

"No," Tramer replied. "I was forced to destroy it for fear that Barker's superior would have found another way to send it out."

"Do you have any idea who this superior is?"

"I have a theory."

"Go ahead."

"I believe the P.A.V. program was created for the sole purpose of conducting espionage. The admiral on the Council in charge of—"

"Jamison?" Steiner asked.

"Yes. Admiral Ralph Jamison."

Chills resonated through Steiner's bones at the mention of the name. He lowered the missile launcher. "I believe you."

"Thank you." Tramer turned and walked to the door. His torso pivoted around to face Steiner. "Captain, I'm also glad that you are still the same man I knew long ago."

Steiner nodded.

After Tramer left the landing bay, Steiner put the missile launcher on the ground. His hands were shaking with the possibility of what he might have done.

He crawled up into the seat of the TRAC, laid his head on the console, and tried to calm himself. What he had expected to be a final bloody stand had turned out to be a startling revelation that he could use to finally avenge McKillip's death. He couldn't wait to bring all of this out at Jamison's tribunal. It wouldn't take much effort for the authorities to dig around in the admiral's past and uncover evidence that linked him to the Separatist Empire.

When he met with Cole, he would tell him of the espionage plot without mentioning Tramer's involvement. The weapons officer would surely be executed for the murder of Barker regardless of his reasons. He didn't deserve such a fate, especially after what Steiner had learned.

An hour and a half later, Tramer announced over Steiner's comlink that the *Marauder* was approaching the rendezvous point.

Three U.S.S. destroyers had gathered around the flagship, the *Magellan*. After receiving transmission of the password, Cole instructed them to dock with the *Magellan*.

When Steiner arrived at the port-side air lock, he found J.R. and Spider lowering Pattie's gurney down the ramp onto the landing of the air lock. Mason and Sam leaned against the storage locker of space suits.

"Did both of you come to say good-bye to Pattie?" Steiner asked.

"Not really," Mason replied. "I've got a bit of morbid curiosity about something else."

"He *thinks* it's the same ship that captured him," Sam explained.

"Slugger," Pattie's voice called softly.

Steiner smiled at both engineers, then moved closer to the patient lying between them on the gurney. "How are you feeling today?"

"I can't wait to get my fists into you."

Steiner laughed. "And I can't wait to see you *try*."

Pattie chuckled.

A hiss of pressure indicated that the *Magellan* had opened its air lock.

Steiner entered into the control panel the sequence to open their end.

Before the door had finished moving aside, a company of heavily armed soldiers burst through the entry. They formed a perimeter around the hatch, training their weapons on Steiner and his shipmates. The hateful looks of the gunmen testified that they wouldn't hesitate to kill everyone at a single command.

"It's them all right," Mason whispered to Sam.

A figure strode through the assembled soldiers. Judging from the medals that decorated the man's uniform, he must have been the *Magellan*'s Executive Officer. He stopped directly in front of Steiner and eyed him with distaste.

"What is the meaning of this?" Steiner shouted.

"Are you the convict in charge of the P.A.V.?" the XO asked.

Steiner clenched his fists so tightly that his nails dug into his palms. "I am the captain of the U.S.S. *Marauder*."

The man grinned. "Murderers, rapists, and thieves don't deserve any title."

"You're lucky I am lyin' down, you bastard," Pattie mumbled.

Steiner bit his lip to keep himself from reacting.

"Captain, surrender your weapon to me," the Executive Officer shouted.

"Call off your troops first," Steiner replied. "We're on the same side."

"I won't tolerate any more insubordination."

"What about common courtesy?"

The man's head turned back to his men. "At the next word from his mouth, open fire."

Steiner's breath caught in his lungs. He glanced at Mason and Sam then at J.R. and Spider, carrying Pattie's gurney. Slowly, he lifted his pistol from its holster. The soldiers surrounding the hatch tensed as he handed it to their leader.

"We are already late," the XO said as he wheeled about to leave. "Follow me."

"What about the injured man you are to take on board?"

"I am to bring you to the commodore, before anything else."

With forced steps, Steiner followed the man through the fan of soldiers into the plush-carpeted corridors of the *Magellan*. One of the gunmen broke ranks and trailed behind him with a pointed rifle muzzle.

The fresh scent of the air gave evidence that this was the flagship, elite and elegant in every detail. Under normal conditions, Steiner would have been impressed by the *Magellan*'s interior, but now, it only reminded him of the respect that had been stolen from him and his crew.

The Executive Officer directed Steiner through a doorway into a massive chamber with a high ceiling. Three other captains, two men and a woman, sat around an oval table that occupied the center of the room. David Cole stood at the head of the table.

"Welcome, Captain Steiner," Cole said. "It's good to see you again. The last time—I believe—was at McKillip's funeral."

"Yes, sir. What about the injured man I told you about?"

Cole shifted his gaze to the man who had escorted Steiner. "Commander Cromwell, please make sure the fallen hero is taken to our infirmary immediately."

"Yes, sir," Cromwell answered, saluting in respect. He departed, closing the door behind him.

"Please have a seat, Captain." Cole beckoned to an empty chair at the far side of the oval table. "Then we will begin."

"I wish to first address how I was greeted."

"I'm sorry, Captain, but our time together is short. I would be happy to confer with you after the meeting."

Steiner nodded and took the remaining seat at the table. As he did so, he scanned the faces of the three other captains in the room. He recognized two of them from his days aboard the *Valiant*. They glared openly at him with the same contempt Cromwell had exhibited. He expected their attitudes would change once they learned of his extraordinary accomplishments.

Cole pressed a keypad on the table. The lights dimmed. A holographic chart of the colonized galactic region appeared on a far wall. A red, illuminated line ran down the middle, designating the border between the U.S.S. and Separatist territories. Blue dots dotted the map on the U.S.S. side, representing the positions of all their warships.

"As you can see, our forces are dwindling along the border in the northern area," Cole told everyone. "From my estimates, we can't hold it much longer. If we lose it, we will eventually lose the war. Therefore, it's essential for our defense to protect it at all costs. Too many planets and resources that are vital for our survival are located there."

Cole sat back down in his chair. "I informed Admiral Barton on the War Council of the severity of the situation, and he has authorized me to proceed as I see fit." With the press of another keypad in front of him, the holographic image zoomed in on the top section of the map. "After studying the information that Captain Steiner and his crew obtained from Hurot IV, I have discovered that the Separatists are planning to sweep through the northern area." The holograph closed in on a single planet just inside the Separatist border. "An enemy base has been constructed on the planet Macrales, capable of outfitting battlecruisers for their invasion."

Whispers of horror rose from around the table.

"If such a plan were initiated, the area would certainly fall," Cole said. "Something must be done about it soon, before the Separatists have the time to reinforce their troops."

The other captains vocalized their agreement.

Steiner's blood ran cold. He hadn't been asked here to be honored.

"This is my plan," Cole said. "The *Manhattan*, the *Excalibur*, and the *Magellan* will be stationed at sector 798. Meanwhile, the *Freedom* and the P.A.V. will be positioned farther down the border."

"Excuse me, sir," Steiner said.

"Do you have something to add, Captain Steiner?" Cole asked.

"My vessel is a thirty-year-old Peacemaker. It would be useless in an engagement."

"We won't need you for the offensive. The P.A.V. and the *Freedom* will be the decoys."

"Decoys," Steiner exclaimed before he could stop himself. "Surely there's another destroyer or assault cruiser that can take our place?"

Cole shook his head. "I'm sure you remember from your days aboard the *Valiant* that immediacy is the key to victory. We can't afford to wait for one to arrive. I haven't even had the time to inform the Council of my plan."

"I see no hope of my ship surviving a run through enemy territory," Steiner said.

"Then you have to ask yourself what is more important, one ship or the entire civilization it protects?"

Steiner couldn't answer. The United Star Systems represented the only form of democracy in the galaxy. It couldn't be allowed to fall, even if it cost his life and those of his crew.

Cole finished the briefing, then brought up the lights in the conference room. Steiner remained in his seat while the other captains left. After saying good-bye to everyone else, Cole sat next to him.

Steiner met the commodore's gaze. "The information my crew fought to obtain signed their own death warrants."

Cole shrugged. "If there were any other way, I would do it."

Steiner turned away. "My men will not be so easily convinced to join in this mission. They may try to mutiny just to save their skins."

"You will find a way to keep them from doing so—of that I am sure. For many years now, I have admired your abilities as a leader."

"If that's true, why wasn't I given any respect when I arrived?"

"I can't be held responsible for what everyone else thinks of you. To most people, you are an ordinary convict in charge of a prison ship." Cole leaned closer. "I know differently. When you served under McKillip, you might have been one of the best Executive Officers in the fleet, but you lost that respect when you attacked Admiral Jamison."

"He murdered McKillip," Steiner exclaimed.

"Why do you believe that?"

Steiner gave a detailed account of his last meeting with McKillip before the *Valiant*'s fatal mission. He also told Cole that the secret McKillip had been murdered to protect was that Jamison was a spy for the Separatist Empire.

Cole considered all that he had heard for a moment. "Do you have any proof that Jamison is a spy?"

"My weapons officer, Maxwell Tramer, observed his involvement in a plot to smuggle U.S.S. military information to the enemy."

Cole's brow creased. "I cannot help you."

"Why?"

"I'm not about to create an uproar among the Council members—not on the word of Maxwell Tramer."

"You know him?"

"Of course. The so-called Killer Cyborg murdered two of my crewmen when one of them made a comment about his former wife. The cyborg snapped both men's spinal cords in half. I suggest you be wary of what it says to you. It may be your spinal cord next time."

Steiner sat there, dumbfounded. He could almost hear himself echoing those same words to Suzanne when he first took command of the P.A.V.

"Don't discount him as easily as I did," he said. "He's still the same man you served with. Talk to him. You'll see—"

"That's enough, Captain," Cole scolded. "You didn't have to face the families of those two innocent men. The Maxwell Tramer I knew would never have done such a thing. As far as I'm concerned, he died in that explosion seven years ago." Cole stood up from the table. "I will always respect his memory." Cole saluted him. "I wish you luck in your mission, Captain."

Steiner returned the gesture, but only out of duty. He stood up and walked out the door. Cromwell and the gunman met him outside in the corridor and led him back to the *Marauder*. Steiner wondered how he would inform his crew that they were to be the sacrificial pawns in a giant chess game to win the galaxy.

CHAPTER

16

"WE'VE been ordered to participate in a military offensive," Steiner said to his officers after they had assembled around a table in the cafeteria.

Bricket shook his head and grumbled. A frown creased Daniels's otherwise-serene face. Mason scowled. Curses erupted from Palmer and Sanchez. Tramer stood quietly at the end of the table, showing no emotion whatsoever.

"I don't like this any more than the rest of you," Steiner told them all. "The commodore has organized an assault against an enemy base under construction on Macrales that would threaten the future of the United Star Systems. Our mission is to draw off any ships guarding that planet."

"That's insane," Mason shouted. "This bucket doesn't stand a chance against any vessel in the Separatist fleet."

Sanchez jumped up from his seat, raising his fist. "We're prisoners—not martyrs."

"That's right," Palmer joined in. "Tell the commodore to go to—"

Tramer stepped forward, intimidating them both into silence. Sanchez eased himself back into his chair.

No one else dared to argue.

After a few seconds, Steiner continued. "If we don't participate in this offensive, the *Magellan* and every other vessel here will destroy us."

Sanchez raised his hand. "What if we pretended to cooperate, then fled at the first opportunity?"

"Or better yet, our engines could suddenly malfunction," Palmer added.

"No," Tramer said with such firmness that he seized everyone's attention. "If anyone attempts to sabotage the mission, he will deal with me personally."

"The rest of us aren't as eager to die as you are, Cyborg," Sanchez replied.

Tramer glared down at the pilot for a long moment.

"The engines will be working at full capacity," Daniels said, relieving the tension.

Steiner knew he could depend on the head engineer's support, no matter how dangerous their assignments got.

"Ironhand, you still haven't told us how we're going to take on a battlecruiser," Mason observed.

"They all have their pulse cannons controlled by computers," Steiner said, aiming his gaze at Bricket. "What are the odds of disabling them?"

The bartender shook his head. "You don't know what you're asking. It would take months to break into a secured system."

"We'll only have a few minutes of contact before they destroy us."

Bricket sighed and rubbed his beard. "I'll do whatever I can."

Steiner nodded, then turned his attention to the weapons officer. "Mr. Tramer, conduct several practice simulations with the gunners."

"It will be done," the weapons officer answered.

Mason raised his hand. "I want to be at the helm during the run. I've been outflying Separatist battlecruisers for years. I already know some of their weaknesses."

"I'll take any advantage I can get," Steiner said. "Sanchez, Palmer, remain on standby during the battle."

The two pilots nodded, grumbling to themselves.

Steiner straightened himself and took a deep breath, hoping to draw encouragement in with it. "Gentlemen, the operation begins at 1800, fifteen minutes from now. Good luck to you all. You're dismissed."

One by one the officers left to prepare their stations for what lay ahead. Steiner looked up at the pale countenance of Tramer. Cole's warning reran within his mind.

"Thank you for your support, Maxwell," Steiner said.

The weapons officer nodded.

SAM wrenched the control bar of the flight simulator back, but the computer-generated *Stormquest* failed to clear the ridge that materialized out of a cloud bank. It disintegrated against the mountainside.

Not again, he scolded himself.

He hesitated before restarting the simulation. A greasy film covered the instruments from an hour of being handled by his sweaty hands. Fatigue demanded him to stop, but he refused to give in to it. Ever since his first solo flight in the *Stormquest*, he had worked harder than ever to improve his piloting skills in the hope he could fly her again.

He glanced about the empty computer room and wondered why Bricket had been called away so suddenly. Several of the terminals chirped softly as if calling out for their master.

Just then, Bricket hobbled into the room, muttering about something being impossible to accomplish. Overwhelmed with curiosity and anxious to be free of the simulator for a while, Sam climbed out of his seat.

"What's wrong?" he asked.

"You might as well know," Bricket said. "We've been ordered on some suicide mission. Our only hope of survival is if I can break into an enemy warship's computer network in a couple of minutes."

"Is that possible?"

The bartender kicked the side of one of the consoles. "Fat chance. Military systems have too many security gates. I'll never break—" He stopped when he noticed Mason standing in the doorway. "Can you believe that, Rick? The military gives us a death sentence for doing so well?"

Mason didn't reply. He extracted a folded slip of paper from one of his pockets.

"What's wrong, Rick?" Sam asked.

Mason fidgeted. "I don't have time to explain." He handed the note to Bricket. "This may help you." He wheeled around and walked away.

"Rick?" Sam called after him, but the pilot was already gone. Sam looked at the bartender in bewilderment. "What does it say?"

Bricket opened the paper and turned it right side up. His forehead wrinkled in puzzlement. "No, it can't be."

"What?" Sam demanded.

Bricket didn't answer. He rushed to the main computer terminal.

STEINER shifted in his chair at the security station, keeping his gaze on the monitors. After his announcement of their mission, he had expected some protests, even rioting, but the convicts were preparing for battle, strapping themselves into each of the gunnery ports. Coming off the high of their mission at Hurot IV, some of them felt pride at their success, despite the odds. It might be they really had no idea how badly outmatched they were.

Steiner looked back into the interior of the command center. Sanchez and Palmer glared back from their standby positions next to the helm while Simmons listened to the communication channels at his station. The sparkle of excitement he had seen in them after the raid yesterday had vanished, replaced by bitterness and resentment. No doubt, they fully understood the situation before them. Steiner suspected they would mutiny if they had the means.

He glanced out the starboard viewport at the *Freedom*, positioned several kilometers away. Both of them had arrived just minutes ago at their assigned starting point along the border and were waiting for the order to begin the mission.

Steiner couldn't help but remember the *Valiant*'s fatal run. Maybe this was how McKillip had felt. Helpless.

Mason climbed up the stairway to the command center.

"You're late," Steiner told him. "You almost lost your chance to pilot this mission."

"I'm sorry," Mason replied. "I had something very important to—"

"Captain, the *Magellan* is signaling us to initiate our run," Simmons interrupted.

Steiner didn't reply for a moment. He thought of how Mary might be beckoning him to join her now. That prospect used to comfort him, but not now. He wanted to live. He wanted to accomplish more as captain of the *Marauder*.

"Sir?" Simmons asked.

Steiner met Mason's gaze. "If you're ready," he whispered, motioning to the helm. "Take us into starspeed on the prearranged coordinates."

The pilot nodded, then maneuvered to his station.

Steiner took one last look at the monitors and saw Tramer heading toward the command center. Satisfied, he stood up and made his way to the command chair.

The stars crept by in the side viewports, gaining speed until they blurred into thin streaks of light. The *Freedom* trailed closely behind in the rear port. Steiner suspected all of its guns were aimed at them in case they tried to deviate from their course.

The destroyer disappeared from sight when Mason phased the *Marauder* into starspeed. Steiner's stomach already felt so tight that he didn't even feel the effects of the dimensional shift. They barreled through the utter blackness with only the navigational sensors to direct Mason along a safe path.

Can we survive the same trip back, blinded? Steiner asked himself as he strapped himself into his seat.

Tramer's heavy footsteps announced his arrival in the command center. He stood at his post in front of the weapons console. "Thirty seconds to the planet Macrales." His synthesized voice rang out through the utter silence.

Steiner could feel the room closing in around him. The desire to be free of his confines grew. He released his safety harness. It wouldn't help him anyway. They would be destroyed too quickly for it to be of any use. He slipped to the edge of the chair in expectation. "Are there any vessels in orbit?" he asked.

"Two Separatist battlecruisers and a dreadnaught," Tramer answered.

A dreadnaught, Steiner thought. A warship more powerful than the other two combined. Once during his tour aboard the *Valiant,* he had seen one defeat two U.S.S. destroyers by itself.

"Both battlecruisers are initiating pursuit," Tramer said.

"Mr. Mason, angle our trajectory back toward U.S.S. space."

Before the words had completely left Steiner's mouth, the pilot guided the *Marauder* into a wide arc and retreated.

The chase was on.

"One of the defending vessels is pursuing us while the other is engaging the *Freedom,*" Tramer announced.

Steiner hoped Cole's attack force succeeded in fighting off the dreadnaught and destroying the base. He didn't want his death to be wasted, not like McKillip's.

"I've just lost navigational sensors."

The hairs on Steiner's arms stood on end. For a moment, he had thought he heard Suzanne's voice instead of Mason's. Should they continue, blinded? Certainly not. History would repeat itself. Steiner refused to die in a retreat. "Reduce speed," he said, then activated the shipwide intercom. "All stations, prepare for combat."

STEINER'S announcement over the speakers in the computer room sent shivers down Sam's back. "How's it coming?" he asked.

"Give me a second to finish the link," Bricket replied, clenching his cigar between his teeth. "Besides, this will probably fail anyway."

On the screen, the enemy vessel's computer prompt appeared.

"Here goes nothing." Bricket typed in the long series of numbers and characters written on the paper Mason had given him.

The screen darkened.

Bricket sighed, creating a small cloud of smoke. "It cut us off just as I—"

Before the bartender could finish, an emblem resembling a silhouette of Emperor Staece wielding a sword appeared. A menu of command functions was listed below the picture.

Bricket gasped. His cigar dropped against the console with a splash of glowing ashes. "I don't believe it. We're in."

"What do we do now?" Sam asked.

The bartender snickered. "Use their vices against them."

CAPTAIN Ronald Peters smiled to himself when he saw the fleeing spacecraft turn to defend itself. His battle-cruiser, *Conqueror*, was monstrous in comparison. The U.S.S. must really be desperate to be utilizing ships as pitiful as these.

"Sir, the enemy vessel is charging up its weapons," Lieutenant Niles said.

"Do the same to ours," Peters replied. "Program into our computer: Attack Response Three."

This battle would be short.

Blasts of orange-red energy beat against the *Conqueror*'s defensive energy shields without any effect.

"Is that the best you can do?" Peters coaxed the vessel on the viewscreen. "Lieutenant, initiate our response."

He turned back for one last look at his opponent. One hit from a megacannon should break it in two. He waited expectantly, but nothing happened.

"What is the delay, Niles?"

"You had better see this for yourself, sir," the young officer muttered in disbelief.

Peters stared at the readout. On the screen, a barely dressed female danced about.

"What is this?" he shouted. "Access the weapons."

The lieutenant pressed several keypads, but the woman continued, uninhibited.

"The computer won't accept any commands. It is receiving an outside signal that is locking us out."

"Outside signal?" Peters exclaimed. "From wher—?" He looked up at the U.S.S. vessel broadsiding them with a fierce blanket of energy bolts. "Send an attack virus into the connection," he demanded.

Immediately, Niles typed out the commands to do so. "How were they able to break into our network, sir?"

"It doesn't matter now," Peters snapped. "Hurry, before it's too late."

BRICKET chuckled like a giddy child who had pulled the ultimate prank. On the screen, purple hair whirled as Princess spun in place, then leapt into the air.

Sam wondered what the Separatist crew might be feeling as they watched her prance around their tactical readouts. Astonishment? Fear? Exhilaration?

"How did Rick get a code that could do all this?" Sam asked. "I had the feeling he was holding something back."

Bricket's mouth crinkled. "I'd rather not think about it now. He may have saved all our—"

A red light flashed on top of the central unit, stopping Bricket cold. He muttered something, then typed out commands rapidly.

"What's wrong?" Sam asked.

The bartender seemed too preoccupied to answer.

Then the control board died into darkness. Princess faded from its screen. Bricket turned toward an unused console at the far end of the room. It sprang to life, with the dancer continuing her stage show. In the same heartbeat, she vanished as the machine erupted into a shower of burning embers. Bricket pressed a keypad on his darkened board, resurrecting Princess on the screen above him. The purple-haired beauty shook her hips as if in celebration.

"What happened?" Sam asked.

"The Separatists sent a destructive program through the link, but I was too quick for them. I diverted it so that it missed us."

"Then they're wise to us?"

"Yeah, but don't worry," Bricket said with a smirk. "They know we have them by the throat."

"ACCESS the weapons," Peters shouted.

"I can't, sir," Niles replied. "The virus wasn't successful."

"Send another one then," he barked.

The small U.S.S. spacecraft lunged at them again, raking into their shields. Each shot ate away at their already weakened defensive grid. He couldn't allow his mighty *Conqueror* to be defeated by a ship half its size.

Peters grabbed Horace, the communication officer, by the sleeve. "Tell the gunners to operate their weapons manually until we have our systems back online."

"Yes, sir," Horace stammered, then relayed the order.

Niles turned around. "The second virus failed, sir."

"Keep sending them," Peters shouted, slamming his fist into the console.

STEINER couldn't understand why the enemy warship hadn't fired a shot in defense of itself.

"The battlecruiser's defensive screen has collapsed," Tramer announced.

Steiner was astonished. Victory lay within their grasp. From there on, every direct hit would cause damage to the other vessel.

At that moment, energy streaks hammered into the *Marauder*'s hull. The ship heaved to the side, throwing Steiner from his chair. He crashed against Simmons's communication console, then propelled himself back into his seat. Less then a second later, he had his harness strapped securely around him. Mason rolled them clear of the assailing bolts.

"Damage report," Steiner ordered, rubbing his shoulder where it had hit the console.

"Nothing severe," Tramer replied, remaining perfectly erect despite the pitching of the ship. "We weren't hit by any of the megacannons. Only normal artillery fire. The pattern of the shots was too random to be a computer-guided assault."

"Do you think their network is down?"

"No. It must be occupied."

Steiner wanted to shout for joy. Bricket must have broken through, somehow.

ANOTHER console exploded five meters away from the main terminal. Sam covered his face against the tiny metal bits that sprayed him and Bricket. The bartender routed the power back to his darkened control board, then looked over at the smoking ruins of the other console.

"I can't keep this up much longer," he grumbled. "There are only two operational units left."

Sam tightened his grip on the bartender's chair, fighting to keep himself on his feet despite the jolts. "What happens when there are none left?"

Bricket frowned. "We lose."

Then they both heard it.

An explosion echoed from somewhere inside the ship.

BLACK smoke billowed from deep within the reactor chamber.

Daniels checked the instrument readouts to see what damage had been done. The cooling system for the reactors had overloaded. If the temperature inside any of the cores rose above nine hundred degrees, a meltdown would occur. The engine chamber had to be sealed and the emergency hatch blown. The vacuum of space would quench the blaze and cool the reactors.

"Code Zero," he yelled into his headset to the other engineers.

Spider, J.R., and Andrew rushed into the control cubicle. Two others were still unaccounted for.

"Don't leave us," a cry sounded from Daniels's headset. It was Charles, one of the missing men. "Fred was injured by the blast. I can't get him out alone."

With all speed, Daniels snatched an extinguisher from the emergency cabinet. "I'll try to contain the fire long enough for one of you to help them," he told his colleagues in the cubicle.

"I'll do it," J.R. replied, then sprinted into the dark cloud.

Slinging the canister over his shoulder, Daniels hurried after him into the forbidding haze.

Visibility dropped to several feet beyond the curtain of smoke. Even though the fumes tried to choke the air from Daniels's lungs, his pace never slowed. He was determined to save his two colleagues, no matter what happened to himself.

The deck shuddered from an impact against the outer hull.

God, grant me the time to save my friends, Daniels prayed.

Finally, he reached the edge of the fire. Flames licked the top of the high ceiling. Intense heat singed his skin. He aimed the nozzle and activated a powerful stream of chemicals. The blaze consumed the extinguisher liquids without any effect to itself whatsoever.

A second stream of chemicals joined his hopeless attack. Daniels turned to find Spider beside him, firing an extinguisher. The aide smiled faintly. Daniels never expected him to come. In the past, Spider had always been afraid of hazardous situations. His loyalty must be stronger than his fears.

A cough broke through the black smoke to his right. Daniels could barely make out the vague forms of J.R. and Charles helping Fred to safety.

"Daniels," Mike shouted over the headset. "The temperature gauge is reading eight hundred degrees and rising. The core is going critical."

Time had run out. The engine chamber had to be sealed for decompression.

"Go now," Daniels screamed at Spider.

The man paled, dropped his extinguisher, and ran back into the black smoke.

Daniels continued to aim his stream of chemicals into the white of the flames. He shielded his tearing eyes from the heat with his arm. *A few more seconds,* he promised himself. *Give them time to escape.*

"Eight hundred and fifty degrees," Mike shouted in the headset.

Daniels knew he couldn't stretch it any farther. Every fiber in his being was telling him to run. Perhaps it was a message from God. Dropping his extinguisher, he fled. He had no idea what direction he was heading in. He coughed and gasped for breath. How could he possibly make it back like this? Yet he kept running.

"Phillip," J.R. said in his earpiece. "We've reached safety."

"Seal the pressure door and blow the hatch before we lose the reactors," Daniels shouted.

"You'll be trapped."

"Do it now."

A motorized whine echoed from somewhere ahead. Daniels used the noise to get his bearings. He still had a chance of making it before the barrier shut. It took twenty seconds to close completely.

As he barreled ahead, each of his feet found solid ground somehow. One misstep would result in death.

Directly ahead, faint lights showed through the haze. A descending wall of darkness covered half the opening. He still had a chance to beat it.

He skidded to an abrupt stop at the foot of something in his path. It was Spider, curled into a ball and whimpering hysterically.

"Spider," Daniels cried, pulling the other engineer to his feet. "We're almost there."

The man sobbed something in reply.

Daniels heaved him over his shoulder and stumbled ahead with all his might. His head began to spin, the first sign of asphyxiation. He knew he would black out soon. He forced each leg forward in short strides.

The world seemed to be falling away from him. Shadowy silhouettes gathered under the shrinking gap. He reached out as if to take hold of them, but they were too far away. He felt himself floating through air, then his face struck something hard and cold. He tried to move but found his body numb.

As he drifted off into a sea of blackness, he felt the sensation of being pulled somewhere. Voices spoke to him, but he couldn't understand what they said. The last thing he heard was an echoing thud.

Within the silence of the darkness, he saw the faces of the people he had assassinated, looking at him through the gloom. Then he saw her. His last victim. A government official he had been contracted to kill. He saw himself standing by the sleeping woman's bed after administering an absorbent poison to her skin. Before she died, she woke up and looked at him. She opened her mouth and started to say something.

"Phillip?" A voice cut through the vision. "Can you hear me?"

Daniels blinked his eyes and saw J.R. smiling down at him. Daniels inhaled deeply of the pure oxygen flowing through the mask over the lower half of his face.

"That was a close call," J.R. said. "Both you and Spider are going to be fine."

Daniels couldn't help but feel guilty. After all the terrible things he had done during his lifetime, he didn't deserve to live.

STEINER sighed with relief as he watched Daniels and Spider begin to move on one of the security monitors. A neighboring screen showed the decompressed engine chamber icing up.

Once the fire had broken out, Mason pulled the *Marauder* back to a safe distance until the engineers could get the situation under control.

"The drive systems have stabilized," Tramer announced. "We are ready for another run."

"Haven't we put up enough of a fight?" Sanchez asked. "Let's flee while our enemy is disabled."

Steiner looked at Mason, who shook his head. "The dimensional drive is down," the pilot replied. "We can't run."

No one argued.

"I doubt we can take many more hits," Steiner told Mason.

"They won't touch us again," the pilot replied. "I'll make sure of it."

"Then take us in for another pass."

Mason dove the *Marauder* back toward the *Conqueror*.

CAPTAIN Peters stared in horror as the tiny U.S.S. ship made another destructive pass. Explosions rocked the bridge, and the interior lighting started to fluctuate. Power reserves were almost depleted. Soon they would be at the mercy of their opponent. He caught another glimpse of the woman on the tactical screen, removing her top.

"She's stripping," Horace muttered.

Before Peters could stop himself, he punched Horace in

the face. It felt refreshing to release some of his pent-up anger. He grabbed Niles by the collar. "Send more viruses."

"It's useless, sir. No matter how many we send—"

He didn't let the young officer finish. He shoved him away from his station. *They'll pay for this,* he swore as he sent another virus through the connection.

BRICKET'S hands raced across the control board so quickly that Sam couldn't tell what keypads Bricket pressed. On a small screen below the one where Princess danced nude, lines of text scrolled so fast Sam couldn't read them.

The main terminal was the last operational unit left in the room. The air stank of burnt wires from all the smoldering consoles.

"If they send another virus, we're finished, aren't we?" Sam asked.

"Not if I can help it," Bricket replied, without losing rhythm in his rapid pace. "I'm planting Princess into the Separatist ship's own computer network, so that they will think that we still control their systems, even after they have destroyed our capability to do so. The only problem is where to put the program so they won't find it."

"Wherever you put it, do it fast."

"Aha, Refuse Control."

The red light above the terminal flashed.

"Bricket," Sam shouted.

"I know—I saw it," the bartender said, working more frantically to finish.

The glowing indicators on the entire board dimmed, warning of an impending overload. With all his strength, Sam pushed Bricket back just as the terminal exploded. They both toppled in a heap as flaming debris rained down on them.

The bartender patted out the patches of fire on his clothes.

"Were you able to finish?" Sam asked.

"I hope so."

The *Marauder* had just completed another charge across the bow of the *Conqueror* when all the instruments in the command center went dark.

"What happened?" Mason said.

"I don't know," Steiner answered. "Use the manual controls to get us out of range."

"On my way," the pilot said, putting distance between them and the other vessel.

Steiner looked back at the weapons officer. "Mr. Tramer, are any of your systems online?"

The weapons officer pressed a few keypads, but nothing happened. "Everything is inoperative. It appears we've lost the computer room."

"Try to contact Bricket."

The cyborg nodded and went to work on it.

Steiner stared out the front viewport at the *Conqueror*, motionless in space. Small fires emanated from the battle-cruiser's hull where the *Marauder* had hit it. It looked badly damaged, yet it still outmatched them.

"Captain," Bricket answered over the ship's intercom. "I succeeded in deadlocking the battlecruiser's network, but it cost me every terminal I had."

"Every unit?"

"Except life support."

"Without the computers, we can't find our way back to across the border," Palmer said.

"He's right," Mason added. "We might be able to guess a direction using the constellations, but we'd never know for sure if we were right."

"The Separatist captain is signaling us," Simmons said from the communication console. "He must be demanding our surrender."

Steiner looked back at Tramer as if searching for an opinion, but the weapons officer remained silent.

"Piece together whatever you can, then get back to me," Steiner told Bricket. "We've got a problem up here." He closed the channel.

"The Separatist captain wouldn't bother asking for our surrender," Mason said. "He would rather destroy us."

"I agree," Tramer said.

"What if it's a trick?" Palmer said.

"I'll speak to him in private," Steiner said. "Maybe he won't be able to detect our current condition.

"Mr. Tramer, if the *Conqueror* tries anything during the discussion, initiate another attack run with manual systems. Maybe we can take them out with us."

The weapons officer nodded once.

Steiner descended the stairwell into the private chamber. Could the Separatist captain be surrendering? It didn't seem possible, yet was there any other logical explanation? If it was true, it might be their only way to get home. If he planned on bluffing the other captain, Steiner would have to project superiority over him.

Steiner sat back in his chair, put his feet up on his desk, and activated the wall monitor.

On the screen, a man in his fifties appeared, his face bright crimson. "Tell me who it was," he demanded. "Who betrayed us?"

Steiner didn't have the slightest idea what the man was referring to. He maintained a confident appearance and smiled, as if toying with the other captain. "You'll find out as soon as you are processed as a prisoner of war."

"I will never allow that," the man shouted.

"Then prepare to become a martyr," he said, reaching to terminate the transmission.

"Wait," the captain shouted. "I'm willing to discuss alternatives."

Steiner knew the man was trying to buy some time in the hope that another battlecruiser would come to his rescue. "Either surrender or fight," he said. "I have no time for negotiating."

"First, tell me who gave you the code to sabotage our weapon systems."

Steiner smiled at Bricket's ingenuity. "Perhaps your computer network needed a few more security gates."

"Don't insult me," the man snapped. "Our records show us that you used a command code. Who gave it to you? Was it Admiral Scheidner, Richina, or that idiot, Patterson?"

"You'll find out once we reach U.S.S. space," Steiner said. "Set a course for the border. Don't try any tricks. My patience has grown too thin."

The Separatist captain glared at him for a few seconds.

"You'd better get moving," Steiner said, then ended the transmission.

Steiner sat in the silence for a few seconds, confused by how Bricket could have accessed the battlecruiser's computer network with a command-level code.

"Captain," Tramer's voice announced through the intercom. "The battlecruiser is beginning to move."

"Have Mason set a course parallel to its. If we're lucky, they should lead us home. Steiner out."

Steiner closed the channel and opened another—one to the computer room. He hoped Bricket could shed some light on how he had accomplished such a miraculous feat.

The hull shuddered as the *Marauder* started to move.

CAPTAIN David Cole stood, looking out a viewport of the *Magellan*. The *Freedom* had arrived at the rendezvous point an hour ago. She had been badly beaten by a Separatist battlecruiser but managed to escape. There was still no sign of the P.A.V.

The mission had been accomplished with great success. The base on Macrales had been completely destroyed. The Separatists would not be invading the Northern Territory anytime soon. Cole's plan had saved the United Star Systems, but none of it would have been possible without the help of Steiner and his team of convicts. What had they gotten in return? Death? It wasn't fair.

"Anything on sensors?" he asked Cromwell.

"Nothing, sir. We've already waited the mandatory length of time. It's useless to stay here any longer."

Cole glared at him. "We'll give them another hour, Commander."

"Yes, sir," the officer said grudgingly.

Cole was frustrated about Cromwell's attitude toward the P.A.V. The commander's opinion wasn't an isolated one. All the other captains had tried to discourage him from waiting as well.

"Sir," Cromwell suddenly called out. "The *Excalibur* has just reported a Separatist battlecruiser heading this way."

Cole's first thought was that there was a retaliation force on the way, but that was unlikely so soon after such a devastating defeat. Maybe the *Excalibur* had made an error.

"Verify it on our sensors, Commander."

"It's there all right, sir."

Cole made his way to the console. "Is there just one ship, or is it the leader of a team?"

"I'm—I'm not sure—sir."

Leaning over the console, Cole analyzed the readout for himself. Indeed, there was another ship trailing behind the battlecruiser. It was the P.A.V.

"Sir?" Cromwell asked. "What does it mean?"

"If I didn't know better, I'd say Steiner captured an enemy ship. Helm, set an intercept course."

The pilot propelled the ship forward toward the target. The two vessels grew in the forward viewscreen.

Cole moved to the communication console and opened a channel. "P.A.V., if you are able, respond with your password."

"This is the U.S.S. *Marauder* reporting back from our run," Steiner's voice replied.

The monitor printed out PAV:73993.

Whispers of astonishment rose from around the command deck.

Unbelievable, Cole thought. In all of his years of service, he had never heard of such an impossible feat. "Transmission accepted, U.S.S. *Marauder*. Welcome home."

STEINER stood silently at the helm next to Mason, watching the other U.S.S. ships discharging their weapons in a salute of respect toward him and his crew.

Simmons, Sanchez, and Palmer shouted cheers. Tramer tried to request repair updates from all sections, but the interfering intercom chatter indicated that the rest of the crew seemed to be so engulfed with elation that no one responded to him.

Steiner wished he could celebrate with them, but that was impossible. He had talked to Mason, and Mason had finally told him the truth—the secret behind their victory. Somehow he had to hide it from his crew and, more importantly, from all the official inquiries that were to come. Everyone would want to know about how a thirty-year-old Peacemaker defeated a Separatist battlecruiser. If the truth were discovered, it could endanger everyone on board.

Mason glanced up at Steiner with evident fear.

Steiner shared it.

CHAPTER

17

IN a restaurant on Earthstation, Steiner drank down the last of his coffee. His gaze wandered over to the large window that currently overlooked the eastern part of the African continent. Even though he had been recalled here to be honored as a hero, the threat of exposure loomed heavy over his head.

A waitress came by, refilled his coffee cup, winked, and walked away. He looked down at his collection of freshly printed magazines lying on the table with his picture prominently displayed. Sinking in his chair, he began organizing the booklets into a stack. The headline of each told him the public's reaction to his and his crew's success. "Convict warriors possibly aided by aliens from a distant galaxy," read one. "Prison raiders in league with Separatists in plot to bring down the United Star Systems." The last theory hit so close to the truth that Steiner squirmed in his chair.

After the capture of the Separatist battlecruiser, when Cole had inquired about their victory over the *Conqueror*, Bricket had conjured up some technobabble that satisfied the commodore, but the phony explanations wouldn't fool Military Intelligence. Only with Suzanne's help did Steiner stand a chance of protecting Mason's secret.

"Jake!"

Suzanne walked toward him, but never as he had seen her before. Her red hair hung loosely down around her shoulders. She wore brightly colored civilian clothes. He got up and held out his hand. She thrust it aside and gave him a long hug.

"You did it," she said. "You made it work. I knew you would. When did the P.A.V. dock?"

"The *Magellan* escorted us in three hours ago, but our ship isn't called P.A.V. anymore. Commodore Cole has officially christened it, the U.S.S. *Marauder*."

She laughed. "You left a convict and returned a hero. Everyone is proud of your accomplishments."

"Not everyone." Steiner read off some of the headlines on the newsdisk.

"That's scandalous trash. The President of the United Star Systems wouldn't be holding an award ceremony for you tomorrow night if he believed that."

"President Lindsey?" Steiner asked, half in disbelief and half in terror.

"Of course. Your initiative saved us from an invasion. You're the biggest war hero to come down the line since Louis Harrison. Thanks to you, we might still prevent the Separatist Empire from forcing its 'New Order' on the rest of the galaxy."

Steiner swallowed hard at the irony of being compared by her to Louis Harrison. Before the civil war had begun, Suzanne had unknowingly met Louie under a different name and thought him to be a scoundrel, loyal only to the highest bidder, unaware that he was secretly part of the Cyrian Defense and played a huge part in defending the United Star Systems on the Day of Betrayal. As far as she knew, Louis Harrison was an upstanding member of Military Intelligence whom she had never met.

"Have you heard about Pattie?" he asked, changing the subject.

"Yes, I've already seen him. Cole brought him here about a week ago on the *Magellan*. We've just been waiting for your slightly slower ship to return. The sergeant really came through for you, I've heard."

"I owe Pattie more than you know. Can you see that he receives better medical treatment than the standard for convicts? I would really like to get him back walking in any manner that you can."

"He's already been provided the very best care available."

Steiner took a second look at her. "The military just put up the money without question?"

"Not exactly. A private donor stepped up to pay for his treatment."

"Donor? What donor?"

"I don't know. Some patriotic citizen who wanted to honor a war hero, despite any mistakes of his past. Everybody is thrilled by what you have accomplished."

Steiner cleared his throat. "Yes, about what we accomplished . . . there's something you don't know yet about our victories."

"What do you mean?"

He struggled with how to answer her, then decided to tell her straight-out. "Someone gave Bricket a Separatist command code to disable the battlecruiser's computer defenses."

Suzanne looked confused. "But your report says he used a special program to break through their security gates."

"I made that up."

"You falsified an official report," Suzanne exclaimed.

"Calm down." Steiner glanced around to make sure no one had heard. "I had no choice. If the truth were known, this person would be in a lot of danger. I can't risk that."

"Why not? What harm would it do as long as this person isn't a member of your— Oh no, it's one of your convicts, isn't it?"

Steiner gave a slight nod.

"How can that be? I did a full background check on all of them." Her eyes widened. "Except for that pilot you asked me to transfer on board. It's him, isn't it?"

"Don't worry. He's not a spy."

"How did he get possession of a Separatist command code? Emperor Staece doesn't just distribute them among his subjects—only to the highest admirals in his fleet."

"He stole it."

"How can you steal something like that? Was he in the Separatist military?"

"Yes." Steiner hadn't been able to believe it when Rick had finally confessed.

Suzanne's expression soured. "You have ruined my otherwise-perfect day. How high up was he?"

"A lieutenant."

"Even a lieutenant in the Separatist military couldn't have stolen a command code. They're kept as secret as our codes. How did he get it?"

"I can't tell you any more than that."

"Why not?"

"It would endanger him. If Military Intelligence ever found out, they would create such a scandal that Mason could end up being wrongfully condemned, maybe worse."

"If it's that bad, why risk falsifying an official report? It automatically makes you his accomplice."

"I don't want Military Intelligence to tear him apart. My crew wouldn't have survived the raid of Hurot IV or the battle with the *Conqueror* if Mason hadn't helped us. You and I are the only protection he has."

"So you want me to be a coconspirator against the truth, is that right?" Suzanne asked.

Steiner's stared into his coffee cup. "I'm asking you to prevent an injustice."

Suzanne shifted her gaze out the window at the landscapes thousands of miles below. She sniffed. "You want me to jeopardize my career without even knowing the whole story."

"I promised Mason I wouldn't tell anyone."

Suzanne shook her head. "If some paranoid official finds out and screams treason, I'll be the first one on the chopping block."

"I wouldn't ask you this if it weren't necessary. Considering the sensation we created, I don't know if I can hold off the inquiries by myself."

She stared down at the table. "Everything that I was raised to believe tells me I should inform Military Intelligence, but I won't. I'll make sure that any investigation into the matter goes nowhere."

"Thank you, Suzanne. Mason would be extremely grateful, too."

"I'm not doing it for him," she said. "I'm doing it for you."

Steiner didn't know how to respond to her admission of affection. He sipped from his cup, revolted by the taste of the lukewarm coffee. He signaled to the waitress and pointed to his mug. When he looked back at Suzanne, he found her staring out the window.

"Where is the award ceremony to be held?" he asked.

She sniffed. "The New York Metropolitan Center."

"Am I confined to the station until then?"

Her confident posture returned. "Not the number one war hero. You've been granted shore leave until Wednesday morning at 0900, Earthstation time, when your ship is scheduled to depart. That gives you over thirty-six hours to visit Earth."

"What about my crew?"

"Be serious. Do you think Earthstation Security will allow forty-four convicts to roam the streets unsupervised?"

"The total is down to forty-two."

The waitress stepped up to the table and exchanged the cold coffee for a fresh cup.

"I'll round up a few replacements before you leave," Suzanne replied.

Steiner burned his lips on the steaming liquid. "How about at least giving my officers some leave time?"

"I doubt Earthstation Security will even allow them off the ship. They're still convicts."

"So am I. If they don't get shore leave, neither do I."

"Don't be unreasonable. You have to attend the award ceremony in New York."

"Not if my officers aren't able to. I couldn't have succeeded alone."

She scowled at him. "You are so stubborn sometimes." She paused and frowned. "Probably as bad as me. I'll talk to Earthstation Security. No promises, though."

"Let's go talk to them right now. Why wait?" Steiner warmed his stomach with two swallows of his coffee before standing up from the table.

She huffed. "I can see my career flashing before my eyes."

After leaving the restaurant, they went to the Earthstation Security Department. It took nearly an hour of arguing with the supervisor to get shore leaves for just the officers but no one else. The man made it clear that if anything went wrong, Suzanne would be held responsible because she ranked higher than Steiner. She accepted reluctantly, then lectured Steiner for twenty minutes about how she wanted his officers to behave and where they could go. Before she left, she told him to meet her outside his hotel an hour before the ceremony tomorrow evening.

When Steiner returned to the *Marauder* to announce the leaves, Daniels turned him down flat, but that came as no surprise. The head engineer usually avoided any type of social activity except for his church services. On the other hand, Bricket, Mason, Sanchez, and Palmer jumped at the opportunity to leave the ship.

The person Steiner most wanted to go to the surface with was Tramer. During the past two weeks of their return voyage, Steiner had met privately with Tramer daily, attempting to rebuild a relationship with him. The weapons officer had remained tightly closed within himself, but Steiner had found one way past his defenses. Tramer liked jokes. He never laughed or smiled, probably because the needed muscles in his face were dead, but his human eye twinkled. Steiner hoped a short leave would bring him out of the shell that had imprisoned him for the past seven and a half years.

Tramer refused to go to Earth at first, but after much persuasion, he agreed to a brief visit.

All of the officers, except Daniels, left the ship together and boarded a civilian shuttle for the New York Transport Station. On the trip down, Tramer received nervous glances from the frightened civilians on board. They spoke to one another in hushed tones tainted with revulsion and terror of the weapons officer.

"They must be envious," Steiner whispered to Tramer.

The gray eye sparkled.

Through the viewports along the passenger compartment, the sun dipped over the horizon. The coming darkness awakened the colorful lights of the metropolis far below. Unused now, ancient bridges spanned the bay, serving only as memorials to the past. Lady Liberty welcomed them with a blazing torch.

After the shuttle landed at the transport station, Steiner and his officers walked out into the crowded streets. Signs hung over each intersection. NO VEHICLES ALLOWED WITHIN THE CITY LIMITS. Steiner remembered seeing pictures of a time when vehicles dominated these pathways, but the advent of the underground transit-tube system had eliminated the need for them and made crowd control more manageable.

Steiner had forgotten how much he enjoyed breathing fresh air rather than the recycled, metallic-scented mixture on the *Marauder*. Aromas of cooked foods emanated from concession stands set up on the curbs.

There on the streets, Tramer didn't receive the attention he had on the shuttle. Many people were dressed so strangely that the weapons officer blended into the cauldron of madness.

Steiner overheard Mason and Bricket talking about visiting a fantasy house, where they could live out computer-generated dreams with women pulled from their mind's eye. His throat tightened. He recalled his last visit to one of those establishments right after Mary's death. He had wanted one final look at her to say good-bye. He found himself twisting his white-gold ring.

"Are you still wedded to Mary?" Tramer asked.

Steiner glanced up at his friend. "Do you remember her?"

"One of the *Valiant*'s assistant chefs, expecting her first child."

"Yes, you correctly deduced that she was pregnant before she knew she was."

"Does she live here on Earth?"

"Well . . . no, I lost her in a shuttle accident."

"What purpose does the ring serve?"

"I'm still her husband."

"She died."

"That doesn't matter to me. I love her." Steiner decided to use this perfect opportunity to ask Tramer about his past. "What about your wife, Candice?"

Tramer fell silent for a long moment. "I died."

Steiner swallowed hard.

Bricket and Mason headed south toward a decoratively lit building with a giant neon sign that read, FANTASIES.

Just then, Steiner realized that might be just what Tramer needed, a chance to be human again for a while. Perhaps that could be his vacation.

He casually led the weapons officer toward the fantasy house. They watched the bartender and pilot enter the "adults only" section.

"Would you like to go inside and try it?" Steiner asked.

"I have no need for imaginary women," Tramer replied.

"I wasn't suggesting you try one of their fantasies. This is your chance to live as you once did, without all the hardware. You could run through a field, climb a mountain—act like a normal man again.

"I am not a man anymore. Why should I subject myself to something I no longer am or ever can be?"

"To relive pleasant memories."

Tramer looked away, wordlessly.

Steiner remembered how much seeing Mary again after her death had helped him. "You could be with your wife again."

Tramer stiffened. His human eye widened with what looked like insane rage.

Steiner backed away in fear. "I'm sorry," he whispered. "I didn't mean—"

Tramer stomped away to a secluded corner and bowed his head. His mechanical fingers jerked. His entire body twitched, expelling short bursts of motorized whines. The seizures lasted for a moment, then subsided.

Steiner's body broke out in a cold sweat. Would Tramer have actually hurt him? Several days ago, he wouldn't have dreamed it possible, yet now he wasn't sure. He remembered Cole's warning him about Tramer killing two innocent people after one of them inquired about his wife.

Three small children scampered out of the kids' section of the fantasy house. Their parents called for them to come back. A small girl ran into Tramer. The child's face whitened at the sight of the deformed head staring down at her. She screamed. Another sound immediately followed, except this one wasn't human. Tramer wailed in agony. The mother of the girl shrieked and snatched up her daughter. Tramer raced through the scattering crowd.

"Maxwell," Steiner shouted at him, forcing his way through the panicking mob.

Tramer moved with inhuman speed. Steiner only caught a glimpse of him dashing down the street before he disappeared completely. Screams from pedestrians sounded far ahead, marking the weapons officer's passage. Steiner sprinted after him, dodging frightened people in Tramer's wake, but soon lost the trail completely.

A tormented wail echoed from out of the distant night.

MAXWELL maneuvered through the streets, avoiding as many people as he could. The few he passed backed away in fear and disgust. A police officer tried to pursue him on foot but wasn't able to keep up. Maxwell couldn't allow anyone to catch him. He might kill more innocent people.

He wished he hadn't come down to the city. In prison and on the P.A.V., he had been safe from his buried past. Now his emotions threatened to tear his sanity away.

The memories that he had hoped were long forgotten came back to haunt him. He saw his wife, Candice, looking at him for the first time after his operation.

"Is it really my Maxwell?" she asked one of the cyberneticists.

"It's the best we could do. There wasn't much left of him to work with. Perhaps, when the ban on genetic manipulation is—"

"That is not my husband. That can't be my Max. You should have let him die with dignity."

Her words cut into his soul. He had no idea what he had looked like at the time, but the fact that his appearance revolted her crushed him. But that was mild compared to the reaction of Veronica.

The scene played out in his mind once more. He staggered through a hall at the medical center, learning how to move his new mechanical appendages. His six-year-old daughter, Veronica, ran around a corner, calling out for her daddy. She stared up at him, then screamed in terror. The bloodcurdling cry lasted for what seemed an eternity. Veronica fell to the ground and covered her face.

"Mommy, Mommy, it's a monster," she shrieked.

Candice raced around the corner, fell down on Veronica, shielding her. "Stay away from her," she shouted hysterically.

Maxwell wanted to die. His own family cowered in fear of him. Didn't they know he would never hurt them? He would have gladly given up his life for either of them.

After that day, he never saw either of them again.

Veronica.

Maxwell came to an abrupt stop in a dark alley and wailed again, hating the sound of his own mechanized voice. Blinded by his fury, he burrowed his fists into a side of a building. The concrete blocks gave way easily to his might, collapsing inward. A burglar alarm rang out from inside the hole. Tramer froze in terror. That was the second time he had lost control of his strength. The first had been in the cargo bay of the *Magellan* seven years ago, when he had acquired the nickname "Killer Cyborg."

He had been working on that ship's weapon systems when his enhanced audio sensors heard two other crewmen talking about him.

"They probably built him some metal genitals, too," one of them whispered.

The other snickered. "His wife must think it's an improvement."

In retrospect, Maxwell realized that both men might have been trying to overcome their fear of his new form. But at the time, all the anger of losing Candice and Veronica flooded back. Maxwell attacked them with the intent of rendering both men unconscious. When he had finished, he stood over two lifeless, broken heaps of flesh.

Maxwell remembered the cyberneticists repeatedly warning him of his new physical abilities. He had thought he could control them, but he had been wrong. In his rage, he had murdered two innocent people, breaking them like dolls.

Seven years in prison had taught him to suppress his emotions. He knew that if they were ever released again, more innocent people might die. He must seclude himself until he could find control again.

Veronica's scream continued to echo inside his mind.

"HE'S missing?" Suzanne nearly shouted at Steiner. The people ahead of them in line at the city transit tubes stared at them as they exited from magnetically driven cars.

Steiner pulled his jacket close about him to shield against a gusty wind blowing in from the Atlantic Ocean. "I searched all night. He could have already left the city."

"I knew something like this would happen, but I didn't expect it to be Tramer," she said. "If he hurts anyone or does any damage, I'll get the blame for it. For goodness' sake, what if he kills someone?"

Steiner stopped her. "Wait a minute. You were the one who said he was emotionally stable enough to work on my ship."

"That was before he scared some kid and went AWOL. What did you say to him to set him off?"

"I asked him about Candice, and if he wanted to live out a fantasy with her."

"His wife? Why would he want to do that? She dumped him right after his transformation. She couldn't bear the sight of him, I'm told."

An empty car stopped in front of them, and they climbed into the open hatch.

"You never told me Candice was a taboo subject," Steiner said, strapping himself into a seat.

"His entire past is a taboo." Suzanne closed the hatch, then entered their destination into the input pad. The magnetically driven car whispered away into the dark tunnels.

"What happened to his little girl?" Steiner asked.

"His wife took her."

"Maybe that's what set him off. He misses his daughter."

"I don't care why he left. I want him back on board the P.A.V. now."

"*Marauder*," Steiner replied.

"Whatever. I'm calling Earthstation Security on this. They can find him before he harms someone."

"Let me go after him alone."

"How will you know where to look?"

Steiner opened his jacket and extracted a small device from an inside pocket. "I purchased this before I came to meet you. All I need is the frequency for the tracers that are planted in all the convicts."

"No. Absolutely not. You're a prisoner."

"A war hero," Steiner shot back. "A former shipmate. You can trust me. I'll find him and bring him back before anyone is the wiser."

"No."

"Suzanne, if you call Earthstation Security, they'll put Tramer back in prison for the rest of his life."

She frowned.

"I can't afford to lose him," he said again. "Please let me talk to him before you throw away his career."

"If anyone finds out that I gave you the frequency for the tracers, I'll lose my rank."

"I haven't betrayed Mason, and I won't betray you."

She sighed. "It's 65150."

He kissed her lightly on the cheek.

She blushed slightly, then her anger returned. "I can't believe all the trouble you're causing me. Here I am, about to mingle with the most influential people in the U.S.S., and I'm under the threat of a possible court-martial."

Steiner replaced the tracker within his jacket. "Just don't think about it."

She rolled her eyes and sighed.

After their car stopped at the New York Metropolitan Center, they passed through a security checkpoint and entered a lift that took them to a luxurious lounge. Flora sprouted from circular planters and scented the air. Colorful holographic artwork decorated the towering walls. Stars glittered through the glass ceiling fifty feet above them.

Suzanne tugged at Steiner's shoulder. He turned in time to see her exchange greetings with Commodore David Cole. She appeared to be holding up well, not displaying any of the fears she had revealed earlier.

"Captain Steiner, it's good to see you again," the commodore said, shaking Steiner's hand. "How is your visit to Earth so far?"

"Uneventful."

"I heard that your officers came down with you," Cole said. "Will they be joining us for the celebration?"

"They are occupied tonight."

Suzanne fidgeted, her gaze dropping to the floor.

"Intelligence officers interrogated Captain Ronald Peters yesterday. He still insists that we have a Separatist admiral in our back pocket." Cole chuckled softly.

Steiner faked a laugh.

"Military Intelligence has requested a copy of that computer program your specialist wrote to break into the battle-cruiser's weapons systems," Cole said. "Drop it off at my office tomorrow before your ship departs."

The color drained from Suzanne's face. "Excuse me." She moved quickly toward the restrooms.

Cole didn't even seem to notice that she had gone. "I think M.I. wants to find a way to re-create your success in future engagements."

"I doubt they will make the same mistake again," Steiner replied.

"That's unfortunate. We could use some more captured battlecruisers." Cole grinned.

Steiner pretended to be amused, thanked the commodore again, and moved to the punch bowl to fill a cup with the bubbling ruby mix.

"Yes, yes, bring us more Separatist battlecruisers for our collection," a familiar voice said. A seven-foot-tall man stood behind a nearby column with his back to Steiner as if he were purposely hiding from the majority of the people in the room. "If you complete a full set, we might obtain a sur-render," the man continued as he turned his head toward Steiner.

The penetrating gaze from the pale face with golden-rimmed spectacles was unmistakable. Professor Isaac R. Steele, whom Pattie used to call "Smarty Pants," among other things. Very eccentric, often misunderstood, Steele had been a silent partner in McKillip's Cyrian Defense. His face looked younger than his forty-five years of age demanded it should. Still free from graying, his blond hair was parted in the middle and feathered back on both sides.

The rims from his spectacles sparkled in the bright room, further distinguishing him in that few people wore optical ware anymore, choosing instead a simple corrective surgery. Steele had claimed all cosmetic surgery was an expression of vanity and that he had too much of that trait already.

Steiner held out his hand. "Isaac, it's good to see you again."

"Yes, yes, let's skip the pleasantries, shall we," Steele said, waving his fingers in disdain. "Always uncomfortable with physical signs of greetings."

Steiner had forgotten the man's aversion to touch. "Are you still teaching at the academy?"

"Yes, yes, never left. Classes in astrophysics, philosophy, and ancient literature." Steele smiled as if talking about his own accomplishments pleased him. "Teaching man's past, present, and future, all in the attempt to forestall the eventual decline of all governments into the chaos of subjectivism. It seems to be working for now since it is a president giving you an award rather than an emperor."

Long before the war, at the early age of twenty-eight, Steele had become the youngest professor of multiple subjects at the academy. At a time when loyalties of all military officers were under question, Steele tested the loyalties of the incoming cadets with carefully designed essay questions to determine who could be trusted not to sell out for a bribe and who would fight for their principles. Steele could remember every essay, word for word, of every student who had ever taken his class and could recite them all back.

"It's strange to see you here," Steiner said. "You used to avoid all social gatherings."

"Yes, yes, but matters of necessity have forced me to come here." When some people approached the punch bowl, Steele shrank back, beckoning Steiner to follow. The professor disappeared behind a spreading plant in an alcove of the room.

Steiner followed him curiously out of sight of the other guests. "Is there anyone in particular you are trying to avoid?"

"Everyone. I do hate reminiscing, and the dreaded small

talk with old acquaintances. Chat. Chat. Chat. How's this? How's that?"

"Have you heard what happened to Captain McKillip?" Steiner asked.

"Yes, yes, of course. I followed the tragic loss of both Fern and Judith."

"I hope you believe me when I tell you that Admiral Jamison had them both killed. He is a spy."

Steiner expected a look of shock from Steele, but the tall man chuckled. "Of course. I know he is. Do you mistake me for some simpleminded dupe?"

Unable to believe what he just heard, Steiner stood speechless.

"I doubt Ralph Jamison was always a Separatist spy. During the invasion on the Day of Betrayal, I do believe he was our ally, but I suspect his relations with the pirating ring put him in a position to be bought."

"You know about the link to the pirates that McKillip was attempting to collect evidence on?"

"Yes, yes, of course. I am certain much of his evidence came from me anyway. McKillip was protecting my involvement in the matter, but I had no choice but to come and speak to the president after the *Valiant* was conveniently sent to a sector of space to face two battlecruisers and a dreadnaught, alone. It was plainly obvious Ralph Jamison had become an enemy agent."

Steiner tried to grasp what Steele was saying. "If that's true, why hasn't he been arrested yet?"

"Michael Lindsey and I both agreed that since Ralph Jamison was in such an influential position, we had to make certain he could do as little damage to us as possible. For the last month, I have been modifying our current jamming buoys near the border to create what I call the 'Steele Net,' which blocks all unauthorized transmissions into the New Order Empire. We only brought it up online today."

Steele's nose twitched. "Why do people insist on having flowers within a closed room?" He pulled out his handkerchief and sneezed. "Until the net became active, we could not risk tipping Ralph Jamison off that he was under suspicion. Our next step goes into effect tomorrow, as each ship will be redeployed from its current location to block off any possible routes back into the New Order Empire. Then we will begin an official investigation."

Steiner soaked in the information for a moment. "So when I attacked Jamison, it was for nothing."

"An emotional overreaction, resulting in the imprisonment of a good officer. I had completely given up hope on you, as I had Patrick Braun, until both of you surprised me by joining the Penitentiary Assault Vessel program and making it a huge success."

"You came here to congratulate me?"

"No, Jacob Steiner. I came to this party to save your career."

"How so?"

Steele reached into his dinner jacket, produced two of the magazines with the scandalous headlines about the success of the P.A.V., and handed them to Steiner. "By tomorrow, these will read 'The son of Admiral Richina, the Emperor's Executioner, in league with Captain Jacob Steiner, convicted attempted murderer.' By this time tomorrow both you and he will likely be tried for treason."

Steiner stood, dumbfounded. "How did—?"

"Surely you didn't think I was an oblivious fool who might believe the alien story or the equally preposterous story you just gave Commodore Cole. It's elementary to any keen observer." He tapped his glasses twice. "I know that the only way to disable a Separatist battlecruiser is to use a command code, one the New Order had installed in each of their ships after the terrible fiasco the United Star Systems had during the Day of Betrayal invasion. If a battlecruiser ever became compromised, an admiral could access its computer with a single command code and shut down its weapon systems. Since an admiral didn't give you the code, it had to be a family member." He paced around the pillar, looking rather proud of himself. "There are three senior admirals in the New Order's fleet, David Scheidner, Francisco Richina, and Matthew Patterson." He held up three fingers. "Patterson isn't married." Two fingers. "Scheidner has three girls, who couldn't be serving on your all-male ship." One finger. "Admiral Richina, on the other hand, had two boys, Mason and Randy. Upon checking your crew manifest, I find a 'Rick Mason,' a poorly constructed alias that interchanged the first and last name of 'Mason Richina.'" His fingers sprang out in the "eureka" expression that Steiner remembered him best for. Steele picked up one of the magazines, looking at the headline, which read "Prison raiders in league with Separatists to gain favor with the United Star Systems." He shook his head sadly. "At the very least, he should have used an anagram."

"He's not a spy," Steiner tried to explain. "He hates his father."

Steele looked up immediately. "Of that, I have no doubt. Fathers often impose a perfect vision of themselves onto their children, resulting in the exposure of the hypocrisies interlaced within their own lives and driving wedges between themselves and the intended clone of their image. I don't doubt his loyalty to you at all." Steele tapped the magazine in Steiner's hand. "But that's the kind of sensational exploitation they'll thrive on."

"What can I do about it?"

"Your only hope is that Commodore Cole explains to everyone at Military Intelligence exactly how your computer specialist cracked a New Order command code, or you'll never make it out of the space docks again."

Steiner shrugged his shoulders, defeated by his situation. Perhaps Steele was right. If the instructor figured it out, the news services would, too. "I wouldn't be able to convince anyone."

"You are precisely right," Steele replied with a smile. "But I can." His hand produced a computer data card from inside his dinner jacket. "This is a little computer program I created last night. It's a 'smart brute-force-attack' cryptographic computer program, based on previously broken Separatist code structures. This could have generated the password he used, as long as he correctly guessed the salted key, the cleartext word or phrase that finishes encrypting the cipher. Do you know what that was?"

Steiner had no trouble remembering the ominous phrase. "The future begins."

Steele let out a single laugh, stifling it immediately, bringing himself came back under control. "So predictable," the man muttered to himself. He handed the card to Steiner. "Give this to Cole and tell him that Bryan Sicket randomly heard another convict in prison mention that same phrase, and you're in the clear. Rick Mason can remain undetected on the P.A.V."

"Thank you, Steele. Rick will probably want to thank you as well. Why are you so willing to believe him?"

"Because I've never told you who my father is," the tall man said with a wink. "And I never will."

Music from an orchestra began playing in the central lobby. The people in the lobby began filing into the auditorium.

Steele straightened up. "I hear you are receiving the 'Louis Harrison' medallion. Frankly, I don't know which Louis Harrison would have enjoyed more, the irony of having an award named after him or your receiving it. After the ceremony, would you care to join me on a visit to Patrick Braun in the hospital?"

"Sorry, I won't be able to. I have another crisis I need to deal with. I heard a private donor is personally overseeing his medical care."

Steele smiled. "You are correct."

"It's you, isn't it?"

"Just don't tell him that—I don't think he could take it. Right now, he thinks the government is doing it because of his heroism."

"Please get him to walk again."

Steele patted him on the back and led him into the conference room. "Even if I have to design the legs myself."

RALPH Jamison stood alone in a cargo hold on Earthstation, contemplating the news he had just received. His plan lay in tatters. All the years he had spent moving the United Star Systems into a new era of freedom, one unhindered by public opinion, seemed to be in vain. Jamison scratched the middle of his hairless scalp. How could he free the galaxy from the bureaucratic chains of democracy if he were exposed as a spy?

He tensed when the door opened, then breathed with relief when Quinn entered the room.

"What is the emergency? I thought you were going to be stationed at Tycus until next month."

"I was called here from Tycus for a special meeting of the Council."

Quinn chuckled. "Are they planning to surrender yet?"

"Haven't you seen any news reports in a while?"

"I just arrived back from the Empire yesterday. I haven't had time. Why?"

Jamison gritted his teeth as he answered. "The Northern Invasion has been defeated."

"The base at Macrales?"

"Destroyed."

The color drained from Quinn's face. "How did the U.S.S. find out about it?"

"Steiner and his crew of convicts deviated from their raiding schedule and overran Hurot IV."

"Impossible."

"Ask the crew of the battlecruiser *Conqueror* what's possible," he said, raising his voice. "Steiner and his wretched band captured them during the attack on Macrales."

Quinn's expression went blank for a few seconds. "He is a powerful man indeed. Where is he now?"

"Down on Earth."

"He is?" Quinn ran his hand through his spiky brown hair. "I'll have the pleasure of gutting him myself."

"Steiner's being presented a medal. You couldn't get near him."

"Find out where his ship will be stationed next week. When I return to the Empire, I'll set an ambush for them."

Jamison shook his head. "You can't get back. New ship placement orders went into effect this morning. All the gaps have been closed off. We can't even send out a message. A new transmission-blocking grid has been deployed along the border regions. Apparently, someone's been listening to Steiner."

Quinn's face hardened. "Had you been informed of these changes beforehand?"

"No. That's what worries me. I suspect they are onto me. That's why I asked you here. We have to act tonight, or all is lost."

"You have a plan?"

"Yes. Since the new battle positioning of the ships needs to be reported to your superiors, and we can't transmit anything to them, we'll have to smuggle a computer disk with all the materials on it into the New Order Empire."

"Yes, but you just said, all the holes we used to use have been closed up. How can we get through without being boarded?"

Jamison smiled. "You served with Joseph Barker on the P.A.V."

"Just for a few days before he was murdered."

"Do you think you can start a mutiny on Steiner's ship?"

The wintry eyes glistened. "Just kill the captain."

"No," Jamison replied. "I mean lead a mutiny, subjugate the crew, and use the vessel to smuggle the computer disk into the Empire. It's the only way. From these revised orders, the P.A.V. will be patrolling the southern border. You'll have to keep Steiner alive until you get to the border, to avoid any suspicion, then kill him."

Quinn ran his fingers through his bristly hair. "It sounds like an interesting challenge. Can you get me on board by tomorrow morning?"

"I'll forge the transfer orders tonight. I have a man I trust, who can switch Steiner's real Orders disk with a phony one, which will contain all the new U.S.S. plans."

"What about the P.A.V.'s passwords? I'll need them."

"Yes. I've already arranged to have someone break into Suzanne Riggs's office and steal them from her personal computer."

"Is he worthy of your trust?"

"Most of the time. He helped me acquire McKillip's files from his late wife. Maybe you remember him? He has a distinctive ponytail."

CHAPTER

18

STEINER looked out from the side of the stage at the multitude of tuxedos and glittering evening gowns within the massive auditorium. The guest list included only the most elite of government officials and their spouses. Commodore Cole sat in one of the front rows, beaming with excitement. Among the row of the president's staff sat Isaac Steele, looking uncomfortable.

Fingering the computer card in his pocket, Steiner was thankful that Mason was going to escape possible prosecution, but his stomach still turned with worry over his missing weapons officer. Why had Tramer run off? Had he gone looking for his wife and daughter? After all, a small girl's scream had incited him to run away. Maybe Tramer had gone to search for them—but then again, how would he know where to look? What would he do if he found them? Nerves sparked a trail from Steiner's head to his feet, making all his body hair stand on end. Would Tramer hurt his wife for taking his daughter away? Worse yet, would he try to take her back? Steiner would have dismissed the thought, but after what had happened the previous night, he couldn't be sure anymore.

The live orchestra began the anthem for the United Star Systems, bringing the entire assembly to their feet. From the opposite side of the stage, President Lindsey strolled out to a podium at the center. A deafening eruption of clapping drowned out all the other sounds in the auditorium. After the gathering reseated themselves, the president gave a speech of how peace and unity would one day be restored to the galaxy. When he finished, he introduced his guest of honor.

Most of the officials rose to their feet and gave him a standing ovation, but a few quietly remained seated.

Steiner walked up to the president and accepted his outstretched hand. Looking into the elderly man's face, he saw earnest gratitude reflected there. This handshake was more than just a token gesture. From out of his suit jacket, the man produced a small case with the initials L.H. on it and opened it. The overhead spotlights played on the surface of the gold medallion contained within.

"Six years ago, Louis Harrison discovered the New Order Empire's plans to invade," the president said. "Because of his intervention, we were able to prevent the First Invasion from moving in any farther than Macrales. I am presenting the medallion named in Harrison's honor to Jacob Steiner, for his initiative in preserving the United Star Systems from another major invasion."

He lifted the ribbon over Steiner's head. In the front row, Cole marched up the center aisle to the front of the auditorium, in view of the entire assembly, and saluted. The cheers increased, and several of the seated admirals rose to their feet also. Steiner held his breath as joy and guilt battled within him.

Tramer, where are you?

Shielding himself with a fake smile, Steiner thanked the crowd. The president invited anyone who wanted to assemble in the courtyard to offer personal congratulations to Steiner. Steiner dreaded the thought. He didn't have time for that. As he retreated behind the curtain, his stomach turned as he envisioned a pack of lions gathering to tear him apart with questions.

Suzanne met him backstage. "What are we going to do

about Commodore Cole needing a computer program to deliver to Military Intelligence?"

"Give him this." He gave her the computer card and told her the key phrase required to make it work.

"Did Bricket make this?"

"Yes," he lied.

"Will this be good enough to fool Military Intelligence?"

"Absolutely."

She breathed with relief. "Oh thank goodness. I thought we were sunk. Let's go give it to Cole together. They are expecting you in the courtyard."

"I can't go with you," he said.

"What are you talking about?" she asked. "They're expecting you—you're the guest of honor."

"I have to find Tramer," he replied.

"I agree, but find him later."

Steiner fingered the gold medallion slung around his neck. "I don't feel right about this. This award belongs to Tramer, not me." He lifted it over his head, but she stopped him.

"By giving this to you, the president is also honoring him for his service," she said. "After all, he is under your command."

"All the more reason I have to go looking for him right now."

"No," she shouted. "You're not leaving." She grabbed his arm and started toward the reception but couldn't move him. "Please, I can't go in there without you."

Steiner held her by the shoulders. "You know as well as I do that the longer it takes to find Tramer, the more the risk that someone will discover he's missing."

"What am I going to say to the others about their guest of honor's being absent?"

He struggled and smiled. "I've never known you to be at a loss for words. If nothing else, tell them I've gone to find the real hero."

She groaned. "Make sure both of you are on that ship at nine hundred hours, Earthstation time." She moved forward, kissed him full on the lips, then stormed away into the courtyard without looking back.

Steiner stood in the corridor, stunned.

* * *

THREE hours passed before the reception died down enough for Suzanne to excuse herself.

She walked through the deserted hallways of the fifty-second floor of the military headquarters on her way to her office. She hoped to finish composing the orders for Jake's replacement convicts before the morning's launch. Questions troubled her mind. *How far has Jake traveled by now? Will he find Tramer? Will they return before they are reported missing?*

She remembered announcing to all the guests that Jake had left prematurely because of a sudden illness. Just as she had feared, they refocused their attention on her. Never once had she lost her composure even when she thought she would. She smoothly evaded all of their questions, pretending to be ignorant of everything.

She wondered if she might actually be in love with him. When she had served under him aboard the *Valiant*, she admired him because he was as ambitious as she, but he never stepped on people like she did to move up. She hated to admit it, but she had even used him as a foothold when she asked him to captain the P.A.V. Much to her surprise, he had again succeeded in boosting his career far beyond hers. Maybe she loved him. He had become everything she wished she could be.

At the entrance to her office, she entered the security code in the control panel. Nothing happened. Upon closer examination, she noticed someone had broken the locking mechanism.

Her blood ran cold. Her fingers slipped through the mouth of her purse and tightened around the handle of a miniature pistol. She used a key to pop out the emergency hand crank. Quietly, she pumped the mechanism until the entrance cracked wide enough for her to squeeze through.

Shadows draped the office, but a light showed through the doorway to the back chamber, where she kept her personal computer. The faint rustling of movement sounded from within it. Every muscle in her body stiffened. Her lungs froze in the middle of a breath.

Common sense instructed her to call the security guards

before confronting the burglar. But by the time they arrived, the intruder might already be gone. Armed with a gun—regardless of its size—and the element of surprise, she figured she'd be more than a match for one thief.

She stepped gingerly past her desk, keeping her small gun trained on the open doorway. A satchel sat just inside the next chamber with the words COMPUTER MAINTENANCE stenciled on it.

She hesitated for a second, unsure of herself. Could it be? No, certainly not. She knew all of the maintenance staff. None of them would have come there so late, not without getting her permission beforehand.

A series of beeps sounded from her computer, indicating that it had started transmitting data to another console. She jolted slightly when she heard footsteps heading her way. She held her breath. Her trigger finger tensed. A man with black hair tied back in a ponytail appeared in the doorway and bent down to retrieve something from his bag. He froze in mid-motion, his hand still in his satchel, and looked up at her.

"I'm sorry," he said, adding an innocent smile. "I didn't mean to frighten you. You must be Suzanne Riggs."

She kept her pistol pointed at him. "The outside door has been forced open."

"Yes, I know," he answered, without moving. "The building's security guards discovered it as it is. I was called in to repair the damage done by burglars in order to ensure you could use this office tomorrow. Weren't you informed I was here?" His hand rummaged through the satchel. "I have a work order, if you don't believe me."

"Put your hands in the air—now," she shouted.

The man's gaze held hers for a split second. Terror squeezed her confidence into mush. The hypnotizing eyes drew her in, seducing her to lower her guard.

With lightning speed, he pulled out a large gun from the bag and aimed it at her. She would have died if it hadn't been for her reflexes. Without even thinking about it, she shot him, striking him in the chest just as he fired his weapon. His bolt sliced the air just centimeters from her right ear. With a look of shock imprinted on his face, the man fell to the floor.

Her heart racing, Suzanne glanced at the large smoldering

hole in the wall behind her. That could have been her head. She nearly lost her balance from the sudden nausea building up inside her.

Gathering up all her remaining courage, she knelt by the fallen man and picked up his weapon. How did an ordinary burglar get an AT-7 past the building's security checkpoints? She searched inside his pockets for identification but found nothing.

Her personal computer emitted another set of tones. She stepped over the man to examine the glowing screen. Sequences of letters and numbers—the P.A.V.'s passwords—scrolled up as the machine transmitted each code out to another destination.

"Jamison," she breathed. No one else would have known how to access her files.

Using the command keys, she tried to cut off the transfer, but the program refused to stop before the completion of its task. She grumbled in frustration when she saw that the computer had already sent out the P.A.V.'s recognition code along with the passwords that protected the command center, armory, landing bay, and other high-risk areas. She couldn't allow it to finish the entire list. It would take days to reprogram them all.

She picked up a chair and smashed it against the console. It flared up in sparks, and the screen went dark. Furious at having to destroy her own terminal, she threw the chair down. Jamison would pay dearly for—

An arm wrapped around her throat, lifting her feet from the ground. She screamed, but only a gurgling noise came out. As she thrashed about, she caught a glimpse of her assailant's reflection in the dead computer screen. It was the man she had shot.

Gasping for air, she put her feet on the corner of the console and pushed away with all her might. Her attacker slammed into the back wall, but his grip remained firm.

Her vision blurred. The room drifted away. She had only a few precious seconds left to free herself from the death hold.

I'll stop him, she promised herself. *I won't die.*

Then she saw her salvation. The vague form of one of her

award statues stood on top of the console. She reached out and took hold of it. With her remaining strength, she thrust the metal pinnacle on top of it into the man's groin. A shriek of pain followed. The iron grip relaxed enough for her to pry herself free.

Coughing and wheezing, she stumbled into the front office, her muscles weak from the lack of oxygen. The room tilted and spun. Escape looked out of her reach. She screamed with all her might. A blow to the back of her head squelched her cry and sent her sprawling to the floor.

She rolled over, her hands flailing out to ward off an attack. The man drove his knee into her abdomen, driving out her breath. The face looking down at her twisted with rage.

"If you want your trophy so much, I'll give it to you," he hissed, reaching for the statue on the ground.

Suzie, don't ever let people get the advantage over you. Her mother's voice rang through her head. *The harder you fight, the farther you'll go.*

"Mother," she sobbed aloud. "What can I do?"

At that moment, she saw her purse lying a few feet away, the miniature pistol sticking out of its flaps. She reached out and grabbed the small gun. The man raised the statue over his head, with the pinnacle pointed at her. She aimed the weapon at his head, closed her eyes, and fired.

She might have lost consciousness for a second or two, because she had no idea what happened next. She opened her eyes. Her attacker's body lay across her legs. To her horror, she saw the award statue protruding from a bloody wound in her chest. Pain followed, excruciating in its intensity before mellowing into a warm sensation. Darkness crept in from all sides of her vision. She fought against it. She must warn Steiner of the sabotage. Numbness enveloped her. She heard voices and saw vague forms, surrounding her, but they became less real to her by the second.

"I'm sorry, Jake," she whispered, then closed her eyes and welcomed the peace of nothingness.

RALPH Jamison stared at his computer screen, expecting more codes to print out, but nothing happened.

"Your man has proven unworthy," Quinn said, looking over his shoulder.

"He got everything except the pressure-door overrides. You won't need them if you plan your mutiny right."

"If someone is onto us—"

"No one knows about you," Jamison replied, losing his patience. "I'm the only one at risk here."

"If you are questioned, they might learn of me."

"Over the years, I've made friends within Military Intelligence who will warn me if I'm in danger of being arrested."

Jamison copied the passwords onto a computer pad and handed it to Quinn.

"Is that cyborg still on board?" Quinn asked as he looked over the list.

"Yes."

"Can you transfer anyone on board with me?"

"As many people as you need."

"Just one other. A cyberneticist friend of mine."

THE New England sky brightened slightly, advertising that dawn had arrived. Gray clouds stretched the horizons, completely masking all but a faint glow of the sun. A light blanket of mist hung across the land, painting everything in dewdrops. Birds danced among the trees, giving praise to the new day. A flash of lightning brightened the haze far to the west.

Steiner maneuvered his rented oversized truck along a seldom-used gravel road, which led to a secluded town. After using public transportation to reach the general vicinity, he had rented a vehicle to approach Tramer from the most secretive angle possible, for fear of bringing attention to himself. Glancing down at the tracker, he located the weapons officer a mile to the north. He parked the vehicle on the shoulder of the deserted road. The rest of the way he would travel on foot. Unstrapping himself from the seat, he stepped out of the truck into the chilled morning air. The scent of the wind promised rain. He zipped up his jacket, folded his arms tightly, and headed off through the damp grass toward Tramer's last-recorded position.

Steiner found his anxiety over the *Marauder*'s upcoming

departure growing like the humidity in the air. Even though Cole had promised their mission schedules would be lighter, a premonition of disaster during the voyage ahead haunted Steiner's thoughts. Maybe the guilt, which hung around his neck with the medallion, had induced the terrible feelings. He couldn't be certain. He looked down at his watch, set for Earthstation time. It told him there were five hours left before the ship was to launch. It had taken him nine hours to find Tramer's location, even with the aid of the tracker.

When he climbed to the top of a hill, he saw the small town nestled in a valley below. Opening one of the pockets in his jacket, he extracted a pair of high-powered binoculars and made a visual sweep of the area. A wave of relief swept through him when he spotted Tramer, standing amidst a collection of shrubbery outside the town. The inhabitants might not even know he was there.

Steiner descended the hill, entering Tramer's sensor range. The weapons officer didn't acknowledge his presence in any way. Steiner stopped outside a gap in the shrubbery.

"Tramer?" he asked.

No response. The faint odor of formaldehyde hung in the humid air.

Steiner forged a path through the prickling branches until he stood next to the metallic body of the weapons officer. The sensor orb cast a blue glaze over the foliage facing the town.

Steiner stood motionless, listening to the respirator on the back of Tramer's neck cycle air.

Steiner aimed his binoculars through the branches, attempting to focus on whatever Tramer stared at. Figures moved around inside the picture windows of a nearby house. Intensifying the distance ratio of the glasses, he could make out a woman inside, bundling up her two children in warm clothing.

"Is that Candice?" he asked, lowering his binoculars.

A breeze shifted the trees overhead. The rustling leaves nearly overpowered the answer.

"Yes."

Steiner sighed with joy. Tramer's response meant that he hadn't lost his mind. "How did you find her?" he asked.

"Candice's parents live in this— Wait, they're leaving now."

With his binoculars, Steiner watched Candice and the two children emerge from the house. When the older girl glanced in his general direction, he saw a slight resemblance to Tramer—the old Maxwell Tramer.

A man stepped out of the building behind the girl and put his arm around Candice.

Poor Tramer.

Candice must have remarried. That would explain the other child, who didn't look anything like Tramer. The family climbed into a sedan and drove off into the hazy distance.

Steiner's throat constricted to the point where he couldn't even swallow. He couldn't stop thinking of what it would be like to see Mary with another man, living out her life in fear of him. It would have been unbearable.

The sky darkened.

Servos whined as Tramer's spiny fingers rose to pinch the stem of a hanging blossom. He plucked the delicate flower and brought it up to his deformed face. The petals changed to a violet hue under the glow of his mechanical eye. "My sensors detect the molecular density of this flower and the dispersal pattern of its pollen, but I can never again savor its aroma." The blossom floated to the ground. "It is forever lost to me, just like the love of my daughter."

Thunder echoed off the hilltops. A light rain rode the breeze.

"Why did you run off?" Steiner asked.

The mechanized torso rotated until Steiner could see Tramer's whole face, wet from rain or tears. "I might have hurt someone in my emotional state—as I did once long ago." He looked up into the heavens, opened his mouth, and let out a barely audible scream that almost sounded human. "I never intended to kill those two men five years ago." His gaze met Steiner's. The torture on his face melted away until he appeared as emotionless as ever. "I had to be alone to regain control over myself."

"Is that why you came here—to find control?"

"I do not know."

"Maybe you came to say good-bye to your old life, so that you could begin anew?" Steiner said.

Water speckles converged on Tramer's breastplate, steaming down the metal surface. "I miss Veronica. I never want to leave her again."

Steiner wiped the rain from his face. "If you stay, you'll lose your career. I need you on the *Marauder*. You're the backbone of that ship."

Lightning flashed from the north.

Tramer's torso swiveled back toward the town.

Steiner took a step closer. "One day, when your daughter learns that her father is still alive, don't you want her to be proud of you?"

"She will always run from me."

"No," Steiner said. "She'll learn to look past your exterior and find the soul of her father, just like I have."

"He died."

"When I first met you on board the *Marauder*, I would have agreed with that statement, yet you care. You feel." Steiner turned toward the direction in which the vehicle had driven away. "And you hurt. Show Veronica you love her by striving to honor her. Don't end it all here."

Heavy droplets pelted the damp earth around them. Tramer continued to stare toward the town.

Steiner sighed. Tramer chose to mourn the passing of his previous life rather than attempt to live again.

Steiner opened his jacket and grasped the medallion flush against his chest. He freed the ribbon from his head, then draped it over the shoulder of the weapons officer. Starbursts of light glistened in the medallion's water-speckled surface.

"Good-bye, Mr. Tramer," Steiner said. "It was a pleasure serving with you." He straightened his posture and gave his best military salute. If Tramer's career ended there, it would be with the dignity he deserved.

Steiner walked back up the hill toward his vehicle. When he reached the apex of his climb, he glanced back and saw the weapons officer frozen in the same position.

Lightning tinged the sky, accented by a low rumble. Sheets of rain rippled through the grayness.

Steiner ran the rest of the way back to the truck. By the

time he climbed into the cab, his clothes and skin dripped water. He started the vehicle, swung it around, and kicked up some gravel as he sped to get back to Earthstation within five hours.

The headlight beams illuminated a dark figure directly in the center of the road. Steiner stomped on the brakes. Rocks ground under the tires of the truck as it slid to a halt. Tramer, his blue sensor light twinkling through the downpour, stepped to the passenger side and opened the door.

"Permission to join you, sir?"

"Always," Steiner said.

The weapons officer climbed into the spacious cab, leaning forward so his head would clear the roof. He handed the Harrison medallion back. "I would prefer to earn one on my own—for Veronica's sake."

Steiner smiled knowingly. "Welcome back, Mr. Tramer."

As they drove off in the direction of the coming storm, Steiner felt at peace. If something terrible did wait on the horizon for the *Marauder*, at least Tramer would be there with him when it happened.

CHAPTER
19

STEINER weaved a reckless path through the flow of military personnel in the corridors of Earthstation. Tramer followed in his wake, people automatically providing him room to pass. Barely fifteen minutes remained before the *Marauder*'s scheduled departure from the space docks. The crew would take three times that amount of time to prep the ship.

When Steiner arrived at the security checkpoint for their ship, he didn't see Suzanne anywhere around. Maybe she had work that needed to be done before the launch? She would probably arrive soon.

He remembered how he had left her the previous evening, frightened about having to go into the reception alone. Maybe the horde of inquisitive people had been too much for her to bear alone? No, if that had been the case, armed guards would have been waiting here to escort him away. She must have made it through without any problems.

He stepped up to the guard behind the counter. "Has Director Riggs been here at all today?"

"No, sir, but Commodore Cole delivered your Orders disk an hour ago."

Steiner accepted the silver wafer from the guard and

slipped it inside his shirt pocket. "Have the rest of my officers returned from their leaves?"

"The last of them reported in this morning. Your two new crew were escorted on board two hours ago." The guard handed Steiner a computer board with a printout of the transfer orders.

"What are the names of the two new convicts?" Tramer asked.

"Travis Quinn and Boon Wong," Steiner read off the miniature screen.

A flash of recognition crossed over Tramer's pale countenance. The sensor orb targeted the guard. "Where are they now?"

The guard blinked under the scrutiny of the beam. "In the ship's bar, waiting to be assigned crew quarters."

Tramer turned to Steiner. "We must find them immediately." Without waiting for a response, he hastened into the docking tube.

Steiner thanked the guard, then chased after the weapons officer. The enclosed walkway shuddered with each impact of Tramer's heavy feet. Steiner raced to match his pace.

"Tramer, what's wrong?" Steiner shouted.

"I have met Travis Quinn before," the weapons officer answered. "He came aboard the P.A.V. with Joseph Barker."

"Stop for a moment."

Tramer halted so abruptly that Steiner overshot him by a yard.

"Why are you so concerned about him?" Steiner asked.

"Quinn claimed to be just another convict, yet he spoke frequently to the captain in private. I found it too coincidental that he left the ship after Barker's death while the rest of the prisoners remained on board."

"Are you implying he might have been working with Barker?"

"Yes."

"What if you're mistaken? Director Riggs authorized his transfer. I trust her judgment—"

"Quinn is dangerous," Tramer said. "Get him off this ship before it's too late."

"I couldn't do that even if I wanted to," Steiner snapped.

"My superior made out his transfer orders. I can't throw him off without authorization from her first."

"Allow me to eliminate him before the launch."

"No," Steiner shouted. "You will not harm him." His hands trembled. "How could you suggest such a thing? Down on Earth, I thought you'd changed."

The deathly pale face glowered at him.

Steiner's anger refused to be held back any longer. "It horrifies me to know that you can justify killing a man so easily. Have you become so desensitized to life that you can only see in black-and-white terms—life or death? Even if this man is as dangerous as you say, I could never kill him based on a suspicion, nor could I look the other way if you did."

"He might destroy everything we've worked to achieve," Tramer replied.

"How could he do that? He's only one man."

"That's how mutinies start. If I had not acted against the two dissidents during the previous voyage, you would be dead, and the United Star Systems would have been invaded a second time."

"I'll assign Quinn to the engine room," Steiner said. "Daniels will keep a close eye on him down there."

"I will watch him as well."

"We do this according to military policy. If you catch him doing anything disruptive, contact me, and I'll throw him in the brig."

"This ship will not be able to operate under normal military guidelines. These are convicts."

"Nevertheless, that's how I intend to run it. Is that clear?"

The weapons officer saluted.

They continued solemnly through the docking tube.

When Steiner opened the air lock into the *Marauder*, he nearly gasped in shock at the sight of crewmen bustling around, preparing for the upcoming launch. He had not expected any of them to be ready. Over the ship's intercom, he heard Daniels giving status reports.

"Just like a normal military ship," Steiner said. "Discipline even when the captain is away."

Tramer didn't respond.

When they reached the bar, Bricket greeted them from behind the counter, where he was securing all his bottles within cabinets. It looked like he was happy to see Tramer.

Two strangers sat alone at a back table, talking softly to one another. Steiner kept one stride ahead of Tramer as they approached the men.

"Gentlemen, I'm Captain Steiner."

Both men rose and introduced themselves.

Quinn, a muscular man in his late thirties, stood over six feet tall. Short, spiky hair covered his head, framing ice blue eyes that stabbed into Steiner.

In direct contrast to Quinn, Boon Wong was a heavyset man in his forties. A thin beard hung from the tip of his chin. He studied Tramer's body from every angle and even probed one of his arm joints with his fingers. Tramer ignored the attention, probably accustomed to overly curious people.

Steiner assigned Quinn to the engineering section just as he had promised. Since Wong had a lot of computer experience, he put him in Bricket's department.

Tramer instructed both men to follow him to their designated cabins. As he led them out of the bar, he glanced back at Steiner as if silently repeating his warning.

"I see you found Tramer," Bricket said, limping out from behind the counter. "The tracker must have worked."

Steiner slapped the device still strapped to his belt. "Perfectly."

"I never thought I would say this, but I'm glad he's back. That tall guy gives me the creeps."

Steiner didn't reply. Meeting Quinn had reaffirmed his premonition about the voyage ahead.

What can one man do? he reminded himself.

Shaking the thought from his head, Steiner used his comlink to call the command center for a status report. Daniels responded, telling him they were fully prepared for the launch three minutes ahead of schedule. Steiner decided to use the extra time to return to the security checkpoint to see if Suzanne had shown up yet.

When he stepped out of the docking tube and didn't see

Suzanne, he checked with the guard to find out if she had sent any messages. She hadn't.

"Suzanne, where are you?" Steiner muttered.

"Sir," the guard said, handing his computer board to Steiner, "I just received this report. It's concerning Director Riggs."

Steiner read the printout, feeling his heart sink. "Not Suzanne, too," he mumbled.

"I'm sorry, sir, but the docks are on a tight schedule."

Steiner returned the computer board to the guard, then stormed back into the docking tube.

AS soon as the outer walkway was sealed up behind Steiner, Jamison stepped out of the shadows and approached the security checkpoint.

"Sir, I did exactly as you asked," the guard said. "I gave the captain the disk you instructed me to."

"Good. Do you still have the one Commodore Cole delivered?"

"Yes, sir. Here it is." He handed it over.

The naive guard grinned with pride, unaware of the treasonous act he had committed. Jamison smiled back. With the disk in hand, Jamison strolled to a nearby window, which overlooked the P.A.V. inside the dock.

The battle-scarred old vessel reversed out of the dock, ferrying with it the disk that held the U.S.S. military data. Soon, Steiner's band of convicts would cause the fall of the U.S.S. to the New Order Empire. Jamison loved the irony.

Once the P.A.V. had maneuvered out of view, he turned back to the guard. "Make sure that you tell no one of the disk switch."

"No, sir. I'm just honored to be aiding a member of the Council."

"One day, history books will tell of what you've done here today."

CHAPTER

20

LEANING against the bar counter in Hell, Steiner watched the bruiseball game on the giant video screen at the far end of the room. Twenty off-duty personnel huddled around the viewer, cheering for their favorite players. Bricket had installed the screen to keep the spectators from interfering with the game. It also provided him with the opportunity of creating gambling pools. Small scraps of paper and napkins posted on the wall blew in the breeze flowing from the ventilation ducts above, each with a handwritten gambled amount and signature.

Steiner lifted his mug up to his mouth, then hesitated. Suzanne's face seemed to shimmer in the liquid surface. He swallowed a mouthful of the high-alcoholic mixture, trying to forget about her. Twelve days had passed since Steiner had learned of her death. According to the report, she had confronted a burglar during a computer theft.

A howl erupted from the screen.

"Oh great," Mason muttered from the barstool next to him. "They're doing it again."

Steiner glanced at the viewer and saw Rex tackle an opponent, snatch up the yellow helmet, and sprint toward his team's goal. He tossed the helmet over to Bo, just before Eddie pounced on him. Jumping over the giant security officer, Bo launched the yellow game ball through the posts, giving their team another score.

The bar patrons exploded into applause and boos.

"I can't believe it," Mason exclaimed. "I've got to invent a defense against those two before our next game."

"Just keep the helmet away from both of them," Bricket said, from behind the counter. "By the way, I don't see Sam anywhere. Doesn't he usually help you plan strategies?"

"Yes." Frustration leaked out through Mason's voice. "I haven't seen him for hours. If he's been spying on people again, I'll kill him."

"Spying?" Steiner cut in.

Mason huffed. "That stubborn kid has the impression he is supposed to protect you from every rumor of a mutiny."

Steiner went rigid. "What rumor are you taking about? Why haven't you told me about this before?"

Mason exchanged an uneasy look with Bricket, then answered reluctantly. "There's always some disgruntled person speaking about wanting to mutiny."

"Usually someone who can't get enough beer because of the regulations on the bar," Bricket added. "It's nothing to be concerned with. I doubt any of them have the audacity."

"Whom did Sam hear?" Steiner asked.

Mason sighed. "Yesterday, he overheard Simmons talking about a mutiny about to happen."

"The navigator is the biggest coward on board," Bricket replied. "He's probably trying to impress people with some fabricated story."

When the *Marauder* had left Earthstation twelve days ago, Steiner wouldn't have believed any rumors of mutiny, but during the course of the voyage to the southern border, the attitudes of some of the crew had become more disrespectful.

Steiner's gaze settled upon Travis Quinn, sitting alone at a table in the corner. The man's cold eyes stared back. Since hearing Tramer's suspicions about him, Steiner had begun to sense something dangerous in his gaze. It was as if he wanted to be suspected of something. So far, he had been a model crewman. Steiner glanced up at the security camera overlooking the bar, which pointed straight at Quinn. If the man ever did try anything disruptive, Tramer would be the first to know about it.

Who, then, is behind this rumor? Steiner wondered.

SAM inched up to the corner of the junction he had seen Simmons turn right at. He suspected that the navigator would use the distraction of the bruiseball game to meet his contact. Sam had learned much about spying on people since Steiner had caught him that first week of the voyage. Glancing up and down the empty passageway, Sam extracted a wire-handled mirror he had constructed for covert viewings. He eased the shimmering circle past the edge of the corner. He adjusted the angle until he could see Simmons talking with Boon Wong twenty feet away. Sam had met Wong on several occasions and didn't care for him much. The man often acted resentfully about his assignment to the *Marauder*.

Wong handed Simmons something too small for Sam to make out. Wong fingered the wispy beard on his lower chin as he whispered to Simmons. Sam strained to hear what was being said, but only could make out the words "cyborg" and "trap."

Simmons smiled brightly and nodded as he slipped the object into his pants pocket. The navigator shook Wong's hand, then whirled toward the junction. Sam whisked the mirror back from the edge, jogged back a few steps, then walked forward casually. Simmons came around the corner, whistling a tune, smiled politely at Sam, and continued toward the command center. Sam passed through the junction, making sure he didn't glance down the corridor Wong was in. After he passed by the other wall, he looked back and saw Simmons dancing with glee down the hall until he was out of sight. Sam crept up to the edge of the junction and angled his mirror around the corner to look for Wong. The computer maintenance man was nowhere in sight.

Sam slipped into the adjoining passageway and went in search of him.

* * *

THE buzzer rang out from the video screen, signaling the end of the match. The BLUE team raised their hands in victory. Despite Eddie's guerrilla runs, Rex and Bo's masterful teamwork had prevailed.

Inside the bar, a surge of convicts rushed the counter, demanding their winnings. Bricket shouted for them to form an orderly line, but the greedy mob continued to push and shove each other. The bartender rolled his eyes and filled the outstretched hands, one by one.

Steiner's comlink chirped right on schedule. After every bruiseball game, Tramer called to inform him that he was on his way to the playing field to secure the body-armor suits.

Standing directly under the active security camera, Steiner stared up into the lens. "Yes, Tramer," he said into the comlink. "I'll meet you at the cafeteria."

A series of shouts rose behind Steiner. He whirled about in time to see one crewman shove another. A burly man jumped on the first man. Without warning, the mob broke out into a brawl. Fists flew. A pile of men tumbled down to the floor, clawing and choking one another.

Hulsey, the smallest of the security officers, sprinted from his post at the door and started immobilizing the men fighting on the outer fringes with his stun gun.

Bricket cried out for help as two convicts climbed onto the counter, reaching for him.

Steiner jumped up onto the polished wooden structure and kicked the two men in the face, knocking them back into the quarreling mass. He whipped out his AT-7. Two bolts rent the air above the brawling convicts' heads, inciting them to silence.

"The betting pool is closed permanently," Steiner shouted. "Disperse immediately or face the consequences."

"What about our money?" one of the men asked.

Steiner aimed at the convict's face. "What good will it do you with a hole fried through your head?"

The man backed away. The rest of the crowd started leaving, grumbling among themselves.

Looking at the scraps of paper littered on the ground, Steiner found it hard to believe these were the same convicts who raided Hurot IV and captured a Separatist battlecruiser. What could have caused the change in attitude?

Among the couple of notes still clinging to the wall was one that he recognized as a type of smuggling code. He snatched up the note, which was pretending to be a bet. He couldn't decipher its meaning—but it had been a message to someone. He looked over to the table where Quinn had been sitting. Only an abandoned mug of beer remained.

IN his mirror, Sam viewed Wong as the computer maintenance man watched Tramer pass through a distant junction, then rushed down the steps leading to the lower level. Sam followed as close as he dared, keeping the heavyset man's image within the mirror's reflective surface. He lost his quarry within the sloping corridor of the lower level. He crept forward until he found Wong sneaking up to the sealed entrance of the armory.

Sam trembled with excitement. The rumor he was investigating might not be a fabricated story after all. He wanted to run and tell Steiner all that he had witnessed, but he didn't want to miss whatever Wong was attempting to do. He positioned himself in a niche in the bulkhead and adjusted his mirror.

Wong pressed a series of keypads in the control panel next to the door of the armory.

Sam's breath caught in his lungs as motors within the wall behind him whined.

The door to the armory parted, and Wong stepped inside.

Sam couldn't believe what he saw.

A slight noise caught his attention coming from the corridor behind him. Sam angled his mirror around the corner in the opposite direction from Wong. Within the reflective circle, Sam saw a face with pale blue eyes grin devilishly at him.

AS Steiner left the bar, he looked sadly at the "S" and "Y" that had almost faded and peeled completely away, leaving only a bar named HELL. He really missed Pattie right then. Carrying the scrap of paper with the smuggling code, Steiner entered the cafeteria and found Tramer already supervising Richards and

Eddie as they finished piling the last of the body-armor suits onto a cart. Steiner stepped over to the weapons officer. The blue orb glistened as it focused on him.

"Have you heard any rumors of a mutiny running through the crew?" Steiner whispered.

"I have," Tramer answered softly.

"Do you believe them?"

"Most rumors have their basis in fact. They surfaced shortly after Quinn's arrival and have been increasing the closer we get to the border."

"Since we left Earthstation, you have not caught him speaking to anyone, but perhaps someone is communicating to him." Steiner handed the note to Tramer. "It's some of smuggler code. I've seen it before a few years back. Pirates used script like this."

Richards and Eddie wheeled the loaded cart of suits toward the lower level. Tramer and Steiner followed, just out of earshot of the security officers.

"For the sake of argument, let's say Quinn is behind the rumors," Steiner said. "What if someone is helping him? Maybe he even wants us to suspect him in order to remove any suspicion from someone else. Maybe you've spent so much time watching him that you've neglected the rest of the crew?"

Tramer remained silent for several strides. "I will increase my surveillance."

"Good."

Tramer halted as if he sensed something. The sensor orb narrowed into a fine ray that shot ahead into the corridor then returned to normal. The pale face turned toward Steiner. "Please return to the command center. I can secure the suits."

"Why?" Steiner asked. "What's wrong?"

"Captain," Richards shouted from ahead, "we've found a murdered crewman down here." The security chief rushed toward a fallen figure in the distance.

"You will not want to see this," Tramer's voice rumbled.

"Why? Do you recognize the victim? Who is it?"

Tramer met his gaze. "The teenager."

"Sam?" Steiner mumbled. Without another word, he sprinted ahead, then stumbled to a halt when he saw the puddle of blood surrounding the body. When Richards turned the head over, Steiner saw Sam's face, the eyes staring out into nothing, just like McKillip's. Steiner's hands trembled as he approached the boy. A wave of nausea swept through him. Leaning his body against the bulkhead, he fought to keep himself from vomiting.

"It looks like his chest was ripped open with a utility laser cutter," Richards said.

Steiner looked at the mutilated corpse with two slash wounds across the chest but couldn't believe it was Sam he was looking at.

"Are you all right, Captain?" Richards asked.

Steiner composed himself, reining his emotions in. There would be time later to grieve for his friend.

"It looks like he tried to write something here," Eddie said, lifting one of the boy's arms from the pool of blood.

Steiner bent over for a closer look. Scribbled in the red ooze was the letter "Q."

Steiner whisked his comlink off his belt. "Hulsey, have you seen Travis Quinn?"

"He entered the bar a few minutes ago," the security officer answered.

Steiner glanced up at Tramer standing motionless in the background. The weapons officer had been right all along. This ship could never operate under military regulations. The only deterrent for convicts was death. Steiner spun around and stormed down the corridor, his common sense sinking into a sea of rage. He remembered his helplessness when he saw the fuel from Mary's shuttle splash onto the launchpad. He could still feel McKillip dying in his arms and being powerless to save him. He would take action this time. Sam would be avenged.

Hulsey shielded the entrance to the bar. When he saw Steiner approach, the small man stepped aside.

Steiner burst into the smoky room, his hand resting on his holster. All voices ceased as the crew stared at him. His gaze zeroed in on Quinn, sitting on a stool at the counter. Steiner's muscles tensed as he traversed the maze of tables.

Bricket approached from the other side of the counter. "Captain?"

Steiner barely heard the bartender. His senses blocked out everything around him except his prey. His fingers clenched the handle of his pistol as he halted directly next to Quinn.

"A young man was killed just now on the lower level," Steiner said. Out of the corner of his vision, he saw Mason swivel around on his barstool, his mouth dropping open. Steiner kept his gaze fixed on Quinn. "He was slashed open with a laser cutter."

Quinn sipped from his mug casually. "What does this have to do with me?"

"Before he died, he wrote the initials of his killer in his own blood."

Quinn's icy gaze met Steiner's. The corners of his lips curled. "I should have aimed for his heart."

Steiner drew his AT-7. "You killed my friend."

With astonishing speed, Quinn snatched the pistol from Steiner's hand and brought the muzzle to bear on him.

Steiner's rage turned instantly to shock. The dark pit of the barrel stared at him, promising death.

"Captain, I've waited a long time for this moment," Quinn said. "I hold in my hands the power to take your life just as I did the boy's." His hand twirled the gun, then slammed it onto the countertop between Steiner and himself. "But, I'm feeling generous. I'll give you another chance. Try to take up your weapon."

Some of the patrons gasped.

Steiner stared at the AT-7 just inches away. To save his image in front of the crew, he had to try. In his mind, he imaged snatching up the pistol, hearing the abrupt blast of energy, the crackle of Quinn's cartilage, seeing the spray of his blood, feeling the victory. He focused on the handle of the gun and—

"Captain," a familiar voice woke Steiner from his madness. He saw Tramer poised at the entrance to the bar. Somewhere beneath the shell of the weapons officer, he could see his old friend Maxwell, who had lost his family, his career, and his body. The air chilled Steiner's sweat-drenched skin. He couldn't muster enough saliva to moisten his parched throat.

Quinn obviously knew that Tramer could rip him limb from limb if he wanted to. "Too bad our little game was interrupted," Quinn said. "We'll play again sometime."

Tramer marched up to Quinn and held out his metallic hand as if demanding something. With his gaze riveted to Steiner, Quinn lifted his uniform shirt, pulled out a laser cutter stuffed under his belt, and gave it to the weapons officer.

Tramer motioned to Benjamin Richards, who stood outside the door. The security chief came forward and shackled Quinn's wrists.

"Which cell do you want him in, Captain?" Tramer asked.

Steiner realized Tramer was trying to repair his shattered image in front of the crew by asking such an unimportant question.

"Cell two."

Tramer saluted, then nodded to Richards, who led away the prisoner.

Steiner could feel the crew members' stares boring into him as he picked up his AT-7 from off the countertop and marched out of the bar. The weapons officer followed in formation a step behind.

When they reached the brig, Richards put Quinn into cell two, then sealed the door. A red light flashed, indicating the locking mechanism had engaged. Richards returned to the murder scene to help Eddie move the body. Steiner and Tramer stood alone in the brig, staring into the cell.

"It was not wise for you to challenge Quinn alone," Tramer said at last. "You have damaged your image."

"Why didn't he just kill me when he had the chance?" Steiner wondered aloud.

"He needed to display his superiority over you in front of the crew. If I hadn't intervened, he would have shot you when you reached for your gun."

Within the cell's window, Quinn's icy stare locked onto Steiner. "I want to kill him now," Steiner said.

"That would not be wise," Tramer replied. "Since he has robbed you of your respect, he must be publicly executed in front of the crew as an example."

"I see what you mean. Schedule a hanging for tomorrow, after a short funeral for Sam."

Tramer nodded.

Steiner could have sworn he saw Quinn grin at him.

CHAPTER

21

STEINER stood over the metal casket, staring down at his young friend's body. The boy's face looked peaceful. It almost seemed like he might awake from a deep sleep at any moment.

Most of the engineers were present for the funeral, as well as Mason, Bricket, and a few other select crew members who had befriended the boy during the voyage. Steiner had taken the *Marauder* out of starspeed so that they could jettison the body into space through the port-side air lock.

A red light glowed from the security camera above. Steiner had invited Tramer to join them, but the weapons officer wanted to keep up his surveillance on the crew in case someone tried to pick up where Quinn had left off.

Steiner missed Sam. In prison, the boy had boosted him out of his depression, giving him someone to care about when everyone else had been stolen from him. How had Steiner repaid his devotion? By letting him die?

Maybe the blame rested on Steiner for allowing Sam to board the P.A.V. in the first place. He should have left him back at the Atwood Penitentiary. At the time, he had reasoned that he was saving Sam from being taken advantage of by Big Al, but he'd had an ulterior motive. He had brought Sam along because he had needed a friend. His selfishness had taken priority over the boy's safety and had stained his hands with innocent blood.

When Spider and J.R. began to sing "Amazing Grace," Steiner's eyes started to burn.

MAXWELL watched the funeral through one of the security monitors while he sped through the rest of the ship's cameras. He hadn't known Sam personally. Steiner seemed to be taking the loss of Sam rather hard. Long ago, Maxwell had resolved never to become that attached to anyone again. It hurt too much.

His sensors detected Simmons approaching from behind. The navigator loved to watch him view the screens, then gossip to other people about whom Maxwell had monitored and when.

In the midst of one of his sweeps, Maxwell detected movement in the reactor chamber. When he zoomed the image in, he saw Boon Wong working near the backup cooling generator. He zoomed in closer, trying to determine what the computer maintenance man was doing down there. Then he saw Boon rummage through a bag and extract an explosive pack—

A sharp prick stung the exposed flesh on the back of Maxwell's neck. His sensors registered a syringe in Simmons's hand.

Infuriated, Maxwell spun around, grabbed the small man by the collar, and lifted him into the air. "What have you done?"

Simmons turned white and stammered something unintelligible.

Maxwell's vision blurred. Control of his autonomic functions slipped away from him. Dropping the navigator to the floor, he attempted to steady himself against the security console. His metallic fingers scratched its surface for a handhold but found none. In desperation, he reached out to activate the ship's alarm, but his hand missed the keypad. He collapsed to the deck of the command center with a heavy thud.

As he drifted out of consciousness, he scolded himself for lowering his guard and allowing this to happen. Simmons smiled down at him, then everything went dark.

SPIDER and J.R.'s duet of the ancient hymn stirred Steiner's soul, giving him hope that maybe the boy had gone to a better place.

All eyes turned to him, waiting for the eulogy.

He took a deep breath. "We have all assembled here to honor our friend, who has passed on." A lump formed in his throat. "His loyalty to those he called his friends was unsurpassed. Regardless of his age, Sam was more a man than most, and I've come here to honor him for it."

Amens arose from a few of the engineers.

Kneeling, Steiner touched Sam's face with his fingers.

Thank you, amigo.

TRAVIS Quinn sat motionless on the cot inside the detention cell. His takeover of the ship was nearly complete. The excitement of the approaching moment built within him.

A faint tapping came from the small window in the door. Boon's face peered through the heavy glass. His hands trembling with exhilaration, Travis stood up from the cot and mouthed the code to the cyberneticist. Boon disappeared from view, and three seconds later, the barrier moved aside.

Stepping out of the cell, Travis shook Boon's hand. "I've been expecting you. Are the charges in place?"

Reaching inside his tunic, Boon produced a tiny transmitter.

"Well then, let's start a mutiny," Travis said.

AFTER closing the coffin, Steiner, Mason, Spider, and J.R. lifted it and placed it inside the open air-lock chamber. Glancing over at Mason, Steiner saw a fiery anger burning in his eyes. Before exiting, the pilot muttered a few words to Sam. Steiner couldn't make out everything he had said, but he definitely heard the word "revenge."

Steiner closed the inner hatch, sealing the casket inside.

The video monitor at the side of the door displayed the metal box.

"And now, we commit the body of our dear friend Sam Perez to the sanctuary of the heavens," Steiner said, then entered the code that opened the outer hatch. The coffin vanished into the eternal abyss of space, gone forever.

"Yea, though I walk through the valley of the shadow of death, I will fear no evil: For thou art with me," Daniels said. "Thy rod and thy staff, they comfort me."

Everyone had bowed his head, except for Steiner. Someone had quoted something like that at Mary's funeral, too, as if God would comfort them in their loss. Lies. God had stolen another friend away, just as he had Mary and Suzanne.

The floor vibrated, causing the air in Steiner's lungs to freeze.

"We can't be under attack, can we?" Mason asked.

"No, that couldn't have been an energy blast from another ship," Daniels answered. "Something on board exploded."

"It must've come from the engine room," J.R. shouted.

"Code Red," Daniels said. All the engineers raced down the corridor.

Steiner grabbed his comlink. "Tramer, what happened? What exploded?"

The comlink remained quiet. The active light still glowed on the overhead camera.

Steiner waved his arms in front of the lens. "Tramer, are you there?"

Again, no response.

The weapons officer should have answered already.

Drawing his weapon, Steiner sprinted toward the command center.

DANIELS reached the control cubicle first. Crimson lights flashed. The fire alarm blared throughout the area. Black smoke billowed from the depths of the reactor chamber. Mike, the attendant inside the cubicle, ran out to meet him.

"It's the backup cooling generator," he stammered. "It exploded for no reason."

"Shut down all the drive systems until we have it contained," Daniels instructed.

Mike sprinted back to his post and carried out the instructions. The exterior lights on the reactors went dark, and the steady drone died out.

Reddish orange bursts continued to flash through the growing haze at the opposite end of the chamber. At any cost, they had to keep the blaze from spreading. As a last resort, they could seal off the massive room and blow the hatch, but it would take more than a day to repressurize it and get the reactors going again. If they could, they had to try to contain it first.

As if reading Daniels's mind, J.R., Charles, Fred, and Andrew opened the fire-equipment cabinet, pulled out the heat-resistant suits, and started to climb into them. Spider took one of the outfits, but just stared at it, making no move to put it on.

"We need all the help we can out there," Daniels said. "Are you up to it?"

Spider gave a weak smile. "I'll be fine."

As he slipped into his own protective gear, Daniels watched Spider dress. He knew the best remedy for the man's fears was to face them again.

After all six of them had suited up, and their extinguishers had been strapped on, they charged out into the engine chamber. The tanks of chemicals strapped to their backs bounced as they sprinted down the center aisle between two of the long cylindrical reactors. Black smoke swirled around the components. When they reached the site, they found flames engulfing the backup cooling generator and threatening to spread to the neighboring units. J.R. fought them back so they wouldn't do so. The rest of the staff took the blaze straight on.

Daniels couldn't figure out what could have caused it. A system that rarely got used shouldn't explode like that. It couldn't have happened by negligence. Someone must have sabotaged it.

A shiver went down his back. Almost as if warned by a sixth sense, he spun around and saw a flash of light inside the control cubicle. He saw the attendant stationed there slump to the ground. Another figure moved into the cubicle.

"Mike, do you read?" Daniels called into his headset.

No one responded.

A distant motor whined. Daniels squinted his eyes and saw the pressure door at the front entrance coming down.

"Dear God," he whispered.

The fire had been the bait for a trap.

GUN in hand, Steiner raced to the top of steps and into the command center. It was deserted. Where could Tramer have—?

"Drop your weapon, Captain," Mack Palmer said from somewhere.

Steiner froze, his eyes searching for the hidden man.

"Do it now," Palmer shouted.

The pilot knelt behind the helm station with an AT-7 pistol muzzle raised over its edge.

Steiner dropped his gun to the floor and slid it across the deck with his foot.

Palmer stood up. "Welcome, Captain—to the end of your short life."

"STOP!" Daniels shouted to the other engineers, and pointed to the door. Everyone ceased fighting the flames and stared in horror.

"Why are they locking us in?" Spider shrieked.

"They must be planning to blow the hatch," J.R. said.

"No, no, I don't want to die," Spider shouted.

Daniels realized they still had a chance to escape. "Everyone to the church! Hurry!"

Shedding their extinguishers, the engineers raced to the ladder that led up into the bulkhead above and began to scramble up it. Daniels brought up the rear, directly behind the whimpering Spider. Rung by rung, Daniels climbed toward safety. A quick glance back at the pressure door found the barrier finishing its trek to the bottom. As soon as the appropriate keystrokes were entered, they would all instantly be sucked into space.

"Put on your oxygen masks," Daniels ordered the others. One by one, they all activated the backup air supplies built into their fire suits.

An explosion shook the ladder. Daniels's left boot slipped from one of the rungs. He dangled, held up only by his hands, until he could get his footing back. Spider screamed wildly. Looking over his shoulder, Daniels saw that the exterior hatch was still intact. The noise had been caused by the backup cooling generator bursting into a fierce inferno.

Spider started gasping in short breaths, his fists frozen tight to the rungs of the ladder.

"Spider, it was the generator, not the hatch," Daniels shouted. "Keep going."

The man shook his head. "I can't."

"If you don't, we're both going to die."

Spider remained still for several heartbeats, then raced up the rungs in a frenzy, catching up with the other engineers in seconds. The abrupt change in behavior stunned Daniels. With all his might, he followed behind him up into the dark tube cut in the bulkhead.

If only they had a moment longer.

The engineers in the lead had already reached the church and begun dragging the others up into the air lock.

Please God, Daniels prayed. *I don't care about myself, but save my men.*

The other engineers lifted Spider out, then their hands reached down and grabbed Daniels. Immediately, he was drawn upward into the lighted chamber. He fell to the floor amidst his rescuers, and they dragged him clear of the hatch.

An earsplitting crack came from below followed by an explosive rush of escaping air. The sheer force lifted them from their feet. The instant it began, it ended. Daniels landed a few feet away, the other engineers falling on top of him. A sharp hiss sounded, and his ears popped. Pushing a boot out of his face, Daniels rose out of the sprawled heap.

Spider lay on top of the closed hatch, shuddering uncontrollably.

WITH his AT-7 muzzle aimed at Steiner, Palmer reached down and retrieved the other pistol and shoved it under his belt. "You can come out now, Simmons. He's disarmed."

The small man's head popped up from inside the stairwell that led to the navigation chamber. His eyes darted about uncertainly, then he came up the rest of the steps.

Palmer moved closer to Steiner, halting within an arm's reach. "Give me your comlink."

With his gaze fixed on the pilot's weapon, Steiner slowly disconnected the device from his belt and handed it over. Palmer threw it to the ground, shattering it.

"We can't have you calling for help," he said with a smirk. "Can we?"

Keeping his temper under tight control, Steiner glared at him.

"I'll inform Travis that we succeeded," Simmons said, moving to the communication station.

Steiner's heart rate jumped. Travis Quinn? How could he be involved in this? He had been locked up in a detention cell.

The navigator pressed a keypad on the console. "Engine room, this is the command center."

"Do you have the captain?" Quinn's voice asked.

Shivers raked through Steiner's bones. How had he gotten free?

"We have him," Simmons answered.

"Good. Our allies have all joined us on the lower level. Daniels and his flock are already dead."

Steiner gasped. His shock melted into rage.

"Bring the captain down here," Quinn said. "We need him to serve as an example to the rest of the crew."

"We're on our way," the navigator responded, then closed the channel and turned to Palmer. "Mack, give me the captain's pistol. I want to be armed when we escort him down."

"Not a chance," Palmer replied. "I wouldn't trust you with it. You might accidentally shoot me."

Simmons's face flushed. "I'm the one who introduced you to Boon. You wouldn't be a part of this if it hadn't been for me. Give me the captain's pistol."

"No."

Without warning, Simmons grabbed the gun from under Palmer's belt and yanked it out. Palmer turned fiery red as he tried to seize it back. In that brief instant, Steiner made his move.

A swift kick sent the AT-7 flying from Palmer's hand. It landed under the helm station. Cursing, the pilot dove after it.

Steiner leapt on top of Simmons and both of them went tumbling down into the stairwell. As they rolled over one another, Steiner's left hand closed around his stolen pistol. His head burst into pain as it hit the edge of a step. His fingers lost hold of the gun. He tumbled into a heap at the bottom of the stairs, with Simmons on top of him.

Bright flashes exploded into the wall above them, showering down burning embers.

Simmons scrambled over Steiner, desperately fleeing into the interior of the room.

Steiner threw himself deeper inside the chamber, barely avoiding another onslaught of searing beams blazing down the stairwell.

Simmons cowered in the far corner, his shaking hands trying to steady the pistol. Steiner pounced on the navigator and tried to pry the AT-7 from his grasp.

Footsteps sounded from the stairwell.

Palmer raced into the chamber, firing blindly. Steiner dropped to the floor as bolts scorched the wall above him. He saw Palmer's pistol level—

A bolt flashed out of Steiner's peripheral vision and struck Palmer's chest. The pilot fell back, convulsed, then went perfectly still.

Simmons whimpered, holding the smoking AT-7. Steiner used the navigator's hesitation to rip the gun from his grasp.

"What are you going to do with me?" Simmons whined.

Steiner aimed the muzzle at the navigator's head and paused, watching the beads of sweat building up on the other's face.

"Please don't kill me," Simmons sobbed. "I can help you."

"You can bet on it." Steiner brought the handle of the gun down sharply against the man's head, knocking him out cold.

Steiner jumped over Palmer's body and raced up the stairwell. Sliding into his command chair, he sealed off all the pressure doors on the lower level. If he had been too late to stop a mutiny, perhaps he could contain it.

It wasn't long before Quinn's voice came back over the intercom. "Palmer, Simmons, what happened up there?"

Steiner activated the channel. "Make a good guess."

"My respect for you has increased, Captain. Maybe you aren't as weak as I first thought. To the death then." The channel went silent.

CHAPTER

22

DEATH looked more like a kaleidoscope of images from life. Faces of family and friends passed by in endless parades. The pressures of existence had faded into unwanted memories. Only a warm sensation remained, whispering to embrace it.

Jacob Steiner strode out of a cloud of swirling mist, dressed in a P.A.V. uniform. He stood at attention and saluted. Behind him, just out of focus, many shadowy figures hunched, like stalking predators.

Look out behind you!

He didn't seem to hear.

Ralph Jamison materialized out of the haze in the background, snuck up behind Jacob Steiner, and pulled out a gleaming knife.

Jake!

Jamison thrust the blade into Steiner.

No!

Suzanne's eyes popped open. The overwhelming glare of the outside world stung them shut again. Knowing only that Jake needed her help, she sat up from where she lay and saw a blurry form looking down at her.

"Miss Riggs?" a female voice gasped.

Blinking to orient her vision, Suzanne focused on a strange woman standing above her, dressed in a white uniform. Nausea swept through her. Her head fell back onto a soft pillow.

The woman leaned over, a smile widening across her face. "Welcome back from the dead. We were afraid that you might never awaken from your coma."

"Where am I?" she asked, not recognizing her own raspy voice.

"Military Intelligence has transferred you to a secure location for your protection. Do you remember anything before you lost consciousness?"

Suzanne searched through the dense fog that shrouded her memory. She recalled a reception with many inquisitive guests. A burglar in her office. A computer transmission. A statue—

A barely audible cry escaped her lips. Her hands came up to her chest, groping for the object that should have been embedded there. Looking beneath her gown, she found that her skin showed no signs of ever being damaged.

The female doctor sat at the end of the bed. "We did a nice job of reconstruction, don't you think?"

"How long have I been unconscious?"

"Almost two weeks."

Suzanne caught her breath. Had she actually been asleep that long?

The doctor leaned forward, and whispered, "Military Intelligence suspected your life might still be in jeopardy so they released a false report of your death. Do you know who attacked—?"

Suzanne grabbed the woman's hand. "Tell them that Jacob Steiner is in danger."

"THIS is the U.S.S. *Marauder* to any vessel in the area, please respond," Steiner repeated into the microphone for the sixth time, his voice becoming despondent. Only static answered him.

Simmons must have sabotaged the entire communication grid to prevent him from calling for help. The intercom system was out, too, except for the channel to the engine room—to Quinn. Steiner's comlink lay shattered on the deck beyond repair. Without any form of communication, he couldn't contact any of his security officers. He didn't even know if they were still loyal to him.

He glanced over at the two blackened holes blasted through the security station. Without the monitors, he had no idea how many people he was up against.

A groan rose from the command chair, where Simmons had been tied up. The navigator opened his eyes. He struggled against the computer wires that strapped him to the chair.

"Good morning, Mr. Simmons," Steiner said, his tone threatening.

The navigator stiffened. "What are you going to do to me?"

"If you answer my questions truthfully, I'll let you live." Steiner yanked him by his collar. "After all, you saved my life earlier."

A frown creased Simmons's lips.

Steiner held up the AT-7 in front of the man's eyes. "Where did this weapon come from?"

"Boon gave it to Mack."

"Boon Wong, the computer specialist?"

Simmons nodded. "Yes, he's Travis Quinn's partner."

Frustrated, Steiner slammed his fist into the armrest of the chair, barely missing his captive's arm. He had been right in suspecting someone else.

"Where did he get the pistol? Steiner asked.

"The armory."

Steiner pressed the muzzle into the navigator's right nostril. "You're lying. Only I have access to the armory."

"That's what I was told," Simmons whimpered. "I don't know any more."

"Was it you who damaged the communication grid?"

"Boon told me to do it."

"Was there anything else he instructed you to do?"

"To steal the ship's Orders disk."

"Why? What did he want that for?"

"I don't know."

Steiner thrust him against the back of the chair and paced around him. "Surely you must be aware that if their mutiny had succeeded, the U.S.S. would have destroyed this vessel. Why would you invite death?"

"Travis Quinn is taking us to the Centri System, where we could be free."

Steiner glowered down at him. "Even if you made it to the outlaw sanctuary, you would have been pursued by bounty hunters."

"Not if Boon removed our tracers," Simmons answered.

"How could he do that?"

"He's a cyberneticist."

The hair on the back of Steiner's neck rose as he realized the implications of what he'd just heard.

"Where's Tramer?" he shouted.

MAXWELL opened his human eye and waited a few seconds for it to focus. He found himself staring up at a ceiling. Where was he? What had happened to him?

He tried to access his digital memory to find out how long he had been unconscious, but it didn't seem to be functioning. It had never failed to work before. He attempted to move his head, yet it remained motionless. None of his appendages responded to his will.

His proximity sensors gave him a picture of his surroundings. He was lying on a table within a closed room, perhaps one of the engineers' quarters on the lower level.

Maxwell vaguely remembered Simmons sneaking up behind him and injecting him with some kind of drug. Since it would have taken several men to carry his heavy metallic body here, a sizable mutiny must be in progress.

The door to the chamber whined open. Footsteps approached. A man—Boon Wong—leaned over into his face.

"You're awake," Wong said. "Wonderful. We can begin."

"Begin what?" Maxwell snapped. "What have you done to me?"

Wong smirked. "I've made you better than you were before."

"How? I cannot move."

"You move when I tell you to," the oversized man answered, seating himself at a table at the side of the bed. "Behold."

A couple of computer tones chimed, then Maxwell's right

arm rose into the air. Maxwell couldn't bring it back down. Another series of chirps commanded his mechanical body to sit upright.

"How have you done this?" Maxwell shouted.

"I've routed all your functions into this command box," Wong answered.

Wong instructed Maxwell's head to turn until he could see the small mobile console that held his body hostage. Wong tilted it up on its side, showing it off.

"It was quite easy to set up," the man boasted. "I installed a bypassing receiver next to your central processing unit that overrides—"

"Release me at once, or I'll destroy you," Maxwell demanded.

Wong pressed some keypads on the box. "You're in no position to be threatening me."

Maxwell's hand lifted up to his face, stopping inches from his human eye. The fingers opened and closed like the teeth of a claw, ready to dig into his flesh and brain.

The door slid aside. Maxwell couldn't believe who he saw enter the room. Travis Quinn.

"What are you doing, Boon?" Quinn scolded. "You may damage our prize."

Maxwell's arm returned to his side.

Quinn stopped a few feet away. A confident smile twisted through his hard features. No doubt he controlled whatever was happening on the ship. For the first time in his life since his transformation, Maxwell felt truly afraid.

"So we meet again, Cyborg. I've waited a long time for this moment. I'm enjoying it immensely."

"Boon Wong," Maxwell said. "You are aiding a Separatist agent. After you have used up your usefulness to him, he will eliminate you."

Wong chuckled softly.

"A waste of time, Cyborg," Quinn answered. "He's been with me from the beginning."

Anger built up inside Maxwell for his failure to see what should have been so obvious. "So you are both spies," he said. "Why would you be here on this ship now? Barker has already been eliminated."

Quinn folded his arms and scowled. "I've always suspected that you were the one who murdered Joseph."

"After I free myself, I will destroy you, too."

Quinn tilted his head. "I've already made precautions for that event if it should occur. See this?" He displayed a miniature device secured to his wrist. "Boon has planted an explosive charge right behind your head. All I have to do is activate this detonator, and you die instantly."

"Why wait then?" Maxwell screamed. "If it's revenge you want, take it now."

A devilish grin cracked Quinn's lips. "I wouldn't dream of depriving you of the glorious end I have planned for you. I need you to take over the ship for us."

Wong typed on the mobile console. Maxwell's body stood up from the table, and his breastplate dropped open, revealing the twin guns.

Maxwell screamed in rage at his helplessness.

"HOW many men are behind the door?" Richards asked.

Steiner scanned through the sealed entryway to the engine room with his tracker. "Eight."

After leaving the command center, he had found Benjamin and his team inside the bar, trying to figure out what was happening. He was thankful none of the security team had joined Quinn's mutiny. As a precaution, he had Eddie round up all the crew members who were not locked on the lower levels, and had them taken to the bar while the other two security officers helped him squelch the mutiny attempt.

"We'll need to find another way down onto the lower level and surprise the renegades," Steiner said.

"I agree," Richards said. "Besides this central passageway, the only other route to the lower level was damaged in the battle with *Conqueror.*"

"What if we used the maintenance shafts at the top of the ship to sneak into the generating station," Hulsey said. "From there, we could climb down onto the lower level."

Steiner had forgotten all about the maintenance shafts. Only Daniels and J.R. ever went in them. Maybe Quinn didn't even know they existed.

"How did you know about the route?" Steiner asked.

"I studied the entire layout of the vessel before coming on board," Hulsey answered with a slight smile. "If I'm going to guard it, I need to know everything I can about it."

"That you do," Steiner said. "Let's go up there and check it out."

"No," Richards snapped. "In order to get down onto the lower level from up there, we'd have to use the maintenance stairway."

"Yeah," Hulsey replied. "What's the problem?"

Richards glared at him. "The stairway is a hundred feet high. If we try to traverse it, we'll be vulnerable to enemy fire."

Steiner held up his tracker. "With this I can determine where each one of the mutineers is. If we act fast, we'll have them under submission before they can fire a shot."

Richards shook his head. "Too many things can go wrong with your plan."

"Don't worry, Ben." Hulsey slapped him on the back. "We can do this."

Richards mumbled to himself.

Steiner led them to the rear of the second level. After he opened the entrance to the maintenance shafts, they crawled through the tight tunnels, past three junctions, until they reached a small room, just tall enough to stand up in. A sealed pressure hatch stood on the far wall.

Steiner hastened to the control panel embedded inside the frame of the doorway and typed in a password. The barrier slid aside, revealing a seven-foot-high, narrow-walled tunnel bathed in bright red lights. Thick cables lined the sides, stretching a hundred feet to a generating station at the opposite end.

"No one is up here, except for us," Steiner said, glancing down at the screen of his tracker.

"I'd feel better if more than one of us were armed," Richards said.

Steiner still had Palmer's gun under his belt. Since the security chief hadn't joined the mutiny, Steiner decided to trust him with the extra AT-7.

With both security officers trailing behind him, Steiner started through the crimson-colored accessway. The walls were little more than three feet apart. The scent of charged air became more pronounced with each step. Flashes of electricity lit the other end of the passageway. Crackles of thunder grew louder.

Inside the generating station, lightning flared among six rows of conductor posts, creating a strobe effect throughout the vast room. The rumbles from the collapsing air pockets ran through the deck plates.

The tracker's display flickered from the magnetic interference. Then Steiner saw them. Six tracer implants registered deep inside the reactor chamber. Since they were perfectly motionless, they must be the bodies of Daniels and his engineers. Steiner forced his sorrow from returning and continued to their goal.

Inching toward the maintenance stairway, Richards searched around the generators with the muzzle of his AT-7.

"No mutineers are anywhere around," Steiner assured him.

"Considering all this electrical interference, I don't trust what that device says," Richards said.

Steiner stepped out onto the balcony that overlooked the top of the stairway. A hundred feet below, the chamber lay empty. No sentries had been posted in this section at all.

Richards locked eyes with Steiner. "If we get caught during our descent, we're all dead," he whispered.

"Would you prefer to stay here until we're done?" Steiner asked.

Richards glanced at Hulsey, then shook his head. "If we must do this, we'll do it together. I'll go first." He started down the steps, keeping his AT-7 trained on the chamber below.

Steiner followed right on his heels, keeping his gaze riveted to the tracker. Hulsey brought up the rear.

When they neared the bottom, Richards climbed over the railing and jumped the remaining ten feet to the floor. He aimed his pistol down the corridor leading to the engine room, waiting until Steiner and Hulsey reached the ground.

Richards handed his gun to Hulsey. "Cover me. I'm going to prepare for the worst."

Richards went under the stairway, where large storage bins had been stacked, and started pushing one out toward the base of the steps. Steiner thought the man was overreacting but decided to help him anyway. Together, they created a small blockade.

When they had finished, Hulsey led them along the corridor leading toward the control cubicle for the engine room. Several tense minutes passed before they arrived at the end of the passageway, where it emptied into the main junction.

People conversed with each another just around the bend to the left. On the right, shadows from a gathering of men danced upon the sealed door to the reactor chamber. They seemed to be working on something.

A distinct hum grew, followed by cheers. Steiner recognized the sound of a laser cannon charging up to fire. How could that be?

Hulsey snuck up to the edge of the corner and peered around the side. "What the hell?" he mouthed.

Steiner hurried to the spot and stole a glimpse. Rex, Bo, Midas, and Sanchez had indeed assembled a laser cannon and were preparing to discharge it. Boon Wong paced around them with an assault rifle slung across his shoulders. The most startling sight was that of Tramer standing perfectly still against a far wall, his human eye fixed directly on Steiner.

His pulse pounding, Steiner drew himself away from the edge and let Richards survey the scene.

The shrill blast of a laser beam pierced the air.

"They're trying to cut through Pressure Door C-3," Richards announced loud enough to be heard over the noise. "Do they have access to the armory?"

Steiner shook his head wordlessly.

"Why isn't Tramer doing anything?" Hulsey asked. "Has he joined them?"

"No," Steiner replied. "He knows we're here but hasn't informed the others."

"Then why doesn't he stop them?"

"Maybe he can't. Simmons also claimed that Boon Wong was a cyberneticist. Perhaps he's been rendered inoperative."

Richards sighed. "If that's true, Captain, we have no other choice but to retreat. Pistols are no match for assault weapons."

"Where will we go?" Steiner argued. "They'll have cut through the pressure door within ten minutes."

"But it would be suci—"

The laser beam abruptly ceased its cry. Richards had cut himself short, but not in time to keep his voice from echoing through the deathly silence.

"It failed again," an irritated voice said.

"Quiet," Wong whispered harshly. "I heard something."

Muttering a curse under his breath, Richards gave a hand signal to Hulsey, then sprinted out from behind the corner. Hulsey rushed after him, discharging his gun into the air. The startled group of men fled toward the armory, calling for Quinn and the other mutineers. Wong raised his rifle, but Richards was on top of him before he could fire. They both tumbled to the ground. A second later, the chief came up with the assault weapon.

"Richards," Tramer shouted from his stationary position. "Disable the cannon—quickly."

Instantly, the chief showered the device in bolts, and it fell from its mount, sparking and sputtering.

Vengeful cries rose from the side passageways, accented by energy blasts.

"Flee at once." Tramer's voice overpowered all the other noise. "They have access to the armory."

Steiner couldn't understand how that could be possible, but considering the number of weapons the mutineers possessed, he wasn't about to doubt it.

"What about you?" Steiner shouted at the weapons officer.

"Go. You cannot help me."

A howl reverberated through the metallic halls.

Richards grabbed Steiner by the shoulder. "Captain, he's right. We must leave."

With a final glance at Tramer, Steiner raced off in the direction of the stairway, with Hulsey and Richards close behind. What had they done to Tramer? Deactivated him?

The cries behind them grew louder and more frenzied.

Richards knelt behind the barrier of storage bins and took aim with his rifle. "Both of you, get up to the generating station as fast as you can. I'll cover you."

When Steiner raced up the steps behind Hulsey, he caught

a glimpse of an army coming around the corner behind which they had been hiding earlier. Richards fired his assault rifle, chasing the mob back. An instant later, bolts slashed into the bins.

Hulsey stopped a third of the way up the stairs and gave a loud whistle.

Richards glanced up from behind his shelter, hesitated for a second, then tossed up his rifle. Hulsey caught it effortlessly and brought it to bear on the mutineers. Dodging enemy energy blasts, Richards sprinted up the stairs.

Steiner paused halfway up to the generating station, furious at himself for allowing the security officers to face all the danger alone.

"Run, Captain," Richards shouted as he bounded past Hulsey.

Steiner dashed up the remaining distance to safety, hearing the intense fight behind him. He looked back in time to see Richards three-fourths of the way up, whistling for Hulsey to throw up the rifle.

A streak of movement at the bottom of the stairway caught Steiner's attention. A missile dug into the barrier of storage bins. With a brilliant flash, the shelter exploded into burning embers. The stairway jolted violently. Hulsey lost his balance and dropped his assault rifle over the railing into the smoke-filled chamber below. The weapon's impact resounded throughout the area.

Sharp cries of victory rose through the haze, followed by the rush of many footfalls.

Hulsey raced up the steps. Richards ran five feet ahead of him, constantly glancing back to make sure his friend stayed with him.

Steiner knew the two men would never make it to the top in time. Drawing his AT-7, he fired blindly through the gray cloud below, hoping to slow the mutineers' approach. A rifle muzzle rose from out of the smoke. Steiner pelted it with bolts before it could come alive. Steiner's hopes climbed when he saw that the two security officers had almost reached the top.

A shrill howl broke out from below, then a fierce onslaught of bolts rained up on them. Richards pulled Hulsey up off the stairs, just as one of the searing beams cut into his friend's back. The man shrieked, falling to the deck of the balcony. Richards hauled him out of range and began examining the wound. The overpowering smell of burnt flesh stung Steiner's nose.

"How is he?" he asked.

Richards glared up at him. "We have to get him out of here—fast."

"Go then," Steiner said. "I'll make a stand here."

The chief picked up his barely conscious friend and dragged him toward the electrical accessway.

Steiner inched up to the edge of the balcony, where bolts from below ate away at the metal railing. The deck plates at the top of the stairway vibrated under the force of many men coming up. Steiner raised his gun muzzle over the lip and fired three times into the leader of the group. The dead mutineer toppled back into the rest, knocking them all down the steps.

Steiner ducked as a new eruption of energy blasts from below sought him out. Covering his ears from the deafening noise, he watched as searing bolts sliced through the railing bars, leaving glowing jagged tips behind. With a groan of fatigue, the top half of the metal assembly dropped to the floor just inches away.

Then, as abruptly as the attack had started, it died. Faint voices floated up in the stillness, but nothing else. The mutineers must be up to something, but what? They wouldn't dare launch a grenade for fear of damaging the generating station.

Steiner shuffled the smoldering rail over the edge of the balcony to see if it would draw any fire. Nothing happened. The new silence made him apprehensive about what was to come.

Another vibration ran through the deck plates, this time much stronger. It was followed by a second, a third, a fourth . . . The twisted metal pieces, scattered about the floor, rattled with each tremor. Some of them tumbled over the edge of the balcony.

When Steiner attempted to fire over the brim of the stairway again, he saw Tramer coming up the steps, wearing a facial shield over his head.

"Flee." The weapons officer's voice echoed from beneath the helmet. "I can't stop myself."

Steiner hesitated. "What have they done to—?"

"Quinn is controlling me," Tramer shouted. "He will use me to destroy you. Run for your life—please."

Steiner didn't waste any time in heeding the warning. He scrambled to his feet and sprinted to the narrow accessway. His shoulders scraped against the tight walls as he ran. About halfway through, he caught up with the crimson-lit forms of Richards and Hulsey, moving much too slowly.

"Richards," Steiner shouted. "You must go faster. Tramer is right behind me."

The chief glanced up. "What? I thought he was immobile."

"No, it's far worse than that. Quinn has control over him, his weapons, his mechanical limbs, everything."

Immediately, Richards dragged his friend faster, causing the man to sob and beg to stop. Picking up Hulsey's feet, Steiner helped with their retreat.

AGAINST his will, Maxwell moved toward the narrow opening into which Steiner had retreated. He hoped his shipmates had enough time to escape.

He ignored the terror and fear that built up within him. If he killed them, he couldn't hold himself responsible—not like when he had murdered the two men aboard the *Magellan*.

It's a monster, Mommy, Veronica screamed inside his mind.

Maxwell began to weep.

One day, when your daughter learns that her father is still alive, don't you want her to be proud of you? Steiner had asked him in New England.

Yes, I do, Maxwell pleaded silently, *but it's impossible. I cannot help myself.*

Stepping into the narrow accessway, he detected Steiner and the two security officers near the far end.

His targeting computer locked on. His breastplate dropped open.

Veronica materialized in front of him, her face panic-stricken. Her mouth opened.

"No, Veronica—please don't," Tramer cried out.

His daughter shrieked at him again as the twin guns ignited.

STEINER, Richards, and Hulsey fell in a heap outside the accessway just as a brigade of energy beams filled its interior.

Heaving with exhaustion, Steiner pulled himself up and stumbled toward the control panel inside the frame of the doorway. When he reached for the keypad to seal the passage, a bolt exploded into it. He retracted his singed hand, ignoring the throbbing pain.

With his pistol drawn, Richards flung himself across the opening to the opposite side as flashes of energy licked the air behind him. Darting back and forth from behind the shelter, the chief returned fire at Tramer.

Inhuman screams and pleas for death echoed from the accessway between weapon blasts. Tramer seemed to be in utter torment, begging for relief. Staring down at the AT-7 in his own hand, Steiner realized he couldn't force himself to shoot at his friend.

Hulsey's lifeless gaze caught his eyes, and Steiner turned away. Horror and guilt threatened to tear his sanity away.

"Captain," Richards screamed, "you must help me. Tramer is more than halfway through the passageway."

Steiner crept to the side of the entrance, then hesitated.

"Fire back," the chief bellowed.

"Forgive me, Maxwell," Steiner breathed, and began shooting at his friend.

MAXWELL'S cries for destruction had been in vain. The pistol fire deflected off his armor without any effect.

His twin guns continued blazing the tight passageway, getting closer to their marks each shot. Wong must be getting accustomed to aiming them with the targeting sensors. It wouldn't be long before he made contact with each of the defenders.

One of Richards's bolts detonated against Tramer's left

hip joint. The implant registered damage. If it could be struck again, it might cease to operate.

"Aim for my left leg," Maxwell shouted.

Richards pelted the location. One of the shots exploded near the same spot. The limb froze up.

It worked, Maxwell thought with relief. *I'm crippled.*

His spirits rose until he saw his arms bracing against the walls and moving him forward again. He wailed in frustration.

Richards whipped around the corner and discharged a slew of blasts into Maxwell's right leg, but failed to retreat fast enough. A beam sliced through his side as he dove for cover. The chief fell backward and rolled behind the door-frame before he could be hit again.

By then, Maxwell stood twenty feet away from his desti-nation. Wong couldn't miss at that range. Nineteen, eighteen, seventeen feet.

Steiner held his gun around the corner and fired blindly.

Then the impossible happened.

One of the captain's bolts impacted under the side of the face shield, damaging a component—Boon's bypass center. Maxwell's right arm flinched and dropped to his side. He attempted to move it and found, much to his surprise, that it obeyed him. Instantly, he used it to rip the control wires from his twin guns. The weapons went still. With his liber-ated limb, he gripped an electrical cable lining the ceiling. As long as he held on to it, Wong couldn't move him any farther forward. His left hand reached up and began prying at the other, tearing into its circuitry.

"Captain," Maxwell shouted. "Try to secure the door. I can't hold on much longer."

STEINER inched around the corner of the entryway and examined the charred remains of the control panel. Two black holes had been burned through the set of keypads. The accessway couldn't be closed with the password, but there might be another way.

"Hurry," Richards warned as he bound his bleeding wound with his shirt. "Someone else could open fire in there at any moment."

Using his pistol, Steiner blasted the outer casing off the panel and pulled out the inner circuitry and cords. He had only one chance. If he could fool the door mechanism into thinking there had been a hull breach, it would close automatically.

"Get back, Captain," Richards screamed. "I see movements on the far side."

Steiner gritted his teeth in determination and continued to randomly connect wire tips together.

MAXWELL'S sensors detected Quinn's men behind him, aiming their assault weapons into the accessway. Using his obedient arm, he shoved his body toward the side wall to shield the captain. An onslaught of rifle bolts slashed into his back. They were twice as powerful as pistol fire. His armor wouldn't withstand them for long.

His body fell forward a few inches as his left hand nearly finished clawing through his right arm.

Just then, a blast to the back of his head blacked out his digital systems.

I'm saved.

His CPU had been damaged. Without it, his human body could not survive. Death would finally embrace him.

Before he slipped away from consciousness, he heard the pressure door beginning its descent.

Then he saw Veronica once again. She ran up to him and hugged him tightly.

"I love you, Daddy."

STEINER watched with despair as Tramer's smoking body was ripped from his right arm and fell forward under the brunt of the bolts assailing him. He dropped less than ten feet from the descending pressure door. His smoldering helmet slid off, giving Steiner one last view of his face before the accessway sealed up.

He could have sworn Tramer was smiling.

CHAPTER

23

TRAMER is finally free, Steiner thought as he lay sprawled out on the floor. Thanks to Tramer's sacrifice, the mutineers had been held back long enough for the pressure door to be sealed.

A barely audible whimper broke the stillness. Richards leaned over Hulsey, gripping the body of his dead friend. Abruptly, he faced Steiner, his watering eyes narrowing. A trembling hand rose until the gun it held aimed directly at Steiner.

Steiner remained motionless, expecting a flash of energy to ignite at any second.

The pistol fell from the quivering fingers. Richards buried his head into his dead colleague's chest.

Steiner almost wished that the chief had pulled the trigger. It would have released him from his own tormented existence and reunited him with Mary.

Breathing in rasps, Richards pried himself away from Hulsey and leaned back against the far wall. Wincing, he untied his blood-soaked shirt from around his abdomen, then looked at his wound.

"How bad is it?" Steiner asked.

Richards glanced up, his brow dotted with perspiration. "Not as bad as Larry." His eyes trailed over to Hulsey's body.

"I'm sorry that you lost—" Steiner's guilt wouldn't allow himself to say Hulsey's name.

"Don't be," Richards snapped harshly. His features softened. "He knew the risks."

"If I had known what we were up against, I would have never—" Steiner stopped himself, realizing that Simmons had told him, but he hadn't believed the navigator. His fist released all his frustration into the wall. "How could Quinn have gotten control of the armory?"

"It doesn't matter," Richards replied. "The real question is, what do you plan to do about it?"

Steiner didn't have the faintest notion. He had never planned for this occurrence. Even though there seemed no hope of defeating Quinn, his pride refused to allow himself to concede.

"I'll find a way to stop them," he answered firmly.

"How? None of the crew will stand with you once they learn of the armament the others possess."

"They will if they want to survive. I've still got the security code to keep us from being attacked by U.S.S. forces."

"How do you know Quinn doesn't have that, too? If he knows one password, he may know others."

Steiner opened his mouth to argue but held his tongue. What if Quinn did know it?

"I've heard Quinn has promised to take the crew to the Centri System," Richards said. "I'm beginning to believe he might be able to do it, and so will the others."

A cold feeling settled over Steiner. "What are you saying?"

"Only that if you force any of the men to help you, they will turn against you for freedom." Richards coughed and almost doubled over from his pain. After a couple of labored breaths, he looked up at Steiner, apparently waiting for a response.

"Anyone not wishing to join me can be sealed up inside the bar," Steiner said.

Richards gave a weak nod. "That would be the wisest course of action."

"Can I expect any help from you or Eddie?"

Richards pursed his lips for a moment, then answered. "Eddie wouldn't support a lost cause, and I'm in no condition for fighting, but we'd be willing to help you escape from the ship."

"No," Steiner shouted, his voice rising a notch. It had come out automatically, without any thought. McKillip would have never abandoned the *Valiant* without a fight.

"You can't possibly stand against a fully armed raiding party on your own."

Steiner picked himself up from the floor. "Nevertheless, I will, if I must."

DANIELS looked around at the other five engineers lying about on the floor, trying to conserve oxygen. Fred, Andrew, and Charles were asleep. Spider huddled in one of the corners, shivering. J.R. whispered a prayer. For more than an hour, they had been trapped in the church, their hopes of rescue fading with each passing moment.

Daniels climbed up from the floor and made his way to the rear of the air lock. The oxygen indicator on the wall told him they had an hour left to live.

Daniels wondered if Steiner still controlled the ship. Probably not. They would have been rescued already. That meant they would have to find a way out on their own, but how?

Then he saw the answer on the far bulkhead. He had overlooked the most obvious escape.

"Everyone, get up," he shouted. "It's time to leave."

"What?" J.R. asked. "Where can we go? The reactor chamber is still decompressed."

Daniels opened a storage cabinet, grabbed a space suit from the rack inside, and tossed it to J.R. "Outside," he declared, pointing to the exterior hatch on the opposite side of the chamber.

Spider climbed to his feet. "There's no way back in from out there."

"We'll break in through another air lock."

"That's impossible."

"Maybe not," Daniels said. "During the battle with the

Conqueror, we received many hits to the starboard side. Maybe one of them left some exposed circuitry?"

"That's a long shot, considering all the repairs we underwent," J.R. replied.

"Would you rather sit around here, waiting to die?" Daniels asked.

J.R., Fred, Andrew, and Charles climbed to their feet. Daniels passed out suits to each of them. Without a word, Spider retreated into a corner by himself.

While the rest of the engineers got dressed, Daniels knelt next to Spider. "We could use your skills to help us break back into the ship."

Spider shook his head. "My biggest fear is to die in space, to float out there forever. I can't go."

"Wouldn't it be more frightening to suffocate in here—alone?"

Spider looked up at him, the terror evident in his eyes. He took the suit.

UNABLE to bear the doubts voiced by the crowd any longer, Travis Quinn exploded several bolts from his rifle into the ceiling. All eighteen of the men surrounding him trailed off into silence.

"I didn't promise you an easy victory," he said. "Freedom is something you must earn. We outnumber and outgun Steiner and his supporters. Why do you still fear him?"

"He destroyed Tramer, didn't he?" one answered back.

"No," Travis snapped, still angry at being cheated out of his greatest prize. "The cyborg killed himself." He paced through the gathering of men, challenging them with his gaze. "Some of you saw what I did to Steiner in the bar. He is weak. Who among you is brave enough to lead a band of warriors against him?"

"Why don't you lead it yourself?" Julio Sanchez shot back.

Travis recognized the challenge to his authority. "I am the only one who knows the passwords. If I am killed accidentally, all will be lost."

Murmurs of agreement rose from the others.

"How about you leading the attack, Julio?" he asked, hoping to bring the pilot under his control again. "It will give you a chance to avenge your friend Palmer, unless you feel it's too heavy a responsibility for you to handle?"

Julio glared at him.

A few others shouted encouragements. Travis knew they admired Julio as one of the smartest of the raiders. In the end, the peer pressure forced Julio to accept.

A faint voice from the control cubicle caught Travis's ear. He rushed inside just in time to hear a message repeat.

"Command center to Quinn." Steiner's voice came from the intercom. "Please respond."

Men rallied around Travis as he pressed a keypad on the console. "Yes, Captain. Are you surrendering to me?"

"Never."

"Why have you called me then?"

"Most of the crew wishes to remain neutral in our dispute. Would you agree to declaring the bar a safe haven?"

Travis read straight through the request. It meant none of the neutral crew wanted to help Steiner.

"No one inside the establishment will be harmed as long as you don't seek refuge there as well," he said.

"Don't worry," Steiner replied. "If it's a fight you want, that's what I'll give you."

The channel disconnected abruptly.

Travis looked over at Julio, wondering if the pilot was cunning enough to kill Steiner. If he was, it might sway the rest of the men into following the pilot. Travis needed to create dissension among the party to keep that from happening. "When we reach the Centri System, I'll give ten thousand credits to whoever brings him back alive," he said.

"What if we're forced to kill him?" Rex asked.

"Five thousand."

Hoots and hurrahs broke out. Rex let out a howl.

Fools, Travis thought. *They believe every word I tell them.* His fingers fondled the Orders disk sitting atop the console.

RICK Mason sat at one of the tables within the bar, watching his drink bubble. Bricket sat across from him, sullen-faced, shuffling a deck of cards.

Across the room, Eddie helped Richards re-dress the wound in his side. Five other crewmen sat at the counter, drinking and singing to Quinn's victory.

One of the drunken convicts staggered over to Mason and Bricket's table. "Your beer tastes great, bartender. Especially since it's free." His four friends at the counter roared with glee.

Bricket stuck his cane out under the feet of the drunken man and tripped him. The group at the counter burst into another round of laughter. Their friend tried to struggle to his feet, then collapsed unconscious on the floor.

"I'm sorry that you're losing your entire stock of liquor," Mason said.

"It's not everything I have. A couple of barrels are locked in a storage room next to the port-side air lock, but I'm sure these lushes or the mutineers will eventually find them, too." Bricket looked over at the men and threw the cards to the floor. "Is life in the Centri System any better than this?"

"Not much," Mason answered. "You must show loyalty to five different overlords, even when they're in conflict with each other."

"That sounds impossible."

"Almost." Mason took another swallow from his mug. "What I can't figure out is why any of them would let Quinn bring a shipful of U.S.S. prisoners in there. They never have liked outsiders."

Bricket rubbed his beard. "How do you know so much about the place?"

"Before becoming a convict, I lived there for five years. I used to be a smuggler for the Overlord Ty."

"It looks like you might be again."

Mason smiled, remembering pleasant memories from when he had worked for Ty. "I could charm him into letting me do whatever I wished. It's quite ironic since, when I first met him, he almost had me killed for being the son of—" He cut himself off just as he realized what he almost said.

"Son of whom?"

"Forget about it."

Bricket leaned over the table. "Perhaps you're the son of a Separatist official," he whispered.

Mason emptied the rest of his mug, pretending not to have heard.

"Don't worry," Bricket continued softly. "I've suspected it ever since you gave me that command password."

Mason shot a sharp look at him. "I told you that I stole it."

Bricket grinned. "Nobody other than family gets that close to Separatist brass."

"You haven't told anyone else that, have you?" Mason whispered.

"Why would I? What do I care about your background? I wouldn't even care if you were a spy."

Mason sighed. "I'm the son of Admiral Richina."

"The Emperor's Executioner?"

Mason squirmed, already regretting having told the bartender.

"No wonder you never told anyone," Bricket said. "Every U.S.S. soldier would probably hold you responsible for the massacre at Macrales on the Day of Betrayal."

"Emperor Staece gave him a medal for that," Mason muttered, remembering how much it had distressed his mother.

"If your name isn't Rick Mason, what is it?"

"Mason Richina."

"Do you have any brothers or sisters?"

Mason hesitated, then lifted a second full mug. "A brother. Sam reminded me a lot of him." He drank the liquor, letting it wash the bitter memories away. He found his hatred of his father rekindled when he remembered his younger brother, Randy. Randy hadn't been as strong as Mason had been in resisting their father. If only Randy had been like—

Sam.

Sam had the strength that Randy lacked, but it also got the kid killed. Maybe death would have been a better fate than what happened to Randy.

Forget him, Mason scolded himself. *Forget them both. They're gone forever.*

Mason reminded himself he would soon be back in the Centri System, smuggling for Ty once again. That didn't seem so appealing anymore. He had enjoyed fighting against the New Order Empire, extracting revenge on his father by using the knowledge with which the admiral had endowed him.

A hush settled over the room. Mason found the source standing at the entrance of the bar. Ironhand. His presence no longer intimidated those around him. He looked tired and broken.

"Are there any volunteers who wish to join me in fighting the mutineers?" Ironhand asked.

The room remained quiet.

"There is no guarantee this ship will reach the Centri System, or that the U.S.S. won't hunt all of you down. This might be the only opportunity to save yourselves."

"We don't have any assault guns," a convict shouted from the counter.

"Ingenuity and bravery are far better than weapons."

Eddie swiped his hand toward him and muttered angrily. The five convicts at the counter giggled.

Ironhand locked eyes with Mason, then wheeled about and left the establishment.

Mason glanced over at Bricket, who had a scowl on his face.

"If I weren't crippled, I'd help him," the bartender said.

"It would be suicide whether you had full use of your legs or not."

Bricket ran his finger over the knife scar on his cheek. "Sam would have joined him."

"Sam is dead."

"Yes, but he died with audacity." Bricket snatched his cane and lifted himself from his chair. "Good-bye, Rick."

"You can't be serious," Mason exclaimed. "You'd be an easy target."

"If I'm going to die, I'm doing it with audacity, too," Bricket snapped back. "Besides, I wouldn't like living in your Centri System." His hand motioned toward the other occupants of the room. "They sound worse than the people in here. If I went there, I *would* be throwing my life away." With that, he headed toward the door, then hesitated and glanced back. "Don't forget. Quinn murdered Sam."

Mason's grip tightened around the handle of his mug. "Go to your death then," he mumbled.

The bartender hobbled out of the exit. The five convicts at the counter bellowed with laughter.

Eddie shut the door, then ignited a laser torch. Sparks flashed as the giant made a blackened trail up the frame, sealing it closed.

Mason stared at the second drained mug in front of him. It symbolized his life—void of meaning. Sam didn't play it smart. He should have acted more like Rand—

Mason threw his glass to the ground, disgusted at himself. He overturned his chair, then stormed to the exit. When Eddie saw him coming, he deactivated the torch.

"I've already started to weld it closed," he said. "It's too late to leave."

"Cut it back open," Mason growled.

Eddie set down his tool and stood up, towering over him. "You lost your chance," he sneered.

No one had ever taken on the Giant and won, but that wouldn't stop Mason. Just before he swung his fist into the massive body in front of him, a voice shouted out.

"Stop!"

From a nearby table, Richards pulled himself to his feet, bandages wrapped around his chest. "Let him go," he ordered his officer. "The fight is out there, not in here."

With a sigh of frustration, Eddie picked up the torch and changed the setting. "Both you and the bartender are insane," he spat at Mason.

"I agree," Mason replied.

DAVID Cole paced back and forth on the bridge of the *Magellan*. About an hour ago, they had reached the spot where the *Marauder* should have been if she were on the correct flight plan.

After Suzanne's testimony, a warrant had been issued for Jamison's arrest, but so far he had eluded capture. According to the admiral's computer's transmission records, not only had the stolen passwords been sent to his personal console but so had many top secret data files from the military's mainframe.

"Sir, a message is coming in from the leader of the Council," Commander Cromwell announced.

"Put it on the monitor."

A small screen on the bridge came to life with the picture of Admiral Barton.

"Commodore Cole, I have some good news and bad news. Admiral Jamison has been captured aboard a cargo vessel believed to have been heading for the Separatist Empire."

"Has he been interrogated yet?"

"Yes, that's the bad news. He has admitted to stealing the military information and storing it on Captain Steiner's Orders disk. Two of the crew on his ship possess the stolen passwords and are planning to take the P.A.V. *Marauder* into Separatist space through the southern border."

"I'll head for that area right now."

Barton frowned. "Not so fast. It gets worse. Since we've had no contact with Captain Steiner, we must assume he is already dead. The stolen data is much too valuable to fall into enemy hands; therefore, I am issuing an order for all ships to destroy the P.A.V. on sight."

Cole went rigid. "But, sir—"

"No arguments, please. The other admirals and I have already decided we can't take the risk. Too much is at stake. I'm sorry. Barton out."

The transmission ended. Cole slammed his fist into the console.

"Commodore?" Cromwell asked with a salute. "Permission to begin targeting drills?"

Cole had to hold himself back from striking the man. "Granted," he forced himself to answer.

If only there was another way.

CHAPTER

24

STEINER searched through the ship's utility closet for potential weapons. The only items he found were a laser cutter and a pair of goggles that the maintenance personnel wore inside dark accessways.

Besides those, he already had a box of grenades in his cabin, two pistols, and the tracker. Somehow, he had to use them all to make an adequate defense.

As he exited the closet, he caught sight of the yellow bruiseball helmet in a corner. It reminded him of what he was up against. The entire voyage had been spent training the crew to fight, and now their skills would be used against him. They did have one weakness which he planned to exploit—no combat experience in the dark.

Steiner knew that the best place to make his stand would be among the crew quarters. His next task was to open each cabin in order to provide more hiding places from which to ambush.

While he moved from door to door, overriding their security locks, he began to question why he was preparing to do battle at all. What reason did he have to survive? All of his true friends had already died, Sam, Tramer, Daniels, and the other engineers. Self-preservation didn't seem a good reason because he would rather be with Mary. Why not just end his own life here and now? One pistol bolt through the head would do it quickly. If he had access to the engine room, he could overload a reactor and destroy the entire ship, taking Quinn and the mutineers out with him.

He stopped and leaned his head against the cold bulkhead, uncertain of what to do. In the past, he had always gone to McKillip to get advice about dilemmas like this. What would his old captain have said now?

He envisioned himself walking into the man's conference chamber back on the *Valiant*. McKillip sat in his oversized chair behind his desk, directly under the painted portrait of his wife. His fingers stroked his silver-tinted beard.

"Come in, Jacob," the captain said. "I've been expecting you."

In his mind, Steiner stepped up to the edge of the desk but didn't know how to begin. "I have no reason to go on," he admitted.

"When I brought you into the Cyrian Defense, I asked you how far you were willing to go to save the United Star Systems."

"I said that I was willing to fight to the death, even to a court-martial."

McKillip looked at him thoughtfully. "How far would Jamison go to cause the United Star Systems to fail?"

"Jamison thinks by killing me, he is protecting himself, but he doesn't know about Isaac Steele."

"Never underestimate your enemy. Your death can't be the only objective; otherwise, Jamison would never have planned something this elaborate, would he?"

Steiner could hear his words in his mind. Captain McKillip would have said that.

McKillip stood up from his desk and moved to the chessboard at the end of it. "Just like in chess, you have to spin the board around and determine what the best moves are for your opponent." The captain's weathered hand twisted the perspective of the game board around so the dark pieces were facing out. "What are Jamison's goals?"

"Overthrow the United Star Systems," Steiner answered out loud.

"What are his resources?"

"He is an admiral."

"Think outside of the box," McKillip said.

Steiner considered what Jamison had sent against him. "He has trained killers." Suddenly, Suzanne's assailant came to mind.

"Keep going," the captain said.

"He has pirate contacts." Then he thought of the smuggling code that had been used on the wall in the bar.

"Keep going."

"By Tramer's testimony, he knew Joseph Barker, and probably Travis Quinn, too."

"Keep going."

"He has access to all the revised troop deployments but no method to get the information out."

Steiner stopped cold. Simmons told him that Quinn had requested the ship's Orders disk that he had received at Earthstation.

Quinn must be one of the pirates Jamison had met. Jamison could have sent an assassin to murder Suzanne, which would allow him to be able to forge documents in her name and place Quinn and Boon Wong on the *Marauder*, arm them with some of the passwords—for the sole purpose of smuggling all the United Star Systems' new ship deployments to the New Order Empire on the Orders disk. The information would most likely lead to another invasion and possible downfall of the last form of democracy in the galaxy.

McKillip smiled. "Good man. Now, fulfill your duty."

Breaking the reverie with newfound purpose, Steiner continued opening cabin doors. He had to find a way to win this battle at any cost, but how could he possibly do it alone?

"Captain," a voice shouted through the empty corridor.

Steiner whipped his pistol out and spun around. When he saw Bricket hobbling toward him, his muscles relaxed. He slipped his gun back into its holster.

"How can a crippled man be of service?" Bricket asked.

"I'm relieved to have an ally." Steiner grasped the bartender's outstretched hand. "The command center needs to be guarded. If what I suspect is true, the whole crew is in great danger."

Steiner explained his theory about Quinn being a Separatist agent trying to smuggle secret military data into the Separatist Empire. To provide Bricket with a defense, he told him the passwords for both the command center and Pressure Door C-1 leading to the forward section.

"That'll hold the cutthroats off for a while." Bricket pulled a cigar out of his pocket and bit the end of it off. "While I'm up there, I'll try to piece together the communication array."

Footsteps echoed from down the passageway. Steiner drew his gun again.

"Don't fire," Mason shouted. "It's just me."

The cigar dropped from Bricket's mouth.

"Consider me Sam's replacement," Mason answered.

A belly laugh exploded from the bartender. "There's audacity under your thick hide after all."

"It's brains that I'm lacking."

"You may not think that after I tell you what Steiner told me. You and I must protect the command center."

"What is Ironhand going to be doing while we're up there?"

Steiner answered for himself. "Confronting the mutineers head-on."

"Alone?" Mason exclaimed.

"I have no other choice—don't worry, I've set a few traps."

Bricket smiled as he leaned over and retrieved his cigar. "Traps, huh? That gives me an idea." He snubbed out the lit end of the butt and dropped the stick into his pocket.

"Do you have any extra weapons?" Mason asked Steiner.

"An extra pistol." Steiner pulled it out from under his belt.

Mason rolled his eyes. "That sure builds my confidence, especially since we'll be up against assault rifles."

"Don't worry," Bricket replied. "I've got an idea for a trap we can use. You won't even need a gun."

"What?" Mason exclaimed.

"I'll tell you my idea on the way because we don't have much time."

Mason stared at Bricket, who limped away at a brisk pace. With a sideways glance at Steiner, Mason took the offered pistol and followed after the bartender.

WITH great care, Daniels picked his way along the outside hull of the P.A.V. Behind him lay the eternal blackness of space, waiting to pull him into its grasp. J.R., Spider, Fred, Charles, and Andrew followed behind him in procession.

Before they had left the church, J.R. had tied a cord to each of their suits to prevent one of them from tumbling off into forever.

When Daniels reached a maintenance hatch that had been hit by a pulse-cannon blast during the battle, he shoved the exterior latch clockwise. The handle moved an inch, then held firm.

J.R. and Spider moved up alongside him.

"It has to work," Spider pleaded, his face dotted with perspiration. It's the last damaged air lock we've found. Try it again—please."

"It's locked tight," Daniels said.

"I knew I should have stayed behind," Spider whined. "I'm going to die in space."

Daniels turned Spider's helmet to face his own. "Relax. There might be another hatch near the front of the ship. We're not lost yet. Are you with me?" When Spider nodded, Daniels patted his shoulder.

J.R. grinned at Spider. "Good ol' Spide."

Daniels started forward again. A quick glimpse at his suit's oxygen indicator told him they didn't have much time left.

WITH a kick of Julio Sanchez's boot, the cutout circle of metal fell through and landed on the far side with a deep thud that vibrated through the floor. Dressed in full body armor and armed with an assault rifle, Julio stepped through the large hole in Pressure Door C-3. Since small arms were useless against his suit, there was no need for caution.

The targeting computer within his helmet searched the empty corridor ahead and found nothing. The captain must be hiding somewhere farther into the vessel.

When he motioned behind him, Rex and Bo rushed through the opening and charged past him, bumping against his shoulder. They raced into the cafeteria, which lay twenty feet away, and began shooting wildly. Startled, Julio sprinted to the entrance, peeked inside, and saw the two raiders hurling bolts into the tables, shattering them into twisted debris. Rex lifted his portable missile launcher. A howl rang out just before a missile launched into the kitchen. A thunderous eruption of flames consumed the section, expelling white-hot fragments in every direction. Julio backed out as black fumes billowed out from the cafeteria's doorway. It took several coughs to clear his lungs of the poisonous vapors.

From out of the dark cloud, the two destructors appeared, laughing and slapping each other on the back.

"You're next, Captain Steiner," Rex shouted into the heart of the ship.

Weapons held ready, they charged ahead.

Julio looked behind him at the confused faces of the six other raiders who had come through the blasted-out hole.

"It's nothing," he announced, motioning them to follow. "The captain isn't anywhere around."

When he turned to lead the team forward, he caught sight of Rex and Bo at the end of the corridor, searing the walls and roaring with glee.

Reckless idiots, Julio thought.

STEINER heard the explosions as he sat at the main terminal in the computer room. He tried not to think anything of it. His fingers danced upon the keyboard, commanding the lights in the crew section to die. Darkness engulfed the room, broken only by the faint glows of instrument panels. Steiner lowered the maintenance goggles over his eyes. The lens painted his surroundings in pale green.

Leaving the computer room, he raced through the green-highlighted corridors until he reached the site where he planned to make his stand.

Rifle blasts echoed from the rear of the ship, getting closer and louder.

Armed with his pistol, tracker, and laser cutter, Steiner knocked one of the ceiling panels aside. He lifted himself into the tight crawl space above, then replaced the panel. Lying perfectly still, he listened to loud taunts growing in volume.

When he twisted his body to a more comfortable position, the sole grenade attached to his belt dug into his side, reminding him of its purpose. If all else failed, he would use it to commit suicide and take as many mutineers as possible with him.

His thoughts then turned to Mary. In his mind's eye, he could still see her, feel her, and even smell her perfume.

"YOU won't be able to hide from us in there, Captain," Rex shouted into the pitch-black entrance to the crew quarters section. "We'll be able to see you."

He and Bo activated the scopes in their helmets and raced down a center aisle of the darkened battlefield, their weapons blazing.

Julio watched with contempt. That kind of cockiness would get both of them killed.

"If we are to succeed, we must be careful not to throw away our advantage," he told the six other raiders. "Fan out in pairs through the other corridors. Use your digital enhancers and targeting computers. Check inside each open cabin. Report immediately if you find anything suspicious."

"Will we have to share the reward?" Dante asked.

Julio sneered. "Let's worry about that later."

Peter and Fritz went down a far right passageway, while Glenn and Dicer disappeared to the left. Midas elected to remain behind in case the captain tried to backtrack. Julio signaled the remaining single raider, Dante, to follow him down another aisle.

The scopes bathed the interiors of the bedchambers in multicolored hues that brought out every detail. There were cots and bags of belongings, but no captain.

When Dante disappeared into one of the cabins for a few minutes, Julio decided to investigate. He found the man pulling a decorative dagger out of one of the bundles. Disgusted, Julio grabbed the knife away and glared at him until the thief went back to his patrol.

When Julio laid the blade down, the glistening jewels from its handle beckoned to him, so he slipped it inside his suit.

STEINER'S legs had cramped up, yet he stayed motionless. The tracker's screen indicated that two mutineers were closing on his position, searching inside each cabin along the way.

Anxiety built within him as each second passed. His blood pumped faster and faster until his head throbbed from the pressure. He swallowed but couldn't wet his throat.

When footsteps sounded near him, he raised the ceiling plate a half an inch, then froze when he heard faint whispers exchanged below. His lungs ached for air, but he feared to fill them. The voices went still.

Holding his breath, Steiner snuck the plate back just enough to provide room for his arm to reach through. Noiselessly, he pulled the laser cutter out from under his belt and held it ready. With his other hand, he drew his gun.

An armor-clad figure moved under the slit, then paused to look down the corridor. Steiner had to act fast—if the raider happened to glance up, all would be lost.

With the cutter's blade enabled, he reached down and sliced through the helmet's power cable. It went dead, blinding its wearer.

Immediately, Steiner exploded some bolts from his pistol into the floor near the man's feet. The startled raider thrashed about, discharging his rifle. A section of the crawl space two feet away from Steiner erupted into fiery debris. A guttural cry sounded. Someone dropped to the floor.

"Fritz?" the mutineer asked. "Where are you?"

No answer.

Steiner thrust the panel aside. He jumped down on top of

the man, jerked his head back, and slit his throat. Blood spilled down the front of the convulsing body.

The other raider, Fritz, lay several feet away, punctured with two smoking holes.

When Steiner pried the assault rifle away from his victim, he heard someone approaching from the far end of the corridor. He flung himself backward a millisecond before the air was rent apart by fiery beams.

His back impacted squarely against the floor inside a doorway. The assault gun flew from his grip into the interior of the chamber.

Curses echoed from outside in the hall, followed by approaching footfalls.

Steiner scrambled after his weapon, snatched it up, and rushed back to the entrance. He lanced out energy blasts at the advancing raider. Two beams ate away at the man's armor before he took cover inside a cabin twenty feet away.

Steiner knew it wouldn't be long before the other mutineers joined in on the attack.

He stepped into the corridor, rapid-firing at the raider, then sprinted in the opposite direction, toward another cabin thirty feet away. Just before he reached it, bolts tore into the doorframe, blocking his way. He dove beneath the searing streaks and rolled through to safety.

A cry of rage from the mutineer testified to the success of his tactic.

Steiner scooped up the single grenade that he had earlier planted on top of a cot, activated it, then stuffed it under the mattress, where a pile of them lay. In nine seconds, they would all ignite.

With his rifle in hand, he squeezed into the open air vent. He pulled the sheet lining the inside of the tunnel until the blast shield it was tied to covered the entry. Darkness shrouded everything except the distant light shining from the life-support station. Steiner crawled toward his escape.

Weapon blasts erupted inside the room behind him. The raider must be shooting blindly, searching for a target.

Then everything went silent.

Teeth clenched, Steiner scrabbled forward in a maddened frenzy, his limbs banging against the walls of the tight passageway. He had lost count of the seconds left on the grenades.

Three feet separated him from his sanctuary, when he heard the blast shield being moved aside.

"Gotcha." A voice echoed into the tunnel.

No, Steiner screamed silently with one final lunge.

Light flooded the shaft, accompanied by a deafening noise. He dropped to the floor of the life-support station as a geyser of fire and debris shot out from the vent like a cannon.

After a few seconds, it died out, leaving the chamber in a smoky haze. Thankfully, the air generator continued its steady drone even though it had been dented in several places.

Among the flaming debris littering the floor, a smoldering helmet rocked back and forth.

JULIO Sanchez reached the source of the explosion, with Dante right on his heels. Glenn and Dicer had already arrived at the site and were staring down at the bodies of Peter and Fritz, lying in pools of blood. Inside the blazing cabin, the torso of another armor-clad figure lay burning in a corner.

"The fools should've called for backup, like I instructed them," Julio growled. "A reward is useless if you're dead."

"The captain must have been better armed than we thought," Dante replied.

Rex and Bo showed up at the site, scowls distorting their faces.

"Who nailed the captain?" Rex asked.

"Nobody, but Midas, Peter, and Fritz are dead," Julio replied.

The two raiders cheered and disappeared back into the darkness.

"Greedy fools," Julio shouted after them. He turned back to the four others. "Are the rest of you willing to work together to capture the captain? We could split the reward four ways. Is it a deal?"

Julio held his hand out in pledge. Glenn and Dicer grasped it, but Dante shook his head and raced off.

"It's the three of us then," Julio proclaimed.

"What's your plan?" Glenn asked him.

"First, let's get the lights back on."

SEATED at the remains of Tramer's damaged security station, Mason pressed keypads until a fiery doorway appeared on one of the monitors that Bricket had repaired upon entering the command center.

On the other side of the room, Bricket knelt by the communication console, opening its maintenance panel.

"I found the explosion we heard," Mason announced. "I don't see any mutineers celebrating, so I'm certain Ironhand is still alive." He switched through several other scenes, but the light level was too low to allow the cameras to register any images.

A sharp clatter made Mason flinch. Turning around, he saw that the bartender had thrown the inner communication assembly to the ground.

"Can you repair it?" Mason asked.

"Not a chance," Bricket shouted in obvious frustration. "Simmons did a fine job of wrecking the unit. I might be able to send out a short-range transmission with what's left, but it wouldn't do us any good way out here."

A muffled response came from the command chair.

Picking up his cane, the bartender whacked Simmons's legs. The captive let out a sharp cry. "That made me feel a little better," Bricket said. He lifted himself and hobbled over to the security station.

A barely visible shadow caught Mason's eye on one of the screens.

"Who was that?" Bricket asked.

"I couldn't tell. It's too dark." Mason let out a sigh. "I wish I knew what was happening down there."

"If you like, we can talk about something else to pass the time."

"Like what?"

"Well, which government would you like to see win the war?"

"I don't care."

Bricket chuckled. "You wouldn't have come on board if that were true."

"It beat rotting away in prison."

"No, I don't believe that either. I'd wager that you want the Separatists to lose the war to get back at your father."

Mason hated it when the bartender was right, so he refused to respond.

"You're too easy to read," Bricket said with a slight smirk.

"I don't want to talk about it," Mason shouted.

"Why not?"

"If these are my last minutes of life, I don't want to waste them talking about him."

"What about your mother? Did you hate her, too?"

Mason fought to keep himself from propelling both fists into the bartender's face.

"No, you loved her deeply," Bricket said. "He did something to her, didn't he?"

Mason turned away, hiding the tears forming in his eyes.

"Did he beat her?" Bricket asked.

Mason fought hard to keep his thoughts from sinking a mire of bitter memories, forgotten tragedies, forsaken loved ones. "Worse."

"It will make you feel better if you get it off your chest."

"It won't change anything. It's best if I don't dwell on it."

"If you try to suppress your emotions, they'll build up inside you until they explode. Confront them now."

Mason wanted to shout a curse at the bartender for torturing him like this but couldn't. He could hear the sincerity in the man's voice.

"My father was promoted to a U.S.S. admiral when I was sixteen. A year later, Christophe Staece convinced him and two other admirals to join his New Order Empire."

Bricket reached into his pocket and extracted his partially used cigar. His eyes never left Mason as he stuck one end into his bearded mouth and lit the other. "What happened to make it go sour?"

The smoke from the bartender's cigar curled and twisted a random course toward the ceiling. Mason could see images from his past dancing within it. His mother's desperate pleas sounded from somewhere far off in time.

"My mother didn't agree with the choice but remained silent. After the U.S.S. succeeded in fending off the first invasion, my father bombarded the planet Macrales. My mother stopped being silent."

Bricket groaned. "That caused problems for your father in the emperor's eyes."

His mother's distant screams echoed in Mason's head. "My father's enemies demanded that he be dismissed from his post for having a conspirator as a wife."

"What did your father do about it?"

"In order to save his career, he released a statement denying all knowledge of his wife's treason, and to prove his loyalty to the emperor, he took the necessary actions against her."

Bricket's face paled. "He didn't . . ."

Mason bowed his head to hide the tears that refused to be held back. "I still remember the day they came for her. My brother, Randy, and I watched as four uniformed thugs dragged her out, while she pleaded to my father to help her. He wouldn't even look at her but held both Randy and me so we couldn't chase after her. He whispered lies about her to comfort us. She was executed that night."

"How old was Randy at that time?"

"Not old enough. He was fifteen, six years younger than I was."

Bricket plucked the cigar from his mouth. "He believed the lies, didn't he?"

Mason sighed and nodded.

"Randy wanted the love of his father so much he deceived himself," Bricket said. "Poor kid."

"When I heard the Centri System needed good pilots, I tried to take him with me." Mason heaved for breath. "He tried to turn me in to our father." The anguish threatened to consume Mason. His pride, the trait that had caused him to survive for so long without family, prevented him from succumbing. "My father stole everything dear to me. I would jump at the chance to hurt him in return."

"Good," Bricket said. "Until now, I wasn't sure where your loyalties lay."

Mason stared at him. "What?"

"During our confrontation with the enemy battlecruiser, you gave me their password to save your own life. I wanted to be sure you wouldn't turn on me if you were given the chance to return to your homeland."

The answer left Mason dumbfounded. He had never thought of it from that perspective before. After all, he was the son of a New Order admiral. Could Bricket have trusted him to fight against his own people?

"Look," Bricket said. "The lights came back on in the crew quarters, which means someone must be in the computer room."

With the press of a couple of keypads from Mason, three body-armored men appeared on a monitor, standing over the main terminal.

"Julio Sanchez," Mason said. "I had a feeling that idiot would eventually mutiny."

"The person on the far left is Dicer," Bricket replied. "I've played several hands of poker with him. Who is the other guy?"

"I don't know, but I've seen him shooting in the targeting range."

"Is he good?"

"Does it matter with weapons like theirs?"

On the screen, Julio stood up and spoke to the other men. When they started to leave the room, Julio looked up at the camera.

"Oh great," Mason muttered. "He can see the red indicator light."

An orange flare ignited from Julio's assault rifle. The screen burst into static.

Mason exchanged a knowing glance with Bricket. The raiders would be coming to the command center next.

STEINER stood on one of the rungs inside a ladder well, just high enough to see above the floor of the upper level. When the lights came on, he had sought a hiding place. With his advantage gone, he would have to rely on surprise from there on. His muscles tightened when he heard voices. A glance down at his tracker found two men proceeding toward his location.

A nearby explosion rocked the area, followed by a howl. Steiner stole a peek around the corner and saw Rex launch a missile into a second cabin. The ladder vibrated under the violent force.

The two hunters appeared determined to disintegrate him rather than hunt for him. He aimed his rifle's muzzle at the edge of the entrance to the well.

Bo appeared in his sights, but Steiner kept himself from firing because Rex remained out of range.

When Bo noticed him inside the well, he shouted and raised his weapon. Two of Steiner's energy blasts tore through Bo's exposed throat before he could fire. The man toppled back against the bloodstained wall behind him.

A venomous scream erupted from Rex.

Letting go of the ladder, Steiner fell down the well. The hiss of a missile launching sounded from above. Steiner tumbled to the floor of the bottom level and rolled away just before the tunnel above him burst into a roaring inferno. He looked up in time to see a backwash of fire proceeding down the chute. He shielded his face as it burst out from the well's entrance. The searing wave swept over him. His skin burned with pain for a second, then the feeling mellowed.

When he lifted his head, he saw that his reddened flesh had first-degree burns—painful, but not serious.

The blackened well smoked. Smoldering metal cinders lay all about the floor amidst the remains of his assault rifle and tracker.

Steiner tried to stand up and winced from a sharp sting in his lower thigh. Blood oozed from where a charred fragment had embedded itself in the tissue.

Boots scraped against metal as Rex began to descend. A foot became visible from out of the roof of the entrance.

Ignoring the pain of his wound, Steiner catapulted himself up and ducked into the first open doorway, which turned out to be the utility closet.

Leaning against the inside wall, he realized the time had come for his suicide plan. He glanced down at the single grenade attached to his belt. His finger poised above the trigger.

Metal cinders ground outside in the hall.

"Captain," Rex bellowed. "Come out and play with me. Maybe I'll let you live."

Play, Steiner thought. *That's it.*

The yellow bruiseball helmet still lay in the corner of the closet. He snatched up the game prop, activated the grenade, and dropped it inside.

"I surrender," he shouted, then stepped out of the closet and tossed the helmet to Rex.

The man's bruiseball instincts seemed to take over. Lowering his missile launcher, Rex caught the prop with one hand. His eyes sparkled.

Steiner flung himself back into the doorway as a white-hot burst cut off a howl in midstride.

AFTER going back to get the laser cannon, Julio, Dicer, and the third man took five minutes to cut through the forward section's pressure door. Mason kept an eye on them the entire time using the security monitors. Julio hadn't shot out any more cameras even though he must have seen them active. Maybe he no longer cared whether they were watched or not.

Bricket sat quietly, savoring the last of his cigar.

Mason rubbed his face. How foolish he must have sounded when he told Bricket his family history.

On the monitor, the three raiders stepped through the burnt-out hole. Bricket grabbed his cane and lifted his body out of the chair. "Let's get ready to show them our hand, shall we?"

With a nod of agreement, Mason followed him down the stairway to the sealed entrance. Bricket whistled as he entered the password into the control panel. The double doors split apart, both halves retreating into the bulkhead. Beyond them, in the middle of the corridor, stood Bricket's secret weapon, right where they had left it.

Mason had to admit the idea had been a brilliant one, but at the same time, it seemed wasteful. His finger ran across the side of the six-foot-high storage container that housed eighty gallons of the bartender's own brand of extrastrength beer. They had used an antigravitational truck to move it.

When Bricket removed the lid on top of it, the overpowering smell of alcohol escaped. The cigar smoke mixed with the aroma of strong liquor, reminding Mason of being back inside the bar. "I'll bet you feel a little bit angry at having to use your stock like this," he said.

Bricket blew several ringlets then smiled. "No, on the contrary, I've never felt more alive than I do now. No profit can ever top this. I'd rather die feeling like this than live as I did, in fear."

When Mason saw the three raiders approaching, he pulled Bricket behind their secret weapon.

Julio halted the other two mutineers thirty feet away.

"Captain," he shouted. "Give yourself up."

"Wrong, Julio," Mason answered back. "I'm not Steiner, and I don't plan on surrendering either."

"Mason?" the man exclaimed. "You can't defeat us. Come out before we start firing."

Bricket's bearded mouth cracked into a giant toothy grin, curling the scar on his cheek. "Let's give them Hell."

Using the floating truck as a pivot, they put their backs against the container and pushed it over. A flood of liquor gushed down the passageway, steaming and bubbling like a brown river, and poured over the mutineers. Dicer and the other man slipped and tumbled under the flow, dropping their laser cannon. Julio kept his footing despite the rushing liquor flowing around his boots.

Bricket removed the cigar from his mouth and flaunted it at the victims. "Crown the new king of audacity."

Julio turned and retreated, splashing through the ankle-deep liquor.

The smoldering cigar made an arch through the air and landed in the river. Flames burst out, racing down the corridor to engulf all three raiders. Dicer and the other man screamed as they struggled to get up from their fiery graves.

Bricket laughed gleefully.

A steady hum grew in intensity. Mason realized that the cannon must have charged itself when it struck the ground. The blaze would heat the core to overload.

"Let's get out of here, your majesty." He grabbed the bartender by the shirt, dragged him back beyond the entrance to the command center, then hit the keypad to seal it.

After the barriers on each side of the entry began to close, a flash of brilliant light shot through the shrinking aperture. Shrapnel pelted the outside of the doors as they sealed the center from the blast.

Out of breath, Mason turned to Bricket, sprawled out on the base of the stairway with a stunned look on his face.

"I guess it worked better than I had planned," the bartender said, then chuckled. "That'll teach them to mess with a crippled man."

Mason replied with a weary nod.

DANTE examined the remains of an armor-clad person in the midst of a charred hallway outside a ladder well.

Seconds ago, he had heard another explosion coming from the forward section of the vessel and wondered what the other three raiders were doing up there. It didn't matter, though, since it was obvious the captain had been here last.

A drop of blood near the utility closet caught his eye. Another one had fallen a few feet away from the first. He could barely contain his joy when he discovered a trail of them leading away.

Steiner must have been injured, making him an easier target.

He followed the path of droplets right up to the sealed door of port-side air lock. The neighboring cabinet stood ajar. One space suit was missing from the rack inside. When Dante activated the monitor for the inner lock, he saw stars glistening through the open outer hatch.

The captain must have escaped onto the exterior of the ship.

Dante grunted in frustration. He had been so close to capturing him, only to lose him again. Maybe he could go out there to find him?

Something moved in his peripheral vision. He spun around in time to see a space-suited figure reach out of the cabinet and press a keypad on the control panel for the air lock.

A shrill alarm pierced the stillness. The pressure doors to each of the adjoining passageways slammed shut. Dante raised his rifle at the figure, but an explosive burst of escaping air stole his attention away.

The inner hatch to the air lock cracked open. Dante cried out in terror. His finger tightened on the trigger of his rifle, searing the floor with bolts as his body was dragged toward the opening. A millisecond later, he was thrust into a never-ending darkness.

A gasp came from Spider, followed by a scream. Daniels turned in time to see his aide lose his grip on the hull. Spider drifted outward, stopping eight feet away, held back by the safety cord tied to his belt. His arms and legs swung about as if they were trying to break free from his torso.

"Stop struggling," J.R. yelled out. "You might break the cord."

Spider's breathing became rapid and quick, signs of hyperventilation.

Using his arms, Daniels launched himself from the bulkhead. His right hand caught hold of Spider's arm. He wrapped the left one around his friend's body. He groped for the control box and lowered the oxygen content in Spider's suit. Spider's breaths became more regulated, but he continued to sob and thrash about.

"Stop it, or you'll kill us both," Daniels told him.

Spider seemed far too panicked to hear him. The cord wouldn't hold much longer under this amount of stress.

"Amazing grace, how sweet the sound," J.R. sang out.

Spider froze. His body began to relax.

". . . that saved a wretch like me."

Daniels turned and saw J.R. and the other three engineers drawing them toward the hull.

"I once was lost, but now am found," Spider whispered along.

Tears clouded Daniels's vision as he joined in. ". . . was blind, but now I see."

Outstretched hands took hold of them and pulled them both to safety. For a long while, the engineers all huddled around Spider, holding him tight. J.R. asked the question that seemed to be haunting everyone's mind.

"Spider, you were doing so well. What caused you to lose control?"

"I had a terrifying vision," he answered. "I saw myself spinning off into space and realized that I had seen my own future." Spider pointed toward the midsection of the port side. "I saw it over the port side."

While the other engineers reassured their friend that he still lived, Daniels moved to a better vantage point to look down the side of the hull. What he saw there was an answer to prayer, an open airlock hatch.

"Spider," he shouted. "You didn't see your death. You saw our rescue."

AFTER giving the area time to pressurize, Steiner removed his space suit and opened one of the adjacent doors, revealing an empty corridor.

He had no idea how many raiders were still searching for him. Six had been killed so far. That meant that there could still be fourteen others out there somewhere.

His eyes caught sight of a glowing red indicator from an active camera overhead. Did Bricket and Mason still hold the command center? Almost in answer to his unspoken question, the light flashed three times. It must be a signal from them that they were still entrenched up there. He smiled and responded with an upward thumb.

A blur rushed at him from an open doorway. Before he could react, the butt of a rifle struck against his side. A second hit to his back sent him sprawling against the cold floor. His body throbbed with intense pain from the blows. The blackened form of Julio Sanchez towered over him.

One energy bolt from the rifle ignited the camera into sparking debris.

Sanchez pressed the muzzle of his weapon hard into Steiner's cheek. "I'd love to kill you, but an extra five thousand credits is too hard to pass up."

CHAPTER

25

STEINER limped through the main corridor leading toward the engine room. The wound in his thigh ached with each step. His hands were tied together behind his back with his own belt. It wasn't too tight, though. If the opportunity presented itself, he might be able to twist free of it.

Steiner turned around and walked backward, facing into his captor's rifle barrel, wrestling against the belt. "Quinn is a Separatist agent. After he is taken back to his empire, all of you will be kill—" Sanchez's booted foot struck him in his gut. Steiner fell back on his struggling hands. He could feel both of them swelling,

"I'm sick of hearing your lies," Sanchez hissed, then drew out an exquisitely crafted, jeweled knife. "Open your mouth again, and I'll cut your tongue out." He lifted Steiner to his feet and shoved him forward. "Move."

Steiner staggered toward the burnt-out pressure door that led to the engine room. When he was about ten feet away, someone inside sighted him and called for Quinn. Steiner almost lost his balance as he tried to step through the jagged edges of the hole. Ten men, five armed with assault rifles, gathered around him. They hurled insults and threats as Steiner stumbled to the center of the room.

A wicked grin distorted Quinn's face as he approached. "It's good to see you alive, Captain. I had feared that they would bring you back in small pieces." He turned to Sanchez and extended his hand. "Good work, Julio."

Sanchez glared back, wordlessly.

Quinn's countenance grew colder. A long pause ensued as each of them stared the other down. Steiner used the distraction to continue to pry at his bonds.

"Where is the rest of your raiding party?"

"They're dead," Sanchez exploded. "That bounty you offered inhibited them from working together as a team. What should have been a simple siege turned into a free-for-all."

"Their greed worked to your advantage," Quinn replied. "You'll be a rich man."

"I'd better be."

Quinn ignored the threat. Instead, he addressed the men who had rallied around them. "Now that the ship is ours, we can begin our voyage to the Centri System."

"Not yet," Sanchez cut in. "Mason and Bricket are barricaded inside the command center."

A flash of annoyance crossed Quinn's face, then his confident smile returned. "Not for long." He shoved Steiner toward the control cubicle. Steiner's ankle twisted wrong, and he toppled to the floor. The onlookers laughed. When Quinn picked him up and threw him against a console near the cubicle, Steiner caught sight of the Orders disk lying next to what looked like the opened case for the Louis Harrison medallion. That small silver wafer could determine the outcome of the whole war. If only he could—

Quinn activated the intercom. "This is the new leader of the crew. We have the captain down here. He has something to tell you." A pistol muzzle pressed against Steiner's temple. "Tell them to surrender," a coarse whisper stung his ear.

Steiner stayed quiet. Quinn kicked the wound in his thigh. The stabbing pain buckled Steiner over.

"Say it," Quinn growled.

Steiner glared up at him, then gave his own wicked smile.

The pistol handle slammed into his right cheek, nearly stealing away his consciousness. A numbing sensation spread through his head. Blood ran down into his left eye. The gun barrel pressed against his forehead.

Quinn's features hardened. The glint of death frosted over his dark eyes. There was no doubt that he was about to kill.

"This is Rick Mason in the command center." A voice shattered the silence.

Quinn pivoted to the console and slammed his fist into an intercom keypad. "Come out of there, or we'll come up and remove you by force."

"You're not going to the Centri System. I doubt you even know the rules for entry. Which overlord is allowing—?"

Quinn cut off the channel.

"Why didn't you let him finish?" Sanchez asked. "Do you know how to enter the Centri System?"

Quinn's gaze narrowed.

Sanchez paced around Quinn. "All the way down here, the captain tried to convince me you were a Separatist agent," he said. "I'm beginning to wonder if that's true."

Quinn stared at him for a moment, then glanced about at the many other faces that mirrored the same doubt. "Don't you see what Steiner has tried to do?" Quinn asked them all. "He has trained you all to be sacrificial lambs of the U.S.S. Now he's trying to appeal to your sense of loyalty by making me out to be the same enemy you've been accustomed to hating." He walked over, picked up Steiner by the arm, and dragged him toward the center of the room. "It was a smart tactic. I'll grant him that. No one would have followed him without it."

Quinn stopped next to a storage bin that had been set out in the middle of the chamber. When Steiner looked up, he saw that the Louis Harrison medallion had been tied to a sprocket embedded in the ceiling above. Its ribbon hung down in a noose.

Too weak to fight Quinn's iron grip, Steiner accepted his own death. Quinn forced him to stand on top of the storage bin, then draped the noose around his neck.

"Wong," Quinn said. "Take Julio and Stiles up to the command center. Contact me when you have secured it."

The desire to protect his friends spurred Steiner to life

once again. With one final effort, he wrestled against the belt. He almost had his left hand free.

Wong and Stiles started toward the door, but Sanchez held back.

"Don't worry, Julio," Quinn added. "Wong isn't motivated by money."

After a brief hesitation, Sanchez followed after the others.

When Quinn turned back, Steiner realized that he had run out of time. No matter how hard he tried, he couldn't get free of his bond.

"Enjoy your medal, Captain," Quinn said. "You've earned it." With that, he pushed the bin away.

Steiner's body fell under the force of gravity and spun. The ribbon bit into his throat.

Mary, I'm coming to you.

AT the sound of approaching footsteps, Daniels shoved J.R. into the doorway to the cafeteria. A burnt, acidic smell greeted them. J.R. gasped. Daniels couldn't help but share his friend's shock. Intense heat had scarred the room. Only ashes and mounds of melted substances remained of the tables and other furnishings. J.R. looked questioningly at Daniels, who responded with a finger to his lips. They pressed themselves against the charred walls as voices, intermixed with the clanking of body armor, passed by. A quick glimpse from Daniels saw several raiders moving toward the front of the ship.

Daniels brought the microphone of his headset close to his mouth. "Spider, are you there?"

"Yeah, we're still at the air lock. Did you find out anything?"

"Affirmative. The ship is in hostile hands. Hide yourselves. Three heavily armed men are coming your way."

"What about you and J.R.?"

"I'm going in for a look inside the engine room."

"Me, too," J.R. whispered into his headset's microphone.

"Be careful." Spider's voice through the earpiece sounded worried.

"You, too. Daniels out."

Daniels led J.R. out of the cafeteria and down the corridor

until they came to a pressure door with a five-foot-wide circle cut out of it. He peeked through the jagged opening.

Steiner hung from the ceiling in the center of the chamber, surrounded by eight mutineers.

THE ceiling spun above Steiner's head, the medallion flashing against the surrounding lights. Pressure built within his head, threatening to explode at any second. Shapes blurred into swirling colors. Noises blended into a ceaseless drone.

Blackness.

Steiner found himself standing in the middle of a luscious field of swaying grass speckled with wildflowers. The sun shone through a couple of sparse clouds. A gentle breeze filled with the scent of springtime caressed him. He glanced around and heard faint laughter from somewhere. He stepped toward a grove of trees, searching out the sound. As he got closer, he began to recognize his surroundings. This was the park where he had proposed to Mary. He saw two people under the shade of an oak embracing. Could it be? He crept closer. The man stood up and raced across a nearby meadow, while the girl laughed merrily.

Steiner knew why the man had left. He'd gone to fetch his holocamera from his vehicle in the parking lot. He planned to take a picture of his new love and put it in a holocard, so he could cherish it for all time.

The woman stood up from the blanket and whipped her dark hair back from her smiling face.

Steiner stopped in his tracks and dropped to his knees. He mouthed the name he was afraid to speak, for it might end his dream. He closed his eyes, not wishing to be tormented with the happy memories that could no longer be. A shadow draped the light seeping through his sealed eyelids.

He opened his eyes and found himself in the back of a crowded church. At the altar stood a man in a black tuxedo with a woman in a flowing white gown. He stepped closer and saw the twinkle of light from the rings as the couple exchanged them.

When he blinked, the people in the chapel vanished. Their voices resonated through the lofty sanctuary for a few seconds before fading into nothingness. The chains holding the chandeliers of smoking candles moaned slightly. Sunlight filtered through a giant stained-glass window in the front wall of the chapel, casting colorful designs across the first six rows of pews.

A sniffle broke the stillness.

In the fourth row, bathed in a blue glow, a woman sat with her head in her lap, her body shaking with silent sobs.

Steiner walked softly forward, stopping three rows behind her within a scarlet patch of light, afraid to approach, afraid to discover who the woman was. The stained glass tinted her dark hair with the color of a twilit evening. Could it be her? Why would she be crying?

A man entered through the double doors at the entrance. A scurry of footsteps resounded within the old building. Steiner saw a younger version of himself in a military dress uniform rush in and sit next to the woman. The man whispered something to her.

Steiner knew what the man had said without having to hear his words. He had just promised Mary that he would come to church with her more often, but not today because he was late for an important meeting that couldn't be missed. Mary smiled and nodded. The man kissed her, then hurried out of the chapel.

Steiner remembered that the appointment had been an excuse in order to play billiards with several high-ranking officials and buck for a promotion.

Alone again, Mary dropped her head into her hands and wept.

Steiner slipped out of his seat and crept closer. If only he could touch her, comfort her. With each step toward her, he could see her fading away into the blue sunlight. He rushed forward, stretched out his hand, and grabbed nothing but the dust floating in the air. He searched around the empty pew where she had been sitting. The echoes of her sobs died into complete stillness. Steiner looked up into the stained-glass tapestry in the window and saw the shape of a cross in the center of a montage of scenes.

"Why did you take her away?" Steiner shouted. "We were happy together."

With a thunderous explosion, the stained-glass window broke into myriads of sparkling fragments. Brilliant light surged through the opening. Steiner blinked. People flowed around him, on their way somewhere. The ambience was different. He no longer stood in the darkened chapel. Above him, a modern lighting tube ran the length of a long room. An old man hobbled around him, glaring at him as he passed. Steiner stumbled out of the way as the crowd continued to pass by. A small boy looked up at him and smiled.

They can see me, Steiner thought.

"Shuttle Nine leaving from Gate D in five minutes," a voice said over a loudspeaker.

Every muscle in Steiner's body stiffened simultaneously. That was the name of the craft that had crashed with Mary on it.

He walked with the crowd as he scanned his environment. This looked like a shuttle depot. A baggage claim lay to the right, a ticket counter to the left. Illuminated signs pointed toward where the gates were. A time display stood in the center of the room, the date on the bottom read February 18, 2429—the day that Mary would die.

No, it can't be.

Was he living out the incident over again? No, it must be a dream. He pinched himself hard on the arm. A stinging red mark swelled up on the skin. Within the glass covering the time display, he saw his reflection. He looked younger. Had he been sent back in time somehow? Could he change the past, or was this a trick to play on his feelings?

"Shuttle Nine departs in three minutes," the person announced throughout the building. "Last call for boarding."

Steiner sprinted toward the gates. If he could rescue her, he would. With a maddened desperation, he forced a path through the slow-moving pedestrians until he found the marker that had a giant numeral 9. Outside the building, passengers proceeded into the craft sitting on the launchpad.

He stepped over to the attendant and asked if Mary Steiner had boarded yet. While the man looked through his list of passengers, Steiner caught sight of a screen displaying the daily news.

"The New Order Empire in the Outer Colonies has increased its aggressive posture," the anchorwoman announced. "Some political analysts fear that war may be inevitable, while still others maintain hope for a peaceful reconciliation."

Bumps rose up his arms, pricking his hairs. He had forgotten that the war had not broken out yet.

"She hasn't arrived yet," the attendant said. "She has two minutes left before the ship departs."

After thanking the man, Steiner inched closer to the screen.

"In brighter news, Ralph Jamison was appointed the newest member of the War Council," the woman said. A hologram of the bald, narrow-faced man appeared behind her.

No, Steiner cried silently. *Not him.*

Jamison raised his right hand. "I pledge to do my best to lead the United Star Systems to a better future."

"To its destruction," Steiner hissed.

A nearby teenager glared at him, probably wondering if he was insane.

Steiner turned away from the screen, unable to bear any more. If Mary came, he would stop her—no matter what.

Almost at that same instant, she ran from the corridor, stepped up to the gate's attendant, and handed in her ticket.

Steiner rushed forward and hugged her. "Mary, I found you—at last."

She pushed away from him. "I told you, Jacob. There is no more discussion. I need to go away for a few months. It'll give us both time to think things through and get our priorities straight."

Steiner stared at her, dumbfounded by her strange behavior. "You're leaving me?" he asked.

"Don't act surprised. We both have known it was leading up to this for some time now."

"You're my wife," he said. "You know that I love you."

"Do you? I feel more like a medal you've won, which you can take down to flaunt whenever it suits you. You love your own selfish ambitions, not me."

Steiner wanted to think this was a gross misunderstanding of some kind but couldn't shake the feeling that what she had said was true. It was like he had heard it before in some distant memory. Desperate to keep her from the shuttle, he clutched her shoulders gently, drew her closer, and gazed deep into her emerald eyes. "Do you remember all the happy times we spent together?" As soon as he had spoken the words, he recalled the scene in the church, where he had left her alone.

Mary sighed. "I will always cherish those memories, but—"

Before she could finish, he kissed her lips. During the caress, Mary remained stiff and unyielding. Steiner drew back. He felt the burning sensation of a single tear running down his face. "I love you."

Mary sniffed. Her eyes glistened with forming tears as she shook her head. "You're infatuated with me, but you don't love me selflessly. I doubt you ever did."

The words stirred Steiner's memory. He'd had this same discussion with Mary on the day she had left for her parents'. He remembered finding her note on the kitchen table, rushing to the shuttle depot, and stopping her there to make a final plea. Every word spoken had been exactly the same as that fateful day. Perhaps the pain of losing her in the shuttle explosion had blocked out the reason why she had boarded the craft to begin with. She died while trying to run away from him.

Steiner glanced down at her swollen stomach. "What about our child?"

"I'll notify you if I go into labor early. I don't think you should miss the birth of your own child, even if the military threatens to court-martial you." She lifted his left hand and kissed the white-gold ring on his finger. "I still love you. Maybe we can try it again after a few months." She backed away toward the shuttle on the launching pad, touching his hand with hers until her fingers lost contact.

The scene dissolved instantaneously before Steiner could do anything else. He saw a glimpse of a flashing gold medallion spinning above him. A gun fired. Steiner experienced a brief moment of weightlessness before landing against a cold, hard surface.

WITH one fluid motion, Daniels grabbed an assault rifle from the nearest mutineer, then used it to sever the medallion's ribbon.

Steiner dropped to the ground in a heap. For a second, he appeared lifeless. Much to Daniels's relief, Steiner's head moved and he gave a barely audible moan.

"Everyone put your hands in the air, and you won't get hurt," Daniels shouted.

"You can't shoot us all," one of the eight men replied.

"No, but who wants to be the first to fall?" Daniels aimed at the speaker. "You?"

Quinn walked forward. "You won't kill anyone."

"Why not?" Daniels replied. "I've killed before." He lowered his tone to the most threatening level.

Quinn shook his head. "I doubt you could do it now, even in self-defense. You no longer see your victims as flesh and bone. You see their souls."

"Stop. I'm warning you."

"Or what? You'll gun me down?" Quinn stepped closer.

Sweat dripped down Daniels's forehead. Within his mind, he could see the woman giving him her Bible just before her life seeped away. He remembered swearing never to take another life. He couldn't bring himself to break that vow. His hand trembled. *I forgive you,* the lady had told him. Even though she had pardoned him, he had never let himself be free from the guilt.

Quinn snatched the rifle away. "Fool. Your belief in the supernatural was your downfall. If you wish to meet your god so badly, here's your chance." He swung the barrel around.

Daniels dropped to his knees. "I forgive you." In that instant, he realized how the woman had felt when she had died. That had been her testimony, and this was to be his. Perhaps it would change Quinn's life as it had his own. "I forgive you," he repeated, weeping tears of joy.

Quinn hesitated in apparent disbelief. Daniels thought he saw doubt in the man's eyes. Doubt about what he was doing. Doubt about what he had become. A second later, the look vanished, replaced by the iciness of a hardened heart. The crossroads had been passed, the choice made. Quinn's finger tightened on the trigger.

"Travis," one of the other men shouted, "the captain's gone."

Daniels glanced to spot where Steiner had lain. Only a belt remained.

Quinn sprang to a console, felt along the top of it, and muttered something about a missing disk. He screamed in rage, shooting fiery bolts into the ceiling, then dashed down the corridor leading to the electrical station.

JULIO inched around the giant hole in the floor of the corridor that had resulted from the overload of the laser cannon. When he looked through the smoldering gape, he could see a pile of rubble and debris mounted in the center of a storage compartment one level down. Vengeance burned within Julio to repay Rick and the bartender for what they had done to Glenn and Dicer.

He glanced back at Wong and Stiles trailing behind him. Could he trust either one of them, especially after the fiasco he had just survived?

Julio tensed when he saw the double doors to the command center ajar. Right away, he sensed another trap. His eyes sought out even the smallest movement ahead.

He led the others up the stairway to the top deck and scanned the room with the muzzle of his rifle. Stiles descended into the navigational quarters, reappearing a second later, shaking his head.

Julio raced down the stairwell and into the captain's conference chamber. He discovered the entrance locked shut. A muffled cry sounded within.

Julio backed away then fired repeatedly at the door. The bolts tore away at the barrier, ripping it into charred shreds. When he burst through the wreckage, he found the chair behind the desk turned away from him. Blood flowed from smoking punctures in the back of it. He swiveled it around and found Simmons's lifeless face gaping up at him. The navigator had been bound and gagged.

Mechanical components lay scattered on the floor everywhere, along with Palmer's body.

"Sanchez, is there anyone down there?" Wong's voice echoed down from the top deck.

"No," Julio answered. "I found Simmons. He's dead. There's no sign of Rick Mason or the bartender anywhere."

Wong came down into the chamber. "They must have doubled back, trying to escape from us."

"I'll find them," Julio said, his need for revenge still aching.

Wong picked up one of the pieces of machinery from the ground. "This looks like part of the communication grid."

Just then, Julio realized where the defenders were.

CAREFUL not to make any noise, Mason removed the maintenance cover for the communication station that Bricket had stripped to provide a hiding place. He snuck up behind one of the raiders, who stared down into the stairwell.

"Stiles," Julio shouted from below, "they're hidden inside the instrument panels."

Stiles turned around just as Mason pounced on him. Mason gripped the barrel of Stiles's rifle and thrust it downward. A blaze of energy ignited into the floor. He wrestled for control of the weapon, but Stiles held it firm. Mason reached down with his left hand, drew his pistol, and fired point-blank into Stiles's face.

Footsteps sounded from the stairwell behind him.

Mason's adrenaline pumped fiercely. He wrenched the rifle free from the dead body's grasp and whirled around, but not before Julio reached the top. Before Julio could fire, a computer panel flew open, and a cane slammed against his helmet. He tumbled back into Wong. They collapsed in a pile of arms and legs at the bottom of the stairwell.

Mason rushed down after them, pointing the muzzle of his rifle in their faces.

"Give me your weapons or die."

Julio surrendered his with a curse. Wong hesitated, then obeyed.

"Rick," Bricket shouted from the main deck, "we've got problems up here."

With both of the captive rifles in hand, Mason ascended toward the main deck. "What's wrong?"

The bartender didn't have to tell him. When Mason reached the top of the steps, through the forward viewport, he noticed the enemy battlecruiser approaching.

CHAPTER

26

JACOB Steiner stumbled down the empty corridor as quickly as his injured leg would take him. When he had first opened his eyes after landing on the cold floor, only one goal shone in his mind: destroy the Orders disk at any cost. While Quinn's attention had been diverted by Daniels, he had wrestled his hands free from the belt, crawled up to the edge of the console, and snatched the silver wafer. He slipped into the corridor leading to the electrical station. He didn't have time to worry about what would happen to Daniels. Above all, the stolen military information had to be erased.

Steiner stopped at the base of the maintenance stairway, where the charred ruins of Richards's defensive barrier still stood. A hundred feet above, flashes from electrical bursts escaped over the edge of the scarred balcony. If he could increase the voltage through the conductor posts up there, it would disintegrate anything at close range.

A rapid series of rifle blasts sounded deep inside the corridor behind him.

Steiner carefully maneuvered up the twisted steps at the base of the stairway, then took the rest of the undamaged ones in giant leaps that brought great pain to his wounded limb. If he landed wrong just once, he might tumble down to the bottom, but there was no longer time to be cautious. Quinn must already be on his trail. Steiner couldn't afford to be caught on the stairway, out in the—

"Captain." Quinn's voice echoed from the chamber below.

Six steps separated Steiner from the safety of the generating station. He might be able to make it. One of his feet missed its mark. He fell forward against the metal slabs. Bolts ate away at the wall above him. The fall had been a blessing in disguise. If he'd been standing, he would've been killed.

The wound in his thigh throbbed. A glimpse behind saw Quinn racing up to the base of the stairway. Steiner knew he could never reach the top in time, so he spun around and crawled backward, holding the disk out in front of him as a shield. Quinn leveled his rifle but didn't fire. That was all Steiner needed. With a cry of determination, he catapulted himself up onto the balcony and rolled clear. Explosions from near misses reverberated in his ears.

FILLED with an inner peace he had never experienced before, Daniels raised his gaze and saw J.R. look through the hole in Pressure Door C-3. The seven mutineers were so preoccupied with what to do with him that they hadn't considered where the rest of the engineers might be. Spider moved into view, pointed to an extinguisher strapped to his back, then at the captors.

Daniels gave a slight nod. His friends intended to attack with the fire equipment. If they stood a chance of success, they would need a diversion.

He fixed his gaze on the two closest armed men. In his mind, he mapped out a precise attack, anticipating their responses. In the next instant, he jumped up and charged at his targets with his arms outstretched. Their eyes bulged. Gun muzzles rose. Before either of them had a chance to fire, he body-blocked both of them, grabbing ahold of their pistols as he made contact. The three of them toppled to the floor in a tangle of arms and legs. He rolled off his stunned victims and was on his feet in the next second, brandishing both weapons.

Another mutineer lifted a rifle, but Spider shot him in the face with a stream of foam before he could discharge any bolts. The blinded convict stumbled backward, coughing and gagging.

Armed with extinguishers, the four other engineers stormed into the room and soaked the rest of the men.

STEINER limped through an aisle of sparking conductor posts toward the opposite end of the generating station, where the power-distribution board lay. He glanced back to see if Quinn had climbed to the top of the stairway yet. The man hadn't, but he soon would.

Steiner knew his only chance was to hide. He hunched down behind the bulk of one of the nearby machines and listened to the sound of his own ragged breathing.

In his mind, he recalled the scene with Mary in the shuttle depot. She had left him exactly the same way as she had on February 18, 2429. He couldn't believe he had blinded himself to the truth for the last seven years. The guilt tried to resurface. He forced it from his mind. He must focus all of his effort into saving the U.S.S.

A loud metallic noise set his nerves on edge. He peeked over the top of his hiding place as it repeated. Quinn was proceeding through the aisles, banging the muzzle of his assault rifle against various assemblies.

Steiner slumped to the ground, ready to give up. It seemed hopeless. How would he be able to destroy the disk before Quinn killed him? He was unarmed and wounded.

A flash of lightning cast his shadow into the aisle. He repositioned himself so that wouldn't occur again.

He glanced up at a sparking conductor above him and understood what he needed to do next. He inched up to the fence surrounding it, stretched his arm through the mesh, and placed the silver wafer at the base of its post. If he could just reach the power-distribution board, he could thrust the control bar up, and the U.S.S. would be saved.

He prepared himself for his desperate charge by tightening the bloody piece of cloth tied around his leg. His mind blocked out the pain and fear. Even the threat of death would not hold him back. All his energy would be focused on one final run.

A glimpse over the side found Quinn standing in a far aisle. The man's dark gaze locked on Steiner, who barely ducked in time before a bolt tore into the top of his shelter.

Rapid footsteps approached.

Steiner's charge had been foiled before it had even begun.

With his head low, he retreated between fences and other apparatuses, fleeing deeper into the maze of electrical machinery. The static discharges around him masked the sounds of his passage.

In his haste, his shoulder clipped the side of a component. A burning sensation flung him to the ground. He picked himself up, stunned. Whatever he had hit had been charged enough to remind him to be more careful in here. Another mistake like that might cost him his life.

He risked another look and sighted Quinn at his former hiding place. It seemed almost unthinkable, but while mighty space battles were being waged, the outcome of the war would be decided by their two-man game of cat and mouse.

Steiner weaved back through the maze of assemblies until he reached an aisle that led to the glimmering power-distribution board thirty feet away.

Sweat trickled down his brow as he sprinted toward his objective, determined to reach it before dying.

Less than ten feet away, his left foot landed wrong. He lost his balance and tumbled onto the unyielding metal surface, three feet shy of the board.

A laugh erupted behind him.

The game had ended.

THE New Order battlecruiser glided forward, slowing until it stood nose to nose with the *Marauder*. Its massive form occupied most of the forward screen in the command center. Printed on the side of its hull was the name WARLORD.

Mason closed his eyes, hoping that when he opened them again he would discover that this was a nightmare of his darkest imagination. His fingernails dug into the flesh of his palms. It comforted him slightly, distracting him from building nausea.

"Enemy vessel, surrender, and prepare to be boarded," someone announced over the speakers.

Mason cringed at the sound of the voice. He turned and locked eyes with the pale bartender. There would be no escape for either of them.

Mason beat the helm in frustration. "This can't be happening—I won't let it."

He stormed toward the weapons console. If the *Warlord* wanted an answer, he would give them one. Then he noticed a pistol aimed at him from inside the stairwell. He froze in midstride.

Wong stepped up to the main deck, keeping the gun trained on him. A spare gun must have been hidden inside his suit. "Drop your rifle," the fat man demanded, climbing to the main deck.

Mason released his weapon, cursing himself for not bothering to frisk his prisoners. How could he have been so foolish?

"Travis Quinn?" the voice from the *Warlord* asked. "If you have secured the vessel, please give a response."

"Pilot," Wong said to Mason. "Flash the ship's running lights."

"Never."

"Do it, or I'll cut you down."

Mason held himself back.

Wong's face turned crimson. "If that's your decision, so be it."

A shadow moved inside the stairwell. Julio Sanchez appeared, grabbing Wong from behind. "Separatist scum," he hissed. Jewels glittered from the handle of the dagger in his hand. He thrust the white of the blade into a gap between Wong's armor pads.

Crying out in pain, the fat man swung his pistol into his assailant and fired it twice. Sanchez's bloodied face sank back into the stairwell.

Mason rushed at Wong, but the fat man's gun muzzle greeted him. An orange beam blazed in front of Mason's face, causing all of his nerves to jolt. Wong dropped to the deck, his head sliced open.

Mason collapsed to his knees in shock.

Bricket stood to the side, holding a smoking rifle. "I never did like him much."

"Neither did I."

Putting the rifle down, Bricket glared at the forward viewer. "What do we do about them?"

With a new strength of will, Mason sprang to his feet and hastened to the weapons console.

Bricket's mouth fell open. "You're going to attack?"

Mason found a functional automatic turret and locked its targeting computer on the *Warlord*. "I'll never surrender to my own father."

"Admiral Richina?" Bricket gasped.

"The one and only." Mason brought a clenched fist down on the firing keypad.

"WHERE'S the Orders disk, Captain?" Quinn asked in an almost playful manner.

Faint discharges sounded from the pulse-cannon assembly. Steiner's breath caught in his lungs. Someone in the command center must be firing at another ship. The Separatists must have arrived to receive the military information.

"Captain?" Quinn asked.

"I destroyed it already," Steiner replied.

Quinn's eyebrows rose in a mocking manner. "How were you able to do that so quickly?" His head tilted toward the sparking conductors behind him as if in answer to his own question. "Perhaps it's hidden up here somewhere?"

Steiner's heart stopped. Quinn had figured out the truth. It wouldn't be long until he found the disk. He had to make a desperate play.

With all the strength he could muster, he launched himself toward the board. When he crashed against it, his left hand moved the control bar to its maximum setting.

Brilliance exploded from behind him. Covering his ears, he slumped to the base of the distribution board and watched the masterpiece of his creation. The entire generating station had come alive with electricity. Lightning streaked all about the ceiling, darting from one conductor to another. One of the pods sitting on top of the cylindrical posts ignited in a shower of sparks, followed by another deeper in the interior. The sight stung his vision, leaving white spots dancing in its wake. He breathed in the charged scent. The most beautiful storm he had ever witnessed played about him. Relief flooded through him, overflowing into a chuckle.

Quinn stared out at the fierce display for a few seconds, then turned back. His lips curled up.

A cold feeling invaded Steiner. Something wasn't right.

Quinn reached into his shirt pocket and retracted a silver wafer.

Steiner cried out hopelessly. After all he had tried to do, he had still failed.

The *Marauder* jolted to one side, almost knocking Quinn off-balance. Several pods overloaded. An alarm rang out. Quinn glanced about in confusion.

Whatever ship they had fired upon must have responded.

The floor rocked violently again. This time, Quinn toppled backward.

Without hesitation, Steiner lunged at him.

MASON straightened up, rubbing his bruised head where it had hit the console. Their defensive shields had withstood two direct hits. A yellow warning indicator lit up, informing him that they couldn't hold up under another. One more well-placed shot should destroy their outdated vessel. The *Warlord* hovered in the front viewer, obviously awaiting the desired response from its victims—one that Mason would never give.

Bricket lifted himself into the chair at the communication station. Blood flowed from a gash in his forehead. "Why didn't they just finish us off?"

"My father isn't about to risk losing the chance to obtain U.S.S. military information. He's trying to intimidate us." Mason bared his teeth at the *Warlord*. "He'll never get that pleasure from me."

"Is anyone in the command center?" The head engineer's voice sounded from the intercom.

Mason sprang from behind the weapons console and responded to the call. "Daniels? Are you in control of the engine room?"

"Yes. What's happening up there?"

"A Separatist battlecruiser is staring us down. How long before we can have starspeed capability?"

There was a short pause. "We'll do the best we can, but it doesn't look good."

Bricket's face whitened. "They'll be jamming our navigational sensors. We can't run blind."

"Do you have a better idea?" Mason replied.

"I might. Give me a second." The bartender hurried to the security station and began typing keypads.

"Enemy ship, this is your last chance to surrender before we destroy you," Richina shouted.

Memories of his mother's arrest came back to haunt Mason, reinforcing his undying hatred for her murderer. He activated the intercom again. "Daniels, we need to leave now."

"The engines are off-line, the reactor chamber sealed up," Daniels replied. "It'll take us more than a day to get it operational."

Mason knew that his father never made empty threats. He would follow through if they didn't signal him immediately.

Mason turned toward Bricket, who rifled through camera images on one of the surviving monitors, apparently searching for something. Whatever the bartender had planned wouldn't make any difference. There was no time left.

Mason stepped to the weapons console and retargeted the automatic turret. With his gaze riveted to the *Warlord*, he pressed the firing keypad.

Streaks of red, intensified energy, lanced out, raking into the shields of the battlecruiser without any effect.

STEINER rolled across the floor with Quinn, struggling for control of the rifle. Only sheer determination kept him going.

His muscles ached from growing fatigue. It would not be long before they gave out completely, leaving him at Quinn's mercy.

He put all of his strength into a punch to Quinn's gut. While Quinn was winded, Steiner yanked the rifle away but lost hold of it. It flew far out of reach and skidded under an assembly.

Quinn's countenance darkened into a crazed expression. He threw Steiner back, then broke into a frenzied assault.

Steiner tried desperately to escape as fists pounded against him. A kick into his bruised side curled him up. Nerves shrieked in agony. He couldn't hold off the attack any longer. His energy was spent. His resistance gone.

Icy fingers weaved themselves around his neck, tightening until no air could be forced through.

Steiner saw a hope. A sparking pod had toppled over against the top of a nearby fence. If he could grab ahold of the electrified mesh, he could take Quinn with him.

He reached out, then froze when he heard something. His ears rang so loudly that they had nearly muffled it. Had it been his imagination, a delusion brought about by his weakened conscious state?

Quinn went rigid, his hands loosening their hold. His gaze rose, widening in surprise—maybe even terror.

Steiner turned his head and saw the impossible. There, twenty feet away, sprawled on the ground, lay Tramer. Steiner blinked hard to see if it was a dream of some kind. It wasn't. Energy burns marred most of the damaged metallic body. One of his legs stuck in the air, frozen at an angle. Charred wires and severed mechanisms protruded from the stub, where his right arm had once been. His left hand propped up the assault rifle that had been lost during the fight, its barrel aimed at Quinn. Even though the pale face seemed distorted by pain, the single human eye held the fire of vengeance.

Quinn climbed to his feet. "You're supposed to be dead, Cyborg." His voice revealed his shock and apparent disbelief. Steiner shared it.

"My creators made me better than even I had expected," Tramer answered back, his synthesized voice crackling badly.

For a split second, Quinn was expressionless, then he broke out in a sly smile. "So you've come back from the grave to kill me, have you?" He held up his left wrist, flaunting a small black instrument secured to it. "Remember this, Cyborg? It has a fail-safe feature programmed into it. If my pulse stops, the explosives in your head automatically ignite."

The rifle remained poised to shoot. "Then we'll die together," Tramer said. His mechanical fingers fumbled with the trigger. The barrel tipped forward. The energy blast erupted into the floor.

Quinn laughed. "It seems you take this trip solo." He reached for a button on the black device.

Steiner coiled his legs in and kicked Quinn into the electrified fence. In that instant, the cold eyes widened in fear. Sparks sprayed as his body made contact. Thousands of volts ripped through him for a second before he bounced off the fence and landed on top of Steiner. His flesh sizzled. The device on his wrist began beeping rapidly in succession.

Steiner crawled up from under the smoking body, stretching his fingers toward the small transmitter. He had to stop it, break it, anything to save his friend.

The beeping turned into a shrill whine.

Tramer lowered his head, willing to accept his fate.

"Maxwell," Steiner uttered in terror.

Steiner wanted to look away so he wouldn't have to see his friend die again, but he couldn't force himself to.

One second passed.

Two.

Three.

Nothing happened.

Perhaps the transmitter had been a phony? No, Quinn would have discarded it after he thought the weapons officer had died. It had to be real, but why hadn't it worked?

A bright flash from above gave Steiner his answer. He watched the lightning arcs playing all about the roof. The strong electrical fields must have interfered with the transmitter's signal.

Without a second thought, Steiner ripped the device off Quinn's smoking wrist and beat it against the ground until it shattered into useless pieces. The Orders disk stuck out of a nearby shirt pocket, the overhead storm reflecting off its exposed surface. Steiner pulled it free, then crawled over to where Tramer lay.

"Maxwell?" he asked.

A low whine sounded as the weapons officer raised his head. "I am alive?"

"Yes," Steiner answered, unable to suppress a smile.

"Is the ship secure?"

Steiner looked down at the disk in his palm, then threw it into the toppled conductor over the electrified fence. The intense heat of the lightning arches melted the silver wafer on contact.

"It doesn't matter now, my friend," Steiner said.

MASON was expecting the *Warlord* to unleash a violent assault. His body quivered in anticipation of his impending death.

"What are you waiting for?" Mason shouted. "Get it over with."

Almost in reply to his plea, the battlecruiser began reversing away, probably preparing to swing about to destroy them. Surprisingly, it pivoted around and sped across the border into the New Order Empire.

"What?" Mason exclaimed. "He's leaving?"

A massive shape passed overhead and pursued the *Warlord*. It was a U.S.S. destroyer.

"The cavalry," Bricket exclaimed.

Another vessel shot by on the starboard side and followed behind the first. The *Magellan*. The two ships chased the battlecruiser until they all disappeared into the distance.

Mason couldn't believe what had happened. "My father should have annihilated us first before retreating."

"You can thank me that he didn't," Bricket said from the security station.

"Why? What did you do?"

The bartender grinned, showing his teeth. "What every good gambler would have done—I raised the stakes." He slapped the console in front of him. "I interconnected the security monitors to what was left of the communications array and sent a low-powered visual transmission."

"Of what?"

"What do you mean 'of what'? Of you."

"Me?"

Mason noticed one of the screens depicting himself at the weapons console.

"I showed your daddy who he was about to kill, betting that he wouldn't be able to do it." Bricket laughed. "What do you know—I was right."

Mason was stunned. If his father had been so quick to execute his wife, why had he spared his renegade son?

"Why do you look so glum?" Bricket asked. "We survived."

"I can't believe he let me live after all I've done to him."

Bricket smiled. "Someday, when you have a child, you'll understand why."

The *Magellan* approached them again, looking as if it might attack.

"*Marauder*, this is Commodore Cole." A voice sounded over the speakers. "We are receiving your visual transmission. Is Captain Steiner alive?"

Mason exchanged an uneasy look with Bricket. "What do we do now?"

"Nothing," Steiner said.

Mason smiled as he watched Daniels helping Steiner up the stairway to the command deck, into view of the camera.

Bricket chuckled.

"Nice to see you again, Captain," Commodore Cole said over the speakers. "Prepare to receive our assistance."

CHAPTER

27

THE man in Earthstation's holding cell was barely a skeleton of the man Steiner remembered. Jamison's mere presence would no longer command respect from all the other military personnel around him. Troops would never again seek his guidance. His status had been reduced to that of a traitor, a betrayer of the United Star Systems. He deserved nothing less.

Two high-ranking officials sat outside the invisible energy barrier, taking turns at grilling the fallen admiral, trying to learn the scope of the damage his treason had caused. The man who had once been the mighty Ralph Jamison sat wordlessly, his hateful stare riveted on Steiner, who stood back behind the interrogators.

Before exiting the detention area, Steiner gave a wink of farewell to his former arch nemesis. A moment later, he was navigating through the bustling hallways on his way to find Suzanne.

He had seen her briefly when, along with all the crew members who had fought against Quinn's mutiny, he had disembarked from the *Magellan* earlier that morning. Cole had brought them here to be honored, while the *Marauder* and the rest of its surviving crew had been escorted to the

Tycus System for debriefing. Because of all the news reporters swarming them, Suzanne hadn't been able to get within five feet. However, now that everything had died down, he could find out from her what the verdict was concerning his future.

His search began in the medical center, in the section marked CYBERNETICS RESEARCH. Bricket and Daniels worked inside, testing a mechanical arm hooked up to a terminal. Tramer lay stretched out on a table on the far side of the room. Cole sat next to him, talking casually, probably reliving old times. During their return voyage, Cole seemed to have put aside his prejudice and fear and had begun daily conversations with the weapons officer. Perhaps he had discovered an old shipmate.

"Just the man I wished to speak to," Cole said, rising to his feet to greet Steiner with a handshake. "The Council has adjourned regarding the matter of Jamison. President Lindsey has taken credit for his exposure; however, I'm still pushing for you and your loyal officers to receive recognition for preventing the U.S.S. strategic plans being compromised."

Steiner's neck ached at the threat of another award. "I've had my fill of medals. Try to get Tramer and the others one."

"I'll do my best." Cole glanced down at the weapons officer. "I've been trying to convince Tramer to inform Candice and Veronica of his part in preserving the Union, but he has refused."

"I will not attempt to contact them," Tramer said. "If Veronica ever becomes strong enough to accept my appearance, she will seek me out."

"That may never happen," Cole pointed out.

"Whatever she wishes."

Steiner knew it was the best decision. Tramer would only hurt worse if they spurned him again. "Would either of you know where Suzanne is?" Steiner asked, changing the subject.

Cole was the one who answered. "The last time I saw her, she was listening to your pilot's recounting of the mutiny. He has an entire audience in the arboretum, glued to every word he says."

Memories of the exaggerated tales Mason used to spin in

prison came back to Steiner, bringing a smile with them. *A showman to the last.*

Once Steiner left the medical center, it took him ten minutes to reach the garden sanctuary. It was housed in a cavernous chamber overgrown with brightly colored plants and trees. A glistening stream flowed down the center, murmuring a relaxing tune. The upper portion of the high ceiling was made up of a transparent material that allowed the stars to show through. At both ends of the room, giant luminescent elements had been suspended from the roof, providing artificial sunlight.

A winding path, twisting through budding flowers and blossoming saplings, led him deeper into the interior. The strong scent of pollen rode the soft man-made breeze. He stopped on top of a wooden bridge spanning a pond dotted with lily pads and encompassed by weeping willows that stretched down to grasp the liquid surface.

J.R. and Spider sat on a far shore, practicing their harmonies. They were scheduled to sing at the station's chapel that night. It was a performance Steiner wasn't going to miss.

In the crystal world below, fish swam idly by. He stared at the wedding band on his finger. Slipping it off, he relinquished it to the water. The ring sparkled as it sank to the sandy bottom.

"I'm sorry, Mary," he whispered.

He stepped off the bridge onto a new path. It guided him into a grove of evergreens. A lieutenant in full-dress uniform approached from the opposite direction. His face lit up in recognition, and he saluted before passing by.

Oh, great, Steiner thought. *Who knows what kind of superhuman picture Mason must have woven of me? If this continues, I won't be able to walk anywhere without drawing attention.*

Farther up the path, in the center of a tree-lined clearing, people of all ranks occupied benches set in a semicircle. Everyone seemed to be listening intently to Mason, who stood in front, most likely telling an exaggerated version of what had really happened.

"You've already missed the best parts," someone said behind him. "The parts with me in them."

Steiner smiled as he turned around to see Pattie step out of the shadows of a tree, gingerly trying not to lose his balance.

Isaac Steele stepped forward and handed the Saint a cane. "You really need to use this. I will not catch you if you fall."

"I'll be fine. Let me be."

"Fine by me."

Pattie looked back at Steiner. "I may not be able to fight today, but soon." The Saint laughed, lost his balance, and Steiner caught him. "Thanks, Slugger. If you don't mind taking me over to one of those chairs so I can hear the rest of the story."

He helped Pattie into one of the chairs in the outer circle.

"Suddenly, I turned around and saw a Separatist battle-cruiser approaching." Mason framed his hands around the imaginary ship. "We knew we were outgunned ten to one, but as you remember, we've been in that situation before." A few cheers erupted. He imitated a very stern, pompous face. "Some hotshot admiral demanded that I surrender, but I wasn't about to do anything of the sort." He waved his fist, and shouted, "I opened fire on him." The gathering went wild.

Suzanne waved to Steiner from one of the back rows. She slid over, beckoning him to join her.

He gave a faint shake of his head and pointed toward the fringe. Just as he was about to escape in that direction, Mason introduced him to the crowd. Suddenly, he had fans surrounding him. After several handshakes and bows, he pried himself away to where Suzanne waited at the edge of the grove. It wasn't until Mason continued the tale that they were finally left alone.

"I still find it hard to believe that any of you survived that ordeal," she said. "Did you know the fleet was under orders to destroy your ship on sight? If they hadn't seen your pilot attacking the battlecruiser, they would have done so."

"Yeah, he probably saved all our lives."

"And there's you, making a stand against thirty mutineers." She shook her head in apparent amazement. "Someone's bound to make a holofeature."

"How would they end it?" he asked.

She pursed her lips together tightly. "Probably happier than I will. Your pardon has been rejected. Regardless of your reasoning, you did assault an admiral and threaten his life. However, you can be allowed to serve the remainder of your sentence here under house arrest."

"Would I be free to roam the base?"

"I'm sure we could work something out with the C.O. In a couple of years, I might be able to get you a pardon and perhaps even command of a destroyer."

"What about my officers? What happens to them?"

"They'll be fine. Your success has guaranteed that the P.A.V. program will survive for a long time."

Steiner turned back and watched Mason for a few seconds. "Can I remain captain of the *Marauder*?"

Suzanne eyed him incredulously. "After the hell you went through, you want to go back?"

"My friends risked their lives for me. I want to repay the favor."

She shrugged. "I guess so, if that's what you want."

"We can discuss the rest of the details over dinner, if you're interested."

She smiled. "I might be able to squeeze in dinner with a war hero."

In the front of the assembly, Mason finished his story. "The Separatist Empire should have known better than to tangle with the crew of the P.A.V. *Marauder*."

ABOUT THE AUTHOR

Michael Bowers lives in Southern California. You can visit him at www.prisonshipbook.com.